PENGUIN CLASSICS

FOUNDER EDITOR (1944–64): E. V. RIEU

MAXIM GORKY is the pen-name of Alexei Maximovich Peshkov, who was born in 1868 in the city of Nizhny-Novgorod, now renamed after him. After his father's death he spent his childhood with his mother and grandparents in an atmosphere of hostility. He was turned out of the house when his mother died and left to work in various jobs – in a bakery, in an ikon-maker's shop, on barges – until his unsuccessful attempt at suicide. For three years he wandered in the south like a tramp before publishing his first story, 'Makar Chudra', in a Tiflis newspaper. After his return to Nizhny he worked on another newspaper, in which many of his stories appeared; he quickly achieved fame and soon afterwards his play *The Lower Depths* was a triumphant success at the Moscow Arts Theatre. By now active in the revolutionary movement, he was arrested in 1905 by the Tsarist government but released following a petition signed by eminent statesmen and writers. While in America in 1960 he savagely attacked American capitalism, and wrote his best-selling novel, *Mother*. During the First World War he was associated with the Marxist Internationalist Group, and in 1917 he founded *New Life*, a daily devoted to left-wing socialism, but which outspokenly attacked Kerensky and Lenin's 'Communist hysteria'. In 1921 he went to Italy, where he wrote *My Universities*, the third part of his great autobiographical trilogy; the other parts are *My Childhood* and *My Apprenticeship*. He returned to Moscow in 1928, and from then on he was a champion of the Soviet cause. In 1936 he died – allegedly poisoned by his political enemies – and was given a hero's funeral in Red Square.

RONALD WILKS studied Russian language and literature at Trinity College, Cambridge. He has also translated 'The Little Demon' by Sologub, *Eugene Onegin* by Pushkin, *My Childhood* and *My Universities* by Gorky and Gogol's *Diary of a Madman*, published in the Penguin Classics.

MAXIM GORKY

MY APPRENTICESHIP

TRANSLATED
WITH AN INTRODUCTION BY
RONALD WILKS

PENGUIN BOOKS

Penguin Books Ltd, Harmondsworth, Middlesex, England
Penguin Books, 40 West 23rd Street, New York, New York 10010, U.S.A.
Penguin Books Australia Ltd, Ringwood, Victoria, Australia
Penguin Books Canada Ltd, 2801 John Street, Markham, Ontario, Canada L3R 1B4
Penguin Books (N.Z.) Ltd, 182–190 Wairau Road, Auckland 10, New Zealand

This translation first published 1974
Reprinted 1976, 1977, 1980, 1983

Set, printed and bound in Great Britain by
Cox & Wyman Ltd, Reading
Set in Monotype Garamond

Introduction

AT the end of *My Childhood* Gorky was sent out 'into the world' at the age of eleven by his wily old grandfather to fend for himself – a tender age indeed at which to face the world. Lesser men than Gorky would have been crushed by what he had to endure until he established himself as a writer. Indeed, as he tells us in the last section of the trilogy he did become desperate enough to attempt suicide. Such was the misery and barbarity of life in Russia during the final two decades of the nineteenth century, which saw the collapse of the small businessman (Gorky's grandfather, originally a prosperous dyer, was eventually reduced to penury) and the rapid growth of industry on a large scale. *My Apprenticeship* forms the second part of the trilogy and most of the events take place in Nizhny-Novgorod, Gorky's birthplace. At the close of the book Gorky states that he can bear life there no longer and moves on to Kazan, where his experiences, hardly less tolerable, are described in the final section of the trilogy, *My Universities*. The whole trilogy covers roughly twenty years of the author's life, from the death of his father from cholera in 1871, to 1892, when he was wandering in the south of Russia and his first published story, 'Makar Chudra', appeared in a Caucasus newspaper.

My Apprenticeship is almost twice the length of *My Childhood*, although the period of time is shorter, and this is what we might expect from a growing boy, now much more receptive to external impressions, more aware of people and their emotions and of the many and often terrifying events rushing past. The book first appeared in serial form, in the journal *The Russian Word*, in 1915, but it was actually written the previous year.

It is highly typical of Gorky that, for all the squalor, misery and violence that were daily features of the life around him, he nonetheless showed a remarkable resilience and strength of character. Indeed, a vein of optimism runs throughout the whole trilogy and the hope is continually voiced that one day people will stop behaving like wild animals, sadistic bullies, drinking themselves silly, fighting, and tormenting each other. Gorky was very much a seeker after truth, trying to find a new and better life, but he was far from being any kind of dreamer. On the contrary, in *My Apprenticeship* he shows how he was able to withstand harsh and bitter reality, and he often reacted quite violently to injustice and cruelty. A good example of this is provided by the scene on the steamboat *Dobry*, when at one moment the passengers cruelly bait a pathetic little soldier who had just joined the crew, and then work themselves into a wild panic when there is an explosion in the boiler-room, allowing themselves to be driven around the deck like sheep by the crew: Gorky acutely describes that strange ambivalence so typical of the Russian temperament:

One noticed before anything else that there was something gentle, timid and sadly submissive about these people and it was strange – terrifying even – when that outer layer of docility crumbled: then they would behave cruelly and stupidly, and those sudden mad fits were never very funny. I thought that these people had no idea where they were being taken and could not care less where they disembarked. Wherever they landed they would stay on the quayside for a short time and then climb on board any ship that happened to arrive and go off somewhere else. They all seemed lost and homeless, and everywhere they went appeared strange to them. And they were all terrible cowards.

This acute characterization can be applied to many of the people that the young Gorky meets in the course of the book, those strange 'outcasts' so brilliantly portrayed in his *Fragments from my Diary*, those aimless people who pass him by like phantoms, drifting through life. In *My Apprenticeship* Gorky tries to help the pathetic soldier on board the steamboat, and it is these same feelings of impotent outrage that lead him to start a fight with a loathsome specimen who deliberately smashes a live cat's head right before his eyes, to provoke him, out of sheer perversity and sadism: it was this very same emotion that had led him to attack his stepfather for insulting his mother. Gorky is typical of that peculiar Russian type, the *ozornik*, who rebels against such outrages and whose feelings boil over into active hostility and pugnacity, with an accompanying desire to shock people out of their complacency and self-satisfaction – a non-acceptance of a dreary monotony, a meaningless life embodied in Foma Gordeev, the hero of Gorky's novel of that name.

In *My Apprenticeship* Gorky tells how this desire to do something about his life, to 'square up to it' and to attack it (at the close of the book he states in a violent outburst of spleen that he wishes to give the earth a 'good kick'), went hand in hand with a desire to escape from it:

There were two persons living within me. One of them had experienced far too much that was filthy and nasty and had as a result become rather timid. This person who was crushed by his knowledge of the horror of everyday life had begun to look upon it distrustfully, suspiciously, with a helpless feeling of compassion for everyone – even for himself. This man dreamed of a quiet, solitary life with books and without any people, of a monastery, of a life as a forest-warden, of living in a railwayman's hut, of going to Persia or working as a night watchman on the outskirts of some town . . . The other man had been baptized by the holy spirit that he had read about in books written by honest and wise men. Although he realized how terrible reality was, how insuperable its horrors were, although he felt that its strength was enough to tear his head off or trample his heart under its filthy boots, he still persisted in defending himself . . . baring his fists, and was always ready for a quarrel or a fight.

In *My Apprenticeship* we see both these men: the pugnacious Gorky, and Gorky the escapist. Indeed, the close of each of the sections of the trilogy is a departure, a move onwards to a new world, with the 'vile abominations' of the old left behind. In the second part of his trilogy Gorky describes the three periods of his life with the Sergeevs (his grandmother's sister's family), his work in an ikon painting shop, and his two journeys on board Volga steamboats as a dish-washer. By far the most insufferable is the suffocating life with the self-satisfied, philistine, complacent Sergeevs. As he tells us: '. . . life was even more boring and cruel than ever before and was strictly controlled by a daily routine that had become immutable. I did not think that there could be any possibility of a better life, different from that which I was condemned to watch unfolding before me every day.'

An escape from a stifling, monotonous existence was

provided by reading, which opened up a new and enthralling world to the growing boy – although even this had to be done furtively. Gorky touchingly describes how he used to hide in the bath-house with the crippled girl Lyudmila, or scraped wax from a candle to make his own candle to read with at night. Later in *My Apprenticeship* Gorky tells us a great deal about how he devoured books, and how he reduced the strong, illiterate men among whom he worked to tears by his reading from Lermontov, Gogol and Pushkin. In the spring of 1880 Gorky decided that he simply could not bear life any longer with the Sergeevs, people who had no culture whatsoever, who subscribed to cheap magazines and who 'considered themselves the finest in the town' and he ran away, down to the wharves by the Volga, and got a job on the steamboat *Dobry*, owned by the same company that had employed his father as a carpenter. Gorky gives some wonderful descriptions of that slow journey on the old paddle-steamer: 'The moon shone brightly, sailing away from the port side of the ship into the meadows. The old reddish steamboat which had a white stripe on its funnel moved slowly and slapped its paddles unevenly in the silvery water. Dark banks seemed to be gently swimming towards it and threw shadows over the river.' But, Gorky writes, like a dark spectre, the convict barge towed by the *Dobry* followed in its wake: '. . . its deck was covered by an iron cage full of convicts sentenced to penal colonies or hard labour. A sentry's bayonet shone on the bows like a candle, and the tiny stars in the blue sky glinted like candles as well . . . The water sobbed and seemed to be crying . . .' Ironically, that very same summer the author Korolenko, who was to play such a great part in helping Gorky establish himself as a writer, was a convict in that barge: part of the long journey east to Siberia was made by river, from Nizhny-Novgorod to Perm, after the 1860s.

It was on the *Dobry* that Gorky met the cook Smury, who kept a trunkful of books of all kinds, an extraordinary collection of almanacs, novels, the poetry of Nekrasov, and old Russian journals. All of this was devoured by Gorky, and in reading adventure stories, travel books and a whole variety of cheap novels he found nourishment for his eager mind.

In the autumn of 1880 Gorky had once again to return to the

Sergeevs and the suffocating atmosphere in that household. He writes how he in fact preferred life with his grandmother and grandfather, which for all the floggings and the fighting between the uncles was infinitely preferable to life with the smug captious Sergeevs, whose family consisted of Gorky's grandmother's sister Matryona, with her two sons Valentin, a draughtsman, who was married, and Viktor, for whom she had an almost pathologically obsessive maternal love. Matryona indeed treated Gorky abominably and brought his brief apprenticeship as assistant draughtsman to an abrupt end – fearing that he might deprive 'her own flesh and blood' of their livelihood by doing their work.

A bright ray among the gloom was the fashionable widow whom Gorky so idolized that he called her Queen Margot after a heroine from one of the French novels he had been able to read: 'That woman had made a deep impression on me, one that I had not experienced before. It was as though a bright dawn had come and for several days I lived in a state of elation.' Like Smury on the steamboat, 'Queen Margot' fed Gorky with books – in this case the works of Balzac, Goncourt, and the Russian poets. But even this vision of radiant, incorruptible beauty was destroyed when Gorky one day found his 'Queen' lying in bed with her lover, and his illusions of purity were rudely shattered. And the heroes in most of the books were in fact far different from those in real life.

In *My Apprenticeship* Gorky describes characters who are truly memorable: once again he gives a loving portrait of his almost saintly grandmother, whom he accompanies to the forests to gather mushrooms; of the imperturbable Smury on the steamboat; of Natalya Kozlovskaya, the simple washerwoman with an amazing stoicism and strength of character who finally dies of tuberculosis; of the extraordinary men in the ikon workshop – Kapendyukhin the gargantuan drunkard, who is at the same time a marvellous singer, Sitanov, the consumptive Davidov, Odintsov, and Zhikharev the wonderful ikon maker; and perhaps most touching of all, of his Uncle Yakov, now a whimpering, drunken wreck of a man who pours out his soul to Gorky in the very last chapter. Equally memorable are the descriptions of the dark and mysterious ikon workshop, of the villages seen from the steamboat, their lights appearing as strings of fiery beads streaming away into the darkness.

In this second part of his trilogy Gorky shows how he was beginning to come to terms with himself and the often crude and horrible reality around him. As in *My Childhood*, the picture painted is not one of unrelieved gloom, of desperate pessimism. For Gorky there is always the hope of something better, and he ends the book with words of defiance and hope as he wanders out on to the fields by the Volga after that final meeting with Uncle Yakov:

I went up to the town and then out into the fields. There was a full moon, and heavy clouds drifted across the sky, blotting out my shadow with their own dark shadows. I bypassed the town, going across the fields instead, and I came out at Otkos, near the Volga. Here I lay down on the dusty grass and for a long time I looked at the river, at the meadows and at the motionless earth . . . Everything around me was half asleep, every sound was muffled. Things moved reluctantly, just out of sheer necessity and not from any passionate love of movement and life. And I dearly wanted to give that earth a hard kick – and myself as well – so that everything, myself included, would start spinning round in one joyful whirlwind, in a festive dance where people were in love with each other, in love with a life which had been begun for the sake of another, which was beautiful, bold and honest. And I thought: 'I *must* do something or I'll be finished.'

On dull autumn days, when one cannot see the sun nor even feel its warmth and when one forgets its existence altogether – on autumn days like these I often wandered through the forest. If I lost my way completely and grew tired of looking for the right path I would grit my teeth and go straight through thickets, through rotting undergrowth, across swamps full of slippery clods of earth and I would always come out on the main road in the end. So I decided to do something. That autumn I went to Kazan in the secret hope that I might somehow manage to enrol as a student there.

Little did Gorky know what hardships this 'main road' was to lead to, as he so vividly recounts in *My Universities*, but it was this seemingly indomitable spirit that enabled him to survive.

As the Soviet writer Paustovsky so acutely remarked: 'For

me, Gorky *is* Russia and just as Russia without the Volga is unimaginable, so Russia without Maxim Gorky is equally unthinkable.' In *My Apprenticeship* Gorky gives a remarkable panorama of Russian life in all its suffering and gaiety, barbarity and deeply affecting stoicism. Each character from this vast gallery is described so graphically, with such convincing detail, that he becomes alive and the reader literally *feels* the physical presence of those ikon painters, cooks, prostitutes, of those men and women broken by life. Tolstoy is recorded as having said of Gorky: '. . . the man seems to be all eyes . . . The wonderful thing is that he saw and noted down things other people were incapable of seeing or, if they saw, were powerless to record.'

It is this that makes Gorky's trilogy one of the truly great autobiographies – a living and memorable record of a boy's growth into a young man.

R. W.

In memory of my mother

Translator

Chapter 1

AND so my apprenticeship began, as a shop-boy in a 'fashionable' shoe shop in the high street. The owner was a small fattish man with a swarthy, tired face, green teeth and eyes the colour of muddy water. He looked as if he were blind and I made funny faces at him to see if he really was.

'Stop screwing your face up,' he would say in a soft, but menacing, voice.

It was very nasty to think that those bleary eyes could actually see me and I just did not believe it. Perhaps he was only *guessing* that I was pulling faces?

'I said stop screwing your face up,' he repeated – this time in an even softer voice. As he spoke his blubbery lips barely parted. Then I heard that rasping, whispering voice again:

'And don't scratch your arms! You're in a high-class shop now, in the high street, so don't forget it! Boys should stand by the door, still as statchers . . .'

I did not know what a 'statcher' was and I could not stop scratching. Both my arms were covered up to the elbows with red patches and sores: those itch-mites were eating away at me and I could hardly bear the pain.

'What were you doing back home?' he asked as he inspected my arms.

When I told him he shook his round head, which was covered with grey hair plastered with oil, and he started showering me with insults:

'Scavenging – that's worse than begging – or stealing even.'

I proudly announced:

'Oh, I used to steal as well!'

At this he planted his hands on the counter like a cat, looked at me with his frightened empty eyes and hissed right into my face:

'Wha-at? Who put you up to that?'

I told him all the details.

'Look, I won't say any more about it now. But if I catch you stealing shoes or money from *my* shop I'll have you put away until you come of age!'

The way he said this, in that calm voice of his, was even more frightening, and I began to dislike him more and more.

Besides the owner, my cousin Sasha (Uncle Yakov's son) helped to sell shoes, and there was a slimy, red-faced smart aleck of a senior assistant. Sasha wore a reddish frock-coat, a starched shirt-front, a tie, and trousers with turn-ups. He was very snooty and almost completely ignored me. When Grandfather brought me to my new master and asked Sasha to teach me the trade Sasha frowned solemnly and issued the following warning:

'Now he'll have to do what *I* tell him!'

Grandfather made me bow to him by pressing my head down hard.

'Listen to Sasha,' he said. 'He's older than you and knows all about the shoe trade.'

Sasha's eyes rolled as he too tried to impress this on me:

'Yes, don't you forget what Grandfather's just told you.'

From the very first day he did all he could to take advantage of his seniority. Once the shop-owner had to tell him:

'Kashirin, stop goggling!'

'Me? But I wasn't sir,' Sasha replied, lowering his head. But my new master would not leave him alone:

'And don't keep lowering your head. The customers will think you're a goat!'

The senior assistant laughed obsequiously and the owner's mouth spread out into an ugly grin. Sasha turned purple and hid behind the counter.

I did not like this way they had of talking, with all those strange words, and sometimes I thought that they weren't speaking Russian at all.

When a lady came into the shop the proprietor would take his hand out of his pocket, smooth his whiskers and plaster his face with an oily smile. But his empty eyes never moved. The senior assistant would stiffen up, draw his elbows in to his sides and let his wrists dangle respectfully. Sasha would blink in a frightened sort of way as though he were trying to hide his bulging eyes. I would stand by the door, scratching my arms so

14

that no one could see, surveying the whole ceremony. Then the senior assistant would kneel at the lady's feet and start trying shoes on. He could spread his fingers out astonishingly wide and his hands would start trembling. He was so careful when he touched a lady's foot that it seemed he was scared of hurting it. But most of the ladies' feet were fat and shaped like bottles with tapering necks, pointing downwards. Once a lady jerked her foot away, wriggled and exclaimed: 'Oo, you're tickling! . . .'

'I was just trying to be polite, madam,' the assistant explained quickly.

It was highly amusing seeing him crawling around the ladies and I often had to stare out into the street to stop laughing. But I usually found it absolutely impossible to keep my eyes off what was going on and the assistant's movements were really very funny. At the same time I thought that I would never learn how to spread my fingers out so 'politely', nor would I ever learn how to fit shoes so skilfully on to other people's feet. The owner would often go into a small room behind the counter and call Sasha in after him. The chief assistant would be left alone with a lady. Once, after touching a red-headed lady's foot, he put his thumb to his first two fingers and kissed them. The lady sighed and exclaimed: 'Oh, naughty, naughty!' This made the assistant puff his cheeks out and produce a deep 'Mm . . . mm . . m!' At this point I laughed so loud that I had to grab the door handle to stop myself from falling over. But the handle turned and I fell against the glass and broke it with my head. The assistant stamped his feet at me and the owner rapped me on the head with his heavy gold ring. Sasha tried to box my ears, and that evening, when we were on the way home, he told me in a firm, authoritative voice:

'You'll get the sack if you carry on like that. What was so funny?'

Then he explained that if a lady happened to take a fancy to the senior assistant it was good for business.

'A lady might not want any shoes at all. But she'll come all the same and buy some – just to have a look at him. Can't you understand? Here we are trying our hardest to teach you . . .'

Every morning our cook, who was a sick, irritable woman,

would wake me up an hour earlier than Sasha. I had to clean the boots and shoes and brush clothes for the owner and his wife, the chief assistant and Sasha, get the samovar ready, fetch fire-wood for the stoves and wash the dishes. When I arrived at the shop I swept the floor, dusted all round and made the tea. Then I had to make deliveries to customers, after which I went home for breakfast. While I was gone Sasha had to stand by the door and this really was beneath his dignity and he would swear at me:

'Lazy little devil! Making me do your work for you!'

Life was hard and boring in that shop. Up to then I had been used to fending for myself, spending whole days in the sandy streets of Kunavino* on the banks of the muddy Oka river or in the fields and woods. Now I did not have Grandmother with me, none of my old friends in fact, and everything conspired to irritate me. I began to see the seamy, deceitful side of life. Very often a lady customer would leave without buying a thing and then all three of them would feel insulted. The owner would wipe the smile off his face, stuff it in his pocket and start order-ing me around:

'Kashirin, put the shoes away!'

Then he would start swearing again:

'Old bag! Sticking her ugly mug in here! The silly old bitch must have got fed up sitting at home. She's got nothing better to do than hang round the shops all day. If she were my wife I'd show her...'

His own wife was a dried-up looking woman with black eyes and a big nose. She would stamp her feet and shout at him as though he were a servant.

Often after they had seen one of the ladies out with their obsequious bowing and oily compliments they would start discussing her in the most obscene, shameless way, which made me feel like running out into the street after her and telling her what they were saying. Of course, I knew very well that people often said nasty things behind one another's backs, but the way those three went on was really disgusting. It seemed that they thought they had been specially chosen, by some power above, to look upon everyone as their inferior and

* A suburb of Nizhny-Novgorod. (Trans.)

to pass judgement on the whole world. At the same time they were envious of nearly everyone and hardly anybody escaped their malicious comments. For example a young lady once came into the shop. She had bright red cheeks and sparkling eyes. She was wearing a velvet sleeveless cloak trimmed with black fur and her face seemed to be blossoming out of it like a wonderful flower. When she had taken her cloak off and handed it to Sasha she looked even prettier. A dress of bluish-grey silk fitted her slim figure very tightly and her ears glittered with diamonds. She reminded me of Vasilisa the Beautiful and I was sure she must be the Governor's wife.

They gave her a particularly servile welcome, bowing low as though she were a holy altar-lamp and choking themselves with their slimy compliments. All three then tore round the shop like demons. I could see their reflections in the showcases and I thought that the whole shop had suddenly caught fire and that everything was about to melt and take on a completely different form. When she had quickly chosen some expensive shoes and left, the owner smacked his lips and said in a whistling voice:

'The old bag! . . .'

'A mere *actress*,' sneered the assistant.

Then they would start telling each other about the lady's lovers and about her drunken sprees.

After dinner the owner went for a nap in the little room behind the counter and I opened his gold watch and poured vinegar into it. I just cannot describe the pleasure of seeing him wake up and leave the shop holding his watch, muttering in complete bewilderment:

'What's happened? My watch has started sweating! Never seen anything like it. Must be an evil omen . . .'

In spite of all the rushing around I had to do and all those household chores, the stifling boredom had a terribly soporific effect on me and the whole time I felt as if I were asleep. I began to think more and more of how I could get myself the sack.

People covered in snow passed by the shop door. They seemed to be late for a funeral and were trying to catch up with the hearse which was already on its way to the cemetery. Horses shivered as they struggled through the snowdrifts. Every day the bells in the church behind the shop rang out drearily for

Lent. They seemed to be beating against my head like heavy cushions – they did not hurt, but they deafened me and made me behave like an idiot. Once when I was sorting out a newly arrived consignment in the yard by the shop door the church watchman came up. He was an old, deformed man, who appeared to have been sewn together from old rags and if his dishevelled appearance was anything to go by it looked as though he had been mauled by dogs.

'*You*'d steal some galoshes for me, wouldn't you, eh?' he suggested.

I did not say a word. The old man sat down on an empty crate, yawned, made the sign of the cross over his mouth and went on:

'You *will* do it, won't you?'

'Stealing is wrong,' I informed him.

'But everyone does it. Have some respect for your elders!'

He made a pleasant change from the people I was living with. I sensed that he *knew* I would steal something for him, and I agreed to pass some galoshes out through one of the window ventilators.

'All right then,' he said calmly, but he was not exactly pleased. 'You won't let me down, will you? No, I can see you won't.'

He sat there silently for a few moments, wiping the dirty, wet snow from his boot-soles. Then he lit a clay pipe and said in a voice that made me jump:

'Supposing I *cheat* you? Supposing I take the shoes straight to your master and tell him you sold them to me for half a rouble? Eh? They're not worth more than two roubles anyway, and I'll say you let me have them for half, just as a present, eh?'

I was speechless and looked at him as though he had already carried out his threat. But he continued in that calm, snuffling voice of his, inspecting his boot-soles and puffing out blue smoke:

'Supposing your boss asks: "Go and test that boy, see if he really does steal" – what then?'

'I'm not going to give you any galoshes,' I said angrily.

'But you've got to now. You promised!'

He pulled me over by my arm, tapped my forehead with his cold finger and said lazily:

18

'Why did you agree then?'

'*You* asked me to steal,' I replied.

'But there's a thousand and one things I could have asked you to do! I could have asked you to burgle the church – would you have done it? Oh, you're such a little fool!'

He pushed me away and stood up.

'*I* don't need any galoshes, only gentlemen wear them. I was only joking. But because you're so stupid I'll let you ring the bells at Easter. You can see the whole town from the top of the belfry.'

'I've seen it already'.

'It looks prettier from the belfry.'

The toes of his boots sank deep into the snow as he slowly went round the corner of the church and I felt depressed as I watched him go. I did not know whether that old man had been really joking or if he had been sent by my master to test me and I was very worried. I felt scared now of going back to the shop.

Then Sasha leaped out into the yard and shouted:

'What the hell are you up to?'

I suddenly went mad and waved a pair of pliers at him. I knew that both he and the other assistant stole from the master. They would hide pairs of shoes or slippers in the stove-pipe and stuff them in their overcoat sleeves as they left the shop. I did not like this and I was frightened, as I had not forgotten the master's threats.

'Do *you* steal?' I asked Sasha.

'Not me, but the senior assistant does,' he said sternly. 'All I do is help him. He'll say to me: "Give me a hand!" And I have to do what he says or else he'll make trouble. It's not so long ago that the boss was a senior assistant himself, so he probably has a good idea of what's going on. So keep your mouth shut!'

He looked into the mirror as he spoke and straightened his tie with his fingers strangely splayed out like the senior assistant's.

He never tired of asserting his authority and power over me, always shouted at me in his deep voice and seemed to be brushing me aside with his outstretched arms when he gave me orders. I was stronger and taller than him, but skinny and clumsy: he was fat, soft and oily. In that frock-coat of his and those trousers with turn-ups he looked important and immovable, but there was something unpleasant and comical about him. He hated the cook, who was in fact a strange woman – it was impossible to make out if she was good-natured or spiteful.

'I like watching fights more than *anything* else,' she used to say, opening wide her fiery black eyes. 'And it makes no difference to me whether it's cocks, dogs or men – I just like fights!'

If there was a cock or pigeon fight in the yard she would drop what she was doing and stand there looking through the window, silent and deaf to the world, until the fight was over. In the evening she would tell Sasha and myself:

'Come on boys, what are you sitting there for when you could be fighting!'

This made Sasha angry.

'You old fool, I'm not a boy, but the junior assistant!'

'I couldn't tell from looking at you! As far as I'm concerned if you're not married you're a boy.'

'You old fool!'

'The devil's clever, but God doesn't love him!' she retorted.

Sasha found some of the things she said particularly annoying. He would tease her, and this made her squint at him contemptuously and say:

'Ugh, you horrible cockroach. God made a mistake letting *you* come into the world!'

Many times he tried to persuade me to smear her face with boot polish or soot while she was asleep, stick pins in her pillow or play some other practical joke on her. But I was afraid of the cook – she was a very light sleeper. She would get up several times in the night, light the lamp, sit on her bed, and peer into a corner of the room. Sometimes she would come over to the place where I slept behind the stove, wake me up and ask me in her hoarse voice:

'I can't sleep, Alexei, something's frightened me. Please talk to me.'

Although I was half asleep I would tell her stories while she sat silently rocking herself. Her warm body seemed to smell of wax and incense and I thought that she was not long for this world. At any moment she might fall flat on her face and just pass away. I would talk very loudly to her – purely out of fear – but she stopped me at once and said:

'Quiet, or you'll wake all that scum up! . . . They might think that we're lovers . . .'

She always sat in the same position when we talked: she would lean forward, her wrists between her knees, pressing them tight between her bony legs. She had hardly any breasts and in spite of her thick linen chemise her ribs stuck out just like hoops on a cracked barrel. For a long time she would sit there without saying a word and then suddenly she would whisper:

'I shouldn't mind dying, though, all this misery . . .'

Or else she would ask someone:

'I've had my life, haven't I?'

At other times she would interrupt me in the middle of a sentence and say:

'Go to sleep!' and her grey figure would silently disappear in the darkness of the kitchen.

Sasha called her a witch behind her back, so I suggested:

'Why don't you tell *her* that?'

'Think I'm frightened, do you!'

All the same he would immediately frown and say:

'I wouldn't say it to her face. She might really be a witch!'

She was contemptuous and intolerant in her attitude to everyone and did not make any concessions as far as I was concerned. At six in the morning she would tug my feet and shout:

'Want to sleep all day, do you! Fetch the firewood! Put the samovar on! Peel the potatoes!'

Then Sasha would wake up and start whining:

'What are you shouting about? I'll tell the boss! It's impossible to sleep in this place.'

The cook rushed round the kitchen and I could hear her bones creaking. Then she would glare at Sasha with eyes that were red from lack of sleep and say:

'Ugh, God's great mistake! If you were *my* step-son I'd show you a thing to two!'

'Bloody bitch,' Sasha would say as we went to the shop. 'We must see she gets the sack. Supposing we put salt in all the food without anyone seeing. Then they'll *have* to get rid of her! Or we could use kerosene instead. Stop yawning!'

'Why don't *you* do it then?'

He snorted angrily: 'Coward!'

The cook died before our very eyes: she was bending down to lift the samovar and suddenly she slumped to the floor as though someone had pushed her on to her back. Then, without saying a word, she rolled over on to her side with her arms stretched out and blood started pouring from her mouth. We both realized immediately that she was dead but we were too petrified to speak, and we just stood there gaping at her for a long time. In the end Sasha tore out of the kitchen. I did not know what to do and pressed my face to the window to be near the light. Then the master came, anxiously squatted by the cook and started pinching her face.

'Yes, she's dead all right. Wonder why?'

He began to cross himself in one corner in front of a small ikon of Nikolai the Miracle Worker. When he had said his prayers he shouted out into the hall:

'Kashirin, go and get the police!'

A policeman arrived, stamped around, and left after the master had given him a tip. Then he came back with a carrier. They took the cook by the legs and carried her out into the street. The master's wife looked out from the hall and told me:

'Give the floor a good wash!'

The master remarked:

'A good thing she died in the evening.'

I did not understand why it was 'a good thing'.

When we went to bed Sasha said in a voice which was strangely timid for him:

'Don't put the lamp out!'

'Frightened then?'

He put his head under the blanket and said softly:

'Let's sleep together over the stove.'

'It's too hot there.'

After a short silence he said:

'Why did she die like that – so suddenly? I told you she was a witch . . . I won't be able to sleep now . . .'

'Nor me.'

He started telling me stories about ghosts, how they left their graves, wandered till midnight through the town, looking for the places where they used to live, or where they had relatives.

'Ghosts can only remember the town in which they lived,' he said softly, 'but not the streets or houses.'

Everything grew much quieter, and it seemed to be getting darker as well.

Sasha lifted his head and asked:

'Like to have a look in my trunk?'

For a long time I had wanted to know what he had in there. He kept it padlocked and always took special precautions when he opened it. If I even tried to have a quick look he would rudely say: 'Well, what do you want?'

When I said that I wanted to have a look he sat on the bed with his feet dangling in the air and literally ordered me to put the trunk on the bed near his feet. The key hung on an old bit of string, together with a cross he wore next to his skin. After looking round the dark kitchen he frowned solemnly, unlocked the trunk and blew on the lid as though it were hot. Finally he lifted it right up and took out various sets of underwear The trunk was half full of pill-boxes, different coloured tea wrappers and old boot-polish and sardine tins.

'What's all that?'

'You'll see.'

He put the trunk between his legs and leaned over it, softly chanting:

'Our Father which art in heaven . . .'

I expected to see some toys. I had never had any myself and I treated them with an outward contempt. But I always felt jealous of boys who had them. I was delighted to see that someone who took himself so seriously as Sasha had some toys, even though he was ashamed of them and hid them away. This I could well understand.

He opened the first box, took out a pair of spectacles without any lenses, put them on, looked at me very sternly and said:

'It doesn't matter if the lenses are missing, the frames are really something special!'

'Let's try them on!'

'They're not your size. They're for dark eyes and yours are bright,' he explained and grunted just like the master. But suddenly he became frightened and looked round the kitchen. In one of the boot-polish tins there were buttons of all descriptions and he proudly explained:

'I found them all in the street. By myself. There's thirty-seven altogether!'

In the next box there were large brass pins which he had also found in the streets, old boot-soles – some of them broken, a few still intact – shoe and slipper buckles, a bronze door handle, a broken cane-head made of bone, a girl's comb, a book called *Interpretation of Dreams and Almanac* and a pile of other similar worthless rubbish. When I had gone collecting rags and bones I could easily have accumulated ten times as much old junk in a single month. Sasha's finds disappointed and embarrassed me and I felt deeply sorry for him. He scrutinized every item very carefully and lovingly fondled it. His fat lips pouted and he gazed at his possessions tenderly, anxiously, with his bulging eyes. Those spectacle frames made his childlike face look very comical.

'What do you need all that junk for?' I asked.

He glanced at me through his spectacle frames and asked in a brittle, treble voice:

'Would you like a present?'

'No, I don't want anything.'

He was clearly offended by my refusal and by my complete lack of interest in his 'wealth'. He did not say anything for a moment and then quietly suggested:

'Get the towel. We'd better give the whole lot a wipe over or everything'll soon be thick with dust.'

When everything was dusted and put away he did a somersault on the bed and lay with his face to the wall. It started raining and water dripped down from the roof. The wind knocked at the windows. Without turning round Sasha said:

'Wait until it's drier in the garden then I'll show you something to make you gasp!'

I got ready for bed and did not reply. After a few seconds he suddenly jumped up, scratched at the wall and said in a voice so convincing that I was scared out of my wits:

'Oh God, I'm frightened! God in heaven, I'm so scared! What was that?'

At this point I was so terrified that I went cold all over. I thought that I could see the cook standing by the windows and looking out on to the yard with her forehead pressed to the glass – just like she did when she was alive and watched the cocks fighting in the yard. Sasha sobbed, dug his nails into the wall and kicked his legs out. I felt I was walking over burning coals, but I managed to cross the kitchen and lie down beside him. At last we fell asleep from the sheer exhaustion of crying our hearts out.

A few days later there was some sort of holiday. The shop stayed open until mid-day and then everyone went home for lunch. When the master and his wife had gone off for a snooze Sasha said to me in a mysterious voice:

'Let's go *now*!'

I thought that I was now going to see something to make me gasp. We went out into the garden. About half a dozen old lime trees stood on a narrow strip of land between the two houses. Their thick trunks were covered with green mouldy lichen and their bare black projecting branches seemed to be dead. There wasn't a single crow's nest in any of them; they looked just like monuments in a cemetery. There was nothing besides those lime trees in the garden – not even a bush or a blade of grass. Along the footpaths the earth was so firmly trodden down and black that it looked like cast iron. There were bare patches among the rotting foliage and one could see that the paths were also covered in mould, just like duck weed on a stagnant pond.

Sasha went round a corner towards a fence near the street, stopped under a tree, and gaped at the dim windows of the house next door. He squatted down and began scraping the leaves away with his hands until I could see a thick root and two bricks planted deep in the earth beside it. He pulled them out. Underneath was a piece of roofing metal and under that was a square board. Finally he uncovered a large hole. Sasha lit a match, then a candle-end, stuck it into the hole and said:

'Have a look, but don't be frightened!'

But one thing was clear – he was frightened himself. The

25

candle shook in his hand, he turned pale and his lips parted very unpleasantly. His eyes became moist as he gently placed his free hand behind his back. His fear infected me and I peered very timidly into the hole beneath the root which formed a little vault over it. Then he lit three candles, filling the hole with a blue light. The vault was fairly large and about as deep as a bucket, only wider. Its sides were completely inlaid with fragments of coloured glass and china. In the middle, where it was a little higher, stood a tiny coffin draped with a piece of red fustian and decorated with bits of tin foil. Something that looked like a piece of brocade was half draped over the coffin, and a bird's grey claws and a sparrow's sharp little head stuck out from underneath it. Behind the coffin there was a pulpit with a little bronze cross and round it burned three wax stumps held by candlesticks wrapped in silver and gold sweet papers. The tapering ends of the candle flames turned towards the entrance to the hole, which was filled with the dim glow of many-coloured patches of light. The smell of wax, warm decay and earth struck my face and a broken rainbow flickered and swam before my eyes. All this startled me so much that my fear vanished.

'Do you like it?' Sasha asked.

'What *is* it?'

'It's a chapel,' he explained. 'Doesn't it look like one?'

'I'm not sure.'

'That sparrow's the corpse! Who knows, its bones might turn out to be holy, because it was a martyr and suffered innocently.'

'Was it dead when you found it?'

'No, it flew into the shed and I covered it with my hat and suffocated it.'

'Why?'

'Well, because...'

He looked me in the eye and asked again:

'Do you like it?'

'No.'

When I said this he leaned over to the hole, quickly covered it over with the board and sheet of metal and stuck the bricks back in the ground.

Then he stood up, brushed the mud from his knees and said threateningly: 'Why don't you like it?'

'I feel sorry for the sparrow.'

He fixed his motionless eyes on me and looked straight through me just as though he were blind. Then he pushed me in the chest and shouted:

'You fool! You're only saying that because you're jealous! Do you think that old thing you made in the garden when we lived in Kanatny street was any better?'

I remembered the little summer house I had built and answered confidently:

'Yes, of course it was better!'

Sasha threw off his jacket, rolled up his sleeves, spat on the palms of his hands and said:

'In that case, we'd better fight it out!'

I did not want to fight. The boredom of the whole afternoon had drained all my strength. I felt awkward when I saw my cousin's furious face. He leaped at me, butted me in the chest and knocked me over. Then he sat on top of me and shouted:

'Do you want to live or die?'

But I was the stronger and I was very, very angry. A moment later he was lying face downwards with his hands pressed to his head, making a hoarse, panting noise. I was frightened and tried to make him stand up again, but he fought me off with his arms and legs, which frightened me even more. I moved away, wondering what to do, while he lifted his head up and said:

'Well, do I win? I'll stay here rolling on the ground like this until the master comes. I'll tell everyone that *you* started it and you'll get the sack!'

He swore and kept on threatening me. What he had said so incensed me that I rushed over to the cave, pulled the bricks out, flung the coffin and the sparrow over the fence into the street, dug everything up and stamped it into the ground.

'There, how do you like that?'

Sasha reacted strangely to this sudden fit of violence. The whole time he just sat there watching what I was doing with lips slightly parted and a frown on his face. He did not say one word until I had finished. Then he slowly got up, shook himself,

27

threw his jacket over his shoulder and said in a calm, menacing voice:

'You wait! I made all this on purpose, to cast a spell on you!'

I sank to the ground as though his words had literally wounded me and everything inside me went cold. He left without looking round and his complete and utter calm made me feel even worse. I decided that next day I would run away from the town, from the master, from Sasha and his witchcraft, from all that tiresome, idiotic life.

Next morning the new cook woke me up and shouted:

'Good God! What's happened to your face?'

'I must be under the spell now,' I thought and I felt terribly depressed. But the cook laughed so gaily that I could not help smiling as I looked into the mirror. My face was thickly smeared with soot.

'Is that Sasha's work?'

'It could have been *me*!' the cook laughed.

I started cleaning the shoes and when I put my hand into one of them a pin stuck in my finger.

'Yes, it's all part of the witchcraft,' I thought again.

Every shoe without exception had pins or needles in it, and they were so cleverly hidden that my hands were soon full of them. Then I took a jug of cold water and with great pleasure poured it over the head of the sorcerer who had either not woken up yet or was just pretending to be asleep.

All the same, I felt terrible. I kept seeing that coffin and the sparrow, those grey twisted claws, that waxen beak pathetically sticking upwards, and all those many-coloured lights that never stopped flickering: it was as though they were trying to form themselves into a rainbow, but just could not. The grave appeared to open up even wider before me and the bird's claws grew larger and larger, and seemed to be alive again as they stretched upwards and twitched in the air. I decided to run away that same evening, but just before dinner, while I was warming up some cabbage soup over a kerosene stove, I became so carried away by these thoughts that the saucepan boiled over. When I tried to put the light out I spilled boiling soup all over my hands and they had to send me to hospital.

I remember what a nightmare of a place it was. In that yellow, hazy emptiness, grey and white figures in shrouds blindly swarmed round me, mumbling and groaning. A tall man on crutches, with eyebrows that looked like moustaches, went around shaking his large black beard and whistling through his teeth as he roared: 'I'll report you to his Holy Eminence!'

The hospital beds put me in mind of coffins and the patients, lying there with their noses facing upwards, looked like dead sparrows. The yellow walls seemed to rock to and fro, the ceiling billowed out into an enormous sail and the floor swelled up like the sea and made the beds slide up and down the ward. The whole place was terrifying, insubstantial. Through the windows I could see branches sticking out and I thought they were going to use them to flog someone. In the doorway a red-haired, thinnish, corpse-like figure danced about, tugging at its shroud with its shortish arms and screeching:

'I don't want any lunatics round here!'

The man on crutches bellowed at him:

'I'll report you to his Ho-oly Emin-ence!'

Grandfather, Grandmother, and in fact everyone I knew said that hospitals kill people and I thought that my life would soon be over.

A bespectacled woman came up to me. She was wearing a shroud like the others and she scribbled something down on the blackboard at the head of my bed. The chalk broke and the pieces rained down on my head.

'What's your name?' she asked.

'Don't know.'

'Haven't you got one?'

'No.'

'Don't you come it with me or you'll get a good hiding!'

I was so sure she meant what she said that I did not reply. She hissed like a cat and looked just like one as she silently glided out of the ward.

Two lamps were lit and with their yellow flames they hung close to the ceiling like two lost eyes, blinking and dazzling me, and trying to merge together.

Over in one corner someone said:

'Like a game of cards?'

'How can I – with only one hand?'

'Aha, so they cut the other off!'

At once I thought they had cut someone's hand off for playing cards. What would they do to *me* before they finally finished me off? My hands ached and burned just as though someone were pulling my bones out. I softly cried to myself from pain and fear and I shut my eyes so that no one could see the tears, but they trickled under my eyelids and rolled down my temples into my ears.

Night came and everyone slumped on to his bed and hid under the grey blankets. It grew quieter every minute; all I could hear was someone muttering: 'No, it's no good. He's scum and so is she . . .'

I wanted to write to Grandmother to ask her to come and help mē escape while I was still alive but I was unable to: my hands were completely useless. Perhaps I might try and slip out without anyone seeing? The night became more and more deathly and it seemed to have settled in for ever. I quietly lowered my legs on to the floor and went over to the door which was half open. Out in the corridor, on a wooden bench underneath a lamp, I could see a grey, bristly head, enveloped in smoke. Dark, sunken eyes were looking straight at me. It was too late to hide.

'Who's that wandering around? Come here.'

The voice was quite soft and not in the least frightening. I went up and saw a round face with short bits of hair growing down the sides. On the scalp the hair was longer and stuck out in all directions, forming a halo of little silvery rays. A bunch of keys hung on the man's belt. If his hair and beard had been any longer he would have looked just like Paul the Apostle.

'What's that – had your hands cooked then? What are you doing wandering around at this time of night? Who gave you permission?'

He blew some smoke into my face, put his warm arm round my neck and pulled me over to him.

'Frightened?'

'Yes.'

'Everyone is at first. But there's nothing to be afraid of. Especially with me, I never harm anyone. Like a smoke? It's all right if you don't want to. It's a bit early, anyway . . . wait a couple of years. Where are your mother and father? You haven't any? Well, you can do without parents, but don't be a coward! Understand?'

It was a long time since I had met anyone who spoke so simply, in such a friendly way, and who used words I could understand. It was incredibly pleasant listening to him. When he led me over to my bed I asked him:

'Please sit with me!'

'All right,' he agreed.

'Who are you?'

'Me? A soldier, a real live soldier, from the Caucasus. I fought in the war – well, what else would you expect? A soldier lives for war. I've fought the Hungarians, the Cherkassians, the Poles – you name them, I've fought them! War, my friend, is no laughing matter!'

For a moment I closed my eyes and when I opened them Grandmother was sitting in his place. She was wearing a dark dress. The soldier was standing by her side saying: 'So they died, the whole lot of them?'

The sun suddenly lit up the whole ward, turning it golden and then it vanished, only to cast its gleam over everything once more: it was just like a mischievous child playing games.

Grandmother leaned over and asked:

'Well, dear? Did they cripple you? I told that red-haired old devil a thing or two.'

'I'll see everything's done according to regulations,' the soldier said as he went away, while Grandmother wiped the tears from her face and said:

'It seems the soldier's from Balakhna.'

I still thought I was dreaming it all and I did not reply. The doctor came and dressed my burns, and in no time I was riding in a cab along the streets of the town with Grandmother who started telling me:

'That Grandfather of yours seems to have gone crazy. He's become so greedy it makes you sick! His new friend, Khlyst the furrier, pinched a hundred rouble note from his psalter. You should have heard the goings-on!'

The sun shone brightly and clouds drifted across the sky like white birds. Now we were crossing a plank-bridge over the

Volga. Below us the breaking ice crackled and heaved upwards and the water gurgled under the wooden boards. The golden crosses of the flesh-coloured cathedral in the fair glinted in the sunlight. A broad-faced peasant woman carrying a bundle of satin-smooth willow twigs passed by. From this I knew that spring was coming and it would soon be Easter! My heart quivered like a skylark.

'I *do* love you, Grandmother!'

This did not appear to surprise her and she told me very calmly:

'That's because we're of the same blood! But I'm not boasting when I tell you that even perfect strangers love me, glory to the Holy Virgin!'

Then she added with a smile:

'Soon she'll be rejoicing, because her son's going to rise from the dead. But my little Varyusha...'

And she did not say any more.

Chapter 2

GRANDFATHER met me in the yard. He was kneeling down making some sort of a wedge with a chopper, which he lifted up in the air as though he were going to throw it at me. Then he took his cap off and said with a sneer:

'Good day, your Reverence! Your Excellency! Finished your apprenticeship? Hm, then you'd better go your own sweet way now. Oh yes! Oh, you-u-u-u . . .'

'All right, we know all about it,' Grandmother said hurriedly as she shooed him away. As she went inside and put the samovar on she told me:

'Your Grandfather's completely ruined now. There was some money but he lent it on interest to his godson Nikolai and didn't take a receipt. I really don't know what happened exactly, but he went bankrupt and all the money disappeared. All because we didn't help the poor or take pity on the unfortunate. God must have thought about us and said to Himself: "Why was I so generous to the Kashirins?" Then He must have decided to take away all we had . . .'

She glanced round and went on:

'I've been trying the whole time to win Him over, to stop Him being too hard on the old man. I've been giving away some of the money that I've earned with my own hands to the poor during the night, and no one knows anything about it. If you like we'll go out *tonight* . . . I've got some money . . .'

Grandfather came in, blinked and asked:

'Been stuffing yourself again?'

'We haven't touched anything of *yours*,' Grandmother said. 'But if you like you can sit with us. There's enough to go round.'

Grandfather sat down at the table and said in a soft voice:

'Pour me some tea.'

Everything in the room was the same as before, except that Mother's corner had a sad emptiness about it. A sheet of paper hung on the wall over Grandfather's head, bearing the following inscription in big, capital letters:

'Jesus be my Saviour! May Thy Holy Name be with me all the days of my life.'

'Who wrote that?' I asked.

Grandfather did not reply. After a little while Grandmother smiled and informed me:

'That piece of paper's worth a hundred roubles!'

'That's none of your business,' Grandfather shouted. 'I'll give all my money away to strangers if I want to!'

Grandmother said calmly:

'There's just *nothing* to give away now. And when you did have some money you kept it all to yourself.'

'Shut up!' Grandfather screeched.

Everything seemed to be following the same old pattern. Kolya woke up in the clothes basket he slept in on a trunk in the corner and looked at us. The blue slits of his eyes were barely visible from below those eyelids. He had become greyer, limp and weak. He did not recognize me, turned away and closed his eyes again.

Out in the street some bad news was waiting for me. Vyakhir had died, suffocated in a flour mill during Passion Week. Khabi had gone to live in the town, and Yaz had lost the use of his legs and did not go out any more.

After telling me all this the black-eyed Kostroma added angrily:

'The boys are dying off very fast nowadays!'

'But didn't you say only *Vyakhir* died?'

'Doesn't make any difference. Anyone who leaves this street is as good as dead. You only get time to make friends with someone, get used to him and he's sent off to work somewhere: then he might as well be dead as far as *you're* concerned. There's some new people at the Chesnokov's, where you used to live, called Yevseenko. They've a little boy, Nyushka, who's not so bad, quite smart really. He's got two sisters. One's still very young and the other's lame and hobbles around on crutches. She's pretty!'

He thought for a moment and added:

'Me and Churka's in love with her and we never stop quarrelling!'

'With her?'

34

'With *her*? No, only among ourselves. Hardly ever with *her*!'

Of course, I realized that big boys and even grown men fell in love and knew its crude implications well enough, and it was unpleasant hearing this. I was sorry for Kostroma and I felt awkward looking at his gangling figure and his angry black eyes.

I saw the lame girl in the evening. When she came down the steps into the yard she dropped one of her crutches and stood there helplessly, a thin, frail-looking creature trying to hold on to the railings with hands so thin that one could almost see through them. I wanted to pick the crutch up for her, but could not do much as my hands were still covered in bandages. I struggled for a long time and finally became very annoyed. She stood there on the steps and laughed softly:

'What's wrong with your hands?'

'Scalded them.'

'And *I*'m lame. Do you live here? How long were you in hospital? I was in hospital for ever so lo-o-ong!'

She sighed and added: 'Oh, such a long time!'

She was wearing an oldish, but clean white dress with a light-blue horseshoe pattern. Her smoothly-combed hair hung over her breast in short thick plaits. A pale-blue fire gleamed in the calm depths of her large, serious eyes, lighting up her pinched face with its sharp nose. She had a pleasant smile, but I did not like her. With that sickly looking body of hers she seemed to be saying: 'Don't touch me! Please!'

How could my two friends possibly fall in love with *her*?

'I've been ill for a long time,' she said eagerly, apparently very proud of the fact. 'A neighbour cast a spell over me, because she'd had a row with mother. That's how she got her own back... Was it awful being in hospital?'

'Yes...'

I began to feel awkward talking to her and I went inside.

Around midnight Grandmother gently woke me up.

'Shall we go then? If you try and help others your hands will heal up much quicker...'

She took me by the arm and led me through the darkness as though I were blind. It was a murky, damp night and the blustery wind never dropped – it was just like a fast-flowing river, and the cold sand seemed to be grabbing me by the feet. Grandmother would creep up to some small houses, very cautiously, cross herself three times, leave a five-kopek piece and three biscuits on the window-sill and cross herself again as she peered up at the starless sky and whispered:

'Holy Queen of Heaven, help the poor! We are all sinners in thine eyes!'

The further we went from the house the more wretched and deserted everything became. The night sky seemed to have hidden the moon and stars for ever in its fathomless depths. A dog ran out from somewhere, stopped near us and started howling. Its eyes shone in the darkness. Like a coward I clung closer to Grandmother.

'Don't worry,' she said, 'it's only a dog. It's too late for the devil to be out walking – the cocks have crowed already.'

She coaxed the dog over to us, stroked it and said:

'Now watch it! Don't go frightening my little grandson!'

The dog rubbed itself against my legs and all three of us moved on.

Grandmother left her 'secret charity' on twelve different window-sills. It began to grow light, grey shapes of houses loomed up out of the darkness and the belfry of the Napolnaya church, which was white as sugar, soared into the sky. The brick wall round the cemetery seemed to be full of holes like a badly-made mat.

'The old girl's tired,' Grandmother said, 'time to go home! When those women get up they'll find the Holy Virgin has left a little something for their children! When you've got nothing a little comes in handy! Ah, Alyosha. People lead miserable lives and no one seems to care!:

> The rich man doesn't think of God,
> He doesn't dream of the Final Judgement,
> He is neither friend nor brother to the poor,
> All he wants is to collect more gold –
> Which will turn to fiery coals in hell!

There you are! We must live for each other. But God lived for everyone. I'm so glad that you've come back . . .'

In a quiet way I was glad too, and I had the vague feeling that

I had seen something that night I would never forget. The reddish dog with its foxlike muzzle and gentle, guilty-looking eyes jogged along at my side.

'Is it going to live with us now?' I asked Grandmother.

'Why not if it wants to? Here's a biscuit for it – I've two left. Let's sit for a bit on this bench. I'm tired!'

We sat down on a bench near the yard gates and the dog lay down at our feet, chewing away at the dry biscuit.

Grandmother told me:

'A Jewess lives over there. She's got nine children, each smaller than the next. When I ask her: "How do you cope with it all, Mosevna?" she answers: "My God helps me. Who else is there?"'

I snuggled up against Grandmother's warm body and fell asleep.

Once more life flowed on in a swift rich stream, and every day brought some new experience, something that both thrilled and disturbed me, that upset me deeply and made me stop and think.

It was not long before I was trying every way I could of seeing the crippled girl as often as possible, of having a talk with her on that bench by the gate or just sitting next to her without saying a word. It was very pleasant just sitting there and saying nothing. She looked as neat and clean as a chaffinch, and she told marvellous stories about the life of the Cossacks on the River Don. She had lived there a long time with her uncle who was an engineer in a refinery. Afterwards her father, who was a locksmith, moved to Nizhny. She told me: 'And then I had another uncle who served under the Tsar himself.'

In the evenings, when there was a holiday, everyone in the street went 'outside the gates' as it was called. Young boys and girls went off to the fields by the cemetery to sing and dance, the men went off to the pubs, while the women and young children stayed behind. Some of them sat by the gates, either on the sand or on little benches and they made a terrible din with their quarrelling and gossiping. The children would play ball games and skittles. Their mothers would watch them, encouraging the good players and making fun of the weak. The noise was deafening and the general gaiety was unforgettable. The presence of the big boys among small fry like us brought a spirit of fierce competition which made all the games particularly lively. But however much Kostroma, Churka and myself were carried away, sooner or later one or other of us would run off and start boasting in front of the crippled girl:

'Lyudmila, did you see me knock all five skittles over?'

She would smile sweetly and nod her head several times.

Previously we had all tried to keep on the same side during the games, but now I could see that Churka and Kostroma always played on different ones, and that each one tried in every way he knew to outdo the other in skill and strength, and this often led to tears and fights. Once they fought so furiously that some of the older boys had to part them and pour cold water over them, as though they were dogs. Lyudmila would stamp her good foot on the ground as she sat on the bench, and when the warriors rolled over to her she drove them away with a crutch and shouted in a frightened voice: 'Stop it!' Her face was almost drained of colour, her eyes had lost their fire and rolled around as though she were having hysterics.

On another occasion Kostroma, who had disgraced himself by losing at skittles to Churka, hid himself behind an oat-bin in a grocer's and stayed there squatting and crying to himself, which was enough to terrify anyone: he clenched his teeth until his cheekbones stuck out and his bony face seemed to turn to stone. Large, heavy tears trickled from his gloomy black eyes. When I tried to comfort him he choked with tears and whispered:

'You wait, I'll sling a brick at his fat head. Then he'll know what's what!'

After this Churka began to show off in earnest. He would swagger down the middle of the street like young men did when they went courting, his hat cocked and his hands stuck in his pockets. He had learned how to spit rather dashingly through his front teeth and he promised me:

'I'm going to learn to smoke soon. I've tried twice already, but I was sick.'

But this did not please me at all. I could see that I was losing a friend and it seemed that Lyudmila was to blame.

One evening when I was sorting out some rags and bones

and other old rubbish I had collected, Lyudmila came to see me, swaying on her crutches and waving her right arm:

'Hello,' she said and nodded three times. 'Did Kostroma go with you today?'

'Yes.'

'And Churka as well?'

'Churka's not friends with us any more. It's all your fault. They're in love with you and they keep fighting over it.'

She blushed and then said in a mocking voice:

'Well, I ask you! Why blame *me*?'

'Why did you make them fall in love with you?'

'*I* never asked them,' she replied angrily and went away saying: 'It's all so stupid. I'm older than them. I'm fourteen. Boys don't usually fall in love with older girls . . .'

'That's all *you* know,' I shouted, trying to annoy her. 'Take the sister of that shopkeeper Khlystov. She's really quite old, but just look how she runs around with all the boys . . .'

Lyudmila turned towards me and dug her crutch deep into the sand.

'You don't know *anything*!' she replied hurriedly, with tears in her voice. Those eyes that I liked so much looked really beautiful when they flared up.

'That shopkeeper's sister's a tart. Do you think I'm like her? I'm still a small girl and nobody's allowed to touch or pinch me . . . If you'd read the second part of that novel *Kamchadalka* you'd be in a position to talk!'

She sobbed as she walked away. I felt sorry for her – there was some truth in what she said, and I had not realized what it was. How could my friends keep on pinching her and still claim that they were in love with her?

The next day, in an attempt to atone for my rudeness, I bought her seven kopeks' worth of barley-sugar drops. I knew these were her favourites.

'Like some?' I asked.

'Clear off, I don't want to be friends with you.'

But she took the sweets all the same and said:

'You might have wrapped them up – your hands are filthy.'

'I didn't have time to wash all the dirt off.'

She took my hand in hers which was warm and dry and examined it.

'Look what you've done to it!'

'But yours has prick marks all over.'

'That's from needles – I do a lot of sewing.'

A few minutes later, after she had looked round first, she suggested:

'Listen, let's go and hide somewhere and read *Kamchadalka*. Would you like to?'

For a long time we tried to discover somewhere to hide, but could not find a place where we would not be disturbed. In the end we decided to go into the front part of the bath-house. Although it was dark there we could sit by the window, which looked out on to a muddy corner between the shed and the neighbouring slaughter-house. Hardly anybody ever went there. Lyudmila sat sideways to the window, her crippled leg propped up on a bench, and her good leg resting on the floor. She hid her face behind the tattered little book and I could hear the trembling in her voice as she read out a lot of incomprehensible and boring words. But I was very excited all the same. As I sat there on the ground I could see those serious eyes moving like light-blue flames over the pages. At times a tear formed in them and her voice started shaking. She hurriedly read out unfamiliar words in phrases that I found impossible to follow. However, I managed to remember some of them and tried to turn them into poetry, twisting them about in every possible way, which ruined any hope of understanding what the book was all about.

The dog would sleep on my lap. I called it 'Wind' as it was hairy and long, ran very fast and growled like the autumn wind in a chimney.

'Are you listening?' she asked.

I nodded silently. That jumble of words made me more and more excited and I wanted to set them out differently, as though they were songs in which each word had a life of its own and burned like a star in the sky. When it grew dark Lyudmila lowered the pale hand in which she held the book and asked:

'Did you like that? Now you can see for yourself!'

From that day on we often went to the bath-house. To my

great delight Lyudmila soon stopped reading from *Kamchadalka*: if she had asked me, I could not have told her what it was all about. It seemed to have no ending, because after part two, with which we had started, there was part three. And later she told me there was a part four as well.

We particularly enjoyed ourselves on rainy days, as long as it was not Saturday, when they used to stoke the boilers. When it rained no one would go outside into the yard and come and find us in our dark hiding-place.

Lyudmila was terrified that we might be caught.

'I wonder what they'd think then?' she asked quietly.

I knew very well and I was terrified of being caught as well.

We would sit there for hours on end, chatting away about different things. Sometimes I would tell her stories that I had heard from Grandmother. Lyudmila would tell me stories about Cossack life on the river Medveditsa.

'Oh, how wonderful it was there,' she would say with a sigh. 'And what's there to live for here? This place is only fit for beggars...'

I decided that when I grew up I must go and see the river Medveditsa.

Soon we found we could do without the bath-house. Lyudmila's mother got a job on Saturdays with the furrier and left the house in the morning. Her sister was at school and her brother worked in a tile factory. On rainy days I would go there and help Lyudmila do the cooking, clean the living-room and the kitchen. She would laugh and say:

'We'll live together, like man and wife, but we'll sleep in different rooms. We'll be far better off that way. Husbands don't usually help their wives!...'

If I had any money I'd buy her some sweets. We would drink tea and pour cold water over the samovar afterwards in case her mother found out we had been using it. Sometimes Grandmother would come over and sit with us, making lace or embroidering. She would tell us wonderful stories. When Grandfather went into the town Lyudmila would come over to our house and then we could relax and enjoy ourselves. Grandmother would say:

'Oh, it's a good life! All you need is a kopek in your pocket!'

She encouraged our friendship.

'It's *good* for a boy and girl to be friends. Only they mustn't get up to any tricks!'

In the simplest possible way she explained what 'getting up to tricks' meant. She explained it beautifully, as though inspired, and I understood from what she said that she did not want us to touch flowers or plants until they had bloomed, otherwise they would lose their fragrance or their fruit.

We did not want to 'get up to tricks' anyway, but this did not prevent Lyudmila and myself talking about what is best left unsaid here. Of course, we only spoke like this because we felt we had to, because we could not avoid seeing the uglier side of the relationships between men and women, which revolted us.

Lyudmila's father Yevseenko was a handsome man of about forty, with curly hair and a moustache, and he was in the habit of twitching his bushy eyebrows in a particularly masterful way. Strangely enough he never spoke – at least I can never remember him saying anything. When he fondled children he made a mumbling noise like a mute and he even beat his wife in silence.

In the evenings, when there was a holiday, he used to walk to the town gates in a blue shirt, baggy velveteen trousers and brightly polished shoes with a large accordion strapped to his back and he would stand there just like a soldier on sentry duty. At that time the 'promenading' past the gates would begin. Girls and women would file past, just like ducklings, giving Yevseenko furtive looks from under their eyelashes, or staring at him quite brazenly with hungry eyes. He would stand there with his lower lip stuck out and pick out those he fancied with his dark eyes. There was something nasty that reminded one of dogs in that silent conversation of eyes, in that slow procession that seemed to be going to its doom. It seemed that he had only to wink in that imperious way of his for any one of them to flop down meekly on the filthy sand as though she had been struck dead.

'Look how the old goat's goggling at them, the filthy devil!' Lyudmila's mother would grumble.

She was a tall, thin woman with a dirty face; with her cropped hair (she had just recovered from typhus) she looked like a worn-out broom. Lyudmila would sit next to her and try, without much success, to take her attention away from the street, and stubbornly kept cross-examining her.

'Leave off, you pest, you miserable little freak,' her mother would mutter, and blink anxiously. Her narrow, mongoloid eyes had a strange brightness and immobility and seemed perpetually fixed on some object.

'Don't worry, mama, it doesn't matter,' Lyudmila would say. 'Just look how the mat-maker's wife has tarted herself up.'

'*I*'d be able to dress a bit smarter if it weren't for you three eating me out of house and home,' her mother would answer savagely, very near to tears, with her eyes riveted on that large stout mat-maker's widow. In fact she looked like a small house and her bosom stuck out just like a front porch. Her red face, which was tightly bound round in a green shawl, resembled an attic window when the sun was shining on it.

Yevseenko would prop his accordion against his chest and start playing. The instrument had innumerable stops and its sounds seemed to lure one away somewhere. Children from the whole street came rushing up to him, threw themselves at his feet and sank in ecstasy on to the sand.

'You wait, one of these days someone's going to bash your face in,' Yevseenko's wife said menacingly. He would scowl at her in silence.

The mat-maker's widow slumped down like a stone on a bench by Khlystov's shop, which was not very far away, and sat there burning with passion, her head flopping on one shoulder. In the fields behind the cemetery the twilight glowed red. Large chunks of brightly dressed human flesh glided down the street as though it were a river. Children dashed around like a whirlwind. The warm air was mild and heady, and the heat of the day had given the sand a certain sharpness. But strongest of all was the fatty, sickly smell of blood from the slaughter-house, while the pungent, salty smell of hides wafted over from the furrier's drying-yard.

Chattering women, men with their drunken bellowing, the shrill cries of children, the music of the low-pitched accordion – all these sounds became one deep rumbling and the ever-fertile earth seemed to give a mighty sigh. Everything was so

43

crude and naked, but it inspired a firm unshakeable belief in a shamelessly animal way of life – a life that seemed to be proud of its immense powers, but which at the same time was anxiously seeking an outlet for them. Now and again the noise would strike right at one's heart and painful phrases would engrave themselves in the memory – to stay there for ever:

'You can't all beat him up at once. Take it one at a time . . .' or:

'Who'll look after us if we don't?'

'Was God having a joke when he created women?'

Night was drawing near. The air grew fresher and the noise died down. Those wooden houses seemed to be swelling out to an enormous size as they became enveloped in shadows. Children were dragged off to bed – some of them slept where they were, underneath fences, on their mother's knees or at their feet: little boys usually become more docile and easier to manage when night comes.

Yevseenko had mysteriously vanished and it was as though he had simply melted away. The mat-maker's widow had disappeared too, and I could hear the deep music of the accordion playing somewhere beyond the cemetery. Lyudmila's mother would sit hunched up on the bench, with her back arched, just like a cat. Grandmother would go off and drink tea with a neighbour who was a midwife and a procuress. She was a large, muscular woman with a nose like a duck's beak and she wore a gold medal 'For saving those in distress' on her flat, masculine chest. The whole street was afraid of her and thought that she was a witch. They said that once when there was a fire she dragged three children belonging to some colonel and his invalid wife out of the flames. Grandmother was firm friends with her. If they happened to see each other coming along the street they would both smile very warmly – even from a long way off.

Kostroma, Lyudmila and myself were once sitting on a bench by the gates. Churka challenged Lyudmila's brother to a fight, and they rolled around on the sand with their bodies locked together, raising clouds of dust. Kostroma squinted at her with his black eyes and started telling stories about the hunter Kalinin, a grey-haired old man with cunning eyes. He

44

had a bad reputation and was known throughout the whole district. Recently he had died. They did not bury him in the cemetery sand however, but left the coffin above the ground, away from the other graves. The coffin was black, and supported by long stilts. A cross, a hunting spear, a stick and two bones were painted in white on the lid. Every night, Kostroma told us, as soon as it was dark, the old man would climb out of his coffin and wander round the cemetery looking for something until the first cocks crew.

'Don't talk about such terrible things,' Lyudmila said in a frightened voice.

'Get off!' Churka shouted as he freed himself from her brother's clutches. Then he said sneeringly to Kostroma:

'You're lying! I saw them bury the coffin myself. They left the surface clear for the tombstone. And as for ghosts walking, that's just the sort of nonsense you would expect from drunken blacksmiths.'

Kostroma did not look at him and said angrily:

'Well, go and sleep in the cemetery if that's what you think!'

They started arguing, but Lyudmila wearily shook her head and asked:

'Mummy, do corpses get up in the night?'

'Yes, they *do* get up,' she repeated, and her voice sounded like a distant echo.

Valyok the shopkeeper's son, a fat red-faced boy of about twenty, came up to us, listened to the argument and said:

'I'll give any one of you who lies on the coffin until dawn twenty kopeks and ten cigarettes. But if he chickens out, then I'm allowed to pull his ears as much as I like. Well? Any offers?'

This remark was followed by an awkward silence. Then Lyudmila's mother said:

'How stupid, encouraging children like that! . . .'

'Give me a rouble and *I'll* do it,' Churka gloomily suggested.

At once Kostroma asked spitefully:

'Too scared to do it for twenty kopeks?'

Then he said to Valyok:

'If you gave him a *rouble* he wouldn't go. All he can do is show off.'

45

'I'll make it a rouble then.'

Churka got up and slowly walked away without saying a word, keeping close to the fence. Kostroma put his fingers in his mouth and whistled piercingly after him. Lyudmila's voice trembled as she said:

'Good God, what a loud mouth!'

'And you cowards have a lot to boast about,' scoffed Valyok. 'Supposed to be the best fighters in the street. Just like little kittens you are!'

We found all this highly insulting. We did not like that well-fed boy and he was always trying to make the younger boys get up to horrible tricks. He would tell them filthy stories about young girls and women, and knew just how to tease them. The young children would obey him and they paid dearly for it. For some reason Valyok hated my dog and used to throw stones at it. Once he stuck a needle in its bread.

The sight of Churka made to look silly and a coward upset us all more than anything else, so I said to Valyok:

'Give me a rouble and I'll go . . .'

He frightened me by his laughter; then he gave Yevseenko's wife a rouble, but she replied sternly:

'I don't want it, I won't take it!'

And she went off in a huff. Lyudmila wouldn't take the money either. All this made Valyok laugh at us even more. I was ready to go without asking for any money at all, but Grandmother came up and when she found out about the bet she took the rouble and said calmly:

'Now, take your small overcoat and a blanket, Alexei, as it gets cold towards morning.'

Her words made me hope that nothing terrible would happen. Valyok made it a condition that I lie or sit on the coffin until dawn without leaving it, whatever happened – even if it started rocking and old Kalinin climbed out. If I jumped off I would lose the bet.

'Be careful,' Valyok warned me. 'I'll be watching you all night long.'

When I got to the cemetery Grandmother blessed me and offered me some words of advice:

46

'If you see anything move keep quite still. Just pray to the Blessed Virgin.'

I rushed along as I wanted to get it all over with as quickly as possible. Valyok, Kostroma and a few other boys came with me. I caught my foot in the blanket as I climbed the brick wall, fell down and immediately leaped to my feet again as if the sand had thrown me up. On the other side of the wall I could hear them all laughing. My heart missed a beat and nasty cold shivers ran up and down my spine. I stumbled over to the black coffin. One side was piled high with sand and on the other I could see the thick little stilts supporting it. It was as though someone had tried to lift it and pushed it half over. I sat on the edge of the coffin, by the stilts, and looked around. The cemetery, with its bumpy surface, was packed full of grey crosses, and their shadows turned into gesticulating arms, falling on the graves and enveloping mounds which bristled with weeds. Here and there, lost among the crosses, gaunt birches stuck out, linking the isolated graves with their branches. Little blades of grass poked through the lacework of their shadows and this grey, ragged growth terrified me more than anything else. The church loomed up like a snowdrift and a small, waning moon shone among motionless clouds. Yaz's father, 'Lousy Peasant', lazily rang the watchman's bell. Each time he pulled the rope it caught on the metal roof and made a mournful scraping noise, followed by the hollow sound of the little bell, which rang out in short, dreary peals. I remembered the watchman's words, 'Lord preserve us from sleepless nights'. It was awful. Then, for some reason, I began to feel hot all over. I broke out into a sweat even though the night was cool. I thought to myself: could I get to the watchman's hut in time if old Kalinin decided to climb out of his coffin? I knew that cemetery very well, and had played dozens of times among the graves with Yaz and my other friends . . . Mother was buried over there by the church . . .

They had not gone to bed yet back in the village and I could hear laughter and snatches of song. An accordion whined and sobbed its heart out in the sandpits by the railway or somewhere in the village of Katyzovka. Myachov the blacksmith, who was drunk as usual, came along by the cemetery wall – I could tell it was him from his song:

> 'Our dear little mother's sins
> Are as small as her,
> She loved no one else,
> Except our father . . .'

It was pleasant listening to these last sighs of life, but each time the bell rang everything became quieter, and the silence flowed like a river over the meadows, submerging and smothering everything. My soul seemed to be swimming round in some fathomless void, fading away like a match-flame in the darkness, dissolving without trace in that vast ocean of nothingness, where only the unattainable stars lived and shone, while everything on earth disappeared, became unwanted – and died.

I wrapped myself in the blanket and sat there looking towards the church with my feet drawn up under me. Whenever I moved the coffin creaked and the sand crunched underneath it. Something struck the ground behind me, once, then again. Then a piece of brick fell quite near me. This was terrifying, but I guessed at once that it was Valyok and his gang flinging things over the wall and trying to frighten me. This only made me feel better, for I knew people were near.

Involuntarily my thoughts turned to Mother . . . Once when she caught me smoking and started beating me I had said: 'Don't touch me. I feel bad enough already. I'm going to be sick . . .' After I had been punished I sat behind the stove and could hear her telling Grandmother: 'That boy's got no feelings . . . he doesn't love *anybody* . . .' This was a terrible insult. Whenever Mother had to punish me I always felt sorry and embarrassed for her sake as she rarely made the punishment fit the crime. And on the whole I had to put up with a great deal in my life. That crowd on the other side of the wall, for instance: they all knew very well that I was afraid of being alone in the cemetery and yet they wanted to frighten me even more. Why? I felt like shouting out: 'Go to the devil!' But that would have been dangerous. Who knew how the devil would take it? Without doubt he was somewhere nearby.

The sand was full of scraps of mica which glinted dimly in

the moonlight and reminded me of the time when I was once lying on a raft on the Oka and looking into the water. A small bream suddenly swam right up to me. As it rolled over on its side it looked just like a human cheek. Then it peered at me with its round bird-like eyes and dived deep down into the water, quivering like a falling maple leaf.

My memory now became more and more active, conjuring up different events from my life to protect me from my imagination, which persisted in creating all kinds of horrors. A hedgehog came rolling over and its firm little paws made a pattering noise on the sand. It was so small and dishevelled it reminded me of a house-goblin. I remember Grandmother once squatting in front of the stove and muttering: 'Kind house-goblin, *please* get rid of the cockroaches . . .'

Far above the town, which was not visible from the cemetery, the sky grew brighter and the early morning breeze pinched my cheeks. I could hardly keep my eyes open and I curled up with the blanket over my head: if anything was going to happen to me – then let it!

The next thing I knew Grandmother was waking me up. She was standing by my side pulling the blanket and she said:

'Get up! You must be frozen! Well, was it *really* terrifying?'

'Yes it was, but don't tell *anybody*, especially those boys.'

'Why not?' she asked in surprise. 'If it wasn't terrifying, then you won't be able to boast to them about it! . . .'

We went home, and on the way Grandmother said in a gentle voice:

'You must try everything out for *yourself*, dear. If you don't then no one's going to teach you.'

By the time evening came I was the hero of the street and everyone asked:

'Weren't you terrified?'

And when I nodded back at them and said: 'It was terrifying,' they all exclaimed: 'Aha. So you see!'

The shopkeeper's wife announced in a loud convincing voice:

'Then it must have been all lies about old Kalinin climbing out of his coffin. If he had got out do you think he would have been scared of a *little boy*? He would have whisked him right away from the cemetery – God knows where!'

Lyudmila looked at me with an expression of tender surprise and even Grandfather was clearly pleased with me and could not stop grinning. Only Churka said in that morose voice of his:

'But it's easy for *him*. His grandmother's a witch!...'

Chapter 3

MY brother Kolya faded away imperceptibly, like a tiny star in the light of dawn.

Grandmother, my brother and myself used to sleep in the small shed, on top of a pile of firewood, using some old rags as blankets. Right next to us, on the other side of a wooden fence full of holes, was the master's henhouse. In the evenings we could hear the well-fed birds flapping their wings and clucking as they dropped off to sleep. In the mornings a golden cockerel would wake us with its loud crowing; Grandmother would shout at it:

'I wish someone would chop you up into little bits!'

By then I was wide awake too. I used to watch the sun's rays filtering towards my bed through the chinks in the woodpile with silvery dust dancing in them: those little specks seemed like words out of a fairy tale to me. I could hear mice rustling in the firewood, and little red beetles with black spots on their wings scurried around all over the place.

Sometimes, to escape from the stifling smell of the hen droppings, I would climb out of the woodpile up on to the roof and watch the house down below where those huge unseeing people were getting up, eyes swollen with sleep. Then that miserable old drunkard Fermanov the boatman would poke his hairy head out of the window. He would blink at the sun through the little slits of his glazed, bleary eyes and grunt like a wild pig. Grandfather would run out into the yard, smooth his thin, reddish hair with both hands and rush into the bath-house to douse himself with cold water.

The talkative cook, who worked for the master, had a sharp nose, and was covered all over with freckles so that she looked just like a cuckoo, while the master himself resembled an old pigeon gone to fat. In fact everyone looked like a bird or some sort of animal.

It was a pleasant, fine morning, but I felt rather depressed and wanted to run off to the fields where I could be alone: I knew

51

very well that those people nearly always soiled bright days with their filthy habits.

When I was lying up on the roof, Grandmother called me over and told me in a gentle voice, nodding towards her bed:

'Little Kolya's died.'

The child had slid down from the red cotton pillow and was lying on a piece of felt. He had turned a bluish colour and his night-shirt had ridden right up to his neck, baring his bloated stomach and his crooked legs which were covered in sores. His hands were very strangely planted behind his back, just as though he were trying to lift himself up. His head had flopped slightly to one side.

'Thank the Lord he's gone,' Grandmother said as she combed her hair. 'How could that poor little devil have survived?'

Grandfather appeared, stamped around the room as though he were doing a dance and then carefully touched the child's closed eyes with one finger.

Grandmother said angrily:

'What are you touching him for with dirty hands?'

Grandfather murmured:

'He was born, he lived, and he ate his food. And what was it all for?...'

'Stop rambling on like that!' interrupted Grandmother.

He looked at her blindly and went outside muttering to himself:

'*I*'ve got no money to bury him with, so you'll have to do it yourself if you want to.'

'Ugh, you miserable old devil!'

I went away and did not come back until it was evening.

They buried Kolya the following morning. I did not go into the church and during the service I sat with my dog and Yaz's father by my mother's grave, which had been opened up. Yaz had done the job cheaply and just could not stop boasting about it.

'It's only because I know you. I'd have charged anyone else a rouble.'

As I looked into the yellow pit, which gave off a strong smell, I could see black, damp planks along the sides. At the slightest movement sand flowed down to the bottom, in thin streams, leaving small channels behind. I moved on purpose, so as to make the sand cover up the planks.

'No larking around,' Yaz's father said as he puffed away at his pipe.

Grandmother appeared bearing a little white coffin. 'Peasant' jumped down into the hole, took the coffin and put it against the black planks. Then he jumped out again and started pushing the sand down with his feet and a spade. His pipe seemed to be smoking just like a censer. Grandfather and Grandmother silently helped him in his work. There were no priests, no beggars, only the four of us in the middle of a dense cluster of crosses. Grandmother told the watchman off when she handed him the money:

'But you've disturbed my Varya's little home all the same.'

'What else could I do? And I stole a little bit of someone else's earth as well. But I shouldn't worry about it!'

Grandmother bowed down to the ground, sobbed and howled, and then she went away and Grandfather followed her, straightening his shabby jacket; the peak of his cap was pulled down low over his eyes.

'We've sown our seed in unploughed land,' he said suddenly and ran on ahead, just like a crow across a field.

I asked Grandmother what he meant.

'To hell with him! He's best left to his own thoughts.'

It was hot and Grandmother had great difficulty in walking. Her feet sank into the warm sand and she kept on stopping to wipe the sweat from her face with her handkerchief. After a great effort I managed to ask:

'That *black* thing in the grave – was that Mother's coffin?'

'Yes,' she answered angrily. 'That sexton's a stupid old fool! It's hardly a year and my Varya's rotted away. The sand lets the water in . . . She should have been buried in clay.'

'Does *everyone* rot?'

'Everyone. Not saints though . . .'

'But *you* won't rot, Grandmother!'

She stopped, straightened my cap and said seriously:

'You mustn't think about such things. Do you hear?'

But I did think to myself: 'Death is so offensive, so revolting. There's nothing more vile!' I felt very bad.

When we reached home Grandfather had already prepared the samovar and laid the table.

'Let's have a cup of tea, to cool us down a bit. I'll make it, and you can all have a drop.'

He went up to Grandmother and slapped her on the shoulder. 'Well, mother?'

Grandmother waved her arm and exclaimed:

'What's there to say!'

'Then I'll tell you! God's angry with us and he's tearing us apart, bit by bit. Families should live close together, like fingers on a hand . . .'

It was a long time since he had spoken so gently, and what he said was clearly intended to comfort Grandmother. I listened to him and hoped that the old man would help me get over my feeling of revulsion and forget that yellow pit with those black, wet clods down the sides.

But Grandmother rudely interrupted him:

'That's enough! You've been saying that kind of thing all your life, but does anyone feel any better for it? You've never *once* stopped gnawing away at people, you're like rust eating iron.'

Grandfather grunted, glanced at her and did not say any more.

That same evening I saw Lyudmila by the gates and told her what I had seen that morning. But it did not make any impression on her as far as I could see.

'You're better off as an orphan,' she said. 'If my mother and father died, I'd leave my sister with my brother and go off to spend the rest of my life in a convent. Where else is there? I can't get married and as I'm a cripple, I can't work. I'd only have lame children anyway.'

She spoke sensibly like all the women in our street and from that evening I must have lost interest in her. As things turned out, I saw less of her anyway.

A few days after my brother's death Grandfather said:

'Go to bed early tonight. I'll wake you up at dawn and we'll all go collecting firewood in the forest.'

'And I'll pick some herbs,' Grandmother announced.

The forest, which was made up of fir and birch trees, stood in a marsh about two miles from the village. It was full of dead, wind-fallen wood. On one side it ran down to the Oka river, while on the other it came out on the main Moscow road and stretched far beyond it. A pine copse called 'Savelov's Mane' rose above its soft, bristling foliage like a black tent. All that wealth belonged to Count Shuvalov and it was very badly maintained. Most of the workers from Kunavino considered it their own property and went there to collect dead wood and to chop up dead trees for firewood but they were not too particular if they found trees that were still growing. In the autumn dozens of people armed with axes and with ropes tied round their waists used to go there to collect firewood for the winter.

When dawn came all three of us went out over the green fields, which were silvery with dew. To the left, beyond the Oka, the lazy Russian sun slowly rose over the reddish slopes of the Dyatlov Hills, over white Nizhny-Novgorod with its green terraced gardens and churches with golden cupolas. A gentle, sleepy breeze blew from the peaceful, muddy Oka, stirring the golden, dew-laden buttercups. Lilac-coloured harebells silently bowed down to the ground and *immortelles* of many different colours stood stiffly on the barren turf. Wild carnations, known as 'beauty of the night', opened up their crimson stars.

The forest moved towards us like a dark army. The fir trees seemed to have wings, just like large birds, and the birches resembled young girls. The acrid smell of the marsh wafted over the fields. My dog trotted along beside us with its pink tongue hanging out and now and again it would stop and sniff and shake its foxy head in bewilderment. Grandfather, who was wearing Grandmother's short jacket and an old cap with its peak missing, blinked and seemed to be smiling at something as he crept along, taking careful little steps as though he were stalking a wild animal. Grandmother, in her blue jacket, black skirt and with a white shawl over her head, bowled along so fast that it was hard to keep up with her. Grandfather livened up as we got nearer to the forest. He drew the air in through his nose and sighed. At first he spoke rather jerkily and indistinctly but then his voice became beautiful and gay – it was as though some drink had gone to his head.

'Forests are the gardens of God. No one ever planted them. It was the wind, the holy breath of God. When I was young I worked as a barge hauler in Zhiguli ... Ah, Alexei, I hope you'll never have to go through what I had to suffer! These forests stretch along the Oka from Kasimov to Murom, and there's more beyond the Volga, right up to the Urals! A miracle – without end!'

Grandmother looked at him out of the corner of her eye and winked at me, while Grandfather stumbled on over little clumps of earth, firing away with his dry staccato sentences so that they stayed in my memory for ever.

'Once we were hauling a barge with a cargo of oil to the Makarius Fair. A man called Kirillo from Puryokh was in charge and the water-pumper was a Tartar called Asaf, from Kasimov. As I was saying, we reached Zhiguli and an up-wind suddenly hit us right in the eye. It nearly killed us, I can tell you, and we were stuck there and we just couldn't move. So we climbed up the bank to cook some *kasha**. It was May and the Volga looked like the sea, with waves dancing all over her, thousands of them in flocks like swans, flowing down to the Caspian. And those hills at Zhiguli, green with spring, reared up to the heavens where the white clouds were grazing ... and the golden sun flooded the earth. We'd lie there next to each other drinking in all that beauty. It was cold on the river, but where we were we felt warm and everything smelled so sweet!

'Towards evening Kirillo, who was a stern man, and getting on a bit, suddenly got up, took his hat off and said: "Look mates, I don't want to be your boss or servant any more, so you can go on without me. I'm off to the forests!"

'We were all pretty shaken by this, I can tell you! But what could we do? How could we face the boss without a foreman? People don't go around without heads! Even though it was the Volga you can get lost on a main road! People are like wild animals really – do they *ever* feel sorry for what they do? We were all scared out of our wits. But the foreman would have his own way: "I've had enough of being your shepherd, so it's off to the forest for me!" Some of us wanted to beat him and tie him up, while the others thought for a bit and started shouting

*A kind of porridge. (Trans.)

56

"Don't leave us!" And then the Tartar shouted: "I'm going as well!" Now we were in real trouble. The boss owed the Tartar for two journeys and we were already halfway on the third. That meant a lot of money in those days. We didn't stop bawling at each other until it got dark, and then seven of the men left, leaving sixteen of us behind – or was it fourteen? That's what forests can do to you!'

'Did they become robbers?'

'I don't know. Perhaps they became hermits. In those days there wasn't much difference.'

Grandmother crossed herself and said: 'Holy mother of God: just thinking about people like that makes you feel sorry for them.'

'Everyone's born with a mind of his own and should know when the devil's trying to tempt him!'

We followed a damp path that led into the forest between wet clods of earth and gaunt fir trees. I thought that it would be wonderful to run off into the forest for ever, like Kirillo from Puryokh. In the forest one did not find people who talked too much, there were no fights, no drunkenness. There one could forget Grandfather's disgusting greediness, Mother's sandy grave – all those things, in fact, which were upsetting and lay heavily on the heart with the dead weight of unrelieved boredom.

When we reached a dry spot Grandmother said:

'Time we had something to eat. Let's sit down.'

In her basket she had rye bread, spring onions, cucumbers, salt, and cheese curds wrapped up in bits of rag. Grandfather looked at all this food rather sheepishly and started blinking at it:

'Ha, dear me, I didn't bring anything for myself, mother!'

'There's enough for everyone.'

We sat down and leant against the bronze-coloured mast-like trunk of a pine. The air was heavy with the smell of resin and a gentle breeze from the fields rocked the horse-tails. With her swarthy hands Grandmother started picking herbs, and at the same time she told me all about the healing properties of St John's wort, betony, ribwort, about the magical properties of fern, the sticky willow-herb and the dusty club-moss.

Grandfather was chopping up dead wood, which I was supposed to collect and pile up in one place. But I managed to slip away without him seeing and followed Grandmother into a thicket. She glided noiselessly among the majestic tree-trunks, and as she bent over she seemed to be bowing down to the earth which was carpeted with pine needles. As she walked along she would mutter:

'The mushrooms are early this year. That means there won't be many. Oh Lord, you don't care for the poor, mushrooms are a luxury for them!'

I followed her in silence, taking great care she did not spot me: I did not want to disturb her conversations with God, herbs and frogs. But she saw me.

'So you've run off and left your poor old grandfather!'

As she bent down to the dark earth, which was covered with a rich, brightly coloured mantle of herbs, she would tell me how God was once angry with the people on earth and flooded it, so that all living things were drowned:

'But the dear Mother of God had already collected every seed in her basket, and had hidden them away. Then she asked the sun: "Make all the land dry up, so that people will sing your praises." The sun dried up the land and she sowed it with the seeds she had hidden away. God looked down and saw that the earth had come to life – herbs, cattle and people were all there once again! God looked and said: "Who did all that – against my will?" and she confessed. But God had felt so sorry when he saw such an empty world that this time he said: "Well done!"'

I liked the story, but it rather surprised me and I said to Grandmother very seriously:

'Surely things didn't happen like that? God's mother was born long after the flood.'

And now it was Grandmother's turn to be surprised.

'Who told you that?'

'They told me at school. And it says so in books.'

This calmed her down a little and she advised me:

'Now you'd better forget those books. They're nothing but lies!'

She laughed quietly and cheerfully and added:

'The things those fools think up! They say there was a God but he had no mother! How did he come to be born then?'

'Don't know.'

'That's very good! So all you learned was "don't know"!'

'The priest said that God's mother was the daughter of Joachim and Anna.'

'You must mean Mary who was daughter of Joachim?'

By now she was getting angry. She stood right next to me and looked me sternly straight in the eye and said:

'If you go on thinking things like that you'll get a good spanking!'

But a moment later she tried to explain everything:

'God's mother has *always* existed, before anyone! She gave birth to God, and then . . .'

'But what about *Christ*?'

She did not reply straight away and closed her eyes in embarrassment. Then she said:

'Christ? Oh, yes, Christ . . .'

I saw I had won, that I had entangled her in theological mysteries, and I must confess that I felt rather bad about it.

We went deeper into the forest, into a bluish haze crisscrossed by the sun's golden rays. The warm, snug forest was filled with muffled dreamy sounds which set one dreaming as well. Crossbills screeched, titmice made a jingling noise and cuckoos laughed. The chaffinch sang its incessant, jealous song and that strange bird the bullfinch sang in its own peculiar melancholy way. Emerald-coloured frogs jumped under our feet, and the grass-snake lay in wait for them among the tree roots, holding up its little golden head. The squirrels clicked away and darted with their fluffy tails among the pine branches.

An incredible variety of things was to be seen there, making one want to see more and to press on even further. Among the trunks of the pines, one could glimpse the transparent, airy shapes of enormous people who then faded away in the thick foliage, through which the bluish silvery sky was visible. A thick carpet of moss lay underfoot, embroidered with red bilberry bushes and the dry creepers of cranberry bushes. Stonebrambles glistened in the grass like drops of blood and a strong tantalizing smell came from the mushrooms.

'Holy Mother of God, shining light of the world,' Grandmother sighed as she offered her prayer. In that forest she seemed just like the mistress of the house and was familiar with every part of it. She looked like a great bear as she walked along, seeing, praising and blessing everything. Indeed, Grandmother seemed to flow through the forest like a warm stream and I particularly liked to see how the crumpled moss stood up again after her feet had flattened it.

As I walked along I thought how marvellous it would be to become a robber, to steal from the greedy and the rich and to hand the money over to the poor; if only everyone were well-fed, cheerful and not envious of one another – perhaps they might stop howling at each other like wild dogs. And how wonderful it would be to go right up to Grandmother's God and to her Holy Mother and tell them the whole horrible truth – about the dreadful lives that people led, and how terribly degrading it was to bury the dead in filthy graveyard sand; and how vile life was in general when it could have been so different. If the Holy Mother of God really trusted me, then she should make a wise person out of me, so that I could change everything for the better. If people only believed what I said: then I would discover the best way of improving life! Being so young was not necessarily a handicap, as Christ could not have been more than a year older than me, and even at his age wise men listened to him.

Once, when I was lost in thoughts like these, I fell straight into a deep hole, scratched my side on a branch and ripped the skin off the back of my neck. I sat on the bottom in the cold mud which stuck to me like tar and I was terribly ashamed when I realized that I could not get out by myself: I did not want to frighten Grandmother by shouting for help. I did start shouting, however, and she came and quickly hauled me out, crossed herself and said 'Thank God! A good thing the bear's den was empty. Supposing the owner had been at home?' And she cried through her laughter. Then she took me over to a stream, washed me and bandaged my wounds with a piece of her blouse after she had pressed some herbs on them to ease the pain. Then we went into a signalman's hut by the railway to rest, as I was too weak to drag myself home.

Almost every day I would say to Grandmother: 'Let's go to the forest!' She would eagerly agree and we passed the whole of that summer, right up to late autumn, gathering herbs, berries, mushrooms and nuts. Grandmother sold what we collected, and with the money we used to buy food.

'Parasites!' Grandfather would screech at us, even though we never even so much as touched his food.

The forest brought me a deep feeling of peace and comfort, which drowned all my sorrows and made me forget all the unpleasant things which had happened. At the same time my senses became particularly acute. My hearing and sight became sharper and my memory more receptive and a far richer storehouse of impressions.

Grandmother surprised me more and more and I grew accustomed to thinking that she belonged to a higher species than anyone else, and was the kindest and wisest person in the whole world. She never failed to convince me that this was so. One evening, for example, we were on the way home after picking white mushrooms and had reached the edge of the forest. Grandmother sat down to rest while I went back into the forest to see if I could find any more mushrooms. Suddenly I heard her speaking to something and then I saw her sitting on the path calmly cutting off mushroom roots while a wiry-looking grey dog stood next to her with its tongue hanging out.

'Off with you now!' she was saying. 'And God be with you.'

Not long before, Valyok had poisoned my dog and I dearly wished to tempt this one over to me so that I could take it home with me. I ran out on to the path and the dog arched itself very strangely without moving its neck, stared at me with its cold green eyes and dashed off into the forest with its tail hanging down. It did not move at all like a dog and when I whistled it leapt wildly into the bushes.

'Did you see it?' Grandmother asked smiling. 'At first I thought it was a dog. Then I had a closer look and saw it had the teeth and neck of a wolf! I was even a little bit frightened so I said: "Well, if you're a wolf, then go away!" A good thing wolves aren't vicious in the summer!'

She never got lost in the forest and she always knew the right way home. She could tell from the smell of the grass what kind of mushrooms grew there and she often used to set me little tests:

'What kind of tree does the saffron mushroom like? And how can you tell if an agaric's poisonous? What mushrooms like to grow near ferns?'

From almost invisible scratches on the bark of trees she could show me where squirrels had made holes in the trunk and I would climb up and take the nuts, stealing all that the squirrel had hoarded for the winter. Sometimes I would find as much as ten pounds of nuts in their nests. Once when I was taking some a hunter planted twenty-seven pellets of snipe-shot in my right side. Grandmother picked eleven out with a needle and the rest stayed in my skin for years afterwards, gradually working their way out. Grandmother was pleased to see that I did not make any fuss about the pain.

'Good boy,' she said approvingly. 'If you can bear pain, then you'll learn a lot!'

Each time she had scraped up enough money from selling mushrooms and nuts she would leave coins on window-sills, her 'secret charity' as she called it. But even on holidays she still went around in old, patched-up rags.

'You make me feel ashamed,' Grandfather snarled. 'You look worse than a beggar.'

'There's no harm in it. I'm not your daughter and I'm not looking for a husband!'

And they would start a fierce quarrel. Grandfather would shout in an injured voice:

'I haven't sinned more than anybody else but I'm the one who's punished most!'

Grandmother would tease him by saying:

'Only the devil knows what people *really* deserve.'

Then she would look me straight in the eyes and say:

'The old man's afraid of devils – it's put years on him! He's afraid of dying, poor wretch!'

That summer I grew a lot stronger and I ran around the forest like a wild animal. I lost all interest in the lives of my friends, in Lyudmila, who bored me because she was far too clever.

Once Grandfather came back from the town soaked to the

skin: it was autumn and the rains had set in. He shook himself at the front door just like a sparrow and said in a triumphant voice:

'Well, you little monkey, tomorrow you'll be going off to work!'

'And where to this time?' Grandmother asked angrily.

'To your sister Matryona, to work for her son.'

'That's a rotten idea!'

'Shut up, you old fool! They might make a draughtsman out of him.'

Grandmother lowered her head without another word. In the evening I told Lyudmila that I was going away to live in the town.

'I'll be going there soon myself,' she said thoughtfully. 'Father wants me to have my bad leg cut right off. He says I'll get well again then.'

During the summer she had become thinner, the skin on her face had turned a pale blue and her eyes had grown much bigger.

'Are you frightened?' I asked.

'Yes,' she said, and she cried quietly to herself. There was nothing I could do to comfort her: I was afraid of the town myself. For a long time we sat there in gloomy silence huddled up against each other. If it had been summer I might have persuaded Grandmother to go out begging, as she did when she was a little girl. Lyudmila could have come with us – I would have taken her around in a little cart. But it was autumn. A damp wind blew down the street and the sky was perpetually overcast with clouds that always seemed heavy with rain. The earth wrinkled up and became muddy and looked terribly miserable.

Chapter 4

ONCE more I was back in the town, in a white two-storeyed house that looked like a communal coffin. Although the house was new it had a sickly, bloated look, and put one in mind of a beggar who had suddenly come into money and had gorged himself with food. It stood sideways to the street and each storey had eight windows, but only four where the front should have been. The lower windows looked out on to a small drive and on to the yard, while the upper ones looked out across the fence on to the laundress's little house and a gully full of mud. There were no streets then in the proper sense of the word. The gully ran past the front of the house and in two places it was crossed by narrow dykes. To the left it led down to the prison. People threw rubbish from their yards into it and the bottom was covered with a thick pool of dark green slime. To the right, at the end, was the stagnant slimy Zvyozdin pond, while the middle of the gully stood right opposite the house. Half of it was filled with rubbish, overgrown with nettles, burdock, and sorrel, while the rest was used as a garden by Dorimedont Pokrovsky, the priest, and there was a little summer house there, made from thin green laths which made a loud snapping sound if you threw stones at them. The whole place was indescribably miserable and disgustingly filthy. Autumn had cruelly mutilated the dirty, clay soil and had turned it into a kind of reddish tar which stuck firmly to one's shoes. I had never seen so much mud in so small a space. Since I was used to the cleanliness of the fields and forests this part of the town left me feeling utterly depressed.

Beyond the gully stretched grey, ramshackle fences and right in the middle of them I could see the little brownish house where I had lived during the winter when I worked in the shoe shop... With that house being so near, I felt even more depressed. Why did I have to live in that same street again?

I already knew my new master, as he used to visit Mother with his brother, who had a comical way of chirping like a bird – 'Andrei-papa, Andrei-papa!' They had not changed at all. The elder brother had a hooked nose and long hair. He was quite pleasant and, so it seemed, good-natured. The younger brother, Viktor, had the same horsy face covered with freckles. Their mother (Grandmother's sister) was very irritable, and had a loud mouth. The elder brother was married, and his wife was a flashy-looking woman, and as white as pure bread. She had large, very dark eyes. During my very first days there she twice said to me:

'I gave your mother a silk gown with glass beads on it.'

For some reason I did not want to believe it, nor did I believe that Mother had accepted the present. When she reminded me yet a third time I told her:

'So you gave her a present! Stop boasting about it.'

This frightened her and she jumped away from me.

'Wh-at? Who do you think you're talking to?'

Her face came out in red blotches, her eyes bulged and she called her husband. He came into the kitchen carrying a pair of drawing compasses and he had a pencil behind one ear. He listened to his wife and then told me:

'Have some respect when you talk to her. I won't put up with any cheek from *you*!'

Then he told his wife rather impatiently:

'And don't you keep bothering me with this nonsense.'

'What do you mean, *nonsense*? If your own flesh and blood...'

'To hell with flesh and blood!' he shouted and stormed out of the room.

I was not pleased either when I discovered that these people were actually related to Grandmother. From what I had seen, relations treated each other far worse than complete strangers, knew more about their weaknesses, had more spiteful things to say, and quarrelled and fought more often.

I liked the master and when he shook his fine hair and smoothed it behind his ears he reminded me of ' Just the Job '.*
His grey eyes often seemed to be laughing from sheer pleasure

* 'Just the Job' appears in *My Childhood* as the pathetic lodger who experimented with acid and different kinds of metals, and was finally turned out of Gorky's grandparents' house in Kanatny Street in Nizhny-Novgorod. The young Gorky had a strong affection for him. (Trans.)

and they had a kind look. Funny little wrinkles would appear round his aquiline nose.

'Enough of your swearing, you stupid ninnies,' he would say to his wife and mother, and his gentle smile would reveal a set of small, strong teeth.

The mother and daughter-in-law had a slanging match every day. I was surprised to see how easily and quickly they picked a quarrel with each other. The moment they got up they would rush around the house, uncombed and with their clothes undone, as though a fire had just broken out. All day long they were busy doing something, taking a break only for lunch, tea or supper, when they used to drink and eat themselves silly. While they were eating they would talk about different dishes and gently insult one another as they built up to a really big row. Whatever the mother-in-law cooked the daughter-in-law would invariably say: 'My mother doesn't make it like that!', to which her mother-in-law would reply:

'Then it can only be worse!'

'No – better!'

'Well, go back to your mummy!'

'*I'm* in charge of this house!'

'And what about me?'

At this point the master would interrupt:

'Stop it, you ninnies! Have you gone mad?'

Everything there was inexplicably strange and comical. To get from the kitchen to the dining-room one had to pass through a small lavatory – the only one in the house. Samovars and food were carried through it to the dining-room and it was the subject of many uninhibited jokes – and often a source of comical misunderstandings. My job was to pour water into the lavatory tank, and I had to sleep in the kitchen, opposite the lavatory door and the front door. The kitchen stove made my head feel hot while a draught from the front door blew on to my feet, so I used to collect all the mats and cover my legs with them when I lay down to sleep.

The large hall, in spite of its two framed mirrors, the gift pictures from the magazine *Niva* in their little gold moulded frames, a pair of card tables and a dozen Vienna chairs, struck me as empty and depressing. The small lounge was crammed full of brightly-coloured soft furniture, cases full of wedding presents, silver and tea sets. It was lit by three lamps, each bigger than the other. Besides a wide bed, the dark, windowless bedroom was filled with trunks and cupboards which smelled of leaf tobacco and Spanish camomile. Nobody ever used these three rooms and the master and his family crowded into the little dining-room and kept on getting in each other's way.

Immediately after morning tea, at eight o'clock, the master and his brother pulled the table out into the middle of the room and spread sheets of white paper, sets of drawing instruments, pencils, and saucers of Indian ink all over it and got down to work. Each would sit at one end of the table, which would then start shaking. It filled the whole room and when the nurse and her mistress came out of the playroom they used to catch themselves on the corner.

'What are you lounging around and interfering with our work for?' Viktor would shout at her.

The insulted mistress would ask her husband:

'Vasya, please tell him not to shout at me.'

'Please don't shake the table,' the master said, trying to make peace.

'I'm pregnant, it's too crowded in here for all of us.'

'All right, we'll go and work in the hall then.'

But the mistress would become indignant and shout:

'Good God, whoever heard of anyone working *there*?'

From the lavatory old Matryona would poke out her evil face, red with heat from the stove, and shout:

'Just think, Vasya. Four rooms aren't big enough for *her* to have her puppies in! Hasn't a thought in her stupid head, for all her fancy upbringing!'

Viktor would laugh spitefully while the master shouted:

'That's enough!'

But when the daughter-in-law had showered her mother-in-law with the most venomous invective, she would slump on to a chair and start moaning:

'I'm leaving! I'm going to die!'

'To hell with you, you're stopping me from working,' the master would bawl, his face pale from the strain. 'It's a madhouse here. And here I am killing myself just to feed you. Stupid ninnies!'

At first these rows frightened me, especially once when the master's wife seized a knife, ran into the lavatory, shut both doors and sat there growling like a wild animal. The house was quiet for a few seconds, then the master leaned with his hands against the lavatory door and shouted to me:

'Climb up, break the window and take the hook off the catch!'

I briskly jumped up on to his back and broke the glass over the door, but when I bent down the master's wife started furiously beating me on the head with the knife handle. Despite this, I managed to open the door and the master dragged his wife out into the dining-room and after a struggle took the knife away from her. As I sat there in the kitchen rubbing my bruised head I soon saw that my sufferings had been in vain. The knife was blunt, it was difficult to slice bread with it even, and it could never have cut anyone's skin. Also, there was really no need to climb up on the master's back as I could have reached the glass standing on a chair. To put it briefly, it would have been easier for a grown-up, with longer hands, to take the hook off. After this incident the rows in that house no longer held any terror for me.

The brothers used to sing in the church choir. They often sang softly while they were working (the elder was a baritone):

> 'My dear beloved's ring I dropped,
> Right into the se-ea!'

The younger had a tenor voice and would take up the song:

> 'And with that ring
> I lost all chance of happiness.'

Then the master's wife would call softly from the nursery:
'Have you gone mad! The baby's asleep . . .'

Or she would say instead:

'You're a married man, Vasya. Why do you have to sing about *girls*? Why? It'll soon be time for evening service anyway.'

'Well, we'll sing some hymns then.'

But she insisted that hymns were not sung just anywhere, least of all in *there* – and she eloquently pointed to the little lavatory door.

'We'll have to move to another flat. The devil only knows what'll happen if we don't!' the master would point out. And he would keep on saying that they needed a new table, something he had been saying over and over for the past three years.

When I heard the master and his wife discussing people I always thought of the shoe shop: there they used to speak in exactly the same way. It was obvious that they thought there was no one like them in the whole town, that they knew all the finest points of etiquette (which I did not understand) and on these they based their cruel and ruthless disapproval of everybody. The way they criticized everybody filled me with a terrible feeling of oppression and made me furious with these rules of theirs: to violate them became a real source of pleasure for me.

They made a perfect slave of me. I had to do a chambermaid's work as well as wash the kitchen floor on Wednesdays and clean the samovar, the pots and the pans. On Saturdays I scrubbed all the floors and the stairs. I had to chop and bring the firewood in for the stoves, wash dishes, clean the vegetables, go shopping with the mistress, drag heavy baskets along after her, and then I was sent off to the chemist's or other shops on errands. My immediate taskmaster was Grandmother's sister, a loud-mouthed, utterly hateful old woman, who got up very early – at six o'clock. After a quick wash she would kneel in her petticoat in front of the ikon and stay there a long time complaining to God about her life, her children, and her daughter-in-law.

'Good Lord,' she would exclaim with tears in her voice, pressing her fingers to her lips. 'Lord, I ask for nothing; I need nothing. Just let me rest, give me peace of mind. By thy holy power!'

She used to wake me up with her wailing. I would look out from under the blankets and listen in terror to her fervent prayers.

The autumn morning dully peered through the kitchen

window, through panes drenched with rain, and on the floor a grey figure rocked to and fro, restlessly waving her arms. All the time she was praying her shawl kept slipping off her small head and her thinning fair hair fell down on her cheeks and shoulders from under it. She would mutter: 'Oh, blast you!' as she tried to pull it back with sharp movements of her left hand. Then she would wildly beat herself on the head, the stomach and shoulders and hiss:

'Oh Lord, punish my daughter-in-law, for my sake. Blame her for all I've had to suffer. And open my son's eyes, so he'll see her in her true colours – and let her see Viktor as well. Good Lord, help my little Viktor, show him thy mercy.'

Viktor used to sleep right next to us in the kitchen, in a bunk over the stove. His mother's moaning used to wake him up and he would shout in a sleepy voice:

'Mama, what are you bawling for at this time of the morning: I can't stand it!'

'All right then, go back to sleep,' she would whisper guiltily.

For a minute or two she would silently rock herself to and fro and then she would suddenly call out vindictively:

'May they be smitten with the plague, and have no roof over their heads, oh Lord!'

Even Grandfather did not pray in such a terrifying way as this.

When she had finished she would wake me up:

'Get up! You won't earn your living dozing all day! Put the samovar on, fetch the firewood. Didn't you cut the kindling wood yesterday! Oh, that boy!'

I tried to get the chores over with as quickly as possible so I would not have to put up with the old woman's hissing and whispering. But she was never satisfied. She rushed around that kitchen like a winter blizzard, howling and hissing:

'Quiet, you devil! I'll give it you, if you wake Viktor up! Run off to the shops – now . . .'

On weekdays I bought two pounds of rye bread and two kopeks' worth of rolls for the young mistress's morning tea. When I came back with the bread the women examined it suspiciously, weighed it on the palms of their hands and asked:

'Did they try and make up the weight with something else? No? Open your mouth!'

Then they would shout in triumph:

'He's eaten some. Just look at the crumbs between his teeth!'

I was a willing worker, and I loved to get rid of the filth in that house, scrub the floors, scour the pots and pans, polish the door handles and clean out the stove flues. More than once, when things calmed down a little, I could hear the women talking about me:

'Works hard.'

'A clean boy.'

'A bit cheeky, though.'

'Well, *who* brought him up?'

Both of them tried to make me respect them, but in my opinion they were half-wits. I did not like them at all, did not listen to what they said and I used to answer them back. The young mistress must have noticed that her sermons had little effect on me and this made her give me much more frequent admonitions:

'Remember, we've taken you in from a family of *beggars*! And I gave your mother a silk gown with beads on it!'

Once I said to her:

'Why do I have to work myself to the bone because of that gown?'

'Good God, that boy might set the whole house on fire!' she shouted in terror.

I was really amazed. Why should I do *that*?

Now and again they would both complain to the master who severely reprimanded me:

'I've got my eye on you, so you'd better look out!'

Once, however, he said rather indifferently to his wife and mother:

'And you're a fine pair as well! You'd think that boy was a horse the way you work him. Anyone else would have run away long ago or died from sheer exhaustion.'

This roused the women to tears. His wife stamped her foot and shouted furiously:

'How can you talk like that in front of the boy, you long-haired idiot! Do I mean anything at all to you? I'm pregnant . . .'

Then his mother started wailing as well:

'May God forgive you, Vasily. Just you mark my words – you'll ruin that boy!'

When they had left in a terrible huff the master told me in a stern voice:

'You little devil, see what a row you've caused? I'm going to send you right back to your Grandfather and you can start collecting rags again!'

I could not take this insult lying down and replied:

'I'd rather do that than stay *here* any longer. You took me on as an apprentice, but what have you taught me? How to empty the slopbucket!'

The master grabbed me very gently by the hair, so as not to hurt me, stared me straight in the eye and said in amazement:

'You are an obstinate boy, you're no good to me, no good at all.'

I thought they would get rid of me after that, but a day later he came into the kitchen with a thick scroll of paper, a pencil, a set-square and a ruler.

'When you've finished the knives you can copy that out.'

On the paper was a drawing of the front of a two-storeyed house with a lot of windows and mouldings.

'Here's a pair of dividers. Measure all the lines, mark them on the paper with dots, then use your pencil and ruler to join them up. First you start across, horizontally, then downwards – those are the verticals. Now get on with it!'

I was very pleased at the prospect of some work which did not mean getting dirty and that my apprenticeship had really started. But I looked at the paper and instruments with a feeling of awe and I felt completely lost. However, I immediately washed my hands and sat down at the table to begin my apprenticeship. I drew the horizontals, checked them against the original and found they were correct, However, I had made three too many. Then I drew all the verticals and to my amazement saw that I had made a terrible mess of the front of the house: windows had changed position – one of them had left the wall altogether and was suspended in mid-air to the side of

72

the house. The front entrance also hung in the air, on a level with the first floor, and the cornice had moved to the middle of the roof; the dormer window turned up in the chimney. For a long time, almost in tears, I looked at these marvels which I would never be able to correct, and tried to fathom out what had happened, but without any success. So I decided to correct my mistakes with the help of my imagination. On all the cornices and along the ridge of the roof I drew crows, doves, sparrows, while down on the ground, by the windows, I sketched in bandy-legged people who were holding up umbrellas, which did not quite hide their ugly faces. Then I drew stripes across the whole page and took my work to the master. He raised his eyebrows very high, ruffled his hair and asked gloomily:

'What's *that* supposed to be?'

'It's raining,' I explained. 'When it rains all houses seem to slant, because . . . the rain falls like that! As for the birds, they've taken shelter in the cornices. They always do that when it rains. And those are people running home for shelter. Look, there's a lady who's fallen down, and there's a lemon seller.'

'My very humble thanks,' the master said as he leaned over the table, swept the papers off with his long trailing hair, guffawed and shouted: 'Oh, I wish someone would take you apart – you wild animal!'

The mistress came in with her belly shaking like a small barrel. She took one look at my work and said to her husband:

'Give him a good thrashing!'

But the master placidly remarked:

'It's nothing. I was no better when I started.'

He marked the ruined façade with a red pencil and then gave me some more paper.

'Try again! You'll keep on drawing until you get it right!'

The second copy came out better, only a window appeared on the front door. But still I did not like seeing the house empty and I populated it with different kinds of people. I made ladies sit with fans in the windows, and drew gentlemen smoking cigarettes. One of them who did not smoke was poking his long nose at everyone. A cabdriver stood at the front door with a dog next to him.

'Why have you gone and spoiled it all again?' my master asked angrily.

I explained that it was very tedious drawing something without any people.

Then he started swearing at me:

'To hell with it! If you want to learn, then learn. But now you're just being cheeky!'

He was quite pleased when I at last managed to make a copy which bore some resemblance to the original.

'There, you did it! We'll get on fine now, you'll see.'

And he started giving me a lesson:

'Draw up a plan of a flat, showing how the rooms are laid out, where the doors and windows are, where everything is. I'm not going to help this time. You can do it yourself!'

I went into the kitchen and thought how best to begin. But at this point my apprenticeship as a draughtsman came to an abrupt end. The old woman came up and asked menacingly:

'Want to draw, do you?'

She seized me by the hair and banged my face against the table so that I split my nose and lips. Then she leaped around, tearing up the plans, throwing the instruments off the table, after which she planted her hands on her sides and cried victoriously:

'Go on, draw! No, I won't have it! I won't have a stranger working here so that an only brother, one's own flesh and blood, has to make room for him!'

The master came running into the room, then his wife sailed in, and a wild scene followed. All three of them jumped at each other, spitting and howling, and it all finished with the women going off to have a good cry and the master telling me:

'You'd better chuck it in. You won't learn anything here. You can see for yourself what happens!

I felt sorry for that dishevelled, defenceless man, perpetually deafened by those bawling women. Already I had realized that the old woman didn't want me to study at all and that she deliberately went out of her way to stop me.

Before I sat down at the table I always used to ask her:

'Want anything done?'

She would answer sullenly:

'I'll tell you if I do! That's about all you're fit for, messing about with those drawings.'

Then she would send me on some errand or say to me:

'Just look at those front steps! There's dust and muck everywhere. Start sweeping!'

I went to have a look, but I could see no dust there at all.

'Arguing with *me*, are you?' she would shout.

Once she poured *kvass** all over my drawings. On another occasion she purposely spilled ikon lamp oil over them. She was just like a naughty little girl, with all the cunning of a child and with a child's inability to conceal it.

Never before nor after did I see anyone who flew into a temper so quickly and easily, and who loved to complain about everyone and everything. People normally like something to grouse about, but she took a particular pleasure in it, and to her it was like singing a song. She had an almost insane love for her son and her religious fanaticism which I can only describe as devilish both annoyed and frightened me. After her morning prayers she would stand on the step in front of the stove, lean on her elbow on the edge of the bunk and furiously hiss:

'My good fortune, my little child, my own flesh and blood, so pure, made of diamonds! Little feather from an angel's wing! Oh, you're asleep! Then sleep, my child, may you have happy dreams of lovely brides, the first beauties in the land, princesses, rich merchants' daughters! May your enemies die before they're born, and may your friends live to be a hundred years. May girls chase after you in flocks, like ducks after drakes!'

It was all unbearably funny. That rude and lazy Viktor looked just like a woodpecker; he had the same bright colouring and large nose, and he was just as stubborn and stupid. His mother's whispering woke him up sometimes and he would mutter sleepily:

'To hell with you, Mamasha, sniffing right into my face! It's just impossible here!'

Sometimes she would meekly climb down from the steps to her bunk and laugh:

'Go back to sleep, you ill-mannered lout!'

*Beer made from rye. (Trans.)

But sometimes her legs would give way and she would flop down on the edge of the stove with her mouth wide open, breathing heavily, as though she had burned her tongue, and her words flowed out in a fiery, bubbling stream:

'Wh-at? Tell your own mother to go to hell, you son of a bitch! Bane of my life! Thorn in my side! The devil himself planted you inside me: you should have rotted away in my womb!...'

She used filthy words, the kind one would expect from drunks in the street, and it was painful listening to them. She never slept very much and was always tossing and turning during the night and jumping down from the stove.

Often she would bump against the couch I slept on and wake me up.

'What do you want?' I would ask.

'Shut up,' she whispered, peering at something in the darkness. 'God in heaven, Holy Elijah the Prophet ... Varvara the Martyr ... spare us all from sudden death.'

Her hand trembled as she lit the lamp. Her round face, with its big nose, swelled up from the strain. Her grey eyes blinked anxiously as she scrutinized objects that had changed their shape in the darkness. The kitchen was spacious, but crammed full of cupboards and trunks. At night it seemed quite small. The rays of the moon lived their quiet little life there, the tiny flame of the everlasting lamp quivered in front of the ikons, and knives gleamed on the walls like icicles. Black frying pans on the shelves reminded me of faces without eyes.

The old woman carefully climbed down from her bunk over the stove, just as though she were going down a river bank into the water, shuffling her bare feet as she went into the corner where a wash-basin that seemed to have big ears hung over the slop bucket like a severed head. Nearby stood a water tub. As she drank she would half choke and sigh. Then she would look out through the window, which was covered with a light blue pattern of frost.

'God have mercy on me,' she whispered. 'God have mercy on me.'

Sometimes she used to blow the candle out, kneel down and hiss in an offended way:

76

'Who loves me, God, who *needs* me?'

When she had climbed back on to the top of the stove she would cross herself by the flues and then feel around to see if the plates were firmly in place. Her hands became covered in soot and she would utter despairing curses and then suddenly go right off to sleep, as though overwhelmed by some unseen power.

When she upset me I used to think it was a great pity that Grandfather had never married her – she would have tormented the life out of him! And *she* would have got what she deserved, too! She upset me frequently, but there were days when that woolly-looking, puffy face became sad, and her eyes filled with tears. Then she would say with conviction:

'Do you think it's easy for *me*? I've borne children, given them a start in life, and for *what*? I'm nothing more than a cook to them, do you think *I* enjoy it? And to cap it all my son brings home a strange woman to take my place, his own flesh and blood. Do you think that's nice. Well?'

'No, not very nice,' I said in all sincerity.

'Aha, so you see *my* point of view.'

Without any inhibitions she would start telling me all about that 'daughter-in-law of mine'.

Once we were in the bath-house together, and I saw her without any clothes on. 'What's my son got to brag about? How can anyone call her *beautiful*?' she said.

She always spoke incredibly obscenely about the sexes. At first this filled me with repulsion, but soon I found myself listening to her stories very attentively, with great interest in fact, and I felt there was some truth in them, however painful they were.

'A woman is strong. She deceived God, so there!'

She droned on and on and slapped her hand on the table. 'Because of Eve everyone has to go to hell!'

She could talk interminably about how strong women were and I always thought that for some reason she was trying to frighten someone: I particularly remember her saying that 'Eve deceived God'.

One wing of our house jutted out into the yard, which was almost as big as the house itself. Officers occupied four of the

77

eight flats in the two houses, with a chaplain in a fifth. The whole yard was full of batmen and orderlies, who were pursued by laundresses, chambermaids and cooks. Every kitchen was the scene of some drama or love affair, often ending in tears, abuse and fighting. The soldiers would fight, not only one another, but the navvies and landlord's workmen. They used to beat the women as well. That yard teemed with vice and promiscuity – rather, with the animal, insatiable sexual hunger of healthy young men. During tea, lunch and dinner, the master and his wife would discuss cynically, without sparing any details, the life that went on there – its cruel sensuality, absurd sadism, and the obscene boasts of those who had made conquests. The old woman always knew everything that was going on in that yard and reported it eagerly and maliciously. Her daughter-in-law would listen to her stories without saying a word and a smile would appear on her puffy lips. Viktor guffawed, but the master frowned and used to say:

'That's enough now, mother!'

'Good God, I'm not even allowed to open my mouth,' the old woman complained.

But Viktor encouraged her:

'Go on, Mamasha, don't be shy. We want to hear . . .'

The elder son treated his mother with a brand of pity that was mingled with repulsion. He was always trying to avoid being alone with her, when she would shower him with complaints about his wife and invariably demanded money from him. He would hurriedly shove a rouble or two or some loose silver into her hand and say:

'It's no good giving *you* any money, Mamasha. Not that I grudge it, but it's a sheer waste!'

'But it's for the poor, for church candles!'

'For the *poor*! . . . I don't think! You'll *ruin* that Viktor in the end.'

'You don't love your brother, and that's a terrible sin!' his mother would reply.

The elder brother would brush her away and leave.

Viktor treated his mother very rudely and never stopped making fun of her. He was a terrible glutton and he was always hungry. On Sundays his mother used to make pancakes and she always hid some of them in a pot under my couch. When he came back from church Viktor would pull the pot out and bellow:

'Couldn't you have left a few more, you tight bastards!'

I would reply:

'Hurry up and get them down you, in case they come back.'

'I'm going to tell them *you* stole the pancakes for me!'

Once I pulled the pot out and ate a couple of pancakes myself, for which Viktor gave me a thrashing. He hated me as much as I loathed him. He would make fun of me, make me clean his shoes three times a day and when he went to bed in his bunk over the stove he parted the planks and tried to spit on me through the cracks. Viktor was obviously trying to copy his brother's remarks – when he said 'stupid ninnies' for instance – but with him they seemed idiotic and meaningless. He would plague me with ridiculous questions:

'Alyoshka, tell me: why do they write *blue*, yet say glue? Why *kolokola* and not *okolo kola**?'

In fact I did not like the way they spoke in that house at all. As I was used to Grandmother's and Grandfather's fine language I could not at first understand combinations of words which were really opposite in meaning, such as 'terribly funny', 'I'm *dying* to eat', or 'frightfully gay'. To my mind what was funny could not be terrible, what was gay could not be frightful, and eating had nothing to do with dying. So I used to ask them:

'How can you say such things?'

They would shout back at me:

'And you're a fine teacher! Your ears need plucking!'

'Plucking ears' seemed wrong as well: I thought only herbs, flowers and nuts could be plucked!

They tried to show me that ears could be plucked as well, but they did not convince me and I announced triumphantly:

'My ears are still there, in spite of what *you* say!'

There were so many vicious tricks being played all round me, so much shameless obscenity that it was far worse than Kunavino which was full of brothels and prostitutes. Behind

* These and other puns are literally untranslatable. For example *kolokola*, meaning 'bells', is turned round to *okolo kola* meaning 'near the stake'. (Trans.)

all the filth and vice there, one felt that there lay something that explained the dirt and the inevitable viciousness that came with it – the hard, half-starved life that people had to lead, and the crippling work they had to do. But here people were well fed and life was easy. Work was replaced by an incomprehensible, totally unnecessary, mad scramble, and a corrosive, exasperating boredom enveloped everything.

Things were hard for me, but I felt even worse when Grandmother came to visit me. She would enter the kitchen by the back door, cross herself in front of the ikon and then bow very low to her younger sister; all of this choked and crushed me like a hundred-pound weight.

'Oh, so it's you, Akulina,' my mistress would say in a cold, indifferent voice when she saw Grandmother, whom I did not recognize at first as she kept her lips meekly pressed together which gave her face quite a different expression.

She would sit quietly on a bench by the door, near the slop bucket, and remain there like a guilty child, only speaking when her sister asked her some questions, to which she would reply in a soft, deferential voice. This was absolute torture for me and I would ask angrily:

'Why are you sitting there like that?'

She would wink affectionately and say in quite a convincing voice:

'You keep your mouth shut, you're not the boss here!'

Then my mistress would start complaining about me:

'However much you beat him and shout at him he's always poking his nose into other people's business.'

She would often spitefully ask Grandmother:

'Why do you live like a beggar, Akulina?'

'What's wrong with that?'

'There's nothing wrong with anything, unless you're ashamed of it.'

'They say Christ lived on charity as well.'

'Only fools and heretics say things like that. Now listen to me, you stupid old woman! Christ wasn't a beggar, but the son of God and, as it is written, he will come back in triumph to judge the living and the dead – remember, *and the dead*! You can't hide from him, even when you are turned to ashes. He'll

80

make you and Vasily pay for being so snooty, for turning me away when I asked for help – and when *you* had money!'

'I helped you as much as I could,' Grandmother replied coolly. 'And you know only too well that God paid us back.'

'But it wasn't enough, not nearly enough.'

For a long time her younger sister went on boring Grandmother with that indefatigable tongue of hers. I listened to her malicious whining and wearily asked myself how Grandmother could stand it. At times like these I really hated her.

The young mistress came out and gave Grandmother a welcoming nod.

'Go on, into the dining-room!'

Grandmother's sister would shout after her:

'Mind you wipe your feet, you old tree stump rotting in a swamp!'

But the master gave Grandmother a gay welcome.

'Well, how's my clever old Akulina? Is old man Kashirin still alive?'

Grandmother gave him one of those smiles that seemed to come right from the depths of her heart.

'Still working your fingers to the bone then?'

'Yes, I'm still working. Like a convict.'

Grandmother spoke to him in a warm eloquent voice, but as though she knew that she was his senior.

At times he reminisced about Mother:

'Ye-yes, Varvara Vasilyevna. What a woman she was – a real heroine, eh?'

His wife would turn to Grandmother and interrupt:

'Remember how I gave her a *cloak*, made of black silk and trimmed with beads?'

'How could I ever forget?'

'It was good as new.'

'Ye-es,' the master mumbled. 'Cloak, shmoak – it's all a joke!'

'*What* did you say?' his wife asked suspiciously.

'Me? Nothing. The good times are passing . . . and so are people.'

'Why do you say such things?' his wife would ask in a worried voice.

81

Later they would take Grandmother to see the new-born baby, while I cleared the dirty dishes. The master would say in a soft, pensive voice:

'A fine woman, your grandmother.'

I was deeply grateful to him for saying this, and when I was alone with Grandmother I would tell her with pain in my heart:

'Why do you come here, why? You can see what they're like.'

'Ah, Alyosha, I can see *everything*,' she would answer and look at me with a kind smile on her marvellous face. This made me feel ashamed. Of course, as she could see *everything* then she would know what was happening in my heart at that very moment.

After cautiously looking round to see if anybody was coming, she embraced me and said in her warm voice:

'I wouldn't have come if *you* hadn't been here – they don't mean anything to me. And Grandfather's been ill. I've been busy looking after him, so I couldn't do any work. Now I haven't got any more money. And Mikhaila threw Sasha out, so *I* had to feed him. They promised to pay you six roubles, so I thought to myself: will you get *one* out of that lot? You've been here six months already.'

Then she whispered in my ear:

'They told me to give you a good telling-off as you don't do what you're told. But you *must* stick it out, dear, for two years, until you can stand on your own two feet. You'll do that, won't you?'

I promised that I would try, but it was very difficult. That boring, wretched life stifled me. Everyone just rushed around and stuffing themselves with food was all they cared about. I seemed to be living in a dream. Sometimes I used to think that I should run away. But the wretched winter had set in, storms howled at night, the wind blew round the attic, and the rafters creaked from the frost. So where could I run to?

They did not let me go out to play and in fact there was no time for it. The short winter's day faded away all too quickly as I rushed about the house doing the chores. But I had to go to church – to mass on Saturdays and to late service on holidays. I liked being in church. I would choose some corner where it was darker and where there was more room. I loved looking at the ikonostasis from the distance: it seemed to be dissolving in the candlelight that flowed in rich golden streams down to the stone floor around the pulpit. The dark shapes of ikons stirred gently and the golden filigree of the holy gates gaily flickered. Candle flames hung in the bluish air, like golden bees, and the heads of women and girls resembled flowers. Everything around me harmonized with the singing of the choir and seemed to be living a strange, fairy-tale existence. The whole church slowly rocked to and fro, like a cradle in that dim emptiness that seemed as thick as tar. Sometimes I thought that the church was submerged in a deep lake and had hidden itself away from the world so it could live its own independent and unique life. It was more than likely that Grandmother's stories about the City of Kityozh aroused these feelings in me. I would often repeat to myself that melodious, sad story as I drowsily rocked backwards and forwards – as everything did around me, almost lulled to sleep by the choir, the whispered prayers and the sighs of the congregation:

> The cursed Tartars have surrounded
> The glorious city of Kityozh,
> With their pagan hordes,
> In the early morning light.
> Oh, God in heaven,
> Most Holy Virgin,
> Have mercy on your slaves,
> Let them say their morning prayers
> And hear thy sacred words!
> Do not let the Tartar
> Desecrate thy holy church,
> Humiliate women, young girls,
> With little children as their sport,
> And our elders doomed to violent death.
> And the Lord Jehovah heard these cries for help
> And so did the Holy Virgin.
> And the great Lord Jehovah said
> To the blessed Archangel Michael:
> 'Now go, Michael,
> Shake the earth under Kityozh,

Drown the city in a lake;
And let the people pray there,
Never stopping to rest one moment,
From morn till night,
Reciting all the sacred prayers of the church,
From here to eternity!'

At that time my head was full of Grandmother's poetry. It was like a beehive overflowing with honey, and even my thoughts seemed to rhyme – just like her poems. I never prayed in church as it was embarrassing reciting Grandfather's angry prayers and mournful psalms in front of Grandmother's God. I was convinced that, like me, Grandmother's God was not at all pleased by them. Moreover, all these prayers were written down in books, which meant God must have known them by heart, like any other literate person. As a result, when I stood there in the church with my heart touched by a feeling of sweet sadness, or when I was smarting from the little wounds inflicted the day before, I used to try and make up my own prayers. All I had to do was reflect on my own miserable existence, and the words would automatically become lamentations:

'Oh Lord, oh Lord, how unhappy I am,
If only I could suddenly grow up.
I can't go on living any more:
If I kill myself, then forgive me.
I can see no sense in learning,
And that old devil, Grandmother Matryona,
Howls at me like a wolf.
My life here is so bitter!'

I remember many of my prayers to this day. The thoughts of a child leave deep scars which a lifetime cannot heal.

I liked the church. For me it was a place to rest in, just like the forest or fields. My vague, fervent day-dreams seemed to purify my heart, which by then had known many upheavals and had been soiled by the savagery of life. But I went to church only when there was a severe frost or when a blizzard raged through the town, when the sky seemed to freeze, and was broken up into clouds of snow by the wind: then it seemed that the earth which lay frozen under the drifts would never come to life again.

On calmer nights, I loved walking around the town more than anything else, from street to street, ending up in the most deserted places. At times I seemed to be flying along, as lonely as the moon in the sky. My shadow glided on before me falling over glinting patches of snow and comically bumping into stones or fences. The night watchman would pace down the middle of the street, wearing a heavy sheepskin coat and carrying a rattle, while his dog jogged along beside him. That clumsy man put me in mind of a kennel which had left the yard of its own accord and was moving off down the street, God knows where, with the angry dog following it. Sometimes I passed cheerful girls with their boy friends and I thought that they had escaped evening service like me. Sometimes peculiar smells drifted from brightly lit casement windows into the pure air – fine, unfamiliar smells that hinted of a life that I knew nothing about. I would stand under a window, sniff hard and try to guess what kind of life the people led in those houses, what they were like. They should have been going to mass but they were all having a gay, noisy time instead, laughing and playing some special kind of guitar, and the air was filled with the rich metallic twanging of their strings.

A single-storeyed, squat-looking house on the corner of the deserted Tikhonovsky and Martynovsky streets particularly caught my attention. I discovered it one moonlit night, just before Shrovetide, when the thaw had set in. Strange sounds blended with the warm air and poured in a single stream from a window ventilator. It was as though a very strong and good-natured person were singing without opening his mouth: I could not make out the words, but the song was very familiar and easy to follow, although that irritating twanging which interrupted the even flow made it rather more difficult to follow. I sat on the kerb and came to the conclusion that some-one was playing an incredibly powerful violin – so powerful that it hurt just listening to it. Sometimes it grew so loud that the whole house appeared to be shaking and the window panes rattled in their frames. Melting snow trickled down from the roof – and tears streamed from my face.

I did not see the watchman come up. He pushed me off the kerb and asked:

'What you doing here?'

'Listening to the music,' I explained.

'So you've nothing better to do! Clear off!'

I quickly toured the whole district and then came back to the same window. The music had stopped, though, and loud sounds of merrymaking flowed out into the street. This was quite different from the sad music of before and I thought that I must have been dreaming.

Nearly every Saturday I ran off to that house but only once in the spring did I hear someone playing a cello right up to midnight, almost without stopping. When I got back home they gave me a terrible thrashing.

Those nightly walks under the stars, along the city's deserted streets, were a rewarding experience. I deliberately chose those streets furthest from the centre, which was well lit and where I might be seen by some of the master's friends, who were bound to report me for missing evening service. Drunks, policemen and prostitutes were a danger as well. In the more remote streets, however, I was able to look into the windows in the lower storeys of houses, if they were not too heavily frosted over or hung with curtains. Those windows revealed many different activities. I saw people praying, kissing, fighting, playing cards, chattering away in anxious, hollow-sounding voices. A mute, fishlike life opened up in front of me – just as though I had put a kopek in a slot machine.

In a cellar I saw two women sitting at a table, one younger than the other. Opposite them a long-haired schoolboy was reading to them and waving his arm about. The younger woman had a dark frown on her face as she listened and leaned back in her chair. The older one, who was slim and whose hair was very thick, suddenly covered her face with her hands, and her shoulders trembled. The schoolboy threw the book down and when the younger woman had leaped to her feet and fled from the room, he fell on his knees and started kissing the other one's hands.

Through another window I could see a large bearded man rocking on his knees a woman who was wearing a red jacket –

86

just as though she were a child. I could tell he was singing as his mouth was wide open and his eyes were bulging. The woman was shaking with laughter and threw herself backwards. The man stopped, sat her up straight and started singing again, which made her laugh all the more. I watched them for a long time and only went away when I understood that they would clearly go on like this all night.

Many similar scenes stayed in my memory for ever and I was often so carried away that I was late getting home. This made the master and wife suspicious and they used to cross-examine me:

'Which church were you in? Who conducted the service?'

They knew every priest in the whole town and what texts were being read. In fact they knew *everything* and it was no problem at all for them to catch me out.

Both women worshipped the same angry God as Grandfather and this was a God who insisted that everyone should be terrified of him. His name was always on their lips and even when they were having a slanging match they would threaten each other with expressions like:

'You just wait! God will punish you. He'll destroy you, you filthy bitch!'

The first Sunday after the fast the old woman fried some pancakes and managed to burn them. Her face was flushed from the heat of the stove and she shouted furiously:

'To hell with the lot of you!'

Suddenly she sniffed the pan and her face clouded over. She flung the slice on the floor and bawled:

'For God's sake! There's some meat left in the damned pan! I forgot to burn it off on the first Monday of Lent. Good God!'

She knelt down and asked tearfully:

'Dear God, please forgive a poor wretch. In the name of all thy sufferings, don't punish an old fool.'

The ruined pancakes were given to the dogs, and the scraps of meat were burned off the pan. But from then onwards her daughter-in-law never failed to mention the incident when she was having one of her quarrels with her:

'So you use frying pans with *meat* on them during Lent!'

God was dragged into everything that went on in that house,

into every little nook and cranny of their meaningless lives, which as a result acquired a certain significance and importance, however superficial: they seemed to be praying every single hour to some higher being. The way in which they mixed God up in their boring, petty lives had a terribly depressing effect on me and I could not help looking round all the time, feeling that some invisible being was watching me.

At night I was smothered by a chilling cloud of fear which floated out from the kitchen, where the everlasting lamp burned in front of the dark ikons. Next to the shelf was a large window with two frames separated by a bar. Through it I could see a bottomless, blue, empty expanse. The whole house, the kitchen, myself even, seemed to be suspended on the edge of that void and I felt that if I suddenly moved everything would tumble into that cold blue desert and would fly up and away, beyond the stars, in deathly silence, like a stone sinking in the water. I would lie there for hours without moving, too frightened to turn on my side and fully expecting a terrible and violent death.

I do not quite remember how I cured myself of this feeling, but I managed to very quickly. Of course, Grandmother's kind God helped and at this time I thought that I had seen the truth, which was really very simple: since I had done nothing wrong, it would have been unfair of God to punish me and make a scapegoat out of me.

I used to miss evening service, especially during the spring, which, by some irresistible power, kept me from going to church. And if they gave me a seven-kopek piece for candles, then this really made a 'lost soul' out of me. With the money I would buy some five-stones and play with them while the service was going on, and I was inevitably late home. Once I managed to lose a whole ten-kopek piece which was meant for prayers for the dead and for Communion bread. As a result I had to steal someone else's offering when the priest brought the plate round.

I was passionately fond of games, and they brought me to a state of frenzy. As I was strong and fairly agile I soon became famous as a five-stones player, ball player, and skittle champion throughout the streets in the neighbourhood.

During Lent I was made to fast and take the sacrament, and off I went to confess to our neighbour, Father Dorimedont. I thought he was a rather forbidding character. As far as he was concerned I had a lot to account for: I had thrown stones at his summer house, fought his children and there were a lot of other nasty tricks I had played on him that he could very easily jog my memory with. All this made me feel very awkward and as I stood there in that poor little church waiting my turn my heart was pounding.

At first Father Dorimedont gave me a warm welcome but then he said rather peevishly:

'Oho, so it's my next-door neighbour! Down on your knees! What have you to confess?'

He covered my head with a heavy piece of velvet. The smell of wax and incense almost choked me and made it difficult to speak, but I did not want to anyway.

'Do you do what your elders tell you?'

'No,' I replied.

'Then repeat after me: "I have sinned."'

To my own surprise I blurted out:

'I stole the sacramental wafers.'

'What? How did you manage that? Where?' he asked slowly after a moment's pause.

'At the Church of the Three Bishops, at Pokrov, at Nikola...'

'All the churches in the neighbourhood! That's very bad, my friend. You have sinned. Do you understand?'

'I understand.'

'Say you have sinned then, you stupid boy! Did you steal because you were hungry?'

'Sometimes. And sometimes I lost money at five-stones. As I couldn't go back home without the bread I had to steal some.'

Father Dorimedont started whispering something in a tired, unintelligible voice, and then he asked me a few more questions. Suddenly he asked in a very stern voice:

'Have you been reading any *underground* books?'

I did not understand the question and asked:

'What are they?'

'Any *forbidden* books?'

'No, none at all.'

'Then your sins are forgiven. Get up!'

I looked at his face in amazement: it seemed thoughtful and kind, and made me feel awkward and very ashamed of myself. Before they sent me off to church the master and his wife had told me about all the horrors and terrors of confession and warned me that I must be honest and confess every single sin.

'I threw stones at your summer house,' I announced.

The priest lifted his head and said:

'That's a sin as well. Off with you!'

'And at your dog!'

'Next please,' Father Dorimedont called out as he looked over my shoulder.

I left with the feeling that I had been made a fool of and insulted. I had been frightened and tense before confession, but now I knew that it was not in the least terrifying, not in the least interesting. The only question that interested me was about those books I had never heard of. I thought of that schoolboy down in the basement reading to the two women and remembered 'Just the Job' who also had several 'forbidden' books, full of drawings that I just could not make head or tail of.

Next day they gave me a fifteen-kopek piece and sent me off to Holy Communion. Easter had come late that year and the snow had thawed a long time before. The streets were dry and dust rose in clouds along the main roads. It was a radiant, sunny day. Near the church wall a large crowd of workmen used to play five-stones. I decided there was still time for a game before Communion and I asked them:

'Can I play?'

'It'll cost you a kopek,' a pock-faced red-haired man proudly announced.

And just as proudly I replied:

'Three kopeks on the second pair from the left!'

'Put your money down then.'

And the game began!

I changed my fifteen-kopek piece and put three under a pair of stones: whoever knocked them off would win, but if he missed he would owe me three kopeks. My luck was in. Two of the men aimed and missed. I had won six kopeks from *grown-up men*, and this raised my spirits considerably. But then one of them said:

'Watch him, mates, or he'll be running off with his winnings.'

I took offence at this and said excitedly:

'*Nine* kopeks under the pair on the far left!'

This, however, did not worry them very much, but some scruffy little brat about my own age gave them a warning shout:

'Watch him, he's a lucky devil. I know him – he's an apprentice draughtsman from Zvezdinka!'

A thin looking man, who was a furrier – judging by his smell – said spitefully:

'*Lucky devil* is he? Ve-ery good!'

He took careful aim and knocked my stake off. Then he leaned over and asked:

'Still feel like playing?'

I answered:

'Three under the last pair to the right!'

'I'll knock those off all right,' the furrier boasted, but he missed.

It was against the rules to stake on the same stones three times in a row, so I began to aim at other people's stakes and won another four kopeks, and a heap of 'chips'. But when my turn came round again I tried three times and lost everything – and just at the right moment too. The service had finished, the bells were ringing and everyone was leaving the church.

'Are you married?' the furrier asked, trying to catch me by the hair. I wriggled away, ran off, caught up with a boy who was dressed in his Sunday best and politely asked:

'Were you at Communion?'

'Well, what about it?' he asked suspiciously.

I tried to persuade him to tell me what happened at Communion and what the sermon was about. The boy looked at me sternly and then bellowed in a terrifying voice:

'So you skipped Communion, you heretic? Well, *I'm* not going to tell you! I hope your father tans the hide off you!'

I ran home quite convinced that they would cross-examine

me and that they were bound to find out that I had missed Communion. But the old woman congratulated me and all she asked was:

'How much did you give the priest?'

I blurted out the first figure that came into my head:

'Five kopeks.'

'You could have kept another three without him seeing. That would have left seven for yourself, muggins!'

Now it was spring. Every day wore a new kind of dress, and every succeeding day was brighter and more pleasant. The young grass and the fresh green leaves of the birches had a heady smell; I felt an irresistible urge to go out into the field to hear the lark, and to lie on my back on the warm earth. But here I was, cleaning the winter clothes, helping to pack them away in a trunk, cutting up leaf tobacco and beating the dust out of furniture. From morning until night I was kept busy doing disagreeable things, things which were of no use to me anyway. When I did have some free time there was absolutely nothing to do. Our miserable little street was deserted and I was not allowed to leave it. Out in the yard there were only angry, tired navvies, dishevelled cooks, and laundresses.

In the evenings the animal-like courting that went on so disgusted and repelled me that I wished I could go blind. I would go up to the attic with a pair of scissors and some coloured paper, cut out lace-like designs and stick them on to the rafters. This only bored me even more. I wanted terribly to go off somewhere where people slept less, where they did not quarrel so much and did not pester God with their tiresome complaints or insult others with their vicious criticism.

On Easter Saturday the miraculous ikon of the Vladimir Virgin was brought from Oran Monastery. It would be left in the town until the middle of June and was carried round to all the houses and flats in every parish.

They brought it to the master's house one weekday morning. I was washing some copper pots and pans in the kitchen when the young mistress shouted to me from her room in a frightened voice:

'Open the front door. It's the Oran Virgin!'

Filthy as I was, with my hands covered in grease and dust from ground bricks, I rushed downstairs and opened the door. A young monk was standing there with a lamp in one hand and a censer in the other, and he said softly:

'Everyone asleep? Give me a hand, please.'

Two of the people in the house appeared and carried the heavy ikon case up the narrow stairs; I helped by supporting one side with my shoulders and dirty hands. Behind us some monks trudged singing 'Holy Virgin, pray for us' in deep voices and without much enthusiasm.

I thought to myself with conviction: 'She'll be annoyed with me for carrying her with my filthy hands. She'll make them wither and drop off!'

They stood the ikon in the front of the room, on two chairs covered with a clean sheet. Two young, handsome monks stood at the sides holding it. They looked just like angels with their bright, joyful eyes and thick hair. Then they started reciting prayers.

'Blessed Mother of God,' a large priest said in a shrill voice as he pinched his puffy ear lobe, almost hidden in his thick hair, with a purplish finger.

'Holy Mother of God have mercy on us,' the monks sang with tired voices.

I loved the Holy Virgin. According to Grandmother's stories, in order to comfort the poor she had planted all the flowers and had brought all joy, all that was good and beautiful into the world. When my turn came to kiss her hand, and as I had never seen grown-ups do it before, I trembled all over and then kissed the ikon right on the lips. A strong arm hurled me into a corner by the door, and I did not remember the monks leaving with the ikon. But I still remember one thing: my master and mistress stood round me while I sat on the floor. They looked terribly frightened and worried as they started discussing what was to be done with me.

'We must have a word with the priest, he knows more about this sort of thing,' my master was saying. Then he started telling me off, but his voice was rather gentle:

'Don't you know it's *forbidden* to kiss the Virgin on the lips. You should have learned that at school!'

For a few days I awaited my doom. I had touched the ikon with dirty hands and kissed the Virgin on the lips. I was certain to pay dearly for that! But apparently the Virgin forgave my unintentional sin, which I had committed only out of sincere love for her. Perhaps the punishment was so mild that it passed unnoticed among the frequent thrashings meted out by my master and mistress. Sometimes I would try and irritate the old woman and I used to say in a grief-stricken voice:

'The Virgin must have forgotten to punish me!'

'You just wait and see!' the old woman replied viciously. 'There's still time.'

While I was decorating the rafters in the attic with cut-outs made from pink tea wrappers, strips of tin foil, leaves and any old rubbish I could lay my hands on, I used to sing anything that came into my head like Kalmuks do when they are on the road. And I tried to imitate the church choir:

> 'I sit in my attic
> With scissors in my hand.
> I just sit and cut paper.
> How bored I am, and such a dunce!
> I wish I were a dog
> So I could run where I like.
> But everyone shouts at me:
> "Sit down, shut up, you urchin,
> If you know what's good for you."'

The old woman would look at my work, laugh and shake her head:

'Why don't you decorate the kitchen?'

Once the master came up to the attic, saw what I had done, sighed and said:

'You really make me laugh, Peshkov,* you little devil! Perhaps you'll be a conjuror one day. But it's hard to say *what's* going to become of you . . .'

He gave me a large five-kopek piece with the head of Nicho-

*Peshkov was Gorky's real surname, and he later adopted the pseudonym Gorky, meaning 'bitter' in Russian. (Trans.)

las I on the back. I put fine wire round it and hung it right in the middle of my gaily coloured decorations. But within one day the coin had disappeared and I am sure that the old woman stole it . . .

Chapter 5

ALL the same I did run away in the spring. One morning I was
sent to buy some sugar and tea. The shopkeeper, who was
having a row with his wife at the time, did not take any notice
of me when I entered and he hit her over the head with a weight
from a pair of scales. She ran out into the street and collapsed.
A crowd gathered immediately and the woman was taken to
hospital in a four-wheeled cab. I ran after the driver and before
I knew where I was I found myself on the banks of the Volga –
with a twenty-kopek piece in my hand. The spring day was
bright and radiant, and the Volga was in full flood. Everything
around me was animated, spacious – and it seemed that up to
then I had been living like a mouse in a cellar. So I decided not
to go back to my master and mistress, nor to Grandmother at
Kunavino. (I had not kept my promise to Grandmother and
felt too ashamed to go and see her: in any case Grandfather
would have gloated over my misery.)

For two or three days I wandered around the quays, scroung-
ing food from kind-hearted porters with whom I spent the
nights. After not very long one of them said:

'You're wasting your time round here! Go to the steamship
Dobry, they need a washer-up.'

So I went. A tall, bearded steward in a black silk peakless
cap peered at me through his spectacles with dull eyes and said
softly:

'The pay's two roubles a month. Where's your passport?'*

I said that I did not have one so the steward thought for a
moment and said:

'Fetch your mother.'

I rushed back to Grandmother who approved of my trying
to get a job and persuaded Grandfather to go down to the
labour exchange and get me a passport while she accompanied
me back to the ship.

'Fine,' the steward said as he looked us over. 'Let's go.'

*In Russia passports were necessary to travel from one town to
another. (Trans.)

96

He took me astern where an enormous cook in a white jacket and hat was sitting at a table sipping tea and puffing away at a thick cigarette. The steward pushed me over to him and announced:

'The new dish-washer.'

Then he immediately left us.

The cook snorted, his black whiskers bristled and he shouted after the steward:

'You'd take on any street urchin, as long as it's cheap labour.'

He angrily shook his head with its short black hair, opened his eyes wide, stiffened up, puffed himself out and shouted in a loud voice:

'And who are you?'

I took a great dislike to that man. Although he was dressed in white, to me he seemed filthy. A kind of wool grew on his fingers and hair stuck out of his big ears.

'I'm hungry,' I said.

He winked and suddenly his fierce expression changed into a broad smile. His chubby, flushed-looking cheeks rippled in waves down to his ears, revealing large, horsy teeth, and his whiskers gently drooped. He looked just like a fat, kindly old peasant woman. He threw what was left of his tea overboard and poured a fresh cup. Then he pushed a whole French roll and a large slice of sausage over to me.

'Tuck in! Got a mother and father? Know how to steal? Well, don't worry, we're *all* thieves here, so we'll teach you!'

He sounded just like a dog barking. His enormous face, which was shaved until it was blue, had thick networks of red veins around the puffy, purple nose which drooped down over his whiskers. His lower lip hung heavily, as if in disgust, and a lighted cigarette stuck to the corner of his mouth. Obviously he had just had a bath, as he smelled of birch branches, and pepper brandy, and heavy beads of sweat glistened on his temples and neck.

When I had drunk my tea he shoved over a one-rouble note.

'Go and buy yourself two aprons with stomachers. No, wait, I'll go and get them myself.'

He straightened his cap and went off, swaying heavily to and fro, feeling the deck with his feet – just like a bear.

97

It was night-time now. The moon shone brightly, sailing away from the port side of the ship into the meadows. The old reddish steamboat which had a white stripe on its funnel moved slowly and slapped its paddles unevenly in the silvery water. Dark banks seemed to be gently swimming towards it and threw shadows over the river. Along their ridges I could make out the red lights of cottage windows. In one of the villages they were singing, girls were dancing, and the refrain *ai lyuli* sounded like 'hallelujah' to me.

Our ship was towing a barge, which was painted dirty red as well, and it moved behind us at the end of a long cable. Its deck was covered by an iron cage full of convicts sentenced to penal colonies or hard labour. A sentry's bayonet shone on the bows like a candle, and the tiny stars in the blue sky glinted like candles as well. No noise came from the barge and it was brightly illuminated by the moon. Behind metal bars I could see dim, round grey figures – these were convicts looking at the Volga. The water sobbed and seemed to be crying, and then quietly laughing. Everything around me reminded me of a church; there was that same strong smell of burning oil.

As I looked at the barge I recalled my early childhood, that journey from Astrakhan to Nizhny-Novgorod, Mother's expressionless face, and Grandmother, who had brought me out into the world of people, which was full of fascination despite its harshness. But particularly when I recalled Grandmother, everything nasty and offensive vanished, and changed into something more interesting and pleasant, and everyone became better and kinder.

The beauty of the night brought me near to tears, and that barge made a deep impression on me. In the brooding silence of that warm night it looked like a coffin and seemed completely out of place in that broad expanse of water in full flood. The uneven line of the bank always rising and falling had a pleasant, stimulating effect on me, and made me want to be kind to people and to feel needed by them.

There was nothing special about the passengers however – young and old, men and women, they all looked exactly the same. The ship moved very slowly (businessmen used to travel then by mailboat) and the people round me were gentle and easy-going. From morning until night they ate and drank and made all the crockery, all the knives and forks dirty; it was my job to wash and polish them, and this kept me busy from six in the morning right up to midnight.

Between two and six in the afternoon, and from ten to midnight there was not so much work, and then the passengers took a break from eating and just drank tea, beer or vodka, and the stewards had some time off. Some of them would sit and drink tea near a hatch – Smury the chef with his assistant Yakov Ivanych, a dish-washer called Maxim, and Sergei the deck steward – a hunchback with oily eyes, prominent cheekbones and a face pitted with smallpox.

Yakov Ivanych would tell filthy stories, laughing with that sobbing laugh of his and showing his rotten green teeth. Sergei would open his froglike mouth until it reached his ears, while gloomy old Maxim would say nothing and just stare at me with those stern eyes, whose colour I find very difficult to describe.

'Asians! Mordvinians!'* the senior chef would say every now and again in his sonorous voice.

I did not like them. All that the fat, balding Yakov Ivanych could talk about was women and he always made obscene remarks about them. His face was vacant and covered with dark blue spots. He had a wart on one cheek, with a little bush of red hair growing on it, which he had twirled into a point. When an easy-going cheeky-looking woman came on board he would follow her around in a very timid, sheepish way, just as though he were begging. Then he would speak to her in his pathetic, sickly voice. Bubbles of saliva would form on his lips and he licked them off with quick darts of his filthy tongue. For some reason I felt these oily specimens were born to be executioners.

'You should learn how to warm women up,' he used to say to Sergei and Maxim, who listened attentively and went red in the face as they puffed themselves up.

'Asians,' Smury would say in disgust as he wearily got to his feet and started giving orders:

* The Mordvinians were of Finnic origin and lived in settlements along the Volga. (Trans.)

99

'Peshkov, get going!'

Back in his cabin he would shove a little leather-bound book over to me, lie down on his hammock by the wall of the ice-box and say:

'Read!'

I would sit on a macaroni box and start reading very conscientiously:

'"*Umbracula* sky, studded with stars, means good communication with heaven, and freedom from ignoramuses and vice."'

Smury would draw on his cigarette, puff the smoke out through his nostrils and bellow:

'Camels, writing muck like that!'

'"A bared left breast means a pure heart."'

'*Whose* bared left breast?'

'Doesn't say.'

'Must mean a woman's breast. Oh, the lecherous devils!'

He would close his eyes and lie there with his hands behind his head. His cigarette, which had almost gone out, would dangle from the corner of his mouth. He used to straighten it with his tongue and then inhale so deeply that something whistled inside his chest and his huge face disappeared in a cloud of smoke. Sometimes I thought he had dozed off, and I would stop reading and have a closer look at that wretched book which bored me stiff. But he would suddenly say in his hoarse voice:

'Carry on!'

'"The Venerable Father answers: Look here, my dear frère Suveryan."'

'Severyan.'

'It says *Suveryan*.'

'Well, it must have been written by the devil. There's some poetry at the end – read that.'

So I would begin again:

> 'Oh, ignorant ones, curious to know our business,
> Your weak eyes will never spy it out
> Nor will you ever discover how brothers sing.'

'Stop,' Smury would say. 'That's not poetry. Give me the book.'

He would angrily turn over the thick blue pages and then stuff the book under his mattress.

'Let's have a look at another.'

Unfortunately he had piles of books in that black iron-bound trunk: *Precepts of Homer, Artillery Memoirs, Letters of Lord Sedengali, Concerning that pernicious insect the bedbug, its extermination, together with an appendix of measures recommended to combat it.* There were books that seemed to have no beginning or end. Sometimes the cook made me go through the whole lot and call out the titles. As I read he would bellow angrily:

'The things they write, the scum! It's as though they are *accusing* you the whole time, God knows why! That Gervasy! The devil must have landed me with *him* . . . Umbracula . . .'

All those strange words and unfamiliar names became terribly tiresome, and I could not get them out of my mind. They made my tongue itch and I wanted to repeat them all over again, every moment of the day: perhaps they had some sort of hidden meaning?

Beyond the porthole the water was eternally singing and splashing away. How wonderful it would be to go forrard, where the sailors and stokers gathered among the crates of cargo, beating the passengers at cards, singing songs and telling interesting stories. It would have been marvellous to sit with them and listen to simple things that I could understand, and to look at the banks of the Kama, at the pines that stuck up like bronze guitar strings, at the meadows, where the flooding had left little pools which looked like pieces of broken glass reflecting the deep blue sky. Our ship seemed to be no longer connected with the earth, but was flying away from it. The sound of invisible bells came from the banks in the quiet of the fading day, conjuring up visions of villages and people. A fisherman's boat rocked on a wave and put me in mind of a piece of bread. Suddenly a little village would come into sight: a crowd of boys were splashing around in the river, while a peasant in a red shirt walked along the strip of golden sand. From the middle of the river everything had a pleasant look, and it amused me to see how distant objects resembled little toys, and looked just as small and gaily coloured. I wanted to shout out some welcoming, friendly words so that the people on the banks and in the barge behind could hear me.

That reddish-coloured barge had an irresistible fascination for me and for hours on end I would stand watching it plough its blunt prow through the muddy water. The steamboat hauled it along as though it were a pig. When the cable slackened it whipped against the water and then pulled tight again, dripping water and gripping the front of the barge. I particularly wanted to see the faces of those people cooped up like animals in that iron cage. When they were taken off at Perm I climbed up the gangways of the barge. Dozens of grey-looking men filed past and they made a loud clinking noise as they stamped their chained feet. The weight of their haversacks almost bent them double. Women and men, old and young, beautiful and ugly – all of them filed past. But for the fact that they were dressed differently and looked so horrible with their shaven heads, they were just like ordinary people. Of course, they were criminals, but Grandmother had lots of good things to say about them.

Smury, who resembled a ferocious bandit more than anyone else on board, would gloomily survey the barge and mutter:

'God preserve us from such a fate!'

Once I happened to ask him:

'Why do you cook while other people kill and steal?'

'I don't cook, but I get the food ready for the kitchens.'

Then he laughed and said:

'The women do the cooking.'

After a moment's thought he added:

'The only difference between people is their *brains*. One is clever, another not so clever and a third is an absolute fool. To be clever you've got to read the right books, black magic – and ... let me see ... what else? You must read *all* kinds of books to find out which ones are best.'

He was always encouraging me:

'Go on, read! If you don't understand a book, then read it seven times. If you still don't understand, then read it twelve times.'

Smury was very abrupt with everyone on board, including the taciturn steward. He spoke in fits and starts, and would drop his lower lip with a look of distaste and make his whiskers bristle, just as if he were throwing stones at them. To me he seemed gentle and attentive, but there was something rather frightening in his concern for me. Sometimes he seemed as halfwitted as Grandmother's sister and he would often say:

'There's plenty of time for books . . .'

For long periods he would lie sniffing in his hammock with his eyes closed. His fat stomach would shake and his hairy fingers, which were covered in burns, and splayed out on his chest as though he were a corpse, seemed to be knitting an invisible stocking with invisible needles. Then suddenly he would start grumbling again:

'Yes, you've got some sense in that head of yours, so use it! Not many of us are blessed with brains, it's all shared out unequally. If everyone had the same amount . . . but no, it doesn't happen like that. One man'll understand, another won't. Some don't even *want* to, so there!'

He stumbled over his words as he told me about army life, stories whose meaning I could never understand. They did not interest me, and to make matters worse he used to leave out the beginning and tell me only what he could remember:

'The colonel would call the soldier over and ask: "What did the lieutenant tell you?" The soldier told him everything as it happened – it's a soldier's duty to tell the truth. The lieutenant looked at him as though he were a blank wall, lowered his head and turned away. Oh, yes! . . .'

The cook angrily puffed at his cigarette and grumbled:

'Do you think I know what people are allowed to say? They carted the lieutenant off to the guardhouse and his mother kept saying . . . – oh God, *I* don't know anything.'

It was hot, and everything around me was shaking gently and humming. On the other side of the metal wall of the cabin I could hear water splashing and the ship's paddles thumping. The river flowed in a broad stream past the ship's lights and in the distance I could see thin strips of meadow on the banks and swaying trees. By then I had got used to all the different noises and it seemed there was nothing to be heard except the sailor standing forrard calling out his melancholy: 'Se-ven. Se-ven.' I did not want to listen or work, or take part in anything, but was content just to sit somewhere in the shade, where I could not smell that greasy stuffy kitchen, and where I could sit and drowsily watch that subdued, weary life gliding over the water. Then the cook would angrily order again:

'Start reading!'

Even the stewards from the first-class cabins were afraid of him, and so was that withdrawn quiet little steward who looked like a fish.

'You pigs!' he would shout at the stewards. 'Come here, you thieves. Asians! Umbracula!'

The sailors and stokers treated him with respect, often very obsequiously. He used to give them pieces of meat from the soup and ask them about life in the country, about their families. Those oily, greasy stokers from White Russia were considered the lowest of the low and were commonly known as *Yaguts*.

When Smury heard them being teased he would bristle, go red in the face and shout at the stokers:

'How *can* you let them take the micky like that, fat-faces! Give them one in the mug!'

Once the handsome, vicious bo'sun said to him:

'Russians or not, they both believe in the same God!'

The cook seized him round the waist, lifted him up and shook him:

'Do you want me to thrash the living daylights out of you?'

They quarrelled frequently and sometimes came to blows, but Smury was never beaten. His strength was superhuman, and besides, the captain's wife, who was a tall, plump woman with a masculine face and hair cropped smooth, like a boy's, often used to have chats with him – and very friendly they were too. He had an insatiable thirst for vodka but never got drunk. He used to start drinking in the morning, as soon as he got up, and polish off a bottle in four swigs. Then he would sip beer until the evening. His face would slowly turn brownish and his dark eyes opened wider and wider in astonishment. Some evenings that enormous white figure used to sit on a hatch for hours without saying a word, gloomily surveying the river disappearing into the distance. At these times everyone was scared stiff, but I felt sorry for him. Smury would come out of that kitchen, flushed and sweating. Then he would stand there and scratch his smooth skull, wave one hand and would either disappear or shout out loud:

'The sturgeon's off.'

'Well, salt it then!'

'Supposing someone orders fish soup or steamed fish?'

'Use anything you've got. *They'll* eat it.'

Sometimes when I went to see him he would give me a weary look and say:

'What do you want?'

'Nothing.'

'That's all right then.'

During one of my visits I asked him:

'Why is everyone afraid of you, when you're such a good man really?'

'I'm only good to *you*.'

But he immediately added in a simple, pensive voice:

'I seem good to *everyone*, I suppose. Only I don't show it. You must never let people see or they'll walk all over you. Everyone likes to trample on a good man as if he were a lump of mud in a swamp. They'll tread you right down. Now go and get me some beer.'

He would drink glass after glass, lick his whiskers and say:

'If you were a little older I'd teach you a lot of things. I've got something to say, I'm no fool, I can tell you. Read books, you'll find everything you need in them. Books must be taken seriously. Want some beer?'

'Don't like it.'

'That's good. Keep off drink, it's a terrible thing. Vodka is the work of the devil. If I were a rich man I'd send you off to school. An uneducated man is like an ox – you'll never teach it anything. All it wants to do is put its head under the yoke, eat and swish its tail.'

The captain's wife gave him a volume of Gogol and I read *The Terrible Vengeance*, which I liked very much. But Smury shouted angrily:

'That's trash! A fairy-tale!'

He took the book away, went to the captain's wife for another, and then told me in that morose voice of his:

'Read *Taras* . . . what's the full title? Can you find out? The captain's wife says it's very good. Might be all right for *her*, but not for me! She's had her hair cut short. Why doesn't she have her ears done at the same time!'

At the passage where Taras Bulba challenged Ostap to a fight the cook burst out laughing.

'Well, what's it all about? All it means is that one had brains, and the other brawn! The things they print these days, the idiots!'

He would listen attentively when I read to him but would often grumble:

'What rubbish! How can you cut a man in half, right from the shoulders to the waist? And it's impossible to lift a man on a spear – it would break! After all, *I* was a soldier once.'

Andrei's treachery really disgusted him.

'That's a fine son for you! And just because of a woman. Ugh, it makes you sick!'

When I read how Taras shot his son the cook lifted his legs out of his hammock, propped himself up with his hands, bent down and burst into tears, which trickled slowly down his cheeks and on to the deck. He sniffed and muttered:

'Oh God in heaven! God in heaven!'

But suddenly he started shouting at me again:

'Why did you stop reading, you little devil?'

He burst out crying once more, even more violently and bitterly, when I read how Ostap, just before his death, cried out: 'Father, can you hear me?'

'That was the last straw!' Smury sobbed. 'Is that the end already? What a terrible thing to happen! But they were real people then. Take Taras, eh? Ye-es, they were *people*.'

He took the book from me and carefully examined it, showering the cover with tears.

'A good book is just like – a holiday!'

After that we read *Ivanhoe*: Smury liked Richard Plantagenet very much.

'There's a *real* king for you,' he said enthusiastically. But I myself found the book rather boring. On the whole our tastes differed. I liked *The Story of Thomas Jones* – an old translation of *The History of Tom Jones, Foundling*, but Smury just grumbled:

'It's all so stupid! What the hell do I care about Thomas! What good is he? There *must* be some other books!'

Once I told him that there were others, that were called 'underground' or 'forbidden' and which one could read only in cellars at night-time. His eyes bulged and he bristled all over:

'Wha-at's that? Lying again?'

'I'm not lying, the priest once asked me about them at confession. I've even seen people reading them and crying.'

The cook stared me gloomily in the face and asked.

'Who was crying, then?'

'A young girl who was listening. But the other one was so frightened that she ran out of the room.'

'Wake up, you must be delirious!' Smury said as he slowly shut his eyes.

After a moment's silence he muttered:

'Of course, there's some things that are hidden away ... But it's *impossible*, impossible to say where . . . I'm too old for that kind of thing . . . But on the other hand . . .'

He could babble on for a whole hour in this very 'eloquent' way.

In the end I got used to reading and it became a pleasure to take books from him. What happened in books was delightfully different from real life, which was becoming harder the whole time. Like me, Smury became more and more carried away by books and he often took me away from my work.

'Read, Peshkov!'

'I've a lot of dishes to wash.'

'Maxim will do them.'

He would very rudely pass on my work to the senior dish-washer, who then started breaking glasses out of spite. One of the stewards, however, gave me a gentle warning:

'I'll have you thrown off the ship!'

Once Maxim deliberately put a few glasses on a tray covered in dirty water and pools of cold tea. I poured the dirty water over the side – and the glasses followed it.

'It's not my fault,' Smury said to the steward. 'I'll pay for them.'

The stewards began to treat me suspiciously and started saying:

'You little bookworm! What on earth do you get paid for?'

They tried to give me as much work as they could and make the crockery dirty on purpose. I could sense that it was all going to end disastrously for me and I was not wrong.

One evening a red-faced peasant woman accompanied by a girl in a yellow dress and a new pink jacket came on board from some small quay. They were both drunk, and the older woman smiled and curtseyed to everyone, pronouncing her 'o's just like a country priest.

'Forgive me, dears, I've had a drop too much. They took me to court and let me off, so I had a few drinks to celebrate!'

The girl was laughing and surveyed everyone with glazed eyes. Then she pushed the old woman forward.

'Get a move on, you filthy slut!' she said.

They sat down near the second-class cabins, just outside where Yakov Ivanych and Sergei slept. The old woman soon disappeared and while she was gone Sergei came up to the girl and sat next to her, greedily opening his froglike mouth.

When I had finished my work and had settled down on a table to sleep, Sergei came up and seized me by the hand:

'Come on then, we'll get you married.'

He was drunk. I tried to pull my hand away but he hit me.

'Come on!'

Maxim came running up. He was drunk as well, and the two of them started dragging me over the deck towards their cabin past sleeping passengers. But Smury was at the door, and Yakov Ivanych was standing just inside, holding on to the post, while the girl pounded him on the back and shouted out in a drunken voice:

'Lemme go!'

Smury pulled me away from Sergei and Maxim, caught them by the hair and knocked their heads together. They went flying on to the deck.

'You Asian,' he said to Yakov, slamming the door in his face. Then he gave me a shove and yelled:

'Get out of here!'

I ran to the stern. It was a cloudy night and the river looked black. In the ship's wake two foaming paths stretched away to invisible shores, and in between them trailed the barge. First to port, then to starboard, glowing red patches would appear and then be hidden by sudden bends in the river, leaving everything in darkness. When they vanished in this way the night seemed blacker and more oppressive than ever. Smury came up and sat next to me. He sighed heavily and lit a cigarette.

'So they dragged you over to *her*, did they? Filthy swine! I heard they tried to . . .'

'Did you save her?'

'*Her*?' He said something very rude about the girl and continued in his weary voice:

'They're all *scum* here. This rotten old ship's worse than the country. Have you ever lived there?'

'No.'

'The country's really a terrible place. Especially in the winter!'

He threw his cigarette over the side, was silent for a few moments and then continued:

'This pigsty'll be the ruination of you! I feel sorry for you, really. And I feel sorry for everyone. Sometimes I just don't know what to do. I could even go down on my knees and say to them: "What are you doing with your lives, you bastards, eh? Are you *blind*?" Just like stupid camels they are.'

The ship gave a long drawn-out whistle and a cable splashed into the water. A lamp showed we were near the quayside and it rocked in the thick gloom. More lights emerged from the black night.

'It's "Drunken Forest",' the cook growled. 'And there's a River Drunk as well. We used to have a quartermaster called Drunkov . . . and a clerk called Boozer! Come on, let's go ashore . . .'

I could see huge women and girls hauling logs from the shore on to the ship on long hand-barrows. Their rope straps made them stoop low and they took little skipping steps. They came down in twos to the stokehole and threw logs that were three feet long into the dark pit and shouts of 'old timber!' filled the air. As they carried the logs down the sailors pinched their breasts and legs, making them squeal and spit. On the return journey they were able to protect themselves with their straps. I saw this happen dozens of times, on every single trip. It was the same at every quay where we took on wood.

I now felt that I had aged terribly and that I had been living for years on that ship. I knew beforehand what was going to happen the following day, next week, next autumn – next year even.

It was already getting light. On the sandy cliffs above the quay I could make out a sturdy looking pine forest. The women went up the path which led into it singing, laughing and shouting. They looked like soldiers with their long hand-barrows. I felt like crying and my heart seemed to be boiling in the hot tears that welled up inside me. It was all very painful. But I felt ashamed of crying and I tried to help a sailor called Blyakhin scrub the deck. He was an insignificant specimen and he seemed literally to be fading, withering away. Blyakhin was always hiding in little corners, and his tiny eyes glinted in the darkness.

'My real name's not Blyakhin . . . Well, you see, my mother was a prostitute. My sister's one as well. It seems that's what they were fated to be. In my opinion, fate is an *anchor* for all of us. You'd better be going now. No, wait a minute.'

He pulled his mop over the deck and said softly:

'Now you can see what insults women have to suffer! If you hold a match to a wet log long enough it'll catch fire. I can't stand goings-on like that, I can tell you! If I'd been born a woman I would have drowned myself in a dark millpond – by Christ I swear it! But no one seems to have any will-power and as a result they get burned. Now the castrates are no fools. They've found the *right* way to live – you must forget all trivial things and serve God with a pure heart.'

The captain's wife made her way past us, lifting her skirt high over the puddles. She was a tall woman with a good figure and such a simple, bright face that I felt like running after her and asking: 'Please say something to me, please!'

The ship slowly swung away from the quay. Blyakhin crossed himself and said:

'We're off!'

Chapter 6

AT Sarapul Maxim disembarked, without saying good-bye to anyone, and he seemed very calm and serious. He was followed by the cheerful laughing peasant woman, and the girl, who now looked terribly scruffy and had swollen eyes. Sergei knelt for a long time in front of the captain's cabin, kissing one of the door panels, knocking his forehead against it and moaning:

'Forgive me, I'm not guilty. It was that Maxim . . .'

The sailors and stewards, even some of the passengers, knew that he was lying, but they urged him on and shouted advice:

'Go in, go in, *he*'ll forgive you!'

The captain chased him away and kicked him, so that he fell flat on his back. All the same, he forgave him. Sergei immediately started running round the deck with his tea-trays, staring people right in the eye as though he were a dog begging for food.

They replaced Maxim with a soldier from Vyatka. He was a skinny man with a small head and reddish eyes. As soon as he came on board the assistant chef sent him off to kill some chickens. The soldier killed two and let the rest run around the deck. The passengers tried to catch them and three flew over the side. Then he sat down on a pile of firewood near the kitchen and cried bitterly.

'What's wrong, you idiot?' Smury asked him in amazement. 'Surely soldiers don't cry?'

'I . . . I was never at the front-line,' he replied softly.

This remark finished him. Within half an hour he was the laughing stock of the whole ship. People would go right up to him, stare him in the face and ask:

'Is *this* the one?'

Then they would collapse in convulsions of imbecile laughter.

At first the soldier did not appear to see anyone or even hear them laugh. He wiped the tears from his face with the sleeve of his old cotton shirt and seemed to be trying to hide them. But soon his reddish eyes began to gleam angrily and he started talking in the rapid Vyatka manner – just like a twittering magpie:

'Wotcher all goggling at? May you all rot!'

This amused everyone even more and the passengers started poking him with their fingers, pulling his shirt and his apron. They played with him just as though he were a young goat and went on tormenting him until dinner-time.

When they had finished eating, someone stuck a piece of dried lemon on the handle of a wooden spoon and tied it to the apron strings behind his back. The soldier walked around with the spoon dangling behind him, and this had everyone in hysterics; he darted about just like a trapped mouse, and he could not understand what they were laughing at.

Smury silently followed him, looking very serious. I felt sorry for the soldier and asked the chef:

'Should I tell him about the spoon?'

He nodded in reply.

When I told the soldier why they were laughing he quickly groped for the spoon, tore it off, threw it on to the deck and stamped it to pieces. Then he clawed at my hair with both hands. We started fighting – much to the delight of the passengers who immediately formed a circle round us.

Smury brushed them aside, separated us, pulled my ears and then caught hold of the soldier's ear. When the passengers saw that little man shaking his head and dancing around under the chef's arm they started to roar like wild animals, whistled and stamped their feet, and split their sides with laughter.

'Up the garrison! Bash him in the belly!'

The animal enthusiasm of that herd of people made me want to throw myself at them and beat their filthy heads in with a log.

Smury let the soldier go, hid his hands behind his back and turned on the crowd like a wild bear, bristling all over and looking quite terrifying with his bared teeth.

'Back to your places. Quick march! As-ians!'

The soldier attacked me again, but Smury seized him round the body with one arm, carried him to a hydrant and started pumping water over his head, twisting the soldier's fragile little body as though he were a rag doll. Some sailors, including the bo'sun and the first officer, came running up, and a crowd soon gathered again. The steward, who was as quiet and subdued as always, stood out a head taller than the rest. The soldier sat down on a pile of wood by the kitchen and his hands trembled as he took his boots off and started trying to wring out his puttees, which were in fact dry. But water dripped from his thin hair and this highly amused the onlookers. Then he said in a thin, shrill little voice:

'I'll kill that little brat!'

Smury held me by the shoulder and said something to the first officer. The sailors dispersed the crowd, and when everyone had gone, leaving the deck empty, the chef asked the soldier:

'What are we going to do with you?'

He did not reply, looked at me with wild eyes and his whole body twitched in the most peculiar way.

'Atten-shun, you twitcher!' Smury said.

The soldier answered:

'Not on your life! You're not in *my* platoon!'

This stunned the cook. His puffed-out cheeks sank and became flabby. He spat and moved off, taking me with him. I felt quite bewildered as I strode after him and kept on looking back to see what the soldier was doing.

Smury muttered in a nonplussed voice:

'Who does he think *he* is? What do *you* think?'

Sergei caught us up and whispered:

'He's going to cut his throat.'

'Where is he?' Smury bellowed and rushed off.

The soldier was standing by the stewards' cabin with a large knife in his hand. It was the one they used for cutting chickens' heads off and cutting up firewood; it was blunt and had notches like a saw. The passengers stood in front of the cabin and stared at that funny little man with his dripping head. His snub-nosed face shook like a jelly, his mouth drooped wearily and his lips twitched. He roared: 'Torturers, torturers!'

I jumped up on something and looked at the people's faces: they were all smiling, giggling and saying to each other: 'Go on, have a look, have a look!'

When he started tucking his shirt into his trousers with his dry little child's hands a respectable looking man who was standing next to me said with a sigh:

'A moment ago he was going to cut his throat, and now he's trying to straighten his trousers!'

The passengers laughed even louder. Clearly, no one thought for one moment that the soldier would cut his throat. Nor did I, nor did Smury, who glanced at him rapidly and then started shoving people away with his belly.

'Clear off, you fool,' he told them. He called them all 'fool' as if he were addressing one person and not a crowd, and he would go up to a whole group of people and shout: 'Back to your places, *fool*!'

This was funny as well, but there was truth in what he said: on that day, from early in the morning, everyone on board seemed to be a big fool rolled into one.

When he had driven the passengers away he went up to the soldier, held out his hand and said:

'Give me the knife.'

'Take it, I couldn't care less now . . .' the soldier replied as he handed over the knife.

The chef put it into my hand and pushed the soldier into a cabin.

'Now lie down and go to sleep. What do you think you're doing, eh?'

The soldier sat down on a bunk without saying a word.

'The boy'll bring you something to eat and some vodka. Do you drink?'

'Only a little.'

'And don't you lay a finger on the boy. *He* didn't make fun of you. Do you hear, not *him*!'

'But why did they all torment me?' the soldier asked quietly.

Smury did not answer for a moment, and then he said gloomily:

'How should *I* know?'

As he went with me into the kitchen he muttered:

'Hm . . . they really did pick on a poor helpless little devil! Did you see it all? People can drive you mad. First they cling to you, like bedbugs, and then they'll leave you. Why did I say *bedbugs*? People are far worse!'

When I brought the soldier some bread, meat and vodka, I found him sitting on his bunk, rocking to and fro and crying like a woman. I put the plate on a little table and said:

'Have something to eat.'

'Shut the door.'

'You won't be able to see.'

'Shut it, or that lot'll get in again.'

I left him. He struck me as an unpleasant character and he did not make me feel at all sorry for him. This was rather awkward, since Grandmother had told me more than once: 'You *must* feel sorry for people, everyone's unhappy, it's hard for them all.'

'Did you take him the food?' the chef asked. 'What's he doing now?'

'Crying.'

'What a damned fool! What kind of soldier's he supposed to be?'

'I don't feel sorry for him.'

'What? What's that?'

'I've been told one *should* feel sorry for people.'

Smury took me by the hand, pulled me over to him and told me:

'You can't *force* yourself. And it's no good lying either – understand? Don't start telling fairy-tales ... be true to *yourself*.'

He pushed me away and added gloomily:

'This is no place for you. Come on, have a smoke.'

I felt deeply disturbed. The way the passengers had behaved made me feel as though someone had been walking all over me. There was something inexpressibly insulting and infinitely oppressive in their cruel soldier-baiting, in their jubilant laughter when Smury pulled his ear. How could they take pleasure in what to me seemed so pathetic and repellent, and find it so funny into the bargain?

Now they had all gone under the low awning where they sat drinking, playing cards, peacefully and earnestly chatting away or looking at the river. One would never have thought these were the same people who only an hour before had been res- ponsible for all that whistling and hooting. Now they were all as quiet and lazy as ever. From morning to night they would slowly stroll round the boat, looking like midges or specks of dust in the sun's rays. When we came to a port a dozen or so of them would jostle at the gangway, cross themselves and disembark, while dozens of other people who looked exactly like them climbed up on to the ship, wearing the same clothes and with their backs bent under the weight of trunks and sacks.

This continual exchange did not alter anything on board: the new passengers would talk about the same things as those who had just left – the weather, work, God, women – and they talked in exactly the same way:

'God meant us to endure suffering, so man has to do what he says! You can't do anything about it, that's what's laid down for us from above . . .'

These remarks bored and annoyed me. I could not bear filth, and I did not want to be treated unjustly, maliciously and have to stand for insults. I was firmly convinced that I had done nothing to deserve them, and I felt this deep down inside me. Neither had the soldier deserved the treatment he had got. Perhaps he *wanted* people to make a fool of him . . .

Maxim, who was really a serious, kind young man, was driven off the ship, but they kept that vile Sergei on. All this was wrong. Why did these people, who were capable of persecuting a man, almost driving him mad, always do what the sailors told them without a word of protest and never take offence when they were sworn at? The bo'sun would screw up his handsome but spiteful-looking eyes and shout at the passengers:

'What are you all leaning over the rails for? Clear off, you devils, you're making the ship list!'

These devils would meekly pile over to the other side and would be chased away again, just like sheep.

'Oh, you bastards!'

On hot nights it was stifling under that iron tent which had been in the sun all day.

The passengers looked like cockroaches as they crept over the deck and lay down in any old place they could find. Just before we came into port the sailors would wake them up by kicking them and shout:

'What are you sprawling all over the place for? Get back where you belong!'

They would get up and sleepily move off in the direction in which they were pushed. The sailors were just like them, except they were dressed differently and ordered them around like policemen. One noticed before anything else that there was something gentle, timid and sadly submissive about these people and it was strange – terrifying even – when that outer layer of docility crumbled: then they would behave cruelly and stupidly, and those sudden mad fits were never very funny. I thought that these people had no idea where they were being taken and could not care less where they disembarked. Wherever they landed they would stay on the quayside for a short time and then climb on board any ship that happened to arrive and go off somewhere else. They all seemed lost and homeless, and everywhere they went appeared strange to them. And they were all terrible cowards. Once after midnight there was an explosion in the engine-room just like a cannon going off. The deck was immediately enveloped in a white cloud of steam which poured from the engine-room in thick swirls and drifted up through every crack. Someone I could not recognize shouted in a deafening voice:

'Gavrilo, get some red lead and some felt . . .'

I used to sleep quite near the engine-room, on a table they used for washing crockery. After the noise and vibration that had woken me up died down, it became quiet again out on deck and hot steam hissed in the engine-room. I could hear the pistons beating fast. But a moment later the place was filled with shouting and howling passengers from the cabin class and suddenly I felt terrified. Bareheaded women and dishevelled men with round fishy eyes rushed around in that white fog, which was lifting quickly, knocking each other over. All of them were dragging their parcels, sacks and trunks somewhere and as they stumbled and fell they called on God and St Nikolai to have mercy on them, and then they started hitting each other. This was absolutely terrifying, but at the same time I found it fascinating. I ran after the passengers and tried to see what they were all doing. This was the first time I had heard the night alarm and at once I realized it had been sounded by mistake. The ship did not slow down at all and veered to starboard. I could see that we were very close to the shore where harvesters' bonfires were burning. It was a bright night and the moon stood high in the sky.

The passengers tore round the deck faster and faster. Then some of the first-class passengers emerged from their cabins. Someone jumped overboard and two others followed suit. Two peasants and a monk levered a bench from the deck with the help of some logs. Some passengers on the stern threw a large cage full of hens into the water. A peasant knelt in the middle of the deck near the ladder up to the captain's bridge, howled like a wolf and bowed to the passengers tearing past:

'True believers, I'm a sinner!'

'Launch the lifeboats, you swine!' shouted a fat gentleman who had nothing on except a pair of trousers and who was striking himself on the chest with his fist.

Sailors came running up, seized some of the passengers by the waist, pummelled them on the head and threw them down on the deck.

Smury lumbered around with an overcoat over his pyjamas and urged everyone on in his rich voice:

'You should be ashamed of yourselves! Have you all gone mad? The ship's still afloat. It's not going down! There's the shore just over there! The harvesters have fished out those idiots who jumped overboard, can you see them in those two boats?'

He hit some of the third-class passengers on their heads, making them slump on to the deck like sacks before they had time to say one word. The panic was still in progress when a lady in a cloak bore down on Smury brandishing a soup spoon which she proceeded to wave under his nose.

'How *dare* you?' she shouted.

A rather wet-looking gentlemen licked his whiskers as he held her back and said to her irritably:

'Leave that idiot alone . . .'

Smury shrugged his shoulders, blinked in confusion and asked me:

'What's the matter with her, eh? What's she got against me? Never even seen her before . . .'

A little peasant with a bleeding nose cried out:

'Call yourselves people! More like bandits!'

During that summer I saw the passengers panic twice and each time there was no actual danger, but just the fear that something terrible *might* happen.

On another occasion the passengers caught two thieves, one of whom was dressed as a pilgrim, and they beat them for almost a whole hour in some quiet spot away from the sailors. When the sailors eventually came and took the thieves away the passengers started hurling insults at them.

'We all know a thief hides a thief!'

'You're thieves yourselves, that's why you're so easy on them!'

The two thieves were beaten until they were almost unconscious, and they were unable to stand up by themselves when they were handed over to the police at the next quay.

This was just one of many similar incidents which were so upsetting that one could not even begin to understand what people were really like, whether they were wicked or good, law-abiding or trouble-makers. I used to ask the cook why this was so but he would only envelop his face in cigarette smoke and often he would say in an annoyed voice:

'What's eating you? People ... well, are just people. One's clever, the next's a fool. Don't talk so much and stick to your books. You'll find all the answers there – providing you read the right ones!'

He did not like theological books or the lives of the saints and he used to say:

'That stuff's all right for priests and their sons ...'

I wanted to bring him some pleasure and present him with a book. On the quayside at Kazan I bought, for five kopeks, *The Legend of how Peter the Great was Saved by a Soldier*. However, the cook happened to be drunk at the time and in a very bad mood, so I decided not to give him the book right away and started reading it myself. I liked it very much, as it was all so simple, easy to understand, interesting and concise. I was sure it would give my 'teacher' a great deal of pleasure, but when I gave him the book he crumpled it up without saying a word and threw it overboard.

'So much for your book, you little devil,' he said gloomily. 'Here I am trying to teach you to be a retriever and then you go and eat the game!'

He stamped his foot and shouted:

'What kind of book do you call that? I've read enough rubbish like that in my time. Is there any truth in it, eh? Tell me then.'

'Don't know,' I replied.

'But *I* do! If they'd cut that man's head off he'd have fallen off the ladder and the others wouldn't have climbed into the hayloft – soldiers aren't fools you know. They would have set light to the hay and that would have been that! Understand?'

'Yes.'

'Right! I know all about Peter the Great. Nothing at all like that ever happened to him. Now clear off. . .'

I saw that the cook was right, but all the same I liked the book. I bought another copy and read it a second time and to my amazement I found that it really was very bad. This rather disconcerted me and subsequently I trusted the cook more and paid more attention to what he said. For some reason he became increasingly irritable and he used to say:

'Ugh, why should *I* have to teach you? This is no place for you!'

I was of the same opinion. Sergei treated me disgustingly. Several times I saw him taking crockery from my table and giving it to the passengers when the stewards were not looking. I knew that he was stealing, and more than once Smury warned me:

'Mind you don't let the waiters take the crockery from your table!'

Worse things lay in store for me and I often felt like jumping off at the next port and running away into the forest. But Smury made me change my mind. He began treating me more considerately. In addition, the perpetual motion of the ship did have an irresistible fascination for me. I did not like it when the ship stopped at a quay, and I was always waiting for it to sail away from the Kama river to the Belaya, to the town of Vyatka, and then along the Volga where I would see new river banks, towns and people.

But nothing like that happened and my life on board came to a sudden and shameful end.

One evening, when we were travelling from Kazan to Nizhny, a steward called me over to his cabin. He shut the door behind me and said to Smury, who was looking very miserable as he sat there on a little stool upholstered in carpet:

'Here he is.'

'Did you give Seryozhka any crockery?' the steward asked me.

'He took some while I wasn't looking,' I replied.

The steward continued in a soft voice:

'He doesn't see a thing but he knows what's going on all right!'

Smury slapped his knee, then said:

'Wait a bit, there's no rush,' and he sat there thinking hard.

I looked at the steward and he looked at me, but behind his spectacles there seemed to be no eyes at all. He was a man who kept very much to himself, went around the ship without making any noise and spoke in a subdued voice. Sometimes his greying beard and empty eyes would pop up from behind some corner and then immediately disappear. Before he went to bed he would kneel for a long time in front of the ikon with the everlasting lamp in the restaurant. I often took a look at him through an eyehole shaped like the ace of hearts, but I could never see him actually praying. He would stay there on his knees, simply looking at the ikon and the lamp and sighing as he stroked his beard.

After a brief silence Smury asked me:

'Did Seryozhka ever give you any money?'

'No.'

'Never?'

'Never.'

'*He* wouldn't lie,' Smury told the steward, who replied in a soft voice:

'Doesn't make any difference. *Now*, if you don't mind.'

'Let's go,' the cook shouted at me as he came up to my table and gave me a gentle flick on the top of my head. 'You're a fool! And the same goes for me. I should have kept a closer eye on you.'

At Nizhny the steward paid me up – about eight roubles, an the first substantial sum I had ever earned.

As he said good-bye Smury told me gloomily:

'Well, now ... Watch out, eh? Keep your eyes open ir future!'

He shoved a brightly-coloured beaded tobacco pouch intc my hand.

'There, that's for you. It's a fine piece of work, my own god daughter made it. Well, good-bye now. Keep on reading you books and you'll be all right!'

He took me under the arms, lifted me, kissed me and firmly set me down on the quayside. I felt sorry for him and sorry for myself. I could not help bursting into tears as I watched him go back to the ship, elbowing his way through the porters – a huge, cumbersome, lonely man. And afterwards I met sc many people who were just like him, people who were kind and lonely, and whom life had left behind ...

Chapter 7

GRANDFATHER and Grandmother once again moved to the town. I arrived back in a very angry, belligerent mood and with a heavy weight on my heart.

Grandmother gave me a warm welcome and immediately went to put the samovar on. Grandfather asked in his usual sarcastic voice:

'Make your fortune, did you?'

'I'm keeping all that I earned,' I answered as I sat down by the window.

I triumphantly pulled a packet of cigarettes out of my pocket and solemnly started smoking.

'Oh, ho!' Grandfather said as he closely watched every movement. 'So that's it! What are you smoking for? – it's the devil's poison! A bit young for that, aren't you?'

'They even gave me a tobacco pouch,' I said boastfully.

'Tobacco pouch!' Grandfather screeched. 'You having me on?'

He flung himself at me, stretching out his thin, strong arms. His green eyes gleamed. I jumped back, then butted him in the stomach and knocked him on to the floor, where he sat looking at me for a few painful moments, blinking in astonishment with his mouth wide open. After a while he asked me calmly:

'So you knocked your grandfather over? Your own mother's father!'

'I've had enough of being flogged by you,' I mumbled, but I saw that I had behaved disgracefully. Grandfather looked withered and fragile as he picked himself up from the floor and sat down next to me. Then he artfully snatched the cigarette from me and threw it out of the window. He said in a frightened voice:

'You wild animal! Don't you see that God will *never* forgive you for this as long as you live?'

He turned to Grandmother and said:

'Mother, he *hit* me! Yes, he did! Ask him yourself!'

She did not ask me anything but simply came over, seized me by the hair and started tugging it.

'Take that . . . and that . . .'

She did not hurt me, but I felt terribly insulted, especially by Grandfather, who jumped up and down on his chair, slapping his knees and croaking with laughter:

'Yes, that's the way!'

I tore myself out of her grasp and ran into the hall where I lay down in a corner. I felt crushed and devastated as I listened to the samovar humming.

Grandmother came up, leaned over me and whispered so softly that I could hardly hear:

'Forgive me, I didn't hurt you, did I? I tried not to! I had to do *something* – Grandfather's an old man and deserves some respect. He's had some beatings in his time and he's drunk the bitter cup of sorrow. You mustn't upset him. You're not a child any more and you should understand these things. Yes, it's time you understood. But Grandfather's *still* a child really.'

What she said seemed to wash me clean, like warm water, and her friendly words made me feel at once ashamed and easier in my mind. I held her tight and we kissed each other.

'Go to him now, it's all right, but don't smoke when *he's* around. At least, let him get used to it first!'

I went back into the room, looked at Grandfather and could hardly stop myself laughing. Grandfather was delighted – just like a little child – and he was beaming all over his face as he folded his legs and beat the table with his little hands covered in that thick reddish hair.

'What do you want, you goat! Come to butt me again? You little bandit! You take after your father! Fancy coming into the house without even crossing yourself, just like a freemason. Then smoking a cigarette before you've been in the room two minutes. Ugh, you cheap little Bonaparte!'

I said nothing. Grandfather ran out of words and he soon became silent as well. However, while we were having tea, he started preaching again:

'Man must fear the Lord like the horse fears the reins. God is our only friend! All men are desperate enemies!'

I felt there was some truth in what he said, that all men were enemies; but the other things he said left no impression on me at all.

'Now you must go over to your Aunt Matryona's, and then back to the ship in the spring. But first you must spend the winter with them. Don't tell them you'll leaving in the spring, though!'

'Why be deceitful?' Grandmother said, but she had been guilty of this herself when she pretended to give me a good hiding.

'You won't get anywhere without deceit,' Grandfather instructed me. 'Is there anyone who makes a living *without* it?'

While Grandfather read his prayer book in the evenings I would go through the city gates with Grandmother and out into the fields. Grandfather's little hut was on the outskirts, behind Kanatny street, where once he too had his own house.

'So this is how we've all ended up!' Grandmother burst out laughing. 'The old man can't find a place he really likes and he's on the move all the time. He likes it here though. But not me!'

Before us some barren fields stretched for about two miles. They were broken up by gullies and bordered by the ridge of the forest; behind a row of birches lay the main road to Kazan. The little branches of bushes stuck up out of the gullies like whips and the rays of the cold sunset turned them blood red. The soft evening breeze rocked the grey grass, and the dim shapes of young men and girls in the nearest gully looked just like blades of grass as they swayed to and fro. In the distance, to the right, I could see the red wall of the Old Believers' cemetery; it was called the Bugrovsky Hermitage; to the left, above one of the gullies, a dark cluster of trees stood out from the fields – that was the Jewish cemetery. Everything around me seemed wretchedly poor and clung silently to the mutilated earth. The little houses on the outskirts of the town seemed to be looking sheepishly with their windows at the dusty road where thin, ill-fed chickens wandered about. A herd of lowing cows passed by the Devichy Convent. I could hear music coming from the camp and the sounds of a blaring military brass band.

A drunk came staggering past tugging savagely at hi
accordion and muttering:

'I'll get to you . . . I must . . .'

'You fool,' Grandmother said, blinking in the red sunlight
'How far do *you* expect to get? Soon you'll fall down and go t
sleep, and then someone will come and rob you. They'll stri
you bare and you'll lose your accordion, your only comfort i
life.'

As I told her about my life on the ship I kept looking roun
me. After all I had seen I felt miserable now, like a fish out o
water. Grandmother listened to me silently and very atten
tively – the way I used to listen to her – and when I told he
about Smury she feverishly crossed herself and said:

'Sounds like a good man, may the Blessed Virgin preserv
him! Don't ever forget him! You should always make sur
that you remember the good things and forget the bad.'

I found it very difficult to explain to her why they had given m
the sack, but in the end I plucked up courage and told her
My story did not make any impression on her whatsoever an
she merely said rather indifferently:

'You're still a young boy and you don't know how to live!

I replied:

'That's what they *all* kept saying, "You don't know how t
live" – the peasants and the sailors. Aunt Matryona says it t
her son. But what is it I should know?'

Grandmother pursed her lips and shook her head:

'Oh, don't ask me!'

'But you keep on saying it!'

'Why shouldn't I?' she said calmly. 'Now don't be angry
You're still a child, you don't *have* to know yet. And who reall
does? Only rogues. That old Grandfather of yours is clever
and can read and write, but he knows nothing really.'

'Have *you* led a good life?'

'Me? Yes . . . And a bad one too! I've led every kind of life.

People went by us without hurrying, dragging shadow
behind them which seemed to be buried in the clouds of dus
they stirred up with their feet. The sadness of evening deepene
and the sound of Grandfather's grumbling voice flowed ou
through the window:

'Oh Lord, spare me the fullness of thy wrath, spare me thy punishment.'

Grandmother smiled and said:

'He must bore God stiff with his complaints! Every evening he starts moaning . . . But he's an *old* man and doesn't really need anything. Yet he never stops complaining and working himself up . . . That God of his must listen to him praying in the evening, laugh and say to himself: "There's that old Vasily Kashirin grumbling again." Let's go to bed now . . .'

I decided to start trapping songbirds, as I thought that this way I could earn enough money to live on: I would catch the birds and Grandmother would sell them. I bought a net, a ring, traps and some cages and soon I was sitting in the bushes in one of the gullies at dawn while Grandmother wandered through the forest with a basket and sack gathering the late mushrooms, guelder-roses and nuts.

The lazy September sun had just risen. Its pale rays would disappear in the clouds and then fall in a silvery arch towards me, into the gully, which was still dark at the bottom, with a whitish mist drifting upwards from it. One steep and clayey side of the gully was dark and bare, while the other had a more gentle slope and was covered with brittle grass and thick bushes bright with yellow and reddish leaves which a fresh breeze ripped away and swept down the gully.

Goldfinches twittered in the burrs at the bottom of the gully and among the grey, tattered-looking high grass I could see those little crimson tufts that resembled hats on the heads of some other lively little birds. Inquisitive tomtits made a clicking noise all around me, and they puffed out their white cheeks in a funny way. With all that noise and rushing about they behaved just like the young housewives from Kunavino at holiday time. They moved quickly, were clever and spiteful and wanted to know and to touch everything; one after the other they fell into my traps. They made a pathetic sight as they struggled to get free, but this was business and I had no time to be sentimental. I transferred the birds to some cages and covered them with a sack since they were usually quiet in the dark.

A flock of greenfinches settled on a hawthorn bush which

was flooded in sunlight. The finches loved the sun which made them sing even more gaily. Their movements reminded me of young schoolboys. The greedy, thrifty speckled magpie, which was late migrating to warmer lands, sat on a supple sweetbriar twig cleaning its wings with its beak and seeking out prey with its dark eyes. Suddenly it soared up like a lark, caught a bee, carefully impaled it on a thorn and settled down again, twitching its grey, crafty-looking head. That prophetic bird the pinefinch silently flew past: to catch just one of those birds had always been my dearest dream! A bullfinch which had left its flock sat on an alder bush, red in the face and as solemn as a general. It chirped away angrily, twisting its black beak.

As the sun rose higher, more and more birds appeared and their songs became even livelier. The whole gully was filled with music, but I could hear the incessant rustling of bushes above all their singing. The lively voices of the birds could never drown that gentle, sweet, sad music in which I could hear the swan song of summer. It seemed to whisper very meaningful words which turned into a song of their own accord. And while I listened my memory would involuntarily conjure up visions of the past . . .

Suddenly I heard Grandmother shouting to me from somewhere above:

'Where are you?'

She came down to the edge of the gully, spread her scarf and laid out bread, cucumbers, turnips and apples. In the middle of all these good things a very beautiful little cut-glass decanter with a crystal stopper shaped like Napoleon's head glistened in the sun. It contained about half a pint of vodka flavoured with St John's wort.

'Oh, God, everything's so wonderful,' she said in gratitude.

'I've written a song!' I said.

'Really?'

And I would recite some verses which bore some resemblance to poetry:

> 'Winter is drawing nearer and nearer,
> Farewell my little summer sun.'

But she would not let me finish:

'There's already one like that, and it's better than yours.'
Then she would recite in a sing-song voice:

> 'Oh, the summer sun is leaving us
> For dark nights and distant forests!
> And here am I, poor maiden,
> Alone, without the joys of spring.
>
> If I go walking in the morning
> I remember those happy days in May.
> Now the bare fields are dreary,
> I gave my youth to him.
>
> Oh, dear friends of mine,
> See how the first snow is falling,
> Tear this heart from my breast,
> And bury it in the snow.'

But this did not dampen my author's pride: I liked her song very much and felt very sorry for the poor girl.

Then Grandmother said:

'That's a *really* sad song! A young girl wrote it, as you see. She went courting in the spring, but when winter came her fond lover left her, perhaps for another, and she wept from this bitter insult. You can never really describe what you've never been through yourself – see what a wonderful song *she's* written!'

When Grandmother first began to sell the birds and got forty kopeks each for them she was very surprised.

'Fancy that! And I thought there was nothing in it – just a boy's game. Just look how well we're doing!'

'But you didn't charge enough.'

'Well, what does it matter?'

On market days she would sell the birds for a rouble or more and never failed to be surprised that she could get so much money for what she had thought was worth almost nothing.

'Women do laundering or scrub floors all day long for a *quarter of a rouble,* you know. But what we're doing is bad. It's wrong to keep birds in cages. You must give it up, Alexei, dear.'

But I became absorbed in my bird trapping and I really liked it very much. It made me feel independent and it did not bother anyone – except the birds. I had made myself some fine traps and cages, and my conversations with some old trappers were a great help and taught me a lot.

I used to go off on my own as far as twenty miles away, to the Kstovsky forest and to the banks of the Volga where I would find crossbills in the pine trees and the highly prized Apollon titmouse, a longtailed white bird of rare beauty. I would go out in the evenings and trudge all night along the main Kazan road; sometimes the autumn rain would teem down as I splashed through the mud. On my back was an oilskin sack containing traps and cages and a decoy bird, and in my hand I had a strong walnut stick. It was cold and frightening out there in the autumnal darkness – *really* frightening. Along the sides of the road stood old weather-beaten birches, spreading their dripping branches over my head. Downhill, to the left, just above the black Volga, lights on the masts of steamships and barges flashed at long intervals and seemed to sail away into a bottomless abyss. I could see paddles thrashing through the water and hear sirens hooting. Little huts in the villages bordering the highway stood out from the iron-hard earth and angry, hungry dogs darted around at my feet.

A watchman beat his bat and cried in a timid voice:

'Who's that? Who's that the devil's brought at this time of night?'

I was very frightened that my traps might be confiscated and I used to keep a five-kopek piece for him.

The watchman at the village of Fokin became my good friend however, though he still used to complain:

'*You* again? Ugh, you restless little nightbird! Not frightened of the dark, eh?'

His name was Nifont, and he was a small, greyish man who looked like a saint. He would often take a turnip, apple or a handful of peas from his pocket, shove them into my hands and say:

'Here, my friend, just a little present. Eat it and enjoy it.'

He would come with me as far as the outskirts of the village and say:

'God be with you!'

I would reach the forest by dawn, set my traps up, hang up

the decoy birds and lie down on the edge of the forest and wait for day to come.

It was quiet. Everything around me seemed frozen in the deep sleep of autumn.

The broad meadows sloping downhill were hardly visible through a greyish haze; the Volga cut across them and on the other side they formed little patches and melted away in the mist. In the distance, beyond the forests on the wooded bank of the river the bright sun slowly rose. Fires flashed on the black manes of the trees and a strange, disturbing movement would begin: the mist rose more rapidly from the meadows and turned silver in the sunlight; bushes, trees, haystacks loomed up; the meadows seemed literally to be melting in the sun and spreading out in all directions in a vast russet sea. When the sun shone on the quiet shallows near the banks the whole river appeared to be flowing towards the spot where the sun's rays had first touched it.

The joyful sun rose higher and higher and blessed and warmed the bare frozen earth, which in turn gave off the sweet smells of autumn. The transparent air made the earth look enormous, as though it had no limits. Everything swam off into the distance and lured one towards that bluish haze where the world ended.

I had seen the sun rise there many times, and always it revealed a new world to me in all its fresh beauty. I particularly love the sun, and its very name* is full of sweet sounds and hidden harmonies. I loved to close my eyes and let its hot rays beat down on my face, and I tried to catch them in the palm of my hand when they jumped like a ball through a hole in the fence or among the branches. Grandfather loved reading *Prince Mikhail Chornigovsky†* and *Fyodor the Nobleman, Who Did Not Bow Down to the Sun*, and I thought that those people were black like gipsies, gloomy and evil, and that they always suffered from bad eyesight, like poor Mordvinians. But I could not help smiling with joy when the sun rose high above the meadows.

Pine trees hummed above me and shook drops of dew from

* The Russian for sun is *solntse*, the 'l' not being pronounced. (Trans.)
† *Chorny* means 'black' in Russian. (Trans.)

their green branches, and the early morning frost sparkled like silver brocade on the delicate tracery of ferns hidden in the shade. The grass, which was turning a reddish brown, had been flattened by the rain and it bowed silently down to the earth; but when the sun's rays fell on the stalks it seemed to quiver slightly – a last attempt perhaps to keep alive.

The birds had woken up by now. Grey tomtits bounced from branch to branch like furry balls. Flame-coloured crossbills pecked away with their crooked beaks at the cones on the tops of the pine trees, and white Apollon birds rocked to and fro on the ends of branches, flapping their long tail feathers, cocking their black beady eyes and squinting suspiciously at my traps. Suddenly the whole forest, which only a moment before had been solemn and thoughtful, was filled with the sounds of hundreds of birds, with the noises of scurrying, living creatures – the purest beings on earth, copied by man, creator of earthly beauty, to provide some comfort for himself in the form of elves and cherubims and seraphims and the whole heavenly host. I did feel rather sorry about trapping those little birds and I was ashamed to put them into cages – I preferred just watching them. But my passion for trapping and the desire to earn some money overcame my feeling of regret.

The birds made me laugh with their cunning tricks. The sky-blue tomtit would carefully, meticulously scrutinize a trap, weigh up the dangers and skilfully pull the seeds out through the little wooden bars by approaching it from the side. The tomtits were very clever, but far too inquisitive, and this proved to be their downfall. The solemn bullfinches were stupid, and whole flocks of them would fly into my nets, like fat townspeople going into a church. When I covered them over, they looked absolutely amazed, their eyes would bulge, and they would nip my fingers with their thick beaks. The crossbills went into the traps without any fuss, in quite a dignified way, in fact. The nuthatch, which bore no resemblance to any other living creature, would sit for a long time right in the net, twitching its long beak and supporting itself on its thick tail. It used to run up and down the tree-trunks like a woodpecker and always kept company with the tomtits. There was something disturbing about that smoky-coloured bird. It seemed lonely, was loved by no one and it did not love anyone in turn. Like the magpie, it loved stealing and hoarding bright, shiny little things.

I used to be finished by midday and would make my way home through the forest and across the fields. If I took the main road which passed through some villages, the boys would steal my cages and smash all my traps. I would arrive home about evening, tired and hungry, but I felt that during the course of the day I had grown up a little, become stronger, and that I had discovered something new. This newly acquired strength made it possible for me to listen to Grandfather's spiteful sneers calmly, without taking any offence, and this in turn made him change his tune and speak to me sensibly and seriously:

'You must give that nonsense up at once. No one ever made a living out of birds! At least, I've never heard of it. You must make your own little niche in life and keep your brain working. Man wasn't born for nothing. He's God's own seed and therefore he must bring forth good grain. Man is like a rouble: use it well and it will treble. Do you think life's easy? It's not! The world is like a dark night, in which everyone must find his own way ... All men are born with ten fingers, but they want to grasp more and more. You must show people you're strong, and if you're not strong you must be crafty. The small and the weak don't go to heaven or hell! You may think there's lots of people on your side, but you must remember that you're really on your own! Listen to everyone, but believe nobody. You'll go wrong if you only trust your eyesight! Keep your mouth shut – towns weren't built with tongues, but by money and axes. You're not a Bashkir or a Kalmuk either: all they have is lice and sheep!'

He would ramble on like this for the whole evening and I knew every sentence by heart. I liked what he said but I was rather sceptical of its true meaning. One thing was clear: two 'powers' stop man from leading the life he wants to – God and people.

Grandmother used to sit for hours by the window twisting thread for lace. Her wheel would hum away under her nimble hands and she would sit there for a long time listening to

Grandfather's sermons in silence, then suddenly she would say:

'Everything will be according to the Holy Virgin's will.'

'What's that?' Grandfather would shout. 'There's God as well!'

'Yes, I haven't forgotten him. I know him all right. Do you think God's filled the world with idiots, you old fool!'

I thought Cossacks and soldiers came off best in this world. Their life was simple and gay. When the weather was fine they used to line up early in the morning in front of our house, on the other side of the gully. Then they scattered all over the bare fields like white mushrooms and began a complicated and interesting game. They were nimble and strong, and they would run around in their white shirts with rifles in their hands, disappear into the gully and then suddenly, when a trumpet blew, spread themselves all over the field again. The drums would beat ominously and with wild 'hurras' they rushed straight at our house, with bayonets bristling, and it seemed that they would lift our house right off the ground and toss it aside just like a haystack. I shouted 'hurra' in turn, and without thinking what I was doing I followed them. That evil-sounding drum aroused a burning desire in me to destroy something, to smash the fence and beat little children up.

During their break the soldiers gave me cheap tobacco, showed me their heavy rifles and sometimes one of them would point his bayonet right at my stomach and shout ferociously:

'There's one for the cockroach!'

His bayonet would glisten so brightly that it seemed to be alive and it twisted like a snake that was about to bite me. Although this was frightening it still seemed pleasant.

The Mordvinian drummer boy taught me how to use the drum-sticks. At first he took me by the wrists and after twisting them until they hurt, he shoved the sticks into my bruised hands and said:

'One – two, one – two. Tra-ta-ta-tam! Left, right, slow . . . quick . . . tra-ta-ta!'

He shouted these commands menacingly, opening his bird-like eyes very wide.

I ran across the field with the soldiers until they had finished their drill and then I went right across the town with them to the barracks, listening to their loud songs and looking at their kind eyes which seemed as bright and as fresh as newly-minted coins. That solid mass of men who all looked the same, gaily flowing down the street as one man, made me want to be friends with them all, to plunge into the middle of them, as though they were a river or a forest. Those men feared nothing, were very brave in everything they did, could overcome any obstacle and achieve anything they wanted. But, most important, they were kind and simple. Once, however, while they were taking a break, a young non-commissioned officer gave me a thick cigarette.

'Have a smoke! It's a special brand. I wouldn't give it to just *anyone*. It's only because you're such a good boy!'

I lit it. The soldier moved a few steps away and suddenly I was blinded by a red flash which burned my fingers, nose and eyebrows. A grey salty smoke made me sneeze and cough. I stamped up and down, frightened out of my wits and unable to see a thing, while the soldiers surrounded me and laughed loud and cheerfully. As I went home I could hear whistles and laughter behind me, and the sound of something cracking like a shepherd's whip. My fingers hurt, my face smarted and tears flowed from my eyes. But the pain did not worry me as much as a feeling of dumb helpless amazement. Why did they do it? Why should such kind men find something like that funny?

When I got home I climbed up to the attic where I sat for a long time recalling all the inexplicable cruelty I had encountered so often in my life. I had particularly vivid memories of that poor little soldier from Sarapul. It was as if he were standing there, right in front of me and asking: 'What? Did you understand what I said?'

Soon I had to endure something even worse, and this upset me even more. I had to visit the Cossacks' barracks which were near the Pechersky Quarter. The Cossacks seemed different from other soldiers, not because they were expert riders and had smarter uniforms, but because they had a different way of speaking, sang different songs and were wonderful dancers. In the evenings, when they had finished grooming their horses, they would gather in a group near the stables and a little red-haired Cossack would shake his wavy hair and sing in a voice that sounded like a trumpet. He would tense himself up and sing soft melancholy songs about the quiet Don or the Blue Danube, closing his eyes like a robin, which will often sing until it drops dead from its branch. His collar bones, which looked like bronze horse-bits, showed through his unbuttoned shirt. In fact he seemed to be cast in bronze from head to foot. He would rock backwards and forwards on his thin legs as though the earth under him were shaking, and he flung his arms out wide. That blind creature with his songs seemed a man no longer but was transformed into a trumpeter's horn or a shepherd's pipe instead. Sometimes I thought that he would fall over backwards and hit his back against the wall and die, just like that bird, because he had poured out his soul and exhausted all his strength in his songs.

His friends would stand round him in a circle with their hands in their pockets or behind their backs, and they would look sternly into his bronze face and follow every movement of his hands which gently hovered in the air. They too would sing solemnly and calmly, as though they were a church choir. At moments like these the soldiers looked like ikons – even those without beards – and they seemed just as frightening and remote from the world of living people. Their songs were long, like a main road, and just as level and broad, and they were full of wisdom. Listening to them made one forget if it were day or night, or if one were a boy or an old man.

The singers' voices would die away and then one could hear the horses sighing, pining for the freedom of the steppes, and the autumn night softly and inexorably crept up from the fields. One's heart seemed to expand and was ready to burst from the richness of these strange sensations, from a feeling of blind love of people, of the whole world.

That little Cossack made of bronze seemed far more important than any ordinary mortal: to me he appeared to be some legendary hero, better and nobler than anyone else. I did not even have the courage to speak to him. When he asked me something I would smile happily, but I felt too embarrassed to reply. I was ready to follow him silently and submissively, like a dog – so long as I could see as much of him as possible and hear him sing.

Once I saw him standing in a corner of the stables examining a silver ring on one of his fingers. His fine lips trembled and his little reddish whiskers twitched. His face had a sad, injured expression.

But one dark evening I took my cages to a pub on the old Haymarket. The landlord was a fanatical songbird fancier and often bought some from me. The Cossack was sitting in a corner by the bar, in between the stove and the wall. With him was a plump woman almost twice his size and her round face shone like morocco leather as she looked at him with the loving eyes of a mother, but rather anxiously all the same. He was drunk and kept scraping his outstretched feet over the floor. He must have trodden on the woman's feet, because she shuddered, frowned and softly said:

'Behave yourself!'

After a great effort the Cossack raised his eyebrows but they immediately drooped again. He was feeling hot and he had unbuttoned his uniform and shirt, leaving his neck bare. The woman let her scarf fall on to her shoulders, put her strong white hands on the table and clenched her fingers so tight that they turned red. The more I looked at that couple, the more the Cossack looked like a prodigal son with his loving mother. She said something affectionate, but in a rather sarcastic voice, and he was too embarrassed to reply: he made no answer to her acid remarks, which he thoroughly deserved anyway.

Suddenly he got up as though someone had stuck a knife in him, pulled his cap low over his forehead, slapped it with the palm of his hand and made for the door without bothering to button himself up.

The woman followed him and said to the landlord:

'We'll only be a few minutes, Kuzmich.'

The people laughed and joked as the couple left. Someone said in a deep, stern voice:

'She'll cop it when the steamboat pilot comes back!'

I followed them. They walked through the darkness about ten paces in front of me, across the square in the thick mud, to the bank that sloped down to the Volga. I could see the woman staggering as she tried to support the Cossack and I could hear mud squelching under their feet.

The woman said softly, imploringly:

'What's going on? Where are we going?'

I followed them through the mud, although it was not my way home. When they reached the footpath near the river bank the Cossack stopped, moved a few steps from the woman and suddenly hit her in the face. She cried out in surprise and fear:

'Oh, what did you do that for?'

I was frightened as well as her and kept close behind them.

Then the Cossack seized the woman round the waist, threw her over the railings, jumped on her and they both rolled down the grassy slope in one black mass. I was stupefied and my heart sank as I heard clothes being ripped down below and the sound of blows. The Cossack bellowed and the woman's soft voice came in short gasps:

'I'll scream!... I'll scream!'

There was a loud, anguished sigh – and then all was quiet.

I felt round for a stone, flung it down at them, making the grass rustle. A glass door in a pub on the square slammed, then I heard a groan – someone must have fallen down coming out of the pub – and once again there was that silence, which seemed to be holding new horrors in store.

Then a large white bundle appeared at the bottom of the slope and started coming up the bank. It was sobbing and sniffing and I could soon see that it was a woman, quietly creeping up towards me. She was on all fours, like a sheep, bare to the waist. With her large breasts hanging down she seemed to have three faces. She managed to reach the railings and sat down almost by my side, breathing like an overheated horse. I could clearly see dark patches of mud on her white face as she started tidying her dishevelled hair. The woman was crying and wiping the tears from her cheeks like a cat washing itself. Then she spotted me and exclaimed softly:

'Good God, who's that? Go away, you *wicked* boy!'

But I could not move for surprise: I felt bitter and sickened by what I had seen. I suddenly remembered that Grandmother's sister used to say: 'A woman is a real power in this world – Eve deceived God himself.'

The woman got up, covered her breasts with pieces of her torn dress, leaving her legs bare, and rushed off.

At the bottom of the slope the Cossack waved a few white rags in the air, whistled softly, pricked up his ears and then said in a gay voice:

'Darya! Cossacks always get what they want – did you think I was drunk? No! And – I proved it, didn't I? . . . Darya!'

He stood there with his feet firmly planted on the ground. He sounded sober and his voice was full of mockery. Then he bent down and wiped his boots with the rags and said:

'Hey, take your blouse, Darya! Don't start acting the lady with me!'

And in a loud voice he called her some obscene name. I sat on a pile of stones and listened to that voice which sounded so lonely in the darkness and at the same time so commanding and masterful.

The lamp lights on the square danced before my eyes. To the right, in the middle of a black clump of trees, stood the white building of the Institute for Daughters of the Gentry. The Cossack crossed the square, lazily calling out one obscenity after the other and waving a white rag. Finally he disappeared like a bad dream.

Down below I could hear steam hissing through an outlet pipe in the waterworks and a four-wheeled cab rolled past. Otherwise there was not a soul to be seen. I felt as though I had been poisoned as I walked along the bank clutching a cold stone which I had not managed to throw at the Cossack.

Near the church of St George I was stopped by the night watchman who angrily asked what I was carrying in that bag slung behind my back. I told him all about the soldier and this made him laugh and shout:

'Well done. I take my hat off to the Cossacks – they leave us standing! That woman's a slut anyway . . .'

He choked with laughter and I went away, completely unable to understand what he found so funny. And I thought to myself in horror: supposing something like that had happened to my mother, or Grandmother even?

Chapter 8

WHEN the snow began to fall Grandfather took me away to Grandmother's sister again.

'Won't do you any harm,' he said.

That summer I had experienced a great deal and I thought I had grown older and wiser. But life with the master and his wife was more boring than ever. They would both make themselves ill by stuffing their bellies – just as before – and they would tell each other, in the same tedious detail, about how they were getting over their illnesses. The old woman still prayed to God in that same frightening, evil way. After she had her baby the young mistress lost weight and she appeared to have shrivelled up. But she still moved around just as solemnly and slowly as she did when she was pregnant. When she was making underclothes for the children she would softly sing that same old song:

> 'Spirya, Spirya, Spiridon,
> Spirya, my brother, my own flesh and blood;
> I will sit on the sledge,
> With Spirya at the back.'

If anyone came into the room she would stop singing at once and shout angrily:

'What do you want?'

I was convinced that this was the only song she knew.

In the evening the master and his wife would call me into their room and demand:

'Come on, tell us what it was like on the ship.'

I would sit on a chair near the lavatory door and tell them all about my life on board. It was pleasant for me to recall a way of life that was so different from that which I was now forced to live. I would become carried away, and forget my audience – but never for very long. The women had never been on a ship and used to ask:

'But weren't you ever frightened?'

I said that I did not understand what there was to be frightened of.

'The ship might suddenly sail into deep waters and sink!' The master laughed.

Although I knew very well that ships do not sink in deep water, I was unable to convince the women. The old woman was sure that ships did not sail over the water but moved along with their paddles pushing against the bottom of the river, just like the wheels of a cart rolling along the road:

'How can they float then, if they're made of iron? Choppers don't float!'

'But jugs don't sink, do they?'

'What a comparison! Jugs are small and empty!'

When I told them about Smury and his books they would look at me suspiciously: the old woman was fond of saying that books were only written by fools and heretics.

'But what about the Book of Psalms? And King David?' I protested.

'The Book of Psalms is Holy Scripture. Anyway King David asked God's forgiveness for writing it.'

'Where does it say that?' I asked.

'On the palms of my hands – for me to catch you with by the the scruff of your neck. Then you'll find out where!'

She thought she knew everything and spoke confidently and always absurdly:

'A Tartar died at Pechorka and his soul poured out of his throat. It was *as black as tar*.'

'But the soul is pure spirit,' I would say, and by way of reply she would shout disdainfully:

'A *Tartar* with a *spirit*? You little fool!'

The young mistress was afraid of books as well.

'They can do a lot of harm, especially if you're young,' she would say. 'When we lived at Grebyoshka a girl who came from a good family just read and read, and she fell in love with a deacon. The way he humiliated her – fills me with horror just to think about it! In the middle of the street, right in front of everyone.'

Sometimes I used words that I had found in Smury's books.

In one of them, which did not seem to have any beginning or end, I had read: 'As a matter of fact, *no one* invented gunpowder. As is always the case, it was the end product of a long series of small experiments and observations.' I do not know why, but that phrase 'as a matter of fact' stuck in my mind, and I particularly liked the way those words were combined: I felt they contained a hidden power and they brought me much suffering – which did have its funny side, however.

Once, when my master and mistress asked me to tell them more about the ship I answered:

'There's really nothing more to tell you, *as a matter of fact*.'

This astounded them and they all started croaking away:

'What? What did you say?'

All four of them laughed out loud, in a friendly way though, and they started mimicking me:

'*As a matter of fact* – good heavens!'

Even the master said:

'What a stupid thing to say, you silly boy!'

For a long time afterwards they kept calling out:

'Come here, *as a matter of fact*! Go and scrub the floor in the nursery.'

I cannot say that I was actually upset by this inane mockery: I was more surprised than anything else.

I lived in a fog of stupefying boredom and worked as hard as I could to try and overcome it. There was no shortage of work in that house, with the two young children there. The master and his wife could not find any nurses who were good enough and they were always changing them. As a result I had to run around after the children myself. Every day I washed their nappies and every week I went to the Zhandarmsky spring to wash the linen – much to the amusement of the laundresses there.

'What are you doing women's work for?' they would say.

Sometimes they teased me so much that I used to slap them with twisted pieces of wet cloth, for which they would repay me generously in kind. But the time I spent with them was gay and very interesting. The Zhandarmsky spring ran along the bottom of a deep gully, down to the river Oka. This gully formed a kind of boundary between the town and a field called after the ancient god Yarilo. Here, on the seventh Thursday after Easter, the people from the town used to go walking. Grandmother told me that when she was young people still believed in Yarilo and sacrificed to him. They used to bring a wheel, smear it with oakum, put a match to it, bowl it down the hill and follow it laughing and singing, hoping it would roll as far as the Oka. If it did, then Yarilo had accepted the sacrifice and the summer would be happy and sunny. Most of the laundresses came from Yarilo Field and all of them were lively and had sharp tongues. They knew everything that was going on in the town and it was fascinating listening to their stories about the merchants and civil servants they worked for. Rinsing linen in the winter, in that icy water, was like hard labour. The women's hands got so cold that the skin cracked. They would rinse their washing out stooping low over the stream which ran through a wooden trough. Also they had to work under an old roof full of holes which gave no protection at all from the snow and wind. Their faces were always flushed and frostbitten. The frost stung their wet fingers so that they could not bend them. Even though tears flowed from their eyes at times those women never stopped gossiping and would tell each other all kinds of stories about the people in the town and they seemed to face the whole world with their own particular brand of aggressiveness.

Natalya Kozlovskaya was the best story-teller of all. She was a little over thirty, healthy and strong, with mocking eyes and a particularly flexible, sharp tongue. She was paid a great deal of attention by her friends, who asked her for advice and respected her because she was a skilful worker, dressed very neatly and had a daughter at boarding-school. When she came down the slippery path, bent double under the weight of two baskets full of wet linen, her friends gave her a warm welcome and asked with genuine concern:

'How's your daughter?'

'Fine, thanks. Studying, thank God!'

'Will they make a young lady out of her?'

'That's why I sent her to college! And where do you think young ladies come from with their faces all tarted up? From *us*, the scum of the earth! Where else? The more you know, the longer your hands grow and the more you earn. And the one who takes most gets the most respect. God sends us into the world as stupid children and wants us back again old and wise. That means we must learn while we're here!'

When she spoke no one said a word and listened silently, paying close attention to her flowing, confident speech. They praised her whether she was there or not, and they were amazed at her powers of endurance, at her deep wisdom. But no one dared copy what she did. She had sewn some leather from a pair of old boots on to her jacket sleeves which protected her arms up to the elbows and stopped her blouse getting wet. Everyone said how clever she was but no one copied her. However when *I* did I became a general laughing-stock. 'Hey you, picking a woman's brains!' they shouted.

They used to talk about her daughter as well:

'Is that really anything special? So, there'll be one more young lady in the world. She might not finish her schooling, she might die even . . . It isn't all honey for people with learning, either. Take Bakhilov's daughter, who studied and studied and became a school-teacher. She'll never be anything else . . . Of course! A man couldn't care less what a woman *knows* – he only wants something he can lay his hands on! . . . A woman doesn't have to use her *loaf*! . . .'

It was strange and embarrassing to hear them talk so brazenly about themselves. I had heard sailors, soldiers and navvies talk about women and I knew that men always boasted to one another about their skill in seducing them, about the way they did not give up until they got what they wanted. I sensed that their attitude to women was really very hostile, but for all their talk about their conquests, with all their boasting, I felt that I was right in thinking that there was more fiction and boasting than fact in their stories.

The laundresses did not discuss their love affairs with one another, but I felt that everything they said about men had something mocking and spiteful about it. In fact I thought that they might be right after all, and that women really *were* a power to be reckoned with.

'However much they run around, whoever they're friends with, men can't help ending up with a woman,' Natalya once said.

Some old woman who sounded as if she had a bad cold shouted out:

'And who else is there? Even monks and hermits abandon God for us.'

These conversations were accompanied by the sound of splashing water, the slapping of wet rags at the bottom of the gully in mud that was so thick that not even the winter snow could cover it with its shining carpet. Those shameless, malicious conversations about the 'secret of life', about the origin of all tribes and nations, filled me with a feeling of nausea that was mingled with fear, and made me feel both physical and spiritual repulsion towards those 'affairs' which were so tiresome and which went on around me all the time. For a long time afterwards 'love affairs', as far as I was concerned, were synonymous with all that was filthy and depraved.

But in spite of all this it was incomparably more interesting being in the gully with those laundresses, in the kitchens with the batmen or in the cellars with the navvies than staying at home, where the frozen monotony of the conversation, the rigid attitude to life, and that dreary succession of events only filled me with a bitter feeling of unrelieved boredom.

The master and mistress lived in a vicious circle of eating, illnesses, sleeping, preparing for meals, and sleeping again. All they could talk about was sin and death, which they feared a great deal, and they raced around like grains of wheat under a millstone, expecting to be crushed by it at any moment.

When I had some free time I used to go and chop wood up in the shed, hoping that I might be left alone. But this rarely happened, and the batmen would come in and talk about life in the yard. Ermokhin and Sidorov visited me more often than the others. The first was a tall, round-shouldered man from Kaluga and he seemed to be sewn together with thick, strong sinews. He had a small head and dullish looking eyes. He was lazy, infuriatingly stupid, moved slowly and clumsily, and whenever he saw a woman he would bellow and lean forwards as though he were ready to fall at her feet. He amazed everyone in the yard by the speed of his conquests among the cooks and chambermaids and the other men there envied him, and were frightened of his bearlike strength. Sidorov was a thin and bony man and came from Tula. He always appeared to be tired of life, spoke softly and he had a way of coughing very cautiously. His bright eyes had a timid look about them and he was always peering into dark corners. He would either whisper some story to me or just sit there saying nothing. But never once did he stop looking into the darkest corner he could find.

'What are you looking at?' I used to ask.

'You never know, a mouse might run out . . . I love mice, the way they scurry around . . . they're so nice and quiet.'

I wrote letters for the batmen to send to their families in the villages, especially for those who were in love, and I liked doing this very much. It was most pleasant of all writing letters for Sidorov, who used to send one every Saturday, without fail, to his sister in Tula. He would invite me into the kitchen, sit down next to me at the table, rub his hands over his cropped hair and whisper in my ear:

'Well, what are you waiting for? We'd better start in the proper way: "My dearest sister, I wish you good health for many years to come" – that's right. Now we'll have: "I got the rouble, but you shouldn't have sent it. Thanks very much. I don't need anything, we all live very well here" – no, put "we don't live well at all, they treat us just like dogs" – no, don't write that either. Tell her that life's very good here! She's very young, only fourteen: she doesn't have to know about such things . . . Now write like they taught you . . .'

He leaned heavily on my left side, and I felt his warm smelly breath in my ear as he kept on whispering:

'Tell her not to let the young boys put their arms round her and *never* let them touch her breasts! Now write this: "If someone says sweet nothings to you, don't believe him, he only wants to seduce you and ruin you."'

His grey face went red as he tried to stop coughing, his cheeks puffed out, his eyes filled with tears, and he fidgeted around on his chair and jolted me.

'I can't write . . .' I said.

'Never mind, carry on: "Trust your master least of all, he'll deceive a young girl like you as soon as he sets eyes on you. Masters are very persuasive, and know just what to say. Once you believe them, then it's the brothel for you. If you manage

146

to save a rouble, give it to the priest, who'll look after it for you – if he's an honest man. Best of all, bury it somewhere, so no one can find it. But don't forget where you put it!'''

I felt very miserable listening to his whispering, which was almost drowned by the screeching of the metal flap in the little ventilation window. I would turn round and look at the sooty mouth of the stove, at the crockery cupboard covered with the marks of squashed flies, at the unbelievably filthy kitchen that was seething with bugs. There was a bitter smell of frying-oil, kerosene and smoke. I could hear the cockroaches rustling in the kindling wood by the stove and my heart would be filled with sadness. Thinking about that soldier and his sister almost moved me to tears. How could people live like that? I would jot things down without even listening to Sidorov's whispering, and write instead about the boredom and oppressiveness of that life while he sighed and told me:

'You've written a lot! Thanks very much! Now she'll know what to look out for.'

'You mustn't be afraid of *anything*,' I would say angrily, although I myself was frightened of a lot of things.

Sidorov would clear his throat and start laughing:

'You're a funny boy! There's lots of people you should fear. There's your master . . . and God . . . That's two people for a start!'

When he received a letter from his sister he would ask me anxiously:

'Please, read it quick!'

And he would make me read the whole infuriatingly short letter, usually written in a terrible scrawl, several times.

He was kind and gentle, but he treated women like he did everyone else – crudely and savagely. Either as a voluntary or involuntary witness of his love affairs, which often began and fizzled out with astonishing rapidity – and it was this that I found really disgusting – I could see right under my very eyes how Sidorov made women feel sorry for him when he started complaining about the hard life of a soldier, and how he intoxicated them with his seductive lies. When he had got what he wanted he would tell Ermokhin about his conquest, frowning with disgust and spitting – just as though he had just swallowed some nasty medicine. This really annoyed me and I would angrily ask him why he seduced women, lied to them and then, when he had made a fool of them, why he handed them over to someone else and, more often than not, beat them into the bargain? But he would only laugh softly and reply:

'You shouldn't be interested in things like that. They're bad, wicked sins . . . You're too young . . .'

But another time I managed to get a more informative reply out of him, and I remembered it for a long time afterwards.

'Do you think they don't know I'm leading them up the garden path?' he said, winking at me and coughing. 'Yes, they know all right! But they *want* to be seduced. In these matters everyone lies, everyone's ashamed, no one loves anyone else – it's all a game! It makes you feel terribly ashamed of yourself, you'll find out! But you should do it at night. If it's daytime then you must be in the dark, in a storeroom . . . yes! It was because of this that God drove man out of paradise and as a result everyone's unhappy.'

He spoke so well, so sadly and regretfully that I took a more lenient view of his love affairs. I was more friendly with him than with Ermokhin, whom I hated and whom I tried in every possible way to annoy and ridicule – and in this I succeeded. He often used to chase me round the yard, fully intending to harm me, but he was so clumsy he rarely managed to catch me.

'Things like that are *forbidden*,' Sidorov continued.

I knew that they were forbidden, but I could not believe that love made people unhappy. I could see that people *were* unhappy, but surely it was not because of their love affairs? Often I saw the strange expression in lovers' eyes, and felt that people in love were particularly kind. It was always pleasant watching that gay holiday of the heart.

In spite of this, life was even more boring and cruel than ever before and was strictly controlled by a daily routine which had become immutable. I did not think there could be any possibility of a better life, different from that which I was condemned to watch unfolding before me every day.

Once the soldiers told me a story which deeply disturbed me. A cutter who worked for the best tailor in town lived in one of the flats. He was a quiet, withdrawn sort of man and not like a

Russian at all. His little wife had never had any children and all she did was read day and night. Right in the middle of all the noise of that yard, which was surrounded by houses full of drunks, that couple lived their own quiet lives, were never to be seen, never had visitors and never went out except on holidays, when they went to the theatre.

The husband worked from morning until late in the evening. The wife, who looked like a young girl, used to go to the library twice a week. I often saw her stumbling along as though she had a bad limp, taking short steps along the embankment like a schoolgirl. She carried her books strapped up and she dressed simply, was pleasant-looking, fresh and clean, and wore gloves on her little hands. Her face was like a bird's with little darting eyes, but to me she was as beautiful as a porcelain figure on a dressing table. The soldiers said that she had a rib missing, which possibly explained her strange limp. But I found this handicap of hers rather pleasing as it immediately distinguished her from all the other women in the yard, who were officers' wives. These women, in spite of their loud voices, gaudy dresses and high bustles, seemed second-hand, as though they had long been forgotten and had been lying for ages in a dark storeroom along with other old rubbish.

The people in the yard thought that the cutter's little wife was a half-wit, and said that books had sent her mad and had affected her so much that she could no longer cope with the house. They said that every day her husband had to tell their cook (who did not look Russian either and was a morose person with one inflamed eye that was always full of tears, and a narrow pink slit where the other should have been) what they wanted for dinner or lunch. They also claimed that this lady could not tell the difference between boiled pork and veal, and that once she had disgraced herself by buying horseradish instead of parsley, which was too shocking for words.

The three of them seemed perfect strangers in that house. It was just as though they had accidentally fallen into a cage in a large henhouse, and behaved just like tomtits trying to escape the frost by flying through the ventilator window into that stuffy filthy place where all those people lived.

Then one day the batmen told me that the officers were playing nasty, malicious tricks on that little woman. Every day one or two of them would send her notes, in which they wrote about their love for her, about their sufferings and about her beauty. She used to answer them, begging them to leave her alone, saying she was very sorry if she had distressed them and she prayed to God to make them fall out of love. The officers would pass these notes round and have a good laugh. Then they would all help to compose a letter, pretending that one of them had written it.

When they told me this story the batmen with me in the shed burst out laughing too and hurled abuse at the cutter's wife.

'Miserable little fool. Cripple!' Ermokhin would say in his deep voice and Sidorov would agree:

'Yes! *Every* woman wants to be seduced. *They* know everything...'

I could not believe that the cutter's wife knew that she had become a laughing-stock and I decided to tell her about it at once. After waiting until the cook had gone down to the cellar I ran up the back-stairs into the little woman's flat and poked my nose into the kitchen, but it was empty. I went into the living-room and found the cutter's wife sitting at the table, holding a heavy gilt cup in one hand and an open book in the other. She was frightened when she saw me, pressed the book to her breast and started shouting, but not very loud:

'Who are you? – Augusta! – Who are you?'

Very rapidly – and rather incoherently – I started telling her who I was, expecting her to throw the book or the cup at me. She was sitting in a large crimson-coloured armchair and she was wearing a blue dressing gown trimmed with velvet at the bottom, and with lace at the collar and cuffs. Her fair wavy hair fell over her shoulders and she looked like one of the angels from the holy gates in a church. As she leaned back in the chair she stared at me with her large round eyes. At first she seemed angry, then she gave me a startled look which changed into a smile. When I had told her everything I started making for the door, as my courage failed me at this point.

'Wait!' she shouted after me.

She put the cup on to a tray, threw the book on to the table, pressed her palms together and said in the deep voice of a grown man:

'What a strange boy you are! Come over here!'

I moved very cautiously. She took me by the hand, stroked it with her cold little fingers and asked:

'Is it true no one actually *taught* you to say that? No one? Well, I believe you now. You must have thought of it yourself!'

She let go of my hand, closed her eyes and said in a soft drawling voice:

'So that's what those foul-mouthed soldiers are saying about me!'

'You should go away from here,' I advised her in a matter-of-fact voice.

'Why?'

'They'll get the better of you in the end!'

She smiled pleasantly and then asked:

'Do you go to school? Do you like reading?'

'Never have time for it.'

'If you *really* liked it you'd find the time. Well, thanks for coming!'

She held out a silver coin in between two fingers and a thumb. I felt ashamed of taking such a present from her, but I did not have the nerve to refuse. On the way out I left it on one of the banisters.

That woman had made a deep impression on me, one that I had not experienced before. It was as though a bright dawn had come and for several days I lived in a state of elation, picturing to myself that spacious room with the cutter's wife sitting dressed in blue like an angel. Everything there seemed to have a strange beauty; a luxurious, golden carpet lay at her feet and the wintry day grew warm as it peered at her through the silvery window panes.

I wanted to look at her again and find out what she would say if I asked her for a book. So I went to see her and once more saw her sitting in the same place with a book in her hands. This time, however, her cheek was bound up with a reddish coloured handkerchief and one eye was inflamed. She mumbled something indistinctly as she handed me a book bound in black.

I felt very downhearted, and the book smelled of creosote and aniseed. I wrapped it up in a clean shirt and some paper and hid it in the attic, as I was frightened that the master or mistress might find it and make it dirty. They took the journal *Niva* for the dress patterns and gift vouchers, but they never actually read it. When they had looked at all the pictures, they put it away in a cupboard in the bedroom. At the end of the year they had all the copies bound and then hid them all under the bed, where there were already three bound volumes of the *Arts Review*. When I washed the bedroom floors dirty water would flow from under them. The master subscribed to the *Russian Courier* and would curse as he read it in the evenings:

'The devil only knows why they write such stuff. What a bore!'

On Saturday, when I sorted out the linen in the attic, I remembered my book, unwrapped it and read the first line: 'Houses are like people: each has its own particular physiognomy.' The truth of this statement amazed me, and I read on, standing by the dormer window until I was nearly frozen stiff. In the evening, when the master and his wife had gone off to church, I took the book into the kitchen and plunged myself into a sea of yellowish, dog-eared pages that looked like autumn leaves. In no time at all I was carried away into another world, where there were new names, new kinds of relationships. The book portrayed good heroes and gloomy villains who were not at all like the people I had seen all around me. It was a novel by Xavier de Montépin and was very long, like all his works, and crowded with people and events. It portrayed a strange, dynamic life. Everything in it was amazingly clear and simple, and a certain light that lay hidden between the lines seemed to illuminate what was good or evil and helped to show me what I should love or hate, and forced me to persevere and follow to the end the destinies of people who were all mixed up together in a thick swarm. Suddenly I had an irrepressible desire to make certain things happen and prevent others, and I completely forgot that this life which had so unexpectedly opened up before me was only made of paper. Those struggles, which fluctuated from day to day, made me forget everything else. On one page everything was suffused with joy, while the next filled me with grief.

I carried on reading until I heard the front door bell ring and it took me some time to realize someone was outside. The candle was almost burnt out and the candlestick, which I had cleaned out that same morning, was filled with wax. The wick, which I was supposed to look after, had fallen out of its holder and gone out. I rushed round the kitchen trying to conceal my crime. I stuffed the book into the space under the stove and tried to light the lamp again. Then nanny suddenly appeared:

'Have you gone deaf? Someone's at the door!'

I rushed to open it.

'Been snoozing again?' the master asked sternly.

His wife heaved herself up the stairs and started complaining that I had made her catch cold, while the old woman cursed me. The first thing she saw in the kitchen was the burnt-out candle and she started cross-examining me. I did not say a word; it was just as though I had fallen from some great height and I felt shattered. I was terrified in case she found the book, but instead she started shouting and accusing me of trying to burn the whole house down. The master and his wife came in for dinner and the old woman complained:

'There, you see, he's burnt a *whole* candle and he'll burn the whole house down next . . .'

While they were eating all four of them kept nagging away at me and they reminded me of all the offences I had committed, intentional or otherwise, and threatened to ruin me. But I knew quite well that there was no real malice in what they said and that they did have my welfare at heart – they spoke like this just out of sheer boredom. It was strange to see how empty and ridiculous they were compared with people in books.

When they had finished eating, they seemed to have suddenly put on weight and they wearily trudged off to bed. The old woman plagued God with her complaining for a while and then climbed up on to the stove and was quiet. At this point I got up, took the book from the space under the stove and went over to the window. It was a bright night and the moon shone straight into the room. All the same, I could not make out the small print, and I wanted terribly to read that book. I took a brass saucepan from the shelf and made it reflect the moonlight on to the pages; but this was even worse than before.

So I climbed on to a bench in a corner where the ikons were and started reading standing up, by the light of the ikon lamp. But I was so tired that I slumped down on the bench and dropped off to sleep. I was woken up by the old woman shouting and hitting me. She had got hold of the book and was banging it against my shoulders, which was very painful. Her face was red with anger and she wildly tossed back her head with its reddish-brown hair. She was barefooted and all she had on was a shift. Viktor started howling again from his plank bed:

'Mamasha, don't shout! It's impossible to sleep in this place!'

'I've lost that book, now they'll tear it up,' I thought.

Sentence was passed over morning tea. The master sternly asked me:

'Where did you get that book?'

The women started shouting and interrupting each other. Viktor suspiciously sniffed the pages and said:

'Smells of scent, my life on it!'

When I informed them that the book in fact had belonged to a priest, they all took another look at it, and were surprised and indignant that a clergyman should read novels. All the same this discovery calmed them down a little, although the master lectured me for a long time on the subject of harmful and dangerous books:

'Some people who read books blew up a railway once and tried to murder someone.'

The master's wife shouted in an angry, frightened voice to her husband:

'You're out of your mind! What are you telling him that for?'

I took the volume of Montépin to Sidorov the soldier and told him what had happened. He took the book, opened a small trunk without saying a word, pulled out a clean towel, wrapped the book up and put it away.

Then he said:

'Don't listen to them. Come *here* to read, I won't tell anyone.

If I'm not in, you'll find the key behind the ikon. Then you can open the trunk and read your book.'

My master and mistress's attitude to the book immediately elevated it in my eyes and I thought that it held some important and terrible secret. I was not interested in the fact that some 'people who read books' had blown up a railway somewhere or other with the intention of murdering someone, but I did remember that question the priest had asked during confession, that schoolboy reading down in a cellar, what Smury had said about 'correct books' and Grandfather's stories about free-masons who read books on black magic:

'During the reign of Alexander the Blessed some petty little noblemen, led astray by black magic and freemasonry, attempted to betray the entire Russian nation to the Roman Pope, the damned Jesuits! And then General Arakcheev caught them in the act, and, irrespective of their rank or title, sent the whole lot to hard labour in Siberia, where they just rotted away . . .'

I remembered the 'Umbracula, speckled with stars', Gervasy, and the solemn, comical words: 'Oh, ignorant ones, curious to know our business, Your weak eyes will never spy them out!' I felt that I was on the threshold of some great secret and I wandered around like a madman. I dearly wanted to finish that book, but I was afraid the soldier might keep it, or that he might damage it. What could I tell the cutter's wife then?

The old woman, who kept a close eye on me in case I went to visit the batmen, started tormenting me again:

'Bookworm! Those books teach nothing but corruption. See what happened to that woman through reading! She can't even go shopping on her own. All she can do is get mixed up with batmen. She lets them come to her flat during the day – I *kno-ow*!'

I felt like shouting 'That's a lie. She doesn't do that . . .' But I was too afraid to defend the cutter's wife, as the old woman would guess right away that the book belonged to her.

For a few days I had a terrible time. I became absent-minded and full of restless longing. I could not sleep for worrying about Montépin's fate. And then the cook who worked for the cutter's wife stopped me in the yard and told me:

'Bring the book back!'

I picked the right moment after dinner, when the master and his wife had gone to their room for a nap, and I turned up at the flat feeling confused and in very low spirits. She looked just the same as when I had first met her, but now she was wearing a grey skirt and a black velvet jacket, with a turquoise-coloured cross on her bare neck. She resembled a female bullfinch. When I told her that I had not managed to finish the book and that I had been forbidden to read it the sense of injury together with a feeling of joy at seeing that woman again brought tears to my eyes.

'Ugh, what stupid people!' she said frowning. 'And yet your master has such an interesting face. Don't upset yourself, I'll think of something. I'll *write* to him!'

This frightened me and I explained that I had lied to my master and mistress and that I had told them that I had not got the book from her, but from a priest, and I said:

'There's no need for that. *Don't* write to them. They'll only laugh at you and curse you. As you know, no one in the yard likes you. They all make fun of you and say that you're a fool and that you've got one rib missing!'

No sooner had I got this off my chest than I realized that I had really gone too far. She bit her upper lip and slapped herself on the ribs, as though she were riding a horse. I lowered my head in embarrassment and wanted the earth to swallow me up. But the cutter's wife leaned back in her chair and laughed gaily as she repeated exactly what I had said:

'Oh, it's all so stupid, so stupid! But what can one do?' she asked herself with her eyes riveted on me. Then she sighed and said:

'You *are* a strange boy, very strange...'

I looked into the mirror next to her and saw a face with a highly placed nose, large cheekbones and a big bruise on the forehead. The hair, which had not been cut for a long time, stuck out in every direction – was this what they called a 'very strange boy'? That strange boy certainly did not look like a fine porcelain figure...

'You didn't take that change I gave you. Why not?'

'I didn't need it.'

She sighed.

'Well, what are we going to do now? If they change their minds and let you read, then come here again, and I'll give you some books.'

There were three on the dressing-table. The one I had brought was the thickest. I looked at it sadly. Then the cutter's wife held out her little pink hand and said:

'Well, good-bye.'

I cautiously touched her hand and left quickly. But they were right to say that she knew nothing: she had called a whole twenty-kopek piece 'change' – just as a child would. But this rather pleased me . . .

Chapter 9

I FIND it both sad and at the same time comical to recall the deep humiliation, the many insults and the anxiety my fast-growing passion for reading had inflicted on me. The books that belonged to the cutter's wife seemed incredibly expensive and as I was afraid of the old woman getting hold of them and burning them in the stove, I tried to forget them and started taking little books with different covers from the shop where I bought bread in the mornings for breakfast. The proprietor was a very unpleasant sweaty young man, with thick lips, a white flabby face covered in pockmarks and pale eyes; his hands were puffy, with short, clumsy-looking fingers. His shop was a meeting-place in the evenings for youths and empty-headed girls from the street. My master's brother used to call on the shopkeeper almost every evening to drink beer and play cards. They often sent me to invite him over to dinner, and more than once I saw that stupid red-faced wife of his sitting on Viktor's or another young man's knees in that cramped little room at the back of the shop. Evidently this did not upset the shopkeeper. And he was not upset either when the choir boys, soldiers – everyone in fact who felt like it – put their arms round his sister, who used to help him in the shop. He did not do very much business and he explained this by saying that it was a new shop and that he had not managed to get things organized although the shop had been open since the autumn. He used to show visitors and customers dirty pictures and let them copy out pornographic verse.

I used to borrow Misha Evstigneev's miserable little books and paid a kopek each for the privilege of reading them. This was expensive and I got no pleasure from them: *Guak, or Invincible Loyalty*, *Frantsyl Venetsian*, *The Battle between the Russians and the Kabardinians, or the Beautiful Mohammedan Who Died on the Coffin of her Spouse* and all that type of literature did not satisfy me and often filled me with annoyance and resentment. It seemed that those books were actually laughing at me, as though I were an idiot to whom they were telling the most improbable happenings in cumbersome sentences. I preferred *The Streltsy, Yury Miloslavsky, The Mysterious Monk, Yapancha, the Tartar Horseman* and similar books that left me with something worth remembering. But the lives of saints attracted me even more. Here there was something serious, which was highly credible and often deeply disturbing. All the martyrs reminded me of 'Just the Job', and the female martyrs put me in mind of Grandmother. The saints reminded me of Grandfather – in his better moments.

I used to read in the shed, where I went to chop the wood, or in the attic, which was just as cold and uncomfortable. Sometimes if a book interested me or if I had to read it quickly I used to get up in the night and light a candle. But the old woman noticed that the candles were growing shorter overnight and started measuring them with a kindling stick which she then hid away somewhere. If the candle was a fraction of an inch short when she examined it in the morning or if I managed to find the stick but did not succeed in cutting it down to exactly the same length as the candle stump, then she would fill the kitchen with her wild shouts.

Once I heard Viktor proclaiming indignantly from his bunk:

'Stop your howling, mother! It's impossible to sleep in this place. Of course he lights candles, because he wants to read his books. He gets them from the shop. I know! You just have a look in the attic . . .'

The old woman rushed upstairs, found a book there and tore it to pieces. This annoyed me of course, but it only increased my desire to read.

If a priest came to the house the master and mistress would start lecturing him and try to make him think their way – just because they had nothing else to do. It seemed to me that if they ever stopped criticizing people, shouting or laughing at them then they would soon lose the faculty of speech altogether, that they would go dumb and that they would not even be able to see themselves as human beings any more. For a man to be aware of his own existence it is essential for him to have some sort of relationship with people. All that my master and mistress knew was how to take a superior attitude towards people and always find fault with them. But if those people had in fact started living and thinking and feeling exactly as they themselves did, then it would not have made the slightest difference and they would still have found something to criticize in them. That's the kind of people they were.

I tried every trick I knew in order to read my books in peace. The old woman destroyed several of the books I borrowed and suddenly I found that I owed the shopkeeper the enormous sum of forty-seven kopeks! He demanded the money and threatened to make me pay with the money they gave me for the shopping. 'What would happen to you if I did that?' he said in a mocking voice.

I found him quite repulsive and, clearly sensing this, he tormented me with threats of various kinds and took a particular pleasure in it. When I entered the shop his spotty face became puffy and he would ask in a friendly voice:

'Have you brought the money?'

'No.'

This appeared to frighten him and he frowned.

'Why not? I'll have to report you to the police now, won't I? Then you'll be sent to a labour camp.'

There was nowhere I could get the money from. My salary was paid directly to Grandfather and I just did not know what to do. But the shopkeeper answered my entreaty for him to wait until I had the money by stretching out his greasy hand which was as puffy as a pancake and saying:

'Kiss it! I can wait for the money.'

But when I seized a weight from a pair of scales on the counter and brandished it at him he cowered and shouted:

'What are you doing, eh? I was only joking.'

But I knew that he was *not* joking and I decided to steal the money to clear the debt.

Every morning when I cleaned the master's suit coins would jingle in the trouser pockets and sometimes they fell out and rolled over the floor. Once a coin fell through a crack in the stairs into the woodpile. I forgot to tell the master and only remembered a few days later when I found a twenty-kopek piece in the wood. When I gave it to the master his wife said to him:

'See? You should count your money if you leave it in your pockets!' But the master smiled and said, turning to me:

'*He* wouldn't steal anything. I know!'

Now that I had decided to steal I could not forget those words and his trusting smile, and I realized how difficult it was going to be. Several times I took some silver from a pocket, counted it, but could not bring myself to steal any. For three days I tortured myself. Then suddenly everything was solved very quickly and simply. Quite unexpectedly the master asked me:

'Peshkov, you seem depressed these days. What's the matter, not feeling well?'

I told him frankly what was worrying me and this made him frown.

'So you see, that's what books can do for you! They always bring trouble in the end.'

He gave me a fifty-kopek piece and strongly advised me:

'Mind you don't go babbling about this to my wife or my mother or there'll be trouble!'

Then he smiled warmly and said:

'You really have guts, damn you! That's a good thing. But leave those books alone. In the new year I'm going to subscribe to a new journal, so you can read that.'

Every evening, from tea-time to dinner, I used to read to the master and mistress from the *Moscow Leaflet* the serialized novels of Vashkov, Rokshanin, Rudnikovsky and other literature for the digestion of people who were bored to death. I did not like reading aloud since then I could not follow the meaning. But the master and mistress always listened very attentively and with a certain awesome hunger. They would sigh, would be amazed at the wickedness of the heroes and used to tell each other proudly:

'*We* lead peaceful lives and don't know anything about all that, thank God!'

They mixed events up, ascribed the behaviour of Churkin the famous bandit to Foma Kruchina the coachman and got all the names wrong. I used to correct their mistakes and this surprised them a great deal.

'What a memory he's got!'

I often came across poems by Leonid Grave in the *Moscow Leaflet*, which I liked very much, and I used to copy some of them into a notebook. But the master and mistress would exclaim:

'An old man like that writing poetry!' or:

'A drunkard and a halfwit. He couldn't care less about anything.'

I liked Struzhkin and Count Memento-Mori's verse, but both women said that poetry was sheer 'clowning'.

'Only Punch and Judy, and actors speak in verse,' they used to say.

Those winter evenings in that little cramped room with my master and mistress were quite unbearable. Outside there was nothing but deathly night. Sometimes I could hear the frost crackling. People sat at the table, as silent as frozen fish. Sometimes a blizzard would buffet the window and the walls, roar down the chimneys and make a banging noise in the dampers. The babies would start crying in the nursery and one felt like sitting down in some dark corner, hunching oneself up and howling like a wolf.

The women sat at one end of the table darning or knitting stockings. At the other was Viktor, sitting there with his back bent, reluctantly copying blueprints and shouting every now and then:

'Don't shake the table! It's impossible here, you wild goats and dogs!'

The master would sit to one side, at an enormous embroidery frame, cross-stitching a tablecloth. Under his fingers there appeared red crabs, blue fish, yellow butterflies and reddish autumn leaves. He had designed the pattern himself and this was the third winter he had been working on the tablecloth, which was in fact boring him stiff. He would very often say to me during the day when I was free:

'Come on, Peshkov, get to work on the cloth!'

I would sit down and start working with the thick needle. I felt sorry for the master and always tried to help him as much as I could. I kept thinking that one day he would give up drawing, embroidering, card playing and start something quite different and interesting, which would make him think.

He would suddenly stop and look at the cloth with motionless surprised eyes, as though it were the first time he had seen it. His hair fell down over his forehead and cheeks, and this made him look like a novice in a monastery.

'What are you thinking about?' his wife asked.

'Nothing,' he would answer, carrying on with his work.

I sat there in silent amazement. How could one ask a question like that, about what a man was actually *thinking*? In my opinion this was impossible, as a person thinks about a lot of different things at the same time, about everything he sees around him at a particular moment, about what he saw yesterday, even a year ago. All these thoughts then become mixed up and are very elusive, moving about and changing the whole time.

As there were not enough articles from the *Moscow Leaflet* to last the evening I suggested reading to them from the magazines underneath the bed and the young mistress said incredulously:

'What's there to read? There's only pictures in them . . .'

But besides the *Arts Review* I found another magazine – the *Little Light* – under the bed, and I started reading Salias's *Count Tyatin-Baltiisky*.

The master particularly liked the imbecilic hero and he laughed until he cried at the sad things that happened to the nobleman's son:

'Well, that's an amusing little story!' he shouted.

'A load of lies,' the mistress answered, trying to prove that she had an independent mind.

The literature I found under the bed came in very useful. I earned myself the right to take journals into the kitchen and it also gave me a chance of reading during the night. Luckily for me the old woman used to go and sleep in the nursery, as the nurse was often dead drunk. Viktor did not get in my way either. When everyone in the house was asleep he would quietly dress himself and vanish until the next morning. They did not give me any light and took the candles away with them – and I had no money to buy any. So I began to scrape wax from the candlesticks, collecting it in a sardine tin, into which I poured some of the lamp oil. I made a wick by twisting some threads together and lit it from the stove; it burned with a smoky flame. When I turned one of the pages over in a very large book the red tongue of the wick flickered and threatened to go out and every minute it sank deeper into the evil-smelling pool of molten wax. The acrid smoke stung my eyes but the pleasure I derived from looking at the illustrations and reading the captions more than compensated for all these discomforts. Those illustrations made the world a larger place, beautifying it with fabulous towns, showing me high mountains and wonderful sea shores. Life blossomed miraculously, the earth became more attractive, richer in people and towns and many different things. And now as I looked at those distant fields beyond the Volga I knew very well that they were not just a desert. Before, I used to look beyond the Volga and found the country there particularly boring. The meadows were flat, and seemed to have been patched all over with dark shrubs. Where they ended rose the ragged black wall of the forests, with a smoky cold blue haze hanging over it. The earth seemed empty and lonely. And as a result my heart became empty, disturbed by gentle feelings of sadness. All desire would disappear and there would be simply nothing to think about. I just wanted to close my eyes, as that depressing void promised nothing and sucked out everything that was in my heart.

The captions to the pictures told me – in a way that I could understand – about different countries, different people, about things that had happened in the past and present. There was a lot I could not understand, and this was sheer torture. Sometimes strange words would stick in my mind – 'metaphysics', 'chiliasm', 'chartist' – and they became an unbearable source of worry, grew into monstrous shapes, and blacked everything out. It seemed that I would never understand *anything* if I did not grasp the meaning of those words that stood like sentries on the threshold of every secret. Often whole phrases would stay in my memory for a long time afterwards like a splinter in my finger, preventing me from thinking about anything else. I remember reading some strange poetry:

> Over the desert, clothed in steel,
> Mute and gloomy as the grave
> Rides Attila, King of the Huns.

And he was followed by a black mass of warriors shouting:

Where is Rome, where is mighty Rome?

I already knew Rome was a town but who were the Huns? I *had* to find out, so I waited for the right moment and asked the master.

'The Huns?' he repeated in amazement. 'God knows! If you ask me – it's all a load of rubbish!'

And he would shake his head disapprovingly and say:

'Your head is full of nonsense and that's bad, Peshkov!'

Whether it was good or bad, I still wanted to know who the Huns were. I thought that Solovyov the regimental chaplain must know, and I stopped him in the square and asked him. He was a pale-faced man, never looked very well and was always in a terrible mood. His eyes were red, without any brows, and he had a little yellowish beard. He poked at the ground with his black staff and said:

'And what's that to do with you, eh?'

When I asked Lieutenant Nesterov he answered fiercely:

'Wha-at?'

Then I decided that I would have to ask the dispenser in the local chemist's about the Huns. He had a clever face and wore gold-rimmed spectacles over his big nose and he was always kind to me.

'The Huns,' Pavel Goldberg said, 'were a nomadic race, like the Kirgiz. They don't exist any more – they've all died off.'

I felt sad and annoyed, not because the Huns had died, but because the meaning of the words that had tormented me was really so simple and in fact conveyed nothing to me. But I was very grateful to the Huns, since after my 'encounter' with them words did not worry me so much, and thanks to Attila I made the acquaintance of Goldberg the dispenser. That man knew the simple meaning of all words of wisdom and he possessed the key to every mystery. He would straighten his spectacles with two fingers, stare me straight in the eye through the thick lenses and speak as though he were hammering fine nails into my forehead.

'Words, my friend, are like leaves on a tree. To understand why a leaf is like it is you must know all about trees. You must study! Books, my friend, are like a fine garden where everything grows; they are pleasant as well as useful . . .'

I often went to his shop to buy soda and magnesium for the grown-ups, who perpetually suffered from heartburn, and for bay-oil and laxatives for the children. The dispenser's brief lessons made me take books more seriously and, without my noticing it, they became as indispensable to me as vodka to a drunkard.

They opened up a different life, a life of deeper feelings and desires, which led people to great exploits – and to crime. I could see that the people around me were incapable of great exploits or of crimes even, and that they lived in a world that had nothing to do with what I read about in books. I could see nothing of interest in the lives they led, and I did not want to live like them – that at least was clear.

I learned from the captions that in the middle of Prague, London or Paris there were no gullies or filthy rubbish dumps, but straight, wide streets and all kinds of houses and churches. In those cities winter did not last for six months, keeping people shut up in their houses, and there was no Lent, when people were allowed to eat only sour cabbage, salted mushrooms, ground oatmeal and potatoes with revolting linseed oil. In Russia during Lent it was even forbidden to read books and they took the *Arts Review* away from me. That empty Lenten life had once more caught up with me and now that I was able to compare it with what I had read about in books, it struck me as even more wretched and ugly.

As I read I began to feel healthier and stronger, and I worked rapidly and skilfully, as I now had a purpose: the sooner I finished my chores the more time would be left over for reading. When they took books away from me I became listless and lazy, and a morbid forgetfulness which I had not known before would take hold of me.

I remember that on one of those empty days something mysterious happened: one evening, when everyone had gone to bed, the cathedral bell suddenly started ringing out with its deep peals and woke the whole house. Half-dressed figures rushed to the windows and asked each other: 'What is it? A fire? A general alarm?'

I could hear people dashing around and doors slamming in the other rooms. Someone ran round the yard with a horse on a lead. The old woman shouted that the cathedral had been burgled, but the master shut her up:

'That's enough, mother. Can't you hear? It's not an alarm!'

'Well, the Bishop must have died then!'

Viktor climbed down from his bunk and muttered as he got dressed:

'I know what's happened. *I know*!'

The master sent me up to the loft to see if the sky was red. I ran up, climbed through a dormer window on to the roof, and could see no redness in the sky. The bell clanged away slowly in the quiet frosty air. The town sleepily clung to the earth. Invisible people ran around in the darkness, crunching over the snow. Sleigh runners screeched and still that bell rang out ominously. I went downstairs and told them:

'The sky's *not* red.'

'Ugh, good heavens!' the master exclaimed. He was wearing an overcoat and a hat; he raised his collar and started shoving his feet into a pair of galoshes without much enthusiasm.

His wife pleaded with him:

'Don't go! Don't go!'

'Stop your nonsense!'

Viktor had got dressed as well and started teasing everybody again:

'*I* know what's happened!'

When the brothers had gone out into the street the women ordered me to put the samovar on and rushed over to the windows, but no sooner had they gone than the master rang the front door bell, ran up the stairs without saying a word and then came back into the hall and said in a deep voice:

'The Tsar's* been assassinated!'

'Assassinated!' the old woman exclaimed.

'Assassinated. An officer told me ... What's going to happen now?'

Then Viktor came back and rang the front door bell. As he reluctantly got undressed again he said angrily:

* Alexander II (assassinated in 1881). (Trans.)

167

'And *I* thought war had been declared!'

Afterwards they all sat down to tea and spoke calmly, but quietly and cautiously at the same time. Everything became quiet out in the street and the bell had stopped. For two days they kept on whispering mysteriously to each other, went visiting, and visitors came to the house. They had long conversations. I tried my best to understand what had happened but the master and mistress hid the newspapers from me. When I asked Sidorov why the Tsar had been assassinated he answered quietly:

'You're not supposed to talk about such things.'

And it was all soon forgotten and submerged in the trivia of everyday life.

Not long after this I had a nasty experience. One Sunday, when the master and mistress had gone to early service and I had put the samovar on and gone off to tidy up the other rooms, the eldest child crawled into the kitchen, pulled the tap off the samovar and sat under the table playing with it. There was a lot of charcoal in the pipe and the hot water flowed out and melted the soldering. I could hear the samovar humming away with a strange viciousness and when I went into the kitchen to my horror I saw that it had turned blue and was shaking furiously, as though it wanted to jump up from the floor. The stopper in the tap had become unsoldered and hung miserably downwards. The lid was now tilting to one side and drips of molten tin were flowing down from under the handles: that lilac-blue samovar now looked like someone who was blind drunk. I poured water over it and this made it hiss and slump sadly on to the floor. Then I heard the front door bell ring and I opened up.

When the old woman asked me if the samovar was ready I curtly replied:

'It's ready!'

Most probably confusion and fear made me say those words: they must have thought I was laughing at them and they doubled the punishment.

I was thrashed unmercifully. The old woman used a bundle of pine twigs, which did not hurt very much, but they left a great number of splinters deep in my skin. By the time evening came my back had swollen out like a pillow and the following afternoon the master had to take me to hospital. When an almost ridiculously tall and fat doctor had examined me he said in a calm, deep voice:

'This flogging must be reported to the police.'

The master went red, shuffled his feet and started saying something in a soft voice to the doctor, who looked over his shoulder and briefly answered:

'No, I'm not allowed to.'

And then he turned to me and asked:

'Do you want to make a complaint?'

Although I was in terrible pain I said:

'No, but get me better as soon as you can.'

They took me into another room, laid me on a table, and the doctor picked out the splinters with some pleasantly cold tweezers. He started joking with me:

'They made a nice job of your skin, my friend. Now you'll be waterproof!...'

When he had finished taking out the splinters, which tickled so much that I could hardly bear it, he said:

'Forty-two splinters, my friend. Remember that, it's something to be proud of! Come back the same time tomorrow for bandaging. Do they beat you often?'

I thought for a while and answered:

'Before they used to beat me *even more*.'

The doctor guffawed.

'Everything improves, my friend, everything!'

When he took me to my master he said:

'Please receive him mended and repaired! Send him to us tomorrow and we'll bandage him up. Lucky for you he can see the funny side of it...'

As he sat in the cab the master said:

'And I was beaten too, Peshkov. What can one do? *I* was thrashed when I was a boy! Although I feel sorry for you, no one felt sorry for *me*. No one! The world's swarming with people, but there's not one bastard who'll take pity on you. Ugh, they're all wild animals!'

He swore all the way home and I felt sorry for him. I was grateful to him for speaking to me as a human being.

Back home they treated me as though it were my name-day. The women made me tell them in the greatest detail what treatment the doctor had given me and what he had said, and as they listened they sighed, sensually licking their lips and blinking. Their intense interest in illness, pain and everything that was nasty astounded me. I could see they were pleased with me for not making an official complaint and as a result they gave me permission to borrow books from the cutter's wife. They dared not refuse now, in fact, and only the old woman exclaimed in surprise:

'Oh, the little devil!'

A day later I was standing in front of the cutter's wife and she said in a warm voice:

'They told me you were ill and had been taken to hospital. The rumours that get around!'

I did not reply, as I felt too ashamed to tell the truth – why should she have to know what was crude and horrible? I thought it was wonderful that she was so different from everybody else.

Once again I started reading fat volumes of Dumas *père*, Ponson du Terrail, Montépin, Zaccone, Gaboriau, Aimard, Boisgobey, and I swallowed them quickly, one after the other, and they all left me in high spirits. I felt I was taking part in a very unusual kind of life, which was pleasantly disturbing and which made me feel aggressive at the same time. Once again my home-made lamp was smoking away and I would read all night long, until morning, and this hurt my eyes.

The old woman would say affectionately:

'You wait, you little bookworm! You'll burst your pupils and go blind!'

However, I came to understand very soon that despite those interesting muddles, despite all those different events and fascinating countries and towns, the stories were always essentially the same: good people were unhappy and persecuted by the wicked, and wicked people were invariably more successful and clever. But in the end something that was quite impossible to pin down would defeat the wicked and the good people would triumph. Love, about which all men and women spoke in the same way, bored me – not only because it was so terribly monotonous but because of the way it made me feel suspicious of everything that happened. From the very first pages I could already see who would emerge victorious, who would be defeated, and as soon as the sequence of events became clear to me I would try to guess the ending with the help of my own imagination. When I had finished a book I would think about it as though it were an arithmetical problem and I was able to guess with increasing accuracy which hero would reach paradise and who would be cast down into hell. But behind all this I could glimpse a living, significant truth, a different life and different relationships from those I knew. It was clear to me that the Parisian cabdrivers, workmen and soldiers and all the 'common rabble' were not the same as in Nizhny, Kazan and Perm. They spoke more boldly to their masters and their relationships with them were much more easy-going.

In one of the stories there was a soldier quite unlike anyone I knew, either Sidorov or the soldier from Vyatka whom I had met on the steamship – and even less like Ermokhin. He was a bigger man than all three of them. He had something of Smury in him, but he was not so animal and crude. In another story there was a shopkeeper but even he was better than all the shopkeepers I had known. And the priests were different: they were more sincere and treated people with much more compassion.

In general, life abroad as it was described in books was more interesting, easier and better than the life I knew. In foreign countries people did not fight so often and so ferociously, nor did they torment others so much with their mockery, like that soldier from Vyatka. And they did not pray to God so fervently as the old woman. I particularly noticed that when they were describing wicked, greedy or loathsome people those authors did not portray the inexplicable cruelty and that pleasure in insulting other people which was so familiar to me and which I had seen so often. Wicked people in books were cruel for some reason and I could almost always understand why they were like this. But in my own life there was only aimless, senseless cruelty, practised merely for amusement and not for any material gain. With every book I read the difference between Russian

171

life and life in foreign countries became more and more evident and filled me with a restless feeling of annoyance, making me more suspicious than ever of the truthfulness of those yellow dog-eared pages that had been read time and time again.

And suddenly I came across Goncourt's novel, *The Zemganno Brothers*, and I read it right through at one sitting, during the night. It left me with a feeling of surprise I had not experienced before, and so I started reading that sad, simple story again. There was nothing complicated in it, nothing even superficially interesting. From the very first pages it seemed serious and dry, like the lives of the saints. Its language, so precise and unvarnished, came at first as an unpleasant surprise, but those sober words, those tightly constructed sentences that settled so easily into my heart, told the story of the acrobat brothers so inspiringly that my hands trembled from the sheer pleasure of reading it. I sobbed as I read how the unfortunate artist with broken legs climbed up to the attic where his brother was secretly busy with his 'favourite art'. When I gave that marvellous book back to the cutter's wife I asked her to lend me another one exactly the same.

'How can I give you the same book?' she asked, smiling.

That smile embarrassed me and I was unable to explain what I really wanted. Then she said:

'That's a *boring* book. Wait a little while and I'll bring you something else, something more interesting.'

A few days later she gave me Greenwood's *True History of a Little Ragamuffin*; this title annoyed me but the very first page made me smile with delight, and I smiled like this as I read the whole book, reading some pages two or three times. So life was as hard as mine and full of torments even for boys abroad at times! Well I was not having such a bad time of it after all, and that meant I should not get downhearted.

Greenwood made me feel much bolder and soon afterwards I came across a book that was really true to life – *Eugénie Grandet*. Old man Grandet bore a striking resemblance to Grandfather and I was annoyed that the book was so short. But I was amazed at the wealth of truth it contained. That truth, with which I was so familiar and which I found so boring in real life, now threw a completely new light on everything – calm and benevolent. All the authors I had read, except Goncourt, criticized people in the same unrelenting, outspoken way as my master and mistress, and very often made me sympathize with criminals and get annoyed with the virtuous. It was always pathetic to see how a man could expend enormous reserves of intellect and will-power, and still not get what he wanted, while the virtuous confronted him from start to finish, as immovable as stone columns. Although all evil and vicious intentions were inevitably dashed to pieces against them those stone columns did not arouse any sympathy in me. Of course, however fine and solid a wall is, one can never admire it if one wants to pluck an apple from a tree on the other side. And already it seemed to me as though the most valuable things in life were hidden somewhere behind that solid wall of virtue.

Goncourt, Greenwood, Balzac did not write about villains or good people, but simply people who were miraculously *real*. They did not allow me to doubt for one moment that everything they said or did could have been said or done in any other way. In this way I came to understand what a great feast a 'good, true' book was. But how could I find one? The cutter's wife could not help me.

'This is a good book,' she would say, offering me Arsène Houssaye's *Hands Filled with Roses, Gold and Blood*, the novels of Belot, Paul de Kock, Paul Féval, but by now I really had to force myself to read them. She liked the novels of Marryat and Werner, which seemed boring to me. Shpilgagen did not give me any pleasure either, but I loved Auerbach's stories. I did not find Sue and Hugo very interesting and I preferred Walter Scott. I wanted books that disturbed me, made me feel glad, like the wonderful Balzac. And I began to like that 'Dresden china' woman less and less.

When I visited her I always wore a clean shirt, combed my hair and tried my best to look smart, if not very successfully. However, I still waited for the time when she would notice how well-groomed I was and would talk to me more simply and in a friendlier way, without that fishlike grin on her made-up, festive-looking face.

But all she did was smile and ask in her tired, sickly voice:

'Finished that book? Did you like it?'

'No.'

She raised her fine eyebrows very slightly, looked at me, sighed and said through her nose as though she were talking to someone she knew very well:

'But why on earth not?'

'I've already read about *that*.'

'About what?'

'About love.'

She screwed her eyes up and laughed with that sugary laugh of hers:

'Oh, but *all* books are about love!'

Then she would sit down in her large armchair, dangle her little feet in their fur slippers, yawn a little, snuggle into her light-blue dressing gown and tap the cover of the book on her knees with her pink fingers. I felt like asking: 'Why don't you leave this flat? The officers write notes to you the whole time and just laugh at you . . .' But I did not have the courage and I would leave with a thick book all about 'love', feeling bitterly disappointed.

In the yard people had started saying much more spiteful and insulting things about her. It upset me deeply hearing those old wives' tales which were so obscene – and certainly untrue. But when I called on her, and saw her sharp little eyes, that feline suppleness of her little body and her face with its perpetual gay smile, my feelings of pity and anxiety for her would vanish like smoke.

In the spring she suddenly disappeared, and a few days later her husband moved as well. When the rooms were lying empty and ready for new tenants I went to look at the bare walls with their square patches, bent nails and nail marks where the pictures had hung. On the painted floor were scattered rags of all colours, scraps of paper, broken pill boxes, scent bottles, and among them glistened a large bronze pin. All this saddened me, and I wanted to see that little cutter's wife again, to tell her how grateful I really was.

Chapter 10

BEFORE the cutter's wife went away, a young black-eyed lady with a little girl, and her mother – a grey-haired old woman who incessantly smoked cigarettes in an amber holder – moved into the flat below the master's. The lady was very beautiful, dominating and proud, with a deep, pleasant voice. She had the habit of screwing up her eyes very slightly, as though everyone was a long way off and she could not see them properly. Almost every day the swarthy soldier Tyufyaev brought a reddish-brown horse with thin legs to her front door and she would emerge wearing a velvety steel-coloured dress, white gloves and yellow boots. She would hold down her skirt with one hand, in which she had a whip with a lilac-coloured stone in the handle, and with the other affectionately stroke the horse's muzzle. The horse would squint at her with a fiery eye, tremble all over and gently beat its hoof on the well-trodden earth.

'Robert, Robert,' she said softly and gave the horse a firm slap on its beautifully curved neck.

Then she put her foot on Tyufyaev's knee, nimbly jumped up into the saddle and the horse went off prancing along the embankment. She sat so skilfully in the saddle she seemed to have become a part of it. Hers was that rare kind of beauty which always seems fresh and strange and always fills the heart with an intoxicating joy. As I looked at her I thought that Diane de Poitiers, Queen Margot, *Mademoiselle de La Vallière and other beauties and heroines from historical novels must have been just like her.

She was perpetually surrounded by officers from the division who were stationed in the town. In the evenings they played the piano, violin and guitar at her place and danced and sang. Major Olyosov, more than all the others, would run around after her on his short little legs. He was a fat greyish man with a red face and he had a greasy look, like an engineer from the

* First wife of Henri IV of France. (Trans.)

ship. An excellent guitarist, he behaved as though he alone were madame's humble and devoted servant.

The curly-haired, plump five-year-old daughter had the same engaging beauty as her mother. Her huge bluish eyes were serious and had a calmly expectant look. There was something very thoughtful about her – quite unlike a child.

From morning until night the grandmother was busy doing the housework with the gloomy taciturn Tyufyaev and the fat cross-eyed chambermaid. The child did not have a nurse and was almost completely left to her own devices. For whole days on end she played on the front steps or on a pile of wood opposite the house. Often in the evenings I used to go out to play with her and I grew very fond of that little girl, who soon became used to me and used to fall asleep in my arms when I told her stories, and then I would carry her off to bed. Soon she began insisting that I came and said good night when she was in bed. When I arrived she would solemnly hold out her puffy little hand and say:

'Good-bye until tomowow! Grandma, is that wight?'

'Bless you, dear,' her grandmother said, blowing out dark-blue streams of smoke through her mouth and sharp nose.

'And bless *you* until tomowow! But I'm going to sleep now,' the little girl repeated as she snuggled into her lace-embroidered blanket.

Her grandmother urged her:

'Not until tomorrow, dear, but *always*!'

'But isn't tomowow the *same* as always?'

She loved that word 'tomorrow' and anything that she liked was turned into the future. She would stick some flowers or twigs into the ground and say:

'That'll be a garden *tomowow*,' and 'Some day, tomowow, I'm going to buy a horsie for myself and go widing, like mama.'

She was a clever little girl, but not very cheerful, and often in the middle of a lively game she would suddenly become very thoughtful and ask quite out of the blue:

'Why do pwiests have long hair, like women?'

If she was stung by some nettles she would point a threatening finger at them and say:

'You watch out, I'll pway to God, and he'll make things vewy bad for you. God can make fings vewy bad for everyone – he can even punish mama.'

Sometimes a calm, serious sadness came over her. She would press close to me, look at the sky with her blue, expectant eyes and say:

'Gwandmother is angwy *vewy often*, but mama never is. She only laughs. Everyone loves her because she never has enough time and visitors keep on coming and looking at her because she's so beautiful. She's lovely, my mama. That's what Olyosov says: "Lovely mama!"'

I was terribly fond of listening to that girl talk about a world which was quite unknown to me. She always liked speaking about her mother and she eagerly told me a lot of things. A new life gradually opened up before me and once again I thought of Queen Margot. All this not only strengthened my belief in books but my interest in life as well.

One evening when I was sitting on the front steps waiting for my master and mistress (who had gone for a walk to Otkos) with the little girl half-asleep in my arms, her mother rode up sprang lightly down to the ground, threw her head back and asked:

'What's going on? Is she sleeping?'

'Yes.'

'All right . . .'

Tyufyaev came up and took the horse while the lady stuck the whip in her belt, held out her arms and said:

'Give her to me!'

'I'll put her to bed,' I said.

'No!' she shouted in the way she shouted at the horse and she stamped her feet on the front door step. The little girl woke up, blinked, looked at her mother and stretched out her arms. They both went away.

I was used to people shouting at me, but it was most unpleasant to have that lady shouting at me as well: everyone did what she said, even if she gave orders in a quiet voice. A few minutes later the cross-eyed chambermaid called me over to tell me the little girl was being difficult and would not go to bed without saying good night to me. I must confess I felt very proud as I went into the lounge where the little girl was sitting on the lap of her mother, who was deftly undressing her.

'Well, so *he's* arrived, that monster!'

'He's not a monster. He's *my* boy!'

'What? That's all right then. Let's give your boy a present. Would you like that?'

'Yes, I would!'

'Fine. I'll give him one. But now it's time for you to go to sleep.'

'Good-bye until tomowow,' the little girl said as she held out her hand. 'Bless you until tomowow!'

The lady was amazed and exclaimed:

'Who taught you that – Grandma?'

'Ye-es.'

When she had gone the lady beckoned me over with her finger.

'What shall we give you?'

I said that I did not want any presents, but that she might let me have a little book. She lifted my chin in her warm, perfumed hands and asked me with a pleasant smile:

'So you like reading then? What books have you read?'

She looked even more beautiful when she smiled. I was very embarrassed and mentioned the names of a few novels.

'What is it you like about them?' she asked, putting her hands on the table and quietly tapping her fingers. She had the sweet, strong smell of certain flowers, which blended strangely with the smell of horse sweat. She looked at me seriously and thoughtfully through her long eyelashes, as no one had ever looked at me before.

Because of the large amount of soft, fine furniture the room was as cramped as a bird's nest. The windows were covered with the thick greenery of plants and snowy-white Dutch tiles in the stove gleamed in the darkness. Next to the stove was a glossy black piano. Some scrolls printed in large, slanting Church Slavonic letters and framed in dullish gold looked down from the walls. Under each one a large dark seal hung on a thick cord.

I explained as best I could that my life was very difficult and boring, but that reading books made me forget it.

'Oh, really?' she said getting up. 'Rather well said. Not at all bad! Well then, what have we got? I'll lend you some books, but I haven't many just now. However, you can start with this one . . .'

She took a tattered volume bound in yellow from the divan.

'Read that and then I'll give you part two. There's four parts altogether.'

I went away with Prince Meshchersky's *Secrets of St Petersburg* and started reading the book very seriously. But from the very first pages it was clear that the secrets of St Petersburg were far more boring than the secrets of Madrid, London and Paris. The only amusing story was the fable of Freedom and the Stick.

'I'm taller than you,' Freedom said, 'and therefore I'm cleverer.'

But the Stick answered:

'No, I'm taller than you, so *I'm* stronger.'

They argued and argued and started fighting. The Stick beat Freedom and I remember Freedom dying in hospital from its injuries.

There were descriptions of nihilists in the book. I remember that according to Prince Meshchersky a nihilist was such a venomous person that he made chickens die if he just happened to look at them. The word 'nihilist' did appear offensive and indecent, but that was about all I understood and I became very depressed since, quite clearly, good books were beyond me. I was convinced however that the book must have been a good one, for surely such a dignified and beautiful lady would not read bad ones.

'Well, did you like it?' she asked when I returned Meshchersky's yellow-bound novel.

I found it very hard to say no, as I thought it would make her angry. But she only laughed as she went behind the screen into her bedroom and brought out a little volume bound in blue morocco.

'You'll like this one, but don't get it dirty!'

It contained the narrative poems of Pushkin. I read them all at one sitting, seized by that hungry feeling that one gets upon finding an undiscovered, beautiful place, when one tries to take it all in at one glance . . . It was the feeling one has after a long trudge over mossy hillocks in a marshy forest, when suddenly a dry clearing covered in flowers and drenched in sunlight opens up. One stands there looking for a moment, enchanted by the sight, and then one walks all over it and each time one's foot touches the soft grass growing on the fertile earth one experiences a calm feeling of joy.

The simplicity and music of Pushkin's poetry amazed me and for a long time prose seemed artificial and I had difficulty in reading it. The *Prologue* to *Ruslan and Lyudmila* reminded me of Grandmother's best stories, all miraculously compressed into one, and several lines startled me with their beautifully expressed truth.

> There, on paths strange and rare,
> Are the tracks of creatures unseen –

I repeated those wonderful lines to myself and I saw those unknown paths which were in fact very familiar to me, those mysterious footprints which had flattened the grass, still laden with dew drops as light as quicksilver.

I could memorize those melodious lines with amazing ease, and always used them when I wanted to describe things in gay, festive colours. They made me feel happy, and my life became easy and pleasant. Indeed, they heralded a *new* life for me. What bliss it was to be able to read! Pushkin's wonderful fairy stories in verse were closer and more comprehensible to me than anything else. After reading them a few times I could memorize them perfectly. I would go to bed and whisper poetry with my eyes shut until I dropped off to sleep. I often told those stories to the orderlies who would listen, guffaw and swear in a friendly sort of way. Sidorov would stroke my head and say softly:

'Isn't that marvellous, eh? Oh God . . . it's marvellous!'

My master and mistress noticed that I had become very elated and the old woman grumbled:

'Been doing nothing but read, the little devil! The samovar's not been cleaned for four days! Just give me a rolling-pin!'

What was a *rolling-pin*? I defended myself against her with the following lines:

> The old witch with her black soul
> Loves all things evil . . .

The beautiful lady stood higher than ever in my eyes when I thought of the books she read. No, she wasn't a simple cutter's wife, a mere piece of Dresden china . . .

When I took the book back and sadly handed it to her she said with conviction:

'So you liked it? Had you heard of Pushkin before?'

I had already read something about him in some journal but I wanted *her* to tell me all about him, so I replied 'No'.

Briefly she told me about Pushkin's life and death and then, smiling like a spring day, she said:

'So you see how dangerous it is to love women!'

From all the books I had read I knew that this was in fact dangerous, but it was good as well, and I said:

'It is dangerous, but everyone loves someone! And women suffer as well . . .'

She looked at me as she looked at everything – with her eyes half closed and she said seriously:

'Oh? So you understand all about it? Then I hope you will never forget!'

Then she began asking me what poetry I liked. I waved my arms and began reciting by heart. She listened to me in silence, seriously, then she got up, walked up and down the room, and said thoughtfully:

'And you, my dear little savage, must go to school now! I'll see what I can do . . . Are you *related* to your master and mistress?'

When I told her that I was she exclaimed: 'Oh!', as though she were criticizing me.

She gave me the *Songs of Béranger* in a fine edition with engravings, gilt-edged pages and a red leather binding. Those songs, with their strange mixture of bitter sorrow and unrestrained gaiety, almost made me go out of my mind. I went cold all over as I read the Old Beggar's bitter words:

> I am a harmful worm: Do I worry you?
> Why don't you crush me underfoot!
> Why feel sorry? You'd do better to stamp on me!

> Why did you never teach me,
> Give me an outlet for my wild strength?
> An ant would have grown from the grub!
> I would have died embracing my brothers,
> An old tramp.
> I call for vengeance on people!

I laughed until I cried when I read after this *The Lamenting Husband* and I remember particularly well Béranger's words:

> The art of living gaily
> Is not difficult for the simple!

Béranger aroused an ebullient gaiety in me, a desire to play the fool, to make impudent, caustic remarks to everyone – and I soon became an expert at this. I learned his poems by heart as well and read them very enthusiastically to the orderlies when I dropped into their kitchen for a few minutes. But I soon had to give this up, since the lines:

> A hat like this does not become
> A young girl of seventeen years!

made those men talk obscenely about girls, which infuriated me almost to the point of madness and I hit Ermokhin on the head with a saucepan. Sidorov and the other soldiers snatched it away from me. But from then onwards I decided to keep away from that kitchen.

They did not allow me to go out in the street, and there was no time for it really, as I had more and more work to do. Besides my usual chores as maid, house-boy and 'errand boy' I had to nail canvas on to wide pieces of wood every day, stick the building plans on them, copy out the master's accounts, and keep an eye on what the subcontractor spent. The master worked from morning till night, just like a machine.

At that time the buildings which had belonged to the state in the fair became the private property of traders and the shopping centre was being hurriedly rebuilt. My master took on contracts for repairing shops and building new ones. He drew up plans for 'altering arches, putting a dormer window in a roof' and so on. I used to take these drawings to an old architect, together with an envelope containing a twenty-five rouble note. The architect would take the money and sign the drawings: 'An accurate drawing; all works supervised by Imyarek.' Of course, he had not even seen that the plans were a true copy and he could never have supervised the work, as he did not leave the house at all, because he was ill. I took bribes round to the fair supervisor as well and to some important people in the town, from whom I received 'authorizations to commit any crime', as the master called them.

For my trouble I was allowed to wait on the front door step for my master and mistress when they went out in the evenings. This did not happen very often, but if they did go out to visit friends they came back after midnight and I would sit for several hours on the landing by the front door, or on a pile of wooden beams opposite the house and look into the window of my lady's flat, eagerly listening to the gay conversation and music. The windows there were kept wide open. Through the curtains and thick foliage I could see the trim figures of officers moving from one room to another, the round major bowling along and 'my lady' floating through space, dressed amazingly simply and beautifully. I invented my own name for her: Queen Margot.

'That's the kind of life they write about in French novels,' I thought as I looked at the windows, and this always made me feel a little sad. With my child's jealousy it hurt me deeply to see all those men near Queen Margot, circling round her like bees around a flower.

A less frequent visitor was a tall, gloomy officer with a scarred forehead and deep sunken eyes. He always brought a violin with him and played wonderfully, so well that passers-by would stop under the windows and people from the whole street would sit listening on piles of beams. Even the master and mistress – if they happened to be home – opened the windows, listened to the musician and showered him with praise. I cannot remember them praising anyone else except the cathedral archdeacon and I knew very well that fish-liver pies were more to their liking than music. Sometimes the officer sang and recited poetry in a muffled, breathless voice as he pressed his palm to his forehead. Once, when I was playing under the window, the little girl and Queen Margot asked him to sing.

183

For a long time he kept refusing and then he said in a clear voice:

> 'Only a song needs beauty
> But beauty needs no songs . . .'

I liked those lines very much and for some reason I felt sorry for the officer.

I found it more pleasant to look at 'my lady' when she sat at the piano and played when there was no one in the room. The music intoxicated me and I would see nothing except the window and, beyond it, the shapely figure and noble profile of a woman in the yellowish lamp light. Her white hands would fly like birds along the keyboard. I looked at her, listened to that sad music and my imagination would run riot: I would go off and find a hidden treasure somewhere and give all of it to her to make her rich! If I were Skobelev I would have declared war on the Turks again, demanded a ransom and built a house on Otkos – the best part of the town – and given it to her, so that she could leave that street and that house where everyone said such insulting and vile things about her. The neighbours and all the servants in the yard, and my master and mistress in particular, all spoke about Queen Margot as maliciously and spitefully as they had done about the cutter's wife, but rather more cautiously, and they would lower their voices and keep looking round the whole time. Perhaps they were afraid of her because she was the widow of a very important man, and the scrolls on the walls of her room had been given to her husband's ancestors by the tsars Godunov, Alexei and Peter the Great. The soldier Tyufyaev, who could read and write and who was always reading the Bible, told me this. Perhaps people were afraid that she might beat them with her whip with that lilac-coloured stone in the handle and they said she had already used it on some important civil servant. But whispered words are no truer than those spoken out loud; 'my lady' lived in a cloud of hostility which I could not understand and which tormented me. Viktor used to say that when he came home after midnight he would look through Queen Margot's window and see her sitting on a couch with only her shift on while the major knelt down, clipped her toenails and dabbed them with a sponge.

When she heard this the old woman swore and spat, while the young mistress screeched and went red in the face:

'Viktor, ugh! Has he no shame! What a disgusting lot they all are!'

The master smiled in silence. I was grateful to him for keeping silent, but I was terribly frightened in case he took sides with them and joined in the general shouting and howling. The women screeched and sighed as they cross-examined Viktor in great detail, asking him exactly where the woman was sitting, how the major was kneeling. And Viktor added some details of his own:

'His face was red and his tongue was hanging out!'

I saw nothing disgusting in cutting a lady's toenails, but I could not believe he had stuck his tongue out, and this seemed a terrible lie. I said to Viktor:

'If it was wrong then why did you look through the window? You're not a child . . .'

This made them all swear at me but it had no effect and all I wanted to do was to run downstairs, kneel in front of the lady like the major and ask her:

'Please leave this house!'

And now, when I knew that there was a different kind of life, different people, feelings and thoughts, that house with all its inhabitants aroused an even stronger feeling of revulsion in me. It was entangled in a filthy network of shameful scandal, and there was not a person there about whom malicious things were not said. The regimental chaplain, a sickly, pathetic specimen, was branded as a drunkard and lecher. According to my employers, the officers and their wives all committed adultery. The stories the soldiers told me about women, which were always the same, repelled me: but my master and mistress disgusted me more than anyone else. I knew very well the true value of the cruel judgements they loved to make about other people. Observing the vices of others was of course the only amusement which was free of charge. My master and mistress amused themselves by subjecting others to this verbal torture and they seemed to be taking it out on others because they themselves had to lead such respectable, hard and deadly boring lives.

When people said filthy things about Queen Margot I went

through emotional upheavals that an ordinary child does not normally experience and my heart burst with hatred for those vile-tongued slanderers. I was overcome by an irresistible longing to irritate everyone, to make trouble and sometimes I was overcome by pity for myself and for everyone else. This silent pity was even more painful to bear than active hatred. I knew more about the 'Queen' than they did, and I was afraid that they might discover this.

On holidays, when the master and mistress went to late mass at the cathedral, I went to see her in the mornings. She would invite me into her bedroom and I would sit in a small armchair upholstered in yellow silk. Her little girl would climb on to my knees and I would tell her mother about the books I had read. The 'Queen' used to lie on a wide bed with her tiny hands crossed under her cheeks. Her body was covered by a veil, which was yellow like everything else in that bedroom, and her dark hair, plaited into one big tress, fell across her dark shoulders and sometimes touched the floor.

As she listened to me she looked into my face with her gentle eyes and said with the faintest of smiles:

'Well, what have you got to tell me?'

Even that friendly smile was only the condescending smile of a queen for me. She spoke in a deep, affectionate voice and she seemed to be saying the same thing over and over:

'I know that I am incomparably better, purer than everyone else and I have no time for any of them.'

Sometimes I found her in front of her mirror. She would be sitting in a low armchair combing her hair: the ends lay on her knees, on the arms of the chair and dropped across its back, almost touching the floor. Her hair was as long and thick as Grandmother's. I could see her dark firm breasts in the mirror and while I was there she would put on her bodice and stockings. Her pure nakedness, however, did not arouse any feelings that I could be ashamed of and all I felt was a joyful pride in her. She always smelled of flowers and this warded off any base thoughts. I was healthy and strong, and I knew the secrets of men's behaviour towards women. But people spoke about those mysteries with such heartless malice, such cruelty, so vilely, that I could not picture her in the arms of a man, and I found it hard to imagine that anyone had the right to touch her impudently and shamefully, that any man could claim that he possessed her. I was convinced that the kind of love that went on in the kitchens and cellars was unknown to Queen Margot, and that she knew a purer, higher joy, a different kind of love altogether.

Once, however, just before evening, I went into the lounge and heard the sonorous laugh of the lady of my heart coming from behind the screen and a man's voice saying:

'Wait please ... Good God, I don't believe it ...'

I knew that I should have left there and then but I just could not bring myself to ...

'Who's that?' she asked. 'You? Come in ...'

There was a strong smell of flowers in the bedroom and it was dark, with the curtains drawn. Queen Margot was lying on her bed with a sheet up to her chin, while beside her lay the officer who played the violin: all he had on was a shirt undone down the front. He had a scar on his chest as well as his face, running in a red line down from his right shoulder and it was so shiny that I could see it quite clearly, although it was dark. The officer's hair was comically rumpled and for the first time I saw a smile on his sad, scarred face. He had a strange way of smiling, and he looked with his large woman's eyes at the Queen as though he were seeing her beauty for the first time.

'That's my friend,' said Queen Margot and I was not sure whether she meant me or the officer.

'Why are you so frightened?' I heard her say in a voice which sounded a long way off. 'Come here.'

When I went up to her she put a warm, bare arm round my neck and said:

'You'll grow up one day, and then you'll be happy ... Off with you now!'

I put the book back on the shelf, took another and left as though I were dreaming. Something went snap in my heart. Of course I did not think for one moment that my queen loved like other women and the expression on the officer's face was living confirmation for me: he was smiling joyfully, like a child when it is taken by surprise, and this brought a wonderful transformation to his sad face. He must have been in love with her –

it was impossible, surely, for anyone *not* to love her. And I could well understand her pouring out her love for him, as he played the violin so wonderfully and read poetry with such feeling. But the very fact that I found I needed to console myself with these thoughts made it clear that all was *not* well, that I was mistaken in my judgement of the situation and in my adulation of Queen Margot. I felt I had suffered some loss and for several days I was deeply depressed.

Once I ran wild and got up to some terrible tricks. When I called to borrow a book my lady said in a very stern voice:

'You're a real terror these days, so they tell me! I would never have thought it.'

I could not remain silent any longer and I began telling her how sick I was of life and how it upset me to hear nasty things said about her. At first, as she stood by me with her hand on my shoulder, she listened to what I had to say seriously, very attentively, but soon she started laughing and gently pushed me away.

'That's enough, I know that already. Do you understand? I *know*!'

Then she took me by both hands and said in a very warm voice:

'The less attention you pay to all that filth, the better it will be . . . Why don't you wash your hands properly?'

But this was unfair: if she had to polish copper, scrub floors and wash napkins *her* hands would have been just as dirty as mine – or so I thought.

'If a man lives respectably people get angry with him and jealous. If he doesn't, then he is despised,' she said thoughtfully. Then she pulled me over to her, embraced me and smiled into my eyes.

'Do you love me?'

'Yes.'

'Very much?'

'Yes.'

'But *how* much?'

'I don't know.'

'Thank you. You're a wonderful boy. I like people loving me!'

She smiled and wanted to say something, but instead she sighed and was silent for a long time – and she did not let go of me.

'You must come here more often. Whenever you have the chance . . . just come along.'

I took advantage of this offer and my visits did me a great deal of good. After dinner when the master and mistress had gone to bed I would run downstairs and if she happened to be home I would sit with her for an hour at a time – sometimes even longer.

'You must read some Russian books. You must know your own Russian way of life,' she told me, sticking pins into her sweet-smelling hair with her nimble, pink fingers.

When she had read out a list of Russian writers she would ask:

'Do you think you can remember them?'

She often spoke in a thoughtful voice, in which I could detect a slight note of annoyance:

'You must study, study. But I've forgotten all about such things! Oh God!'

After I had sat with her I would run upstairs with a new book and I felt as though I had been inwardly cleansed. I had already read Aksakov's *Family Chronicle*, that wonderful epic *In the Forests*, the marvellous *Hunter's Notebook*, a few slim volumes of Grebyonka and Sollogub,* the poetry of Venevitinov, Odoevsky, Tyutchev. Those books purified my soul, cleansing it of the superficial layer of impressions produced by that bitter, miserable reality. I came to appreciate what good books really were and realized how much I needed them and they gradually gave me a stoical confidence in myself: I was not alone in this world and I would not perish!

When Grandmother arrived I was in raptures as I told her about Queen Margot.

Grandmother took a sniff of tobacco, savoured it and said as though she really meant it:

'Well, that's very good! There's a lot of good people in this world but you have to look hard to find them!'

*Count V. A. Sollogub (1814–82), memoirist and author of the satirical novel *The Coach*. (Trans.)

Once she suggested:

'Do you think I should go and thank her for all she's done?'

'No, it's not necessary.'

'All right then ... Good God! How wonderful everything is! I'd like to live for ever and ever!'

Queen Margot did not succeed in making me go to school, as by Whitsun something quite horrible happened which was very nearly the end of me.

Not long before the holiday my eyelids swelled up terribly and my eyes closed completely. The master and mistress were frightened that I was going blind. I was frightened too and they took me to a well-known doctor, Henrich Rodzevich, who made incisions on the inside of my lids. For a few days I lay with my eyes bandaged, in terrible, unrelieved boredom. On the evening before Whitsun they took the bandages off and I got up again. It was just as though I had risen from a grave in which I had been buried alive. Nothing can be more terrible than losing one's sight. Blindness is an indescribable handicap, an insult to man, depriving him of nine tenths of his world.

When the gay Whit Sunday arrived I was let off all my duties after lunch, since I had been ill, and I was free to wander round the kitchens and visit the orderlies. Everyone, except that strict disciplinarian Tyufyaev, was drunk. Before evening came Ermokhin hit Sidorov on the head with a log and he fell down unconscious in the hall. The terrified Ermokhin ran off into the gully.

The 'news' that Sidorov had been killed quickly spread round the yard. People gathered outside the front door and looked at the soldier who lay motionless across the entrance to the kitchen with his head on the hall floor. They whispered to each other that someone should fetch the police, but no one went, and no one could bring himself to touch the soldier. Natalya Kozlovskaya, the laundress, who was wearing a new lilac-coloured dress and a white shawl over her shoulders angrily pushed the crowd away, went into the hall, squatted down and said in a loud voice:

'You idiots, he's alive! Get some water!'

The crowd started telling her:

'Don't poke your nose into other people's business!'

'I said get some water!' she shouted, just as though a fire had broken out.

She lifted her new dress above her knees, straightened her petticoat and propped the soldier's bleeding head on her knee. The crowd left, very timidly, muttering their disapproval. In the darkness of the hall I could see the angry glint of the laundress's tear-stained eyes and her round, white face. I brought a bucket of water and she told me to pour it over Sidorov's head and chest, at the same time warning me:

'Now don't pour any over *me* . . . I've got to go out this evening.'

The soldier regained consciousness, opened his dull eyes and groaned.

'Lift him up,' Natalya said, as she caught hold of him under his arms and held him away from her in case her dress got stained. We carried him out into the kitchen and laid him on a bed. The laundress wiped his face with a wet rag and told me as she left:

'Keep wetting the rag and hold it to his head while I go and find that fool Ermokhin. Those stupid devils'll drink themselves into hard labour, you mark my words!'

She pulled off her dirty petticoat, flung it into a corner, carefully adjusted her rustling, crumpled dress and went out.

Sidorov stretched himself, hiccuped and groaned. Thick dark drops of blood trickled down on to my bare feet. This was not very pleasant, but I was too frightened to move. It was really horrible.

Outside, the day was radiant and festive and the steps and gates were decorated with young birch twigs. Each door post had freshly cut maple and ash branches tied to it. The whole street was gay with greenery and everything looked young and new. From early morning it had seemed that the spring holiday had come to stay and from that day onwards life would be purer, brighter and gayer.

The soldier vomited and a stifling smell of warm vodka and green onion filled the kitchen. Now and again dim, broad faces with flattened noses pressed against the windows and with a hand on each cheek they seemed to have grown monstrous

191

ears. The soldier tried to remember what had happened and muttered:

'What? How did I get here? Did Ermokhin hit me? A fine friend!'

Then he started coughing, cried drunken tears and moaned:

'My little sister . . . my little sister!'

He got to his feet, slimy, wet and stinking, staggered and slumped on to his bunk. His eyes rolled strangely as he said:

'Nearly killed me, he did.'

All this seemed very funny to me.

'What the hell are you laughing at?' the soldier asked, giving me a stupid look. 'How can you laugh? They nearly finished me off!'

He pushed me away with both hands and murmured:

'First was Elijah the Prophet, then came St George, and then . . . don't come near me. Clear off, you little wolf!'

I told him not to be so stupid. He really looked absurd when he lost his temper. Then he shouted and shuffled his feet.

'They've nearly killed me and all you can do . . .'

Then he hit me hard over the eyes with his limp, filthy hand and I screamed. I could not see any more but somehow I managed to leap out into the yard where I bumped into Natalya. She was leading Ermokhin by the hand and shouting:

'Come on, you old horse.'

Then she caught hold of me and asked:

'What's the matter with you?'

'He's been fighting me.'

'Fighting, eh?' she said in a surprised, drawling voice. Then she gave Ermokhin a tug and said:

'Well, you devil, you'd better thank God he's still alive!'

I washed my eyes and looked out through the hall door where I saw the two soldiers making it up, embracing each other and crying. Then they both tried to embrace Natalya who pummelled them with her fists and shouted:

'Get your paws off, you filthy dogs! What do you think I am — one of your tarts? Lie down and try and sleep it off before your masters come home. Hurry up or you'll be for it!'

She put them to bed like little children, one of them on the floor, the other in the bunk, and when they were snoring away she went out into the hall.

'I've got blood all over me and I was dressed to go out! Did he hit you? The idiot! That's what a drop of vodka does ... Don't touch it ... ever ...'

Afterwards I sat with her by the bench near the gates and asked her why she was not afraid of drunks.

'And I'm not afraid of men when they're sober, either. I know how to keep them under control!'

She showed me a tightly clenched red fist.

'I had a husband once, he's dead now. He drank like a fish as well. When he was drunk I'd tie his arms and legs up and when he'd slept it off I'd take his trousers down and give him a good thrashing with some strong twigs. Then I'd say to him: "Don't drink, don't ever get drunk again. You married me, so you should enjoy your wife, not vodka!" Yes! I'd whip him until I had no strength left and after that he was like putty in my hands.'

'You're a strong woman,' I said, remembering Eve, who deceived God.

Natalya sighed and said:

'A woman needs more strength than a man, she needs enough for two, but God did not give her a fair share! You can never trust men ...'

She spoke calmly, without any malice, and sat there with her arms folded across her large breast, leaning back against the fence, sadly staring at the embankment which was littered with filth and broken bricks. I listened with delight to her clever words, forgot all about the time, and suddenly saw my mistress and master walking arm in arm at the other end of the embankment. They were walking slowly, solemnly, just like a turkeycock with its hen, and they seemed to be saying something to each other as they stared at us. I ran to open the front door. As she came up the steps the mistress said to me in a venomous voice:

'Flirting with laundresses? Is that what the woman downstairs taught you?'

This was such a stupid remark that it did not even upset me. I was more insulted when my master grinned and said:

'Well, it's about time!'

Next morning as I went to the shed for firewood I found an empty purse near the little opening in the door for cats. I had seen Sidorov carrying it dozens of times and I immediately took it to him.

'Where's the money?' he asked as he felt inside the purse. 'There should be one rouble thirty. Hand it over!'

He had a towel wrapped round his head like a turban. His face was yellow and thin and he blinked his swollen eyes angrily and just would not believe that the purse was empty when I found it. Ermokhin appeared and started trying to convince him I was lying. He nodded towards me and said:

'*He* stole it, take him to the master. Soldiers don't steal from each other!'

From what he said I guessed that he had stolen the money and had thrown the purse into that part of the shed where I went for the firewood. Straight away I shouted right in his face:

'You're lying! *You* stole it.'

And I became firmly convinced that I had guessed correctly. His oaken face started trembling with fear and rage, he spun round and screeched.

'Prove it then!'

But how could I? Ermokhin shouted and dragged me out into the yard. Sidorov followed us and shouted as well. A few heads were poked out of the windows, and Queen Margot's mother calmly looked on, puffing her cigarette. I realized that I was finished as far as they were concerned and this made me nearly go out of my mind. I remember the soldiers holding me by the arms while the master and mistress stood opposite us, each agreeing with the other and listening sympathetically to the complaints. The mistress said with great conviction:

'Yes, that's *his* work all right! Only yesterday he was flirting with the laundress by the gates. That means he had money, for you won't get anything from *her* without paying for it!'

'Quite right,' Ermokhin said.

The ground sank beneath me and I got into such a mad rage that I roared at my mistress, for which I was well and truly flogged. But the beatings did not bother me so much as the thought of what Queen Margot thought of me now. How could I prove my innocence? It was a bitter time for me then.

Fortunately the soldiers quickly spread the story round the whole yard and street and by the time it was evening I could hear Natalya Kozlovskaya shouting down below as I lay upstairs in the attic:

'No, why *should* I keep my mouth shut? Come on! I said come on, or else I'll go to the master myself. He'll make you come!'

At once I realized that I was the subject of the uproar.

I could hear Natalya shouting near the front door and her voice became louder, and more and more triumphant.

'How much money did you show me yesterday? Where did you get it? Tell me!'

I was breathless with joy when I heard Sidorov wailing:

'Oh, it was Ermokhin...'

'So you blackened the boy's name and got him a flogging as well!'

I wanted to run down into the yard, dance with joy and gratefully kiss the laundress's hand, but at that moment my mistress shouted out from one of the windows:

'The boy was beaten for *swearing*. No one accused him of being a thief, except you, you slut!'

'My dear lady, you're a slut yourself – *and* a cow if I may be permitted to say so.'

Their slanging-match was like music to my ears and my heart felt as if it had been scalded with boiling tears prompted by both the injury done to me and by my gratitude towards Natalya. I almost choked trying to hold them back.

Then the master slowly came upstairs to the attic, sat on a rafter near me and said smoothing his hair:

'Why are you always so unlucky, Peshkov?'

I turned away in silence.

'All the same, you *do* use filthy language.'

But I quietly answered:

'When I'm able to get up again I'll be leaving this place.'

He sat for a little without saying a word, smoking his cigarette and after he had scrutinized the stub he said softly:

'That's your affair! You're no longer a child and you should know what's best for you.'

And he left me. As always, I felt sorry for him.

Four days later I left that house. I very much wanted to say good-bye to Queen Margot, but I did not have the courage to call on her, and I must admit that I was expecting her to invite me over herself.

As I said good-bye to the little girl I asked her:

'Please tell mama that I'm very grateful to her, *very*! Promise to tell her?'

'Yes,' she said, giving me a warm, tender smile. 'Good-bye until tomowow then, yes?'

I met her twenty years later, when she was married to an officer in the gendarmerie.

Chapter 11

AND once again I became a dish-washer, on the *Perm*, a fast spacious steamship as white as a swan. This time I was an 'assistant' dish-washer or 'galley boy' and I was paid seven roubles a month to help the cooks.

The waiter in charge of me was fat, bloated with conceit, and as bald as a rubber ball. He would place his hands behind his back and pace wearily round the deck for days on end just like a bear looking for a shady spot on a hot day. The restaurant was 'embellished' by his wife, a woman of over forty. Although she was very pretty she went around looking rather scruffy and she used so much powder it used to fall from her cheeks on to her dress in a white sticky dust. The galley was in the charge of a chef with the nickname 'Bearcub'. He was a small fattish man with a hawk-like nose and mocking eyes. He was something of a dandy, wore starched collars and shaved every day. His cheeks were bluish and he kept his dark whiskers twisted upwards. In his free time he never left these whiskers alone for one moment, straightening them with his red fingers that looked as if they had been roasted, and continually peering into a round hand-mirror.

The most interesting person on board was the stoker Yakov Shumov, a broad-chested man with a squarish figure. His snub-nosed face was as flat as a shovel and his tiny bearlike eyes were hidden under his thick eyebrows. His cheeks were covered with fine ringlets of hair resembling moss from a swamp and the hair on his head was matted into a thick cap so that he had difficulty running his crooked fingers through it. He was an expert card player and he amazed everyone with his capacity for food – he would hang round the galley like a hungry dog, begging for pieces of meat, for bones, and in the evenings he would drink tea with Bearcub and tell startling stories about himself.

When he was a boy he used to help the town shepherd of Ryazan. Then a monk who happened to be passing lured him away to a monastery, where he served as a novice for four years.

'And I'd still be a monk now – God's black star!' he said very quickly and breezily, 'if a pilgrim from Penza hadn't turned up. Funny little thing she was, completely turned my head. "You're a fine strong man," she said, "but I'm an honest widow, all on my own now. You can come and work for me if you like. I've my own little house and I make my living selling feathers and down." "All right then," I said and she took me on as a house porter. I became her lover and lived off her very nicely for three years . . .'

'You're a barefaced liar!' Bearcub interrupted as he anxiously inspected the pimples on his nose. 'If people paid you for lying, you'd be worth thousands!'

But Yakov just kept chewing away. The dark grey ringlets danced on his empty-looking face and his hairy ears twitched. Then he continued his story in that same measured, rapid voice:

'She was older than me and I got sick of her. So I latched on to her niece. But the widow found out and threw me out by the scruff of my neck.'

'And that's the least you deserved,' the cook said in the same easy, flowing voice as Yakov's.

After he had stuffed a piece of sugar into his mouth the stoker carried on with his story: 'I messed around for a bit and then hooked myself on to an old pedlar from Vladimir and off we went round the whole world. We went to the Balkan mountains, visited the Turks and Rumanians, the Greeks and Austrians – we went to every country, selling to some people or buying from others.'

'And what about *stealing*?' the cook asked seriously.

'What? Why, the old man told me I must behave honestly in foreign countries. The law's so strict they'll cut your nut off for the least thing! True, I did try stealing, only I wasn't very good at it. I tried to steal a merchant's horse, but I was caught and of course they beat the living daylights out of me and hauled me off to the police station. There were two of us in the same cell, one a regular horse-thief and just me there more out of curiosity than anything else!

'I had worked for that merchant, put a new stove in for him in his bath-house and then he became ill. He had a bad dream about me and he got frightened and off he went and told the prison authorities "Let him go", which really meant: "Let him go or else he'll start dreaming that I won't get better! He's a wizard!" I ask you – a wizard! Well, the merchant was well known in that town, so they let me go.'

'They shouldn't have let you go – they should have put you in a tub of water for a few days to soak all that nonsense out of you!' the cook said.

Yakov immediately agreed:

'Yes, there's a lot of nonsense in me. To be honest with you, there's enough for a whole village!'

The cook stuck his finger inside his collar, which was too tight for him, and angrily pulled at it, shaking his head and bitterly complaining:

'What a load of rot! A convict like you goes guzzling, drinking, lounging around doing nothing and for. what? Well, tell me, what are you living for?'

The stoker chewed away and said:

'I don't know. I just live. One man lies down, another walks around. A clerk sits on his backside.'

This infuriated the cook even more:

'That means you're such a pig there's no words to describe you! And you eat just like one . . .'

'What are you shouting about!' Yakov would reply in surprise. 'All men are acorns from the same tree. Please don't swear – it won't make me any better! . . .'

Right from the start that man had a magnetic attraction for me. I would look at him in astonishment and listen to his stories with my mouth wide open. I thought he had some deep knowledge of life that no one else possessed. He spoke to everyone very familiarly, without standing on ceremony, kept peering at us all from underneath his bushy eyebrows with a most independent look, and it seemed that he was reducing everyone – the captain, the steward, even important passengers travelling first class – to the same level as himself, as the sailors and waiters and the third-class passengers. He would stand in front of the captain or one of the engineers with his long apelike arms behind his back and listen silently while he was told off for being lazy or for coolly cheating someone at cards. He would just stand there silent and motionless and it was quite obvious abuse had no effect on him and that any threats to throw him off the ship at the next port did not frighten him in the least. There was something about that man that made him different from everybody else and like 'Just the Job'. He was clearly aware of this and realized that people did not understand him. I never saw him upset or deep in thought, and cannot remember him keeping quiet for very long. Words always flowed from his hair-fringed mouth in a continuous stream and sometimes it seemed he was powerless to stop them. When people told him off, or if he was listening to some interesting story, his lips would start twitching as though he were repeating what he had just heard or was quietly carrying on saying something of his own. Every day when he came off watch he climbed out of the stoke hatch – barefooted, sweaty, smeared with oil and wearing a damp shirt without a belt, with the thick curly hair on his chest showing through the unbuttoned front. And then his even, monotonous, rather hoarse voice would start flowing over the deck, scattering words like drops of rain.

'How are you, dear? Where are you going? To Chistopol? I know it, I worked for a rich Tartar there. He was an old man, called Usan Gubaidulin, and he had three wives. Very healthy he was, with a red face. One of his wives was an amusing little Tartar girl. I sinned with her . . .'

He had been everywhere and wherever he had been he had 'sinned with women'. He never talked spitefully about anything and he would usually speak calmly, as though he himself had never been insulted or abused.

After a few minutes I would hear his voice coming from somewhere astern:

'Card players are a fine crowd! And there's no end of games you can play! They are a really great comfort. You can earn money sitting down just like merchants do.'

I noticed that he rarely used the words 'good', 'bad', 'nasty', but 'amusing', 'comforting' and 'curious', instead. For him a beautiful woman was an 'amusing butterfly', a fine sunny day – a 'comforting little day'. But his favourite expression was: 'To hell with it!'

Everyone thought he was lazy, but it struck me that he did

that difficult job right at the mouth of the furnace, in hellish, stifling heat, just as conscientiously as anyone else, and I cannot remember him ever complaining of exhaustion like the other stokers.

Once someone stole a purse from an old lady passenger. This happened one bright, calm evening when all the passengers were in a good mood and feeling very friendly. The captain immediately gave the old woman five roubles and the passengers made a small collection. When they gave the money to the old woman she crossed herself, bowed down to the ground and said:

'Dear friends, you've given me too much!'

Someone shouted cheerfully:

'Take as much as you can, and don't make a fuss. A three-rouble note is never too much!'

Someone added very pointedly:

'Money's not like people – you can *never* have too much of it!'

But Yakov went up to the old woman and said very seriously:

'Give me what's over then and I'll play cards with it.'

All the passengers laughed, thinking that the stoker was joking, but with great determination he went on trying to talk over the old woman, who did not quite know what to do.

'Hand it over, dear. What do *you* need it for? Tomorrow you might be in your box!'

At this everyone swore and drove him away. He shook his head and said to me in amazement:

'People *are* strange! Why do they poke their noses into what doesn't concern them! After all she herself said that they'd given her too much. And I could have done with a little extra!'

The sight and feel alone of money must have fascinated him. As he talked, he loved polishing silver and copper on his trousers so that the coins gleamed. Then he would twitch his eyebrows and closely examine the coin as he held it up in front of his snub-nosed face with his crooked fingers. But he could not be called greedy. Once he suggested I play cards with him, but I didn't know how to.

'Don't know?' he said in amazement. 'How's that? You

can read and write. I must teach you then. Let's play for lumps of sugar.'

He won a half pound of sugar and stuffed the lumps into his hairy cheeks. Afterwards, when he thought that I had learned enough, he said:

'Let's play seriously now. Have you got any money?'

'Five roubles.'

'And I've two and a bit.'

Of course, he won all my money but I wanted to get it back and staked my coat worth five roubles, and lost. Then I put my new shoes, worth three roubles, and lost them as well.

Yakov then said in a dissatisfied, almost angry voice:

'No, you can't play, you're too hot-headed. Off with your coat and shoes! No, I don't really need them. Take your clothes and your four roubles back. I'll keep one – for the lesson. All right?'

I was extremely grateful to him, and I said so. But he answered my gratitude with:

'To hell with it! A game's only a game, to pass the time, and you're trying to make a big issue out of it! You mustn't get mad or pick a fight. Just make sure you come out even! You're a young boy and you must take a firm grip on yourself. If you don't succeed the first time or the fifth, then say to hell with it – but only after you've tried for the seventh! Then you must clear off out of it. If you catch cold, then try again. That's what the game's all about!'

I began to dislike him more and more. Sometimes his stories made me think of Grandmother. There was much about him that was appealing, but his indifference to people, which would clearly never leave him as long as he lived, really disgusted me.

Once, when the sun was setting, a drunken passenger from the second class – a fat merchant from Perm – fell overboard and started splashing about in the reddish-gold water. The engines were quickly stopped and the ship came to a halt, its paddles beating up clouds of foam which the setting sun turned red. A dark body, already a long way astern, floundered in the blood-coloured foam and a wild, heart-rending scream echoed down the river. The passengers screamed as well and jostled each other at the rails and crowded the stern. His friend, a red-faced, bald man who was also drunk, pummelled everyone with his fists, dashed to the rails and roared:

'Clear off! *I*'ll save him!'

Two sailors had already dived overboard and were striking out towards the drowning man. A dinghy was lowered astern and above the shouting of the crew, the screaming of women, I could hear the calm, measured flow of Yakov's husky voice:

'He's going to dro-own because he's wearing a coat. You're bound to drown in a long coat. Just take an example: why do women drown more often than men? Because of their skirts. As soon as a woman falls into the water she goes straight to the bottom like a thirty-six-pound weight. See for yourself! He's drowned already! I know what I'm talking about!'

The merchant had in fact drowned. They searched for two hours or more but could not find him. His friend, who had sobered up by then, was sitting astern, panting away and mumbling pathetically:

'So that's the end of *his* journey! What am I going to do now? What shall I tell his family, eh? He's *got* a family . . .'

Yakov stood in front of him with his hands behind his back and tried to comfort him:

'Don't worry! After all, no one knows when he's going to die. One man can eat some mushrooms and two seconds later he's dead! Thousands of people eat mushrooms to keep healthy, but for one man they can mean death. And what *are* mushrooms, after all?'

He looked broad and strong as he stood there like a millstone in front of the merchant and showered him with words as though they were oats. At first the merchant cried without saying anything in reply and he wiped the tears from his beard with his broad palms, but then, after he had listened to Yakov for a while, he began howling:

'You devil! Why do you have to torment me, why? Fellow-believers, please take him away, or I'll do him an injury!'

Yakov calmly said as he went away:

'People are crazy. I try and help him and he starts picking a fight with me.'

At times I thought the stoker was an idiot but more often

than not it seemed that he was deliberately pretending to be stupid.

I was determined to find out about his travels around the world, about what he had seen, but I never managed to get anything out of him. He would toss his head back, barely open his dark, bearlike eyes, stroke his hairy face and start speaking in that drawling voice:

'People are like ants, my friend. They're all the same! I'm telling you, where there's people there's trouble. Most people are just like peasants. The world is covered with them, like autumn leaves. You ask about Bulgarians? I've seen them, and Greeks too. And Serbs and Rumanians and all kinds of gipsies! What are people really like? Well, in towns they're townspeople, in villages they're peasants! They're all very much alike anywhere you go. Some even speak our language – although very badly – like the Tartars for example, or the Mordvinians. The Greeks can't speak Russian, and they babble away any old how. You think they're using words, but it's impossible to understand them and you have to use sign language. But the old man I worked for pretended he understood the Greeks and used to mumble *Karamara* and *Kalimera*. He was a cunning old boy. He could tell them what was what! So you want to know what people are really like? You're a strange boy. What do you expect people to be like? Of course, some are black. The Rumanians are black, but they have the same faith as us. The Bulgarians are black as well, and they believe in the same God too. But as for the Greeks – they're like the Turks.'

It struck me that he was not telling me everything and that he was hiding something that he did not want to talk about. I knew from illustrations in journals that Athens was the capital of Greece and that it was a very ancient and beautiful city. But Yakov sceptically shook his head and dismissed Athens:

'That's all lies, my friend. There's no such town. But there's *Athos*, only it's not a city but a mountain with a monastery on it. It's called holy mount Athos. There's pictures of it and I've seen an old man selling them. There's also a city called Belgrade on the Danube – it's just like Yaroslavl or Nizhny. The cities there are ugly but the villages are another matter. And their women ... well ... a *comfort* to last you all your days! I very nearly stayed abroad because of one – what on earth was her name now?'

He firmly pressed his palms against his blind-looking face and his wiry hair made a soft crackling noise, while from somewhere deep down in his throat came the sound of laughter which reminded me of the jangling of a cracked bell.

'Men tend to be forgetful. And when I was with *her* I used to . . . She cried when it was time to say good-bye. And *I* did too, oh yes!'

With a calm arrogance he started teaching me how to treat women. We would sit at the stern of the ship while the warm moonlit night swam towards us. The meadows along the shore were barely visible beyond the silvery water of the river. From the hilly banks yellow lights winked and they were just like stars captured by the earth. Everything around me was moving and trembling, never resting, but leading a quiet purposeful life all of its own. Yakov's rasping words would break that sad, enchanting silence:

'Yes, she would throw her arms out like she was being crucified.'

Yakov's story was a shameless one, but it did not revolt me. There was nothing boastful or cruel about it and it struck me as simple and rather sad. The moon in the heavens was just as shameless in its nudity and just as disturbing and it made me feel very sad. I would try and remember only the good things that I had known in my life – Queen Margot and those lines of poetry which contained so much truth that I could never forget them:

> Only a song needs beauty
> But beauty needs no song.

I would rouse myself from my dreamy mood as though I had just woken up and once again I would start questioning the stoker about his life, about what he had seen on his travels.

'You're a strange boy,' he would say. '*What* can I tell you? I've seen everything. Ask me if I've seen a monastery and I'll say yes. And pubs? I've seen them as well. I've seen how gentlemen live and how peasants live. I've eaten plenty in my time, and I've gone hungry.'

He would reminisce just as if he were slowly crossing a deep river by a shaky, dangerous bridge:

'Well, then, I was in prison once, for horse stealing, and I was thinking to myself I was bound for Siberia. But the police officer started swearing away, saying that the stove in his new house was smoking. So I said to him: "That's something I can mend, your honour." But he said: "Shut up! The best workman couldn't do anything with *that* stove." But I replied: "It sometimes happens that a shepherd is cleverer than a general." I was capable of saying anything then – it was all the same to me, with Siberia waiting for me! So he said: "Go and have a try then, but if you make it worse I'll break your bones into little bits."

'I finished the job in two days and he was very surprised and started shouting at me: "You fool! Blockhead! You're a master craftsman and yet you have to go stealing horses. Why?" I said to him: "That, your honour, was just stupidity on my part." "Yes, that's precisely what it was. I'm sorry for you!" Yes, he was *sorry* for me. Ever seen anything like it? A policeman, who must show no mercy with people, was *sorry* for me!'

'Well, what happened?' I asked.

'Nothing. He took pity on me. What else would you expect?'

'How can anyone feel sorry for *you*? You're just like a stone!'

Yakov replied good-humouredly:

'You're a strange boy! A stone eh? You should feel sorry for stones as well. They serve their purpose and streets are paved with them. You should feel sorry for all things: *everything* is here for some reason. What's sand for? Blades of grass grow in it!'

When the stoker spoke like this it became abundantly clear that he knew something that was beyond my understanding.

'What do you think of the cook?'

'Old Bearcub?' he replied rather indifferently. 'What do you expect me to think? Not much.'

He was right. Ivan Ivanovich was so terribly upright and correct in all he did, so faultless that he left no impression at all. The only interesting thing about him was that he did not like the stoker and always swore at him. But he always invited him to drink tea with him.

Once he said to Yakov:

'If serfdom came back and I were your master I'd have you flogged seven times a week, you lazy devil!'

Yakov observed solemnly: 'Seven times is a lot!'

While the cook told the stoker off he would feed him some scraps, rudely shoving a piece of meat in front of him and saying: 'Eat!' Yakov would take his time, chew it and say:

'I'll grow up to be a big boy, thanks to you, Ivan Ivanych!'

'And what do *you* need strength for, you lazy devil?'

'Why? Because I'm going to live a long time!'

'And why should *you* live? You hobgoblin!'

'Hobgoblins have to live as well. Now tell me, being alive is very amusing, isn't it? It's a great *comfort*, being alive, Ivan Ivanych!'

'What an idiot you are!'

'*What* did you say?'

'Id-i-ot.'

'What a word to use!' Yakov said in astonishment.

But Bearcub added:

'Well, listen then. *We* sweat blood, dry our bones up in that hellish heat in the kitchen, while *he* stuffs himself like a wild pig!'

'Well, that's how it goes,' the stoker said as he chewed away.

I knew very well that stoking the furnace was more difficult and hotter than working at the kitchen stove. Several times during the night I tried to help Yakov stoke the furnace and I was surprised that he never wanted to show the cook how difficult his job was. No, that man knew something nobody else did . . .

Everyone used to tell him off – the captain, the engineer and the bo' sun – everyone, in fact, for whom this was not too much of an effort. I thought it was very strange that they did not give him the sack. I could see that the stokers treated him much better than the others, although they too laughed at his incessant chatter and card-playing. I used to ask them:

'Is Yakov a *good* man?'

'Old Yakov! He's all right. He's not what you would call touchy, so you can do what you like with him, even stuff hot coals down his shirt!'

Because of the way he slaved down in the boiler-room and because of his horse-like appetite, the stoker got very little sleep. He would come off shift sweaty and filthy all over and hang around the stern all night, chattering with the passengers or playing cards – often not bothering to change his clothes at all. When he stood there in front of me he looked like a locked trunk which had something hidden away in it and I stubbornly tried to find a key to open it.

'I can't understand what you're trying to get out of me,' he said as he surveyed me with those eyes that were almost completely hidden by his bushy eyebrows. 'Yes, I've covered a lot of ground in my time. What *else* do you want to know? Listen, then, and I'll tell you what happened to me once.'

And he would start telling me about his life:

'Once upon a time there lived in some provincial town a young judge who suffered from consumption. He had a healthy German wife, who had borne him no children. Now this German fell in love with a textile merchant, who was also married, to a beautiful woman, and he had three children.

'Now the merchant saw that the German girl had fallen for him, so he decided to make a fool of her. He arranged a meeting with her in the garden one night, invited along two of his friends as well, and told them to hide in the bushes. It was wonderful! The German girl turned up and there she was – all ready to go away. The merchant said to her: "My hands are tied, as I'm a married man. But I've brought two of my friends along for you. One's a widower, the other's a bachelor." The German gave him one in the face and he fell backwards over a bench. Then she started hitting his face with the heel of her shoe. I had followed her, as I was the judge's house-boy, and I looked through a hole in the fence and saw things were really beginning to happen. Then the two friends jumped out and caught hold of the woman by the hair. But I leaped over the fence and separated them and said: "That's no way for gentlemen and merchants to behave!" That German girl had really believed him and it was a dirty trick to play on anyone! As I led her away they hit me on the head with a piece of brick.

'The German was very miserable now and started wandering round the house and saying to me: "I'm going back to Germany to my own people, Yakov. As soon as my husband dies I'm off!" So I said to her: "Yes, of course you must go back." The judge died and off she went. She was kind and gentle and so sensible. And the judge was a gentle person as well, God rest his soul!'

I could not understand the moral of the story and remained speechless. I felt there was something familiar, cruel and absurd in it, but what could I say?

'A good story?' Yakov asked.

This would make me angry and I would start telling him off but he would calmly explain:

'People are well fed and content. Well, sometimes they like to have their little joke but it falls flat. Tradespeople are a serious lot, of course. You need a lot of brains to be in business. But it's boring just living on your wits. Now and again you want to have some fun...'

The foaming river rushed swiftly past the stern and I could hear the seething of flowing waters and the dark shore seemed to be flowing slowly along with them. Passengers were snoring away on the deck and a tall, dried-up looking woman in a black dress and with nothing on her grey head silently picked her way towards us between benches and sleeping bodies. The stoker nudged me with his shoulder and said:

'Look, *she's* fed up.'

Now I thought that he really found it amusing when other people were sad.

He told me a lot of things and I listened eagerly. I remember all his stories very well, but cannot recall one that was cheerful. He sounded much more dispassionate than books, in which I could often actually sense what the author was feeling himself – whether he was angry or gay, sad or in a mocking mood. The stoker never laughed or passed judgement, and it was quite plain to me that nothing really offended him or made him feel glad. He used to sound like an apathetic witness in front of a judge, like a man for whom defendants, prosecutors, judges were all strangers. This indifference irritated me even more and aroused feelings of strong hostility towards him. Life appeared to burn away before him like the fire in the furnace under the boilers, where he would stand with a wooden mallet in his leathery, bearlike paw and gently tap the nozzle to regulate the flow of oil.

'Has anyone ever insulted you?' I asked.

'Who would dare to do that? I'm too strong, you should see how I can hit back!'

'I'm not talking about fighting. I mean – your *soul*.'

'It's impossible to insult the *soul*. You can't reach it. You can't touch the human soul with *anything* . . .'

The third-class passengers, the sailors, everyone on board in fact, spoke as often about the soul as they did about the earth, work, bread and women. The soul was a common word in the vocabulary of simple people, in constant use, like a five-kopek piece. I did not like those slimy tongues using that word so much, with so much familiarity, and it broke my heart when men spoke obscenely and reviled it. I remember very clearly how careful Grandmother was when she talked about the soul, which for her was a mysterious repository of love, beauty and joy. I firmly believed that when a good man died white angels carried his soul up into the blue sky, to Grandmother's kind God, who warmly welcomed it and said: 'Well, my dear, my pure one, have you suffered much and worn yourself out with work?' And he would give the soul seraphim's wings – six white ones.

Yakov Shumov spoke about the soul as carefully and as reluctantly as Grandmother. When he swore he never even mentioned the soul and when others started arguing about it he remained silent, keeping his red bull's neck bent low. When I asked him what the soul was he would reply:

'The soul is the breath of God.'

That did not mean much to me and I would ask something else. The stoker would then lean forward and say:

'Even *priests* don't understand much about the soul, my friend. It's something quite mysterious . . .'

I constantly thought about him, wracking my brains in an effort to understand him, but in vain. Apart from him I could see nothing and his broad body blotted everything else out.

A stewardess called Gavrilovna was so friendly towards me that it made me very suspicious. In the morning she made me fetch the water for her wash-basin, although that was really the job of Lusha, a clean-looking, jolly chambermaid from the second-class cabins. When I stood there in that cramped cabin next to that woman who would be stripped to the waist and looked at her yellow body which was as flabby as sour dough I could not help comparing it with Queen Margot's dark body, cast from bronze, and it made me feel disgusted. The stewardess would keep talking about something the whole time, often in a plaintive, grumbling voice, or else angrily and mockingly.

I could never grasp what she was trying to say, although I seemed to be able to guess and it was really pathetic, miserable and shameful. But I did not let it upset me as I lived in a world far from the stewardess and from everything that was happening on board, and I seemed to be screened from it by Yakov, who was like a large mossy stone blocking out that world from me, a world that appeared to be floating away somewhere night and day. I seem to hear Lusha's mockery even now: 'Our Gavrilovna's fallen head over heels for you' and as though in a dream I can hear her say: 'Wake up and take your happiness while you can.' Not only did Lusha make fun of me, but all the stewards and waitresses knew of Gavrilovna's 'weakness', which made the cook frown and say:

'That woman's tasted everything. She just wanted a little pastry, *un baiser*! . . . Ugh, pe-ople! Keep your eyes open wide, Peshkov – very wide!'

And Yakov also started giving me paternal advice:

'Of course, if you were two years older I would have spoken to you differently, but at your age . . . it's . . . best not to give in! But if you really feel like a little bit of what you fancy! . . .'

'Stop it,' I said. 'It's disgusting!'

'All right then.'

Then he would immediately start pouring out his sharp little sentences again as he tried to ruffle up his flattened hair:

'You must see it from the woman's point of view as well . . . her job's wretched, miserable . . . If a dog likes being stroked, a human being likes it even more. A woman *thrives* on affection, just like a mushroom loves the damp. She should be ashamed of herself, I know, but can she help it? The body needs petting, that's all.'

I would stare expectantly at his darting eyes and ask:

'Are you sorry for her?'

'Me? What is she, my mother, eh? You don't feel sorry for mothers . . . you're a strange boy!'

He laughed and sounded like a cracked drum. Sometime when I looked at him I seemed to be falling into a deathly void, a bottomless pit, into complete and utter darkness.

'Everyone else is married. Why aren't you, Yakov?'

'What for? I can always get a woman . . . it's easy. A married man has to stay in the same place and be a good peasant. But my land is poor because my uncle came and took the little I had. My little brother came home from the army just to have it out with him and to take him to court. And then he gave him one on the head with a stick. The blood just poured out. He got eighteen months for that and there's only one road after you've been in prison! Straight back to prison again. His wife was a *comforting* young girl . . . Oh, what's the use of talking? When you're married you're boss of your own kennel, but a soldier is never his own master.'

'Do you pray to God?'

'You're a funny boy! Of course I do.'

'How?'

'All sorts of ways.'

'What kind of prayers do you say?'

'I'm not too well up on prayers. I know the simple ones "Lord Jesus, spare the living, let the dead rest in peace, save us, oh Lord, from sickness." And some other ones . . .'

'Such as?'

'Come off it! Whatever you say reaches God in the end.'

He was kind to me, and took a lively interest in me, as though I were a smart puppy which could perform clever tricks. I used to sit with him at night-time, when he smelled of oil, burning, and onions . . . He loved onions and used to gnaw away at the moist bulbs as though they were apples. Then he would suddenly ask:

'Come on, Alyosha, let's hear some poetry!'

I knew a lot of poetry by heart and besides, I had a thick exercise book in which I had copied out my favourite poems. would read *Ruslan* and he listened without so much as budging, appearing to have gone deaf and dumb and trying to stop wheezing. When I had finished he would say softly:

'There's a *comforting* little story and well put together! Did you make it up? Did you say it's by *Pushkin*? There was some gentleman called Mukhin-Pushkin, I saw him once...'

'Not *him*. This one was killed a long time ago!'

'Why?'

I told him the story briefly, in the way Queen Margot used to tell me.

Yakov listened and then said calmly:

'A lot of men seem to be ruined through women.'

I often told him the different stories that I had found in books, and they had all become mixed up and fused together into one very long story about a restless, beautiful life, abounding in fiery passion, full of mad exploits, lofty nobility, fabulous triumphs, duels and deaths, pure words and vile deeds. In my interpretation Rocambole acquired the knightly features of La Mole, of Hannibal and Colonna; and Louis XI came to resemble Père Grandet. Cornet Otletaev became one with Henri IV. This long story in which, as though inspired, I had changed people's characters, mixed up events, represented a world where I was free to do what I wanted – like Grandfather's God, who played around with things as he liked. However, that literary chaos of my own creation did not prevent me from seeing reality as it truly was, did not dampen my desire to understand real living people and it protected me with its transparent but impenetrable veil from the infectious filth and deadly poison of life. Books made me invulnerable to many things. Since I knew how people really loved and suffered, I found it impossible to visit brothels. The idea of a few kopeks' worth of debauchery filled me with revulsion – and with pity for the people for whom it was so sweet. Rocambole taught me how to be strong, how not to surrender to the force of circumstances; the heroes of Dumas made me want to dedicate myself to some important, lofty task. My favourite hero was gay Henri IV, and I thought Béranger's wonderful song must have been written about him:

> He gave the peasants many privileges
> And liked a drink himself.
> Yes, if all the nation was happy,
> Why shouldn't the King drink?

213

Novels portrayed Henri IV as a good man, close to his people. He was as bright as the sun and convinced me that France was the most beautiful country on earth, the country of knights, who looked noble whether they were dressed in royal cloaks or in peasant's clothes. Ange Pitou was the same sort of knight as d'Artagnan. When Henri was assassinated I cried bitterly and gnashed my teeth in anger at Ravaillac. That king was almost always the hero of the stories I told the stoker and it seemed that Yakov had also fallen in love with France and 'Henrik' as he called him.

'That King Henrik was a good man. You could have gone fishing with him if you liked.'

Yakov never got excited, never interrupted me with questions, but listened in silence, with lowered eyebrows and motionless face – which made him look just like an old stone covered with mould. But if I stopped for some reason he would immediately ask:

'Is that the end?'

'Not yet.'

'Well, why did you stop?'

He used to sigh when he talked about the French:

'They live where it's nice and cool.'

'Why's that?'

'Well, where we work it's hot, but they're always in the shade. They have no businesses to look after, all they do is drink and lounge around – a *comforting* life!'

'But they work too.'

'You wouldn't think so from your stories,' he said quite rightly, and suddenly it became clear to me that the overwhelming majority of books I had read said absolutely nothing at all about how those noble heroes worked or how they earned their living.

'Well, I'm going to have a nap,' Yakov would say, leaning back exactly where he was sitting. A moment later his nose would start whistling at regular intervals.

In the autumn, when the banks of the Kama had turned reddish brown and when the trees were gold and the slanting rays of the sun became white, Yakov left the ship quite unexpectedly.

The evening before he went he told me:

'The day after tomorrow we'll be in Perm. We'll go into a bath-house and have a good steam and then we'll go off to a pub where there's music – that will be a *comfort*. I love watching them playing the accordion.'

A fat man came on board at Sarapul. He had a flabby face, just like a woman's, without any beard or whiskers. His warm, short coat and his cap with ear mufflers made from fox fur made him look even more like a woman. He immediately sat down at a table near the galley where it was warmer, asked for a cup and saucer and started drinking some yellow infusion without unbuttoning his overcoat or taking his cap off. The whole time he sweated profusely.

A perpetual drizzle came down from the autumnal clouds and it seemed that it would slacken off when this man wiped the sweat from his face with his checked handkerchief and that it would fall heavier when he started sweating again.

Yakov soon sat down next to him and they both began looking at a map. The new passenger ran a finger over it while the stoker said in a calm voice:

'Well? What of it? It's nothing. To hell with it . . .'

'Very good,' the passenger replied in a thin little voice as he stuffed the map back into an open leather bag at his feet.

Before Yakov went on duty I asked him who the man was. He grinned and said: 'He's a castrate. From Siberia – a lo-ong way away! Funny man, travels up and down the convict routes.'

He left me and stamped over the deck with his dark boots, which sounded as heavy as horses' hoofs. Then he stopped again and scratched his side.

'I'm going to work for him. So when we get to Perm – it's good-bye! I'll be going by train first, then along the river and then perhaps by horse even! The journey might take five weeks – it's a long way! . . .'

'Do you know him?' I asked, surprised by Yakov's sudden decision.

'How could I? Never seen him before. Never even been where *he* comes from . . .'

In the morning Yakov appeared dressed in a short, dirty

215

coat, old boots and Bearcub's tattered brimless straw hat. He squeezed my hand in his iron-like fingers and said:

'Coming with me? He'll take you as well if you like. Want me to ask? He'll give you more money if you let him cut something off! For them it's a form of worship mutilating a man and they'll pay you for it . . .'

The castrate stood by the rails with a little white parcel under his arm and stared at Yakov with his dead eyes. He had a heavy bloated look about him – just like a drowned man. I told Yakov what I thought of him, in not too loud a voice, and the stoker kept squeezing my hand.

'Well – to hell with him! Each man has his own god to pray to – whom do *we* have anyway? Well, good-bye then, and the best of luck!'

And Yakov Shumov went away rolling along from one foot to another, just like a clumsy bear. He left a strange, uneasy feeling in my heart. I was sorry and annoyed with him at the same time and perhaps just a little envious. I thought anxiously to myself: why had that man gone off to a place he knew nothing about?

And – what kind of a man *was* Yakov Shumov? . . .

Chapter 12

AT the end of autumn, when the steamboats stopped running, I became an apprentice in an ikon workshop. I had not been there a day when my drunken old mistress said to me in her Vladimir accent:

'The days are short now and the evenings are long. During the day you'll be working in the shop and in the evenings you'll study!'

I was put in the hands of a small, nimble-footed assistant. He was a young man with a face that was handsome in a sickly sort of way. In the cold darkness of dawn I used to go right across the town with him along the steep Ilinka street, where the merchants lived, to Nizhny market.

The ikon shop was on the first floor. It was a converted warehouse, very dark, with an iron door and one small window looking out on to a gallery covered in with an iron roof. The shop was crammed full of ikons of different sizes, ikon cases, and books printed in Church Slavonic and bound in yellow leather. There was another shop next door to ours which sold ikons and religious books as well and it was owned by a black bearded relative of a Bible scholar from the Old Believers, who was well known on the other side of the Volga, especially in the Kerch region. The shopkeeper was helped by his dried-up looking, quick-witted son who had the small grey face of an old man and the darting eyes of a mouse. After opening the shop I had to fetch hot water from the pub. When they had drunk their tea I had to tidy up, dust the ikons and then hang around in the gallery outside to keep an eagle eye on prospective customers and stop them from going into the shop next door.

'Customers are *idiots*,' the assistant used to say in a voice full of conviction. 'They couldn't care less where they buy, as long as it's cheap, and they haven't a clue what they're paying for.'

He would snap his finger on some ikon boards, boast about his expert knowledge of the trade and start giving me lessons:

'This is a fine little piece and cheap at the price. Six or seven inches high ... doesn't need a stand ... and another, ten to

eleven inches high . . . doesn't need a stand either . . . Do you
know your saints? Remember: Vonifaty guards against drunk-
enness. Varvara the Martyr against toothache and sudden
death. Vasily the Blessed against fevers. Know your Virgins?
Look: there's the Virgin of the Sorrows, the Virgin of the
Three Arms, the Virgin of the Abalatskaya Apparition, Do not
Mourn for Me, Soothe my Grief, the Kazan Virgin, Pokrova,
Semistrelnaya . . .'

I soon memorized the value of the different ikons according to
their size and the quality of their craftsmanship, and I learnt
how to tell the difference between ikons representing the different types of Virgin. But it was very difficult to remember
what each saint stood for. I would be standing by the door lost
in thought when the assistant would suddenly start testing my
knowledge:

'Who helps with a difficult birth?'

If I answered wrongly he would disdainfully ask:

'What have you got a head for, eh?'

It was even harder enticing customers into the shop. I did
not like those crudely painted ikons and it was awkward
selling them. From what Grandmother told me I imagined
the Holy Virgin as young, beautiful and kind. She looked like
this in pictures in journals, but in ikons she was old and forbidding, with a long crooked nose and wooden arms. On
Wednesdays and Fridays – which were market days – trade was
brisk and now and again peasants and old women appeared in
the gallery, sometimes whole families. All of them were Old
Believers from across the Volga, and they were a distrustful,
gloomy lot who lived in the forests. One would see a cumber-
some-looking man draped in a sheepskin and thick home-made
clothes making his way along the gallery so slowly that he
seemed frightened of falling through. He made me feel awkward and ashamed. After a great effort I would bar his path,
dart around his heavy boots, buzzing like a mosquito:

'What would you like, sir? Psalters with commentaries, the
works of Efrem Sirin, Kirillov's canon law, prayer books?
Please have a look round, sir. Any kind of ikon you like at all
prices, best workmanship, fine dark colours. We can paint any
ikon to order, all the saints and Virgins. Perhaps an ikon for a

birthday or for the family? This is the best workshop in Russia! The busiest shop in town!'

The apathetic, phlegmatic customer would stand for a long time without saying a word, eyeing me up and down as though I were a dog and then he would suddenly brush me aside with the dead weight of his arm and go into the shop next door, while the assistant would rub his big ears and growl angrily at me:

'You've gone and lost a cust-om-er . . .'

Next door I would hear a soft, cloying voice droning away, and intoxicating words:

'We don't sell sheepskins here, or shoes, but God's blessing, which is purer than silver or gold! You can't put any price on it!'

'To hell with it!' my assistant would whisper with envy and admiration in his oily voice. 'He knows how to smooth that old peasant over all right! Take a lesson from him!'

Now I was a very conscientious apprentice: if one did a job then it had to be done properly. But I had little success in luring customers into the shop and selling the ikons. I really felt sorry for those gloomy taciturn peasants, those little rat-like women who seemed in a perpetual state of terror with heads downcast. I wanted to tell them, in secret, what the ikons were really worth and I just did not want to try and get an extra twenty kopeks out of them. All of them struck me as poor and hungry, and it was strange to see them paying three and a half roubles for a psalter – a book that they used to buy more than any other. They amazed me with their knowledge of religious books and ikon painting. Once a greyish old man whom I had managed to coax into the shop said to me abruptly:

'It's just *not* true that your workshop makes the best ikons in Russia. The best is Rogozhin's, in Moscow!'

I was so taken aback that I stepped to one side but he quietly went on his way without even going into the shop next door.

'Did he rise to the bait?' the assistant asked me spitefully.

'You didn't tell me about *Rogozhin's* workshop.'

He started swearing:

'Those bloody hypocrites loaf around all day and think they

know everything! To hell with them! They understand *everything*, those old dogs!'

He was a handsome, well-fed, proud man and he hated peasants. At times he would complain:

'I'm *clever*. I like clean things, nice smells – like incense, *eau de cologne*. And yet I have to bow and scrape to some stinking peasant just to make him cough up another five kopeks for the mistress! Do you think I like it? What is a peasant anyway? Moth-eaten wool, a louse . . . but – they're *our living*!'

He lapsed into angry silence.

I liked the peasants and I felt that each one had something mysterious about him, like Yakov. A ponderous looking figure in a kaftan would come creeping into the shop. He would be wearing a half-length fur coat, a shaggy cap, and would cross himself with two fingers as he looked into the corner where the everlasting lamp flickered, trying not to lay his eyes on the unsanctified ikons and peering round the shop. Then he would say:

'Give me a psalter with a glossary.'

He would roll up the sleeves of his kaftan and stand there a long time reading the title page, twitching his dark, cracked and bleeding lips.

'Haven't you anything *older*?'

'Old ones cost thousands of roubles, you know very well.'

'Yes, I know.'

He would wet a finger and turn over a page, leaving a dark smudge where he had touched it. The assistant would glare down at him and say:

'*All* holy writings are ancient . . . God never changed his word!'

'Yes, so I've heard. God didn't change his word, but Nikon* did.'

And the customer would shut the book and leave without saying another word.

Sometimes those people from the forests would quarrel with

---

* A famous archbishop of the seventeenth century who revised the spelling in church books, and varied points of ritual. This led to a great schism in the Church. Those who opposed him were called 'Old Believers'. (Trans.)

the assistant and it was clear to me that they knew their Bible better than he did, and he would snarl and say:

'Those heathens from the swamps!'

I could see as well as he did that although peasants did not like new books, they treated them with respect, touched them carefully, half-expecting them to fly away at any moment like a bird from their hands. I loved to see them do this, since for me books were indeed something wonderful, and I thought that the soul of the writer was locked away in them: when I opened a book I was able to set this soul free and then it would have a secret conversation with me.

Very often old men and women would bring ancient books from the times before the Schism or copies of them which they wanted to sell. These books were beautifully made by hermits in Irgiz or Kerzhenets. They would bring copies of prayer books without Dmitry Rostovsky's corrections, ikons bearing ancient inscriptions, crosses, enamelled bronze triptychs which had been cast in village workshops, and silver ladles presented by the princes of Muscovy to wine merchants. All of these were offered in secret and the people who brought them kept anxiously looking round the whole time and hid them under their clothes. Both the assistant and our neighbour kept a close watch on them and tried to stop them going into each other's shop. They would both buy ancient objects for ten roubles and sell them in the fair to rich Old Believers for a hundred. The assistant used to give me instructions:

'Follow those devils and sorcerers, watch them as hard as you can! They bring happiness with them!'

When one of them turned up the assistant would ask me to go and fetch Pyotr Vasilich, a Bible scholar and an expert in old books, ikons and all kinds of church antiquities. He was a tall, old man with a long beard like Vasily the Blessed, clever eyes and a pleasant face. A bone in one foot had been cut away and he walked with a limp and had to use a long stick. Winter and summer he went around in a light coat that looked like a cassock, and wore a weird velvet cap resembling a saucepan. He was a strong, healthy old man, and as he strode into the shop he would stoop a little, gently sigh and frequently cross himself with two fingers, mumbling prayers and psalms. This mixture of piety and senile decay at once inspired confidence.

'How's business?' he would ask.

'Someone brought an ikon, said it was a Stroganov.'

'What?'

'A Stroganov!'

'Oho . . . I'm hard of hearing . . . The good Lord's made me deaf, so I can't hear those filthy things Nikonites keep saying . . .'

After he had taken his cap off he would hold the ikon horizontally, look at the wording from the side, at the joint in the back-board, blink and mutter:

'Those godless followers of Nikon knew how we loved ancient workmanship and were taught by the devil to practise malicious deceit. Now they forge holy images. They're very good at it, very good! At first sight one of their ikons really looks as if it's a Stroganov or an Ustyug, even a Suzdal, but if you examine it with your *inner* eye, then you'll see it's a forgery!'

If he called an ikon a forgery, it meant it was rare and valuable. A system of signals worked out beforehand told the assistant how much he should offer for an ikon or a book. I knew that 'gloom and dejection' meant ten roubles, 'Nikon the Tiger' meant twenty-five. I was ashamed to see how these people were taken in, but the Bible scholar's clever game fascinated me.

'Those followers of Nikon, that black offspring of Nikon the Tiger, are capable of *anything*, and are led by the devil. Now you might think this priming was genuine and the clothes painted by the same hand. But just take a closer look at the face – that's the work of a different brush. The old masters, even if they were heretics, like Simon Ushakov, painted the whole ikon themselves, including the clothes and face. And they planed the lynch-pin and primed the woodwork. But nowadays the miserable devils aren't up to it. Ikon painting used to be *holy* work, inspired by God, and now it's just another form of painting.'

Finally he would carefully place the ikon on the counter, put his cap on and say:

'It's a sin,' which meant: 'Buy it!'

The seller would be drowned by a river of words which were

sweet to him and he would be astonished by the old man's knowledge. Then he would ask respectfully:

'What about the ikon itself then, holy father?'

'The ikon . . . it's the work of the Nikonites.'

'That's impossible! My grandfather and great-grandfather prayed to it!'

'Old Nikon lived before *your* great-grandfather.'

The old man would lift the ikon up to the seller's face and say solemnly:

'Don't you see how *gay* it is? Call *that* an ikon? It's nothing but an ordinary picture, the work of a blind man, something the Nikonites painted to amuse themselves. It has no soul! Do you think *I* would lie to you? I'm an old man, I've been persecuted for my faith, my time will soon be up, so what have I to gain by being hypocritical?'

He would go out on to the gallery terribly offended by the fact that people did not trust his judgement. The assistant would then pay a few roubles for the ikon and the customer would bow low to Pyotr Vasilich as he left. They would send me off to the pub for some hot water for tea. When I came back the Bible scholar would be in a lively and cheerful mood, lovingly scrutinizing his purchase and telling the assistant:

'Look now: disciplined workmanship, finely painted from *the fear of God*. Nothing that would remind you of a mere mortal in *that* . . .'

'*Who* painted it?' the assistant would ask, beaming all over and jumping up and down.

'That's none of your business.'

'But how much would an *expert* give?'

'That I don't know. Come on, I'll offer it to someone.'

'Oh, Pyotr Vasilich! . . .'

'If I sell it, there'll be fifty roubles for you and anything above that'll be mine!'

'Oh!'

'Stop your oh-ing.'

They would drink their tea, shamelessly haggling and looking at each other with roguish eyes. The assistant was completely at the mercy of the old man, that was clear, and when the old man had gone he would·say:

223

'You there, mind you don't go blabbering to the mistress about what I've bought!'

When they had agreed on the price the assistant would ask: 'Any news from the town, Pyotr Vasilich?'

The old man would smooth his beard back with his yellow hand, revealing his oily lips, and start telling stories about the lives of rich merchants, about their business successes, their drunken sprees, illnesses, and weddings, about the infidelity of husbands and wives. He would tell those colourful stories swiftly and skilfully, like a good cook making pancakes, and his hissing laughter made a piquant sauce for them. The assistant's little round face would turn greyish brown with envy and rapture, and his eyes would mist over dreamily. Then he would sigh and say pathetically:

'Some people *know* how to live! But as for *me* . . .'

'Everyone has his allotted destiny,' the old man would drone away in his deep voice. 'One person's destiny is forged by the angels with little silver hammers, while another's is made by the devil, who uses the blunt end of an axe . . .'

That strong, sinewy old man knew everything that was going on in the town, all the secrets of the merchants, clerks, priests and townspeople. His eyesight was as sharp as a bird of prey and he had something of the wolf and fox in him. I always tried to annoy him but he would merely look at me as though he were standing a long way off and peering at me through a mist. He seemed to be surrounded by a boundless void: if I went close up to him I was sure I would fall into some deep hole. I felt that he had something of the stoker Shumov in him. Although the assistant deeply admired his intellect when he came to the shop or when he was away in the town there were times when, like myself, he wanted to provoke and insult the old man:

'You *like* cheating people,' he said suddenly, looking the old man straight in the face.

The old man smiled lazily and retorted:

'Only God doesn't live by cheating, but we ordinary mortals have to make our living from fools: if you can't swindle a fool then he's no use to you . . .'

The assistant flared up:

224

'But not *all* peasants are fools. Even some merchants were peasants once.'

'I'm not talking about merchants. Fools don't live by swindling: A fool is holy, only his brain's asleep!'

The old man spoke more and more lazily and this was exceedingly irritating. He seemed to be standing on a clump of earth surrounded by a quagmire. It was impossible to make him angry: either he was completely impervious to insults or he was an expert at controlling his temper. But very often he himself would start teasing me and he would come right up to me, grin into his beard and say:

'What was the name of that French writer? *Ponos**?'

This filthy trick of distorting names almost drove me mad but I just managed to control myself and answered:

'It's *Ponson* du Terrail.'

And he would make another horrible pun.

'Don't be so stupid, you're not a child,' I would exclaim.

'True. I'm not a child. What are you reading there?'

'Efrem Sirin.'

'And who writes better, your godless authors or this one?' I could not answer this question.

But he persisted:

'What do your godless authors write about mostly?'

'About everything that happens in life.'

'Then they must write about dogs, horses ... they're all part of life!... they all *happen*...'

The assistant guffawed, but I was fuming. All this was very trying and most unpleasant for me, but if I made any attempt to leave, the assistant would stop me.

'Where do you think you're going?'

Then the old man would start testing me:

'Come on, you're supposed to be able to read and write. Get your teeth into this one: a thousand nude people are standing in front of you, 500 women, 500 men, and among them are Adam and Eve. How would you find Adam and Eve?'

He would try for a long time to get an answer out of me and in the end would triumphantly announce:

*An untranslatable pun on the name Ponson. *Ponos* means diarrhoea in Russian. (Trans.)

'You fool, they weren't *born* but *created*, which means Adam and Eve don't have navels.'

The old man knew countless 'conundrums' like that and used them to torment people.

During my early days in the shop I used to tell the assistant about the few books I had read, and now they were turned against me and the assistant retold the stories in them to Pyotr Vasilich in a deliberately garbled and distorted version. The old man was very good at helping him by asking obscene questions. Their sticky tongues showered filthy words on Eugénie Grandet, Lyudmila, Henri IV. I realized that they did not do this from malice, but out of sheer boredom. But this did not help matters as far as I was concerned. They created piles of muck and wallowed in it like pigs, grunting delightedly from the pleasure of soiling and dirtying all that which was beautiful and therefore totally alien, incomprehensible and comical to them.

The whole shopping centre, all the people who lived there – the merchants and their assistants – lived strange lives, full of stupid, childish amusements which nonetheless caused much misery. If a peasant who had come up from the country for the day happened to ask the quickest way to some part of the town they invariably gave him wrong directions: they were so used to this 'diversion' that they no longer derived any pleasure from it. They would catch a pair of rats, tie their tails together, put them down in the road and watch them bite each other as they tried to free themselves. Sometimes they poured kerosene over a rat and set fire to it. Then they would tie a broken metal bucket to the tail of a dog so that it yelped and tore off in mad terror while the people looked on and laughed. There were many other pastimes like these and it seemed that everyone, especially the people from the country, lived solely for the amusements offered by the shopping arcades. One felt that they had an insatiable desire to laugh at other people, to hurt and embarrass them. And it seemed rather strange to me that those books I had read said nothing about the way people were always trying to make laughing-stocks of one another.

One of the amusements in the market was particularly disgusting. Below our shop there was an assistant who worked for a woollen and felt shoe merchant and he amazed the whole of the Nizhny market with his gluttony. His master used to boast about his assistant's 'talent' in the same way people boast about a fierce dog or a strong horse and he often used to place bets with neighbouring merchants.

'Who'll bet ten roubles? I bet you Mishka can eat ten pounds of gammon in two hours.'

But everyone knew that Mishka was capable of this and they would reply: 'We don't want the bet. Buy the ham though, and let him eat it. We'll watch! Only it must be all meat and no bones.'

They would argue lazily for a short while and then a thin, beardless boy with prominent cheekbones would emerge from the dark warehouse wearing a long overcoat made from thick cloth, tied round with a red sash and covered all over with bits of wool. He would respectfully take his cap from his little head and, without saying a word look vaguely with his deep-sunken eyes at his master's round face, which was flushed purple and overgrown with thick, wiry hair.

'Can you eat ten pounds of gammon?'

'In how long?' Mishka would ask in a businesslike, thin little voice.

'Two hours.'

'That's a tough one!'

'But not for *you*.'

'Give me two glasses of beer then.'

'Get weaving,' the master said, boasting to everyone for all he was worth. 'Don't you think for one moment that he's going to do this on an empty stomach. Far from it. Only this morning he stuffed himself with two pounds of bread and he had lunch as well of course . . .'

They would bring the ham and a crowd would gather round – stout merchants, tightly wrapped up in heavy fur coats and looking like enormous weights, and people with big bellies. All of them had tiny eyes misted over with a film of sleepiness and insurmountable boredom. They would sit round the champion glutton in a small circle, with their hands in their pockets, while he armed himself with a knife and a large crust of rye bread. He would fervently cross himself, sit down on a

227

bale of wool, put the ham on a box next to him and measure it with his vacant eyes. After cutting off a thin slice of bread and a thick lump of meat he would carefully make a sandwich out of it and lift it to his mouth with both hands. His lips would tremble as he licked it with his long, doglike tongue, showing his fine, sharp teeth. He looked just like a dog as he bent over the meat.

'He's started!'

'Keep an eye on the clock!'

All eyes were riveted on the glutton's face, on his lower jaw, on the round swellings near his ears. They would watch his pointed chin rise and fall regularly and emptily remark:

'Eats just like a bear!'

'Have you ever seen a bear eat?'

'You know very well I don't live in the forest! But that's what they say: "guzzles like a bear".'

'You mean a *pig* don't you?'

'Pigs don't eat ham . . .'

They would laugh grudgingly and immediately some expert would correct them.

'Pigs eat *everything*, including their piglets and their own sisters.'

The glutton's face grew browner and browner, his ears turned blue, his bulging eyes seemed to roll out of their bony sockets. He breathed heavily, but his jaw still kept moving with a regular rhythm.

'Get a move on, Mikhailo, not much time left!' they said, egging him on.

He anxiously estimated how much meat was left, drank some beer and started chewing again. The crowd livened up, and looked more often at the watch that Mishka's master was holding. Then they started giving orders:

'Mind he doesn't turn the watch back!'

'Take it away from him.'

'Watch Mishka doesn't stuff some ham up his sleeves.'

'He'll *never* finish in time.'

But Mishka's master would urge him on:

'I bet you twenty-five roubles! Mishka, *please* don't let me down.'

The crowd provoked the master more and more but no one placed any bets.

Mishka kept on chewing and chewing, and his face began to look like a piece of ham; his sharp, gristly nose made a mournful whistling sound. It was terrible watching him and I thought that at any moment he would shout out loud and start screaming: 'For God's sake, have pity!' or that he might get a piece of meat stuck in his throat, fall down at the people's feet and die.

In the end he ate everything, and his drunken-looking eyes bulged as he gasped:

'Give me something to drink!'

But his master looked at the watch and growled:

'You're four minutes over, you devil.'

And the crowd started teasing him:

'Good job we didn't make any bets, we would have lost!'

'But what an *animal* of a boy!'

'Yes, he should be in a circus.'

'The freaks that God sends into this world!'

'Come on, let's go and have some tea.'

And off they would sail to the pub, just like barges along the river.

I wanted to find out what had made those heavy people, who seemed to be made of cast iron, gather round that unfortunate boy and why his morbid gluttony amused them so much.

It was dark and miserable in that narrow gallery piled high with wool, sheepskins, hemp, rope, felt shoes, saddles and harness. It was separated from the passage-way by clumsy looking stout brick pillars that were eaten away by time and spattered with mud from the street. I must have made a mental note of every brick and the chinks in between them thousands of times, and the monotonous network of their ugly patterns settled in my memory for ever. People walked between the shops without hurrying, and carts and sleighs laden with merchandise moved slowly down the street. Behind the street there was a square formed by two-storeyed red-brick shops and it was always littered with boxes, straw, torn wrapping papers, and covered with filthy trampled snow. Everything there, despite the movement of people and horses, seemed motionless

229

to me – lazily rotating on the same spot to which it appeared to be fastened by invisible chains. I suddenly felt that this was an almost completely silent life, sadly lacking in any sounds of animation. The sleigh runners would screech, shop doors would slam, women selling pies and spiced tea would call out, but those voices were dreary, apathetic and monotonous, and one quickly grew so used to them that one did not even hear them. The church bells hummed as though they were ringing for a funeral and for a long time afterwards I could hear that mournful sound. It seemed to be perpetually floating in the air above the market, from morning till night, insinuating itself among all my thoughts and feelings, stifling every sensation, like a thick deposit of metal filings. Wherever I went I could sense a cold, tedious boredom which drifted upwards from the earth beneath its layer of filthy snow, from the grey drifts on the roofs, from the flesh-coloured bricks of the buildings. Boredom rose from the chimneys in a grey haze and climbed up into the greyish, empty, low sky. The horses sweated boredom, people breathed it. It had its own peculiar smell – the dull, heavy smell of sweat, fat, linseed oil, oven-baked pies and smoke. That smell seemed to press heavily against one's head, like a warm, tight-fitting hat; it seeped down into the chest and brought with it a strange feeling of intoxication, arousing a vague desire to close one's eyes, cry out loud in despair, to run off, to take a running jump head first at the nearest wall. I would peer into the merchants' fat, well-fed faces, which were flushed with thick rich blood and bitten by the frost, and quite motionless, as though they were all dreaming. The people there would never stop yawning, opening their mouths wide like fish thrown up on to dry sand. In the winter business was slack and the traders did not have that alert, predatory sparkle in their eyes which lent a little life to their faces during the summer months. Those heavy fur coats only cramped their movement and made them stoop towards the ground. They had a lazy way of speaking and when they became angry they would have arguments. I thought that they did this on purpose, just to show each other that they were alive! It was obvious that they were stifled by boredom, killed by it, that their cruel, stupid amusements could only be interpreted as a futile struggle against its all-consuming power.

Sometimes I would chat with Pyotr Vasilich about them. Although he usually mocked and ridiculed me, my passion for books appealed to him and sometimes he would condescend to have a serious talk with me, just like a teacher.

'I don't like the way those merchants live,' I would say.

He would curl some hair on his beard with a long finger and ask me:

'How do *you* know what kind of life they lead? How often do you go and watch them? This is a street and men don't *live* in it. Here they only do their trading and then clear off home as quick as they can. People dress up when they come out into the street, but you don't know what they're like under their clothes. A man lives openly in his own house, within his own four walls, but you can never know what kind of life he *really* leads there!'

'But don't people have the same thoughts, whether they're at home or in the streets?' I asked.

'Who knows what the next person's thinking?' he said, opening his eyes wide and speaking in a deep bass voice. 'Thoughts are like fleas – you can never count them. That's what old men say. Perhaps, when a man gets home, he falls down on his knees and cries, and asks God: "Forgive me, oh Lord, I've sinned on your holy day." Perhaps his house is a kind of monastery for him and he lives there alone with his God. Yes! Each little spider must know its place, weave its own web and know how much weight it can take . . .'

When he spoke seriously, his voice sounded even lower and deeper, as though he were telling some very important secrets.

'Here you are arguing away! You're too young for that! At your age you should rely on your eyes, not your brain. You should look, remember and keep your mouth shut. The brain's for *practical* things, but for the soul you need faith! Reading books won't harm you, but you must not overdo it – as with anything else. Some people read until they go mad and lose their faith in God.'

To me he seemed immortal and it was hard to imagine that he would ever grow old and look different. He loved telling stories about merchants, bandits and banknote forgers who had become famous. I had already heard many similar stories from Grandfather, who was better at telling them than the

Bible scholar. But their meaning was the same: riches are always acquired at the price of sinning against people and against God. Pyotr Vasilich had no compassion at all for people, but he spoke about God with deep feeling and he would sigh and cover his eyes.

'Some people manage to deceive God, but the Lord Christ sees it all and weeps. My people, oh my poor people, hell is waiting for you!'

Once I had the impertinence to tell him:

'But *you* swindle peasants as well . . .'

But he took no offence at this and gave me an answer:

'But is that very important?' he said. 'I might steal three or five roubles – but I don't keep them for very long.'

When he caught me reading he would take the book from me, ask carping questions about what I had read, and then tell the shop assistant disbelievingly:

'You see, he *understands* books, the little devil!'

And he would start lecturing me very sensibly, trying to make sure that I would never forget:

'Listen to my words, they'll come in useful some day: There were once two Kirills, both of them bishops, one from Alexandria, the other from Jerusalem. The first fought against the cursed heretic Nestorius, who was responsible for the obscene story that the Virgin was an ordinary woman and therefore couldn't have given birth to God, but bore a human being instead who was Christ in name and deeds, that's to say the saviour of the world. Of course, she couldn't be called mother of *God* but mother of *Christ* – understand? That is what you call heresy! The Kirill who came from Jerusalem fought against the Arian heresy . . .'

I was enthralled by his knowledge of church history. He would tug his beard with his smooth priestly hand and boast:

'I'm an expert in these matters. Once, at Whitsun I went to Moscow to take part in a verbal argument with those venomous learned followers of Nikon, with priests as well as laymen. Although I was only a young man then, I even discussed these things with professors. Oh yes! I flayed one of those priests with my verbal whip until his nose bled, so there!'

His cheeks grew flushed and his eyes sparkled. Making an

opponent's nose bleed was considered the peak of his success, the brightest ruby in the golden crown of his fame and he spoke about it almost voluptuously.

'He was a handsome little priest and very strong! He was standing in front of the pulpit and the blood just dripped from his nose! But he was blind to the disgrace of it all. He was a violent man, like a lion in the desert, and his voice was like a great bell! I attacked him very slyly and aimed straight at his soul. My words stabbed him right between the ribs, like awls! He got very heated up inside with all that heretical evil – just like a stove! Ah, we had *real* arguments in those days! . . .'

Other Bible scholars used to come into the shop: Pakhomy, a big-bellied man who wore a soiled, sleeveless coat; he was blind in one eye, fat and flabby, and he grunted like a pig. Then there was Lukian, a friendly, lively little old man who looked as smooth as a mouse. He would come with a large gloomy-looking man, who resembled a cabdriver, with a black beard, a lifeless, unpleasant but nonetheless handsome face, and eyes that never moved.

They almost always brought old books for sale, ikons, censers, and various kinds of chalices. Sometimes they brought some people with things to sell – usually old men or women from across the Volga. When business was over they would sit by the counter like crows on a hedge, drinking tea with rolls and boiled sugar and they would tell each other about the way the Church of Nikon was persecuting everyone: in one town a church was raided, and prayer books were confiscated. In another the police closed a chapel and arrested the priests in charge under Article 103. This Article was the most frequent topic of conversation, and they spoke very calmly about it, as though it were something inevitable, like the winter frosts. Again and again I heard the words 'police', 'raid', 'prison', 'court', 'Siberia' in their discussions about religious persecution and they burned my soul like hot coals, kindling sympathy and compassion for those old men. The books I read had taught me to respect people who persevered until they achieved their goal and to value steadfastness and firmness of spirit. I forgot all the bad things I saw in those people who taught about life and I was conscious only of their calm persistence, which concealed – or so it seemed to me – an unshakeable belief that what they were teaching was the truth, and they were ready to suffer all sorts of torment for it.

Later, when I had the opportunity of seeing many similar custodians of the old faith, both among the common people and the intelligentsia, I came to understand that this stubbornness was really the passiveness of people who had nowhere to go, and who in fact did not want to go anywhere, as they were firmly fettered by archaic words and outmoded ideas which had finally stupefied them. Their will had become static, incapable of any movement: when some blow from the outside world shifted them from the places they were used to, they would mechanically roll downwards, like stones on a hill. They were kept in the graveyard of their own obsolete beliefs by the sheer inertia of their memories, by their morbid love of suffering and oppression. But if one tried to deprive them of any *possibility* of suffering, then this would destroy them and they would disappear like clouds on a fresh windy day. The faith for which they were ready to suffer willingly and very proudly was undeniably strong, but it put me in mind of a worn-out dress which was so thickly soiled with every kind of filth that it would never be touched by the destructive power of time. In both thought and feeling they had grown used to their tight, heavy cocoon of prejudices and dogmas: although they had lost their wings and had been mutilated in their struggles they still had a cosy, comfortable resting-place. A belief which is based on force of habit is one of the saddest and most harmful phenomena of our time – as in the shade of a stone wall everything new grows slowly, becoming stunted, lacking the sap of life. There were too few rays of love in that faith, too many insults, too much animosity and too much envy, which always goes hand in hand with hate. And the light emanating from that faith was nothing but the phosphorescent glow of putrefaction.

But to convince myself that this was so I had to live through many difficult years, stamp out many things in my soul and erase them from my memory altogether. And when I first met those 'teachers of life' in the midst of that boring and shameless reality that surrounded me they seemed to be people of great spiritual strength, the best people in the world. Each one of them was awaiting some verdict, was in prison or in exile, wandering with convicts along the road to Siberia. They all lived cautiously and were continually in hiding.

However, I could see that while they complained of spiritual persecution at the hands of the Nikonites, the elders themselves were quite ready to persecute each other and even took pleasure in it. When the one-eyed Pakhomy was drunk he loved to boast about his memory, which was really quite staggering. He knew a few books by heart, just like a pious Jew knows the Talmud. He could put his finger on any page and start reading by heart in his soft, snuffling little voice. When he recited he always looked down at the floor and his one eye would scrutinize it anxiously, as though he were looking for something very valuable. He liked most of all to show off with Prince Myshetsky's *Russian Vineyard* as he knew the 'very patient and very brave sufferings of wonderful and valiant martyrs' particularly well. Pyotr Vasilich was always trying to catch him out:

'You're lying. That wasn't Kiprian the Blessed Fool but Denis the Chaste.'

'What Denis? It says Dionysus...'

'Don't make a fuss over one word!'

'And don't you start teaching *me*!'

A minute later they would be staring at each other, boiling with rage and saying:

'You glutton, look at the belly on you, old fat-face!'

Pakhomy would answer him just as though he were counting on an abacus:

'And you are a lecher, a randy goat and womanizer!'

The assistant would hide his hands in his sleeves, smile maliciously and encourage those guardians of ancient piety just as though they were boys:

'Go on, at him! Again!'

Once they came to blows. Pyotr Vasilich slapped his friend on the cheeks with a sleight of hand that was totally unexpected and forced him to beat a hasty retreat. He wearily wiped the sweat from his face and shouted as Pakhomy ran from the room:

'Watch out, that's another sin to account for! You

devil, you made me sin with my hand. To hell with you!'

He was particularly fond of telling his friends that their faith was not strong enough and that they were all succumbing to 'negativism'.

'That's all Alexander's work – crowing just like a cock.'

'Negativism' annoyed him and, so it seemed, frightened him as well, but when he was asked what the essence of it was he was unable to give a very intelligible reply:

'Negativism is the worst kind of heresy. It acknowledges reason alone, with no place for God. Down where the Cossacks live they don't read anything except the Bible, but it's the Bible preached by the Germans in Saratov, the Bible of Luther, about whom it is said: "Luther is the right name for you, coming from '*Lut*'*." The people who preach negativism are usually called a load of idlers, and also Stundists.† All of this comes from those heretics in the West.'

He would stamp his crippled foot and say in a cold, weighty voice:

'*They*'re the ones the Church of the new order should persecute! They're the ones who should be burned! But not us, we've always been Russian. *Our* belief is the true one. It comes from the East and it is the original Russian faith. But all that nonsense from the West is distorted free thinking! What good ever came from the Germans or the French anyway? Take 1812 for example . . .'

As he grew more and more carried away he would forget he was talking to a little boy. He would put his firm arm round my waist, pull me towards him and then push me away, talking in that fine, excitable, passionate young voice of his:

'The human reason can go astray in the thick undergrowth of its own fantasies. Like a fierce wolf it wanders about in the power of the devil who tortures the soul, which is God's gift to man! What did those diabolical monks think up, do you imagine? The Bogomils, through whom all this negativism was

* An untranslatable pun: *luty* means 'fierce'. (Trans.)

† The Stundists were a religious sect who lived in the Southern Ukraine. Their teachings were based on those of the German Baptists. They broke away from the Russian Orthodox Church in 1870. (Trans.)

handed down, taught that Satan was the son of God, the elder brother of Jesus Christ – that's what they came to believe in the end! They also taught that one shouldn't obey authority, that one shouldn't work, and that one should abandon one's wife and children. They say man needs nothing, no laws, but should live just as he likes, as the devil directs. It's that Alexander again – Oh . . . you worms!'

At that moment the assistant would give me a job to do and I would leave the old man, who remained in the gallery talking to the blank walls:

'Oh, souls without wings, oh, blind kittens, how can I escape from you?'

Then he would toss his head back, rest his hands on his knees and stay quite still for a long time without saying anything, simply staring into the grey winter sky.

Later he began to pay more attention to me and treat me more affectionately. When he found me reading a book he would stroke my shoulder and say:

'Read, read, my boy, that's very good! You seem to have brains. A pity you don't respect your elders! You pick fights with everyone! Do you think you'll get far with your impudence? As far as the convict battalions, that's where! Keep reading books, but remember that a book's only a book, and you should learn how to think for yourself. Those Flagellants had a teacher called Danilo and he got the idea in his head that neither old nor new books were necessary, so he collected all he could in a sack and then threw them in the river. Yes, I know that's just as stupid. Now that devil Aleksasha's* started stirring things up . . .'

He mentioned that Aleksasha more than anyone else and once, when he came into the shop with a worried, forbidding look on his face, he announced to the assistant:

'Alexander Vasilyev is in town, arrived yesterday. I looked and looked but couldn't find him. He must be hiding somewhere! I'll wait a bit, and see if he pokes his nose out somewhere . . .'

The assistant replied in a hostile voice:

* Diminutive form of Alexander. (Trans.)

'*I* don't know anything, don't know anyone!'

'All right then. For you everyone's a buyer or a seller, and no one else exists! Now, how about some tea?'

When I brought in the large brass pot full of hot water some other visitors had turned up. There was the old man Lukian, who smiled cheerfully, while on the other side of the door, in a dark corner, sat someone I did not know. He was wearing a warm overcoat and high felt boots, a green belt and a hat which was awkwardly pushed over his eyebrows. His face was rather insignificant and he seemed quiet, withdrawn, like a shop assistant who had just lost his job and was feeling very miserable. Pyotr Vasilich did not look at him and said something in a stern, weighty voice, while the newcomer kept on moving his hat forward with convulsive movements of his right hand. He would lift it as though he was about to cross himself and push it back, more and more, until it almost touched the crown of his head. Then he would pull it down tight towards his eyebrows. That convulsive movement reminded me of the fool 'Igosha Death in the Pocket'.*

'There are different fish swimming about in the muddy river and they are making it even muddier,' Pyotr Vasilich said.

The man who looked like an assistant asked in a soft, calm voice:

'Are you talking about *me* then?'

'Do you think I'd want to talk about *you*?'

'So you must mean yourself then, my man?'

'I only talk about myself to God, and that's my affair.'

'No, it's mine as well,' the new visitor said solemnly and convincingly. 'Don't hide your face from the truth, don't blind yourself *deliberately*, man, that's a great sin before God and people!'

I liked to hear him call Pyotr Vasilich a man but his gentle, solemn voice worried me. He spoke as good priests do when they read 'Lord of my soul' and he would keep leaning forward all the time, almost falling off his chair and brandishing his arm . . .

'Don't criticize *me*. . . . I'm no more guilty than you when it comes to sinning . . .'

*Igosha – the pathetic 'holy idiot' who appears in Chapter 7 of *My Childhood*. (Trans.)

'The samovar's boiled, just listen to it puffing away,' the old scholar said disdainfully, but the speaker was not deterred and did not let himself be interrupted for one second.

'Only God knows what sullies the springs of the holy spirit. Perhaps that's *your* sin, you people who read books. I don't read books or anything made of paper . . . I'm a simple, *living* person.'

'I know all about *your* simplicity!'

'You confuse people, distort simple thoughts. You people who read books are Pharisees. Come on, what are you trying to make me say?'

'Heresy!' Pyotr Vasilich said, but the other man moved the palm of his hand in front of his face as though he were reading something on it and said excitedly:

'Do you think that chasing people from one barn to another makes them any better? No, I say, set yourself free! What do your house and wife and all your possessions mean in the face of God? Free yourself from all the things people fight and kill each other for – from gold, and silver, from any kind of possession, for they are nothing but corruption and filth! The soul will not be saved on the fields of this earth, but in the valleys of paradise! Abandon all this, I say, break all ties and bonds, break the net of this world, these snares made by anti-Christ . . . I'm following the straight and narrow, and I am no hypocrite. I don't accept this dark world . . .'

'But what about bread, water, clothing – do you accept them? Surely they're *worldly* things!' the old man said spitefully. But Alexander ignored this interruption and continued his speech more enthusiastically than before. Although his voice was not very loud he seemed to be blowing into a brass tube.

'What's dear to you? God alone is dear. Stand before him, unsullied, tear those earthly fetters from your soul and see the Lord. You're alone in this world and so is he! Get close to God, there's only one path! That's where salvation lies. Leave your father and mother, tear out that eye that's leading you into temptation! For the sake of God, strip yourself of material things and live in the spirit. Then your soul will keep burning for ever and ever.'

'Now *you* go back to your stinking dogs,' Pyotr Vasilich said as he got up. 'I was beginning to think you'd got a little sense in your head after last year, but you're worse than ever . . .'

The old man tottered out on to the terrace, which worried Alexander and he quickly asked him in a startled voice:

'You're going! How can you?'

But the kind-hearted Lukian gave him a reassuring wink and said:

'It doesn't matter, it's nothing . . .'

Then Alexander started on him:

'And as for you, you busybody, you're spreading muck all over the place! Where's the sense in it? The hallelujah with two fingers, three fingers *. . . well?'

Lukian smiled at him and joined him on the terrace outside, while Alexander turned to the assistant and said confidently:

'They can't stand me! They'll disappear, like smoke after a fire . . . you'll see!'

The shop assistant gave him a sullen look and observed in a dry voice:

'I refuse to get mixed up in those things!'

This seemed to startle him and he moved his hat forward and mumbled:

'How do you mean, won't get mixed up? But you *should* try to understand these things . . . they're very important . . .'

He sat silently for a minute with his head bowed. Then the other old men called him and all three left without saying good-bye. Alexander would flare up like a bonfire in the night, burn brightly and then disappear. This made me feel there was some truth in his rejection of life.

When evening came I chose the right time and very excitedly described him to the quiet, friendly Ivan Larionovich, the master craftsman in the ikon shop. He listened to what I had to say and then he explained:

'He must be a *runner*. There are sects like that, and they don't recognize *anything*.'

'How do they manage to live then?'

* One of the major points raised during the seventeenth-century church controversy was whether a blessing should be made with two fingers – representing the dual nature, divine and human, that hung on the Cross – or with three – representing the Trinity. (Trans.)

'By running away from everything, wandering over the earth. That's why they're called *runners*. They say that the earth and anything to do with it means *nothing* to them. But the police think they're dangerous and try to hunt them down.'

Although my life was very hard I could not understand how one could actually run away from everything. Often there was much that was interesting in the life around me and much that was dear. And soon Alexander Vasilyev completely faded from my memory. Later, when life was difficult, I would often picture him walking across the fields, along a grey path leading to a forest, violently jerking his stick with his white hand which was not like a workman's at all and muttering: 'I'm taking the *straight and narrow*. I don't accept anything! I must break the bonds...'

And at the same time I would remember Father as Grandmother used to describe him from her dreams – with a walnut stick in his hand and a spotted dog running after him with its tongue hanging out.

Chapter 13

THE ikon workshop consisted of two rooms in a large house
half built of stone. In one of them there were three windows
looking out on to the yard and two on to the garden. The other
had one window looking on to the garden as well and the other
on to the street. They were small square windows, and the
glass, which had become rainbow-tinted from age, reluctantly
allowed the pale, diffuse light of those wintry days to filter into
the workshop.

Both rooms were crammed with tables and one or two ikon
painters would be stooping over them. Glass balls hung from
the ceiling on little ropes. They were filled with water, which
made them reflect the lamplight in cold white rays on to the
square ikon boards below.

It was hot and stuffy in that shop. About twenty 'God-daub-
ers' from Palyokh, Kholui and Mstera used to work there. They
all wore cotton shirts, undone at the front, short linen trousers,
and were either barefooted or wore old shoes. Over their heads
floated a thick, bluish haze of tobacco smoke and the air was
filled with the smell of drying oil, varnish and rotten eggs. That
mournful song from the town of Vladimir flowed slowly from
them like molten tar:

> 'How shameless the people have become;
> They watched a boy seduce a girl . . .'

They would sing other songs as well – all of them sad ones – but
they sang this one most often. Its leisurely rhythm did not
interfere with the men's thoughts or distract them from drawing their fine ermine-hair brushes over the ikon sketches, colouring in the folds of the vestments and painting the fine wrinkles
on the bony faces of saints. Beneath the level of the windows
Gogolev the engraver hammered away. He was a drunken old
man with a huge blue nose. The tapping of his little hammer
continually interrupted the lazy flow of that song, and it
sounded just like a worm nibbling away at a piece of wood.

None of the men had any enthusiasm at all for painting

242

kons, since a spiteful, clever craftsman had once divided the
work up into a long series of tedious little operations which had
no beauty in themselves and which would not arouse any love
of the craft or any interest in it. The one-eyed carpenter, Panfil – a
vicious man – would bring in the glued boards of varying sizes
made from cypress or lime wood which he had planed down. A
consumptive boy called Davidov would prepare them for
priming. His mate Sorokin would apply the undercoat. Mil-
yashin would make pencil sketches from the original and old
Gogolev would emboss a gold pattern and some other men
would paint in the landscape and vestments and then the
ikon was placed against the wall, faceless and armless, ready for
the 'body' painters. Those large ikons for the ikonostasis and
altar doors looked very unpleasant as they stood there, without
faces, without arms or legs, with only the vestments or armour
and little blouses for the archangels painted in. Those bright
boards had the smell of death about them. They had not
yet been given the touch of life by the final painting of
the faces; what should have given them life was not there;
it seemed that it had been there once but had now been
miraculously spirited away, so that only those heavy vestments
remained.

When the flesh had been painted in by the face-painter, the
ikon was handed over to the master, who made an embossed
enamel pattern. There was also a special craftsman for inscriptions. Ivan Larionych, a quiet man and the manager of the
workshop would do the final varnishing himself. He had a grey
face, a grey beard with fine silky hair, and grey eyes which were
strikingly deep-set and sad. He had a fine smile but one felt
awkward smiling back at him and he looked like the ikon of
Simon Stylites and had the same dried-up, emaciated appearance; his motionless eyes seemed to be looking at something
far off, straight through the walls and everyone in the
workshop.

A few days after I started work there Kapendyukhin, a
handsome, very strong Don Cossack who painted the church
banners, turned up dead drunk. He pressed his lips tightly
together, screwed up his soft feminine eyes and without saying
a word started hitting out at everyone with his iron-like fists.

He was short and well built, and he rushed around that workshop like a cat in a cellar full of mice. The workmen panicked, tried to hide in the corners and shouted to each other:

'Hit him!'

Evgeny Sitanov, who painted the faces on the ikons, managed to stun the maddened Kapendyukhin by hitting him on the head with a stool. The Cossack slumped down on the floor and was immediately turned over and tied up with pieces of towel. He started gnawing and tearing away at them with his teeth like a wild animal. This made Evgeny lose his temper: he jumped on a chair, pressed his elbows to his sides and got ready to jump on the Cossack. He was tall and muscular and he would certainly have crushed Kapendyukhin's chest. But at that moment Larionych appeared in an overcoat and cap. He pointed a threatening finger at Sitanov and told the painters in a soft, businesslike voice:

'Take Kapendyukhin out into the hall to sober up.'

The Cossack was dragged out of the workshop, the tables and chairs put back in place and the men got down to work again, making brief remarks to each other about the terrible strength of their friend and prophesying that one day he would be killed in a fight.

'It would be a hard job killing *him*,' Sitanov said very calmly as though he were discussing a subject he was already very familiar with.

I looked at Larionych and wondered why those strong violent men submitted so easily to him. In his work he set an example for everyone else. Even the best craftsmen eagerly listened to his advice. He would spent more time instructing Kapendyukhin than any of the others.

'You, Kapendyukhin, are supposed to be an ikon painter which means you must paint gaily, like the Italians. For oil painting you need a lot of warm colours. Look, there you've gone and used too much white, so the Virgin's eyes have turned out cold and wintry. The cheeks are rosy as apples, yet the eyes seem to belong to someone else. And they're not placed correctly. One's looking towards the bridge of the nose while the other's painted too near the temple, so that the face does not look holy and pure as it should do, but cunning and earthly instead. You don't think about what you're doing, Kapendyukhin!'

The Cossack would twist his face up as he listened, smile frozenly with his woman's eyes and then say in his pleasant voice which had gone hoarse from drinking:

'Ah, Ivan Larionych, that's not *my* business. I was born a musician and they sent me off to be a monk instead!'

'You can do *anything* if your heart's in it.'

'I don't agree. What do you think I am? I should have been a troika driver...'

At this point he would stick his Adam's apple out and sing in a despairing voice:

> 'Oh, I will harness a troika
> Of swift dark hazel horses
> Oh, then I will tear off into the frosty night
> Yes, straight to my beloved's arms!'

Ivan Larionych would smile humbly, straighten his spectacles on his grey, sad-looking nose and go away, while a dozen voices would take up the song, all of them blending in one powerful stream. These voices seemed to lift the whole workshop up in the air and rock it to and fro with regular movements.

> 'Horses know from habit
> Where the young la-ady lives...'

Pashka Odintsov, an apprentice, would stop pouring out egg yolks for the primer and stand there with a shell in each hand singing a supporting part in his wonderful treble voice. All the men would become intoxicated by the singing, almost unconscious in fact, and they seemed to be breathing and feeling as one person as they glanced at the Cossack. When *he* sang he was the acknowledged lord of the workshop, and all the men were irresistibly drawn towards him and followed the broad sweeping movements of his arms which he flung out as though he were about to fly. I was sure that if he suddenly stopped singing and shouted 'Smash everything up' then everyone, even the most serious craftsmen, would have smashed the whole workshop to smithereens in a few minutes.

He sang rarely, but his rousing songs had an irresistible, triumphant power. However depressed people were he would lift them up and stir their passions. Everyone became alert, acquired a new strength, a burning enthusiasm, when he sang.

These songs filled me with a deep feeling of envy towards the singer and his wonderful power over people. Something painfully disturbing flowed into my heart, making it swell until it began to hurt. I felt like crying and wanted to shout out to all those singing people: 'I love you all!'

The consumptive, yellow-faced Davidov, who had a ragged mop of hair, opened his mouth as well and spluttered some words out, just like a newly hatched crow leaving the egg. We sang cheerful, noisy songs only when the Cossack was there to lead the men, and most often they sang depressing long drawn-out songs about the 'shameless people': 'Oh, in the little forest' or about the death of Alexander I: 'How our Alexander went to inspect his army.'

Sometimes, at the suggestion of the best face-painter, Zhikharev, they tried hymns, but that happened rarely. Zhikharev always sang in a particularly harmonious style of his own and this always made the others stop. He was forty-five, dry-looking, bald, with a half halo of curly black gipsy hair and large black eyebrows that looked just like moustaches. His sharp, thick little beard made his fine, dark, un-Russian face look very handsome but thick whiskers stuck out from under his hooked nose and spoiled the effect of those bushy eyebrows. His blue eyes were different from each other, the left one being noticeably larger than the right.

'Pashka!' he would shout in his tenor voice to my apprentice mate, 'let's sing "Let us praise the Lord". Now listen everyone!'

Pashka would wipe his hands on his apron and start singing.

'Let us pra-ise...'

A few voices took up the song:

'The na-ame of the Lord'

while Zhikharev shouted anxiously:

'Lower, Evgeny! Let your voice come from the very depths of your soul.'

Evgeny Sitanov began to sing in a dull hollow voice and it sounded as though he were beating a barrel:

'Slaves of the Lord...'

'No, not like that! You should sing loud enough to make the earth tremble and doors and windows fly open!'

Zhikharev was so excited he kept twitching, and this bewildered me. Those amazing eyebrows moved up and down his forehead, he could hardly speak and his fingers played invisible strings.

'Slaves of the Lord – understand?' he said very meaningly. 'You *must* feel it, right down to the kernel, right through the shell! Sla-aves, praise the Lord! Can't you understand? You're alive, aren't you?'

'We can *never* get that right, you know very well,' Sitanov said politely.

'Well, leave it then.'

Zhikharev would start work again, with an offended expression on his face. He was the best craftsman and could paint faces in the Byzantine, Phrygian and 'Picturesque' Italian style. When he took orders for ikonostases Larionych would consult him, since Zhikharev was a real expert on original ikons and all valuable copies of miracle-working ikons: those from Fyodorovsk, Smolensk, Kazan and others – all of them went through his hands. As he rummaged away among the originals he used to grumble loudly:

'These originals have put chains on us ... Yes, that's the only word...*chains*!'

In spite of his important position in the workshop he was not so overbearing as some of the others, and he was very kind to apprentices such as Pavel and myself. He really wanted to teach us the craft and he was the only one who bothered about us. He was a difficult man to understand and was usually very morose. Sometimes he did not say a word for a whole week, just as though he had suddenly gone dumb. He would look at the others with a surprised expression, as though they were strangers whom he was seeing for the very first time. And although he was very fond of singing, when he was in one of these moods he would not sing at all and did not seem to hear the others even. Everyone would watch him and wink at one another. He would bend over an ikon which had been propped up against the wall, put the board on his knees, lean the middle on the edge of the table and with his fine brush carefully paint a dark, remote face, just like his own. Then he would suddenly say in a distinctly offended voice:

'*Predtecha** – What's that? *Tech* is the old word for "to go". So *predtecha* means someone who comes before, and *nothing else*!'

The whole workshop would become quiet and everyone would squint in the direction of Zhikharev and smile and many strange words could be heard in that darkness.

He would say to himself:

'You should paint an angel with wings, not in a sheepskin jacket.'

'Who are you talking to?' the men would ask.

He would say nothing, either not hearing the question or just ignoring it. Then his words would once more break that expectant silence:

'You *must* know about the lives of the saints, but who really does? What *do* we know? We live without growing any wings. And where's the soul, where is it? There are originals for those ikons we paint, yes, but there's no soul in them . . .'

These thoughts spoken out loud brought sneering smiles to everyone's face, except Sitanov's. And someone was sure to whisper spitefully: 'On Saturday he'll go and get drunk!'

The tall, muscular Sitanov was a young man of about twenty-two, with a round face, no whiskers or eyebrows, and the habit of sadly peering into corners. I remember that when Zhikharev finished a copy of the Fyodorov Virgin, meant for Kungur, he put the ikon on the table and said in a loud, excited voice:

'The Virgin's finished! For your chalice is bottomless and now the bitter, heartfelt tears of the world are poured into it . . .'

Then he put his overcoat on and went off to the pub, while the young apprentices laughed and whistled. The older ones sighed and enviously watched him leave. Sitanov went back to the ikon he had been working on, looked at it carefully and explained:

* 'Forerunner'. *Pred* means 'before'. (Trans.)

248

'Of course, he'll go and get drunk now, because it hurts terribly handing over your work when it's finished. But not everyone feels like that.'

Zhikharev's drunken sprees always started on Saturdays, but his was no ordinary workman's binge. He would begin the day by writing a note and sending Pavel somewhere with it, and before supper he would tell Larionych:

'I'm going to have a bath today!'

'Will you be away long?'

'Only the Lord can tell . . .'

'Well, please try to get back by Tuesday!'

Zhikharev would nod that bald skull of his in agreement and his eyebrows would start twitching again.

When he came back from the bath-house he spruced himself up and put on a false shirt front and a cravat; a silver chain dangled over his velvet waistcoat. He would leave in silence after giving orders to myself and Pavel:

'Tidy up the workshop in the evening. Give the large table a good wash. Scrub it!'

Everyone was in a festive mood on that Saturday and the men smartened themselves up, had a bath and ate their food quickly. After dinner Zhikharev would appear with trays of savouries, beer and wine and he would be followed by a woman whose measurements were so exaggerated in every direction that she looked quite ugly. She was over six feet tall and she made all the chairs and stools look like toys. Even the tall Sitanov seemed a mere boy next to her. She had a very good figure, but her breasts rose like hillocks towards her chin and she moved slowly and clumsily. She was over forty, but her round, fresh and smooth, motionless face, with its enormous horsy eyes and little mouth, seemed to have been painted on, so that it resembled a cheap doll's. She would smile affectedly, thrust out her broad warm hand for every one to shake and say a great deal that seemed unnecessary:

'Hullo. Frosty today. Smells a bit strong in here. Must be the paint. Hullo.'

It was pleasant looking at that woman who was as calm and powerful as a large river in full flood, but in what she said there was something that made me feel sleepy, something superfluous and tiresome. Before she spoke she would take a deep puff and her cheeks, which were almost purple, became even rounder. The apprentices would grin and whisper:

'What a size!' . . . 'Just like a belfry!'

Then she would form her lips into a bow and sit down near the samovar with her hands under her breasts, and give everyone a benevolent look with her horsy eyes.

Everyone treated her with great respect and the young apprentices were even a little afraid of her. One of them who was a young man would look at her large body greedily, but when his eyes met her all-enveloping glance he would look down in embarrassment. Zhikharev also treated his guest with respect, used the polite form of address, called her 'dearie' and bowed low as he served her with food.

'Now don't you worry,' she would say in her sugary voice. 'What a fidget you are! Can't keep still a minute!'

She never seemed to hurry herself, and she only moved her arms from the elbows down to the wrists, keeping her elbows firmly pressed to her sides. She had a heady smell, which was rather like hot, freshly-baked bread.

Old Gogolev would stammer with delight and praise the woman's beauty as though he were a deacon reading a service. The woman would listen with a friendly smile and when he could not get his words out she would start telling everyone about herself:

'When we were little girls we were ugly. Just look what a woman's life has done for me! We were so beautiful by the time we reached thirty that even noble gentlemen were interested and one provincial marshal promised me a coach and pair . . .'

The drunken, dishevelled Kapendyukhin would look at her hatefully and rudely ask:

'What did he expect in return?'

'Love, of course,' she explained.

'Love?' Kapendyukhin muttered. 'What love?'

'Such a fine-looking man as you must know all about love,' she said quite simply.

The whole workshop shook with laughter, but Sitanov bellowed at Kapendyukhin:

'She's a fool. Worse! That kind of love only comes from deep longing, as anyone knows.'

The wine had made his face turn white. Pearls of sweat rolled down his temples and his clever eyes gleamed uneasily.

Old Gogolev twitched his ugly nose, wiped away the tears with his fingers and asked:

'How many children did you have?'

'We had one.'

A lamp hung over the table and another over the stove. They did not give much light and thick shadows filled the corners of the workshop, where unfinished headless figures looked out. Those flat grey spots where hands and heads should have been were frightening and I was more certain than ever that the saints' bodies had mysteriously left those freshly painted vestments and disappeared from the cellar altogether. The glass balls hanging close to the ceiling were enveloped in small clouds of smoke and now they had a bluish glow. Zhikharev moved restlessly around the table, serving everyone, and I could see his bald skull bowing to one person, then another, and his thin fingers constantly moving. He looked thinner, and his nose, like that of a bird of prey, had grown sharper. When he stood sideways to the fire his nose cast a black shadow over his cheek.

'Drink and eat, my friends,' he said in a sonorous tenor voice.

And the woman would say in a singing voice, as though she were mistress of the house:

'What are you getting so busy for? Everyone here can help himself and knows when he's had enough!'

'Relax, everyone!' Zhikharev shouted excitedly. 'My friends, we are all slaves of God, so let us sing "Praise His name..."'

But no one felt like singing. Everyone had become a little stupefied and intoxicated by all that food and vodka. Kapendyukhin had a two-tiered accordion in his arms and young Viktor Salautin, who was as dark and as serious-looking as a young crow, took a tambourine and drew his finger across the tight leather, making it give a dull hum. The little bells on it jingled gaily.

'Let's have a Russian song,' Zhikharev ordered. 'Come on, dear!'

The woman sighed as she got up and said:

'I wish you'd relax for a minute!'

She chose an empty space and stood there, looking as immovable as a chapel. She was wearing a broad, brown skirt, a short yellow linen jacket and had a crimson shawl on her head. The accordion would sob passionately, and its little bells jingled out loud, while the tambourine made a heavy, dull, sighing sound. This was unpleasant to listen to: it was as if someone had just gone mad and was groaning and sobbing and beating his head against the wall.

Zhikharev could not dance and all he did was take short steps, tapping the heels of his brightly polished boots, jumping around like a goat, completely out of time to the music. He seemed to have borrowed someone else's legs and he made an ugly, depressing sight as he twisted his body about, struggling like a wasp in a spider's web or a fish in a net. But everyone, even the men who were drunk, followed his convulsive leaping about and watched his face and arms in silence. Zhikharev's face could change expression amazingly quickly – at one moment it was kind and had an embarrassed look and then it became proud. But a second later he would frown sternly, and then, suddenly, he seemed to be startled by something, groaned, closed his eyes for a moment – and when he opened them his face was sad again.

He would go up to the woman with his fists clenched, stamp his feet, drop to his knees with his arms outspread, raise his eyebrows and smile warmly. She would look down at him with an affectionate smile and give him a mild warning: 'Stop it, dear!' She would try to cover up her eyes and look sweet and imploring; but those eyes were the size of three-kopek pieces and she could not hide them, with the result that her face wrinkled up and looked most unpleasant. She could not dance either – all she could do was slowly sway her enormous body and silently move it from one place to another. Then she languidly waved a scarf in her left hand and kept her right hand against her side, which gave her the appearance of a huge jug.

Zhikharev would dance round that woman who seemed to be made of stone, altering his expression every second. It looked as if not only Zhikharev was dancing out there, but ten different men, all at the same time. One of them was reserved and subdued, the next angry and terrifying, the third frightened of something, gently groaning to himself and wanting to slip away unnoticed from that large unpleasant woman. Then he would pretend to be somebody else, baring his teeth and twisting convulsively like a dog that had been hurt. That boring, ugly dance made me feel very depressed and stirred up horrible memories of soldiers, laundresses and cooks and their animal-like fornication. I can still remember Sidorov's gentle voice: 'Everyone's lying, yes, they're all lying and pretending, every one of them. They should all be ashamed of themselves. No one really loves *anybody*, they're just playing a game ...'

I did not want to believe that everyone was lying and playing games. What about Queen Margot? – And of course, Zhikharev never told lies. I knew that Sitanov had fallen in love with a prostitute and that she had infected him with some shameful disease. But he did not follow his friends' advice and beat her, but rented a room for her instead, gave her medical treatment and always spoke about her warmly and with much embarrassment.

And now that huge woman kept on swaying to and fro and waving her handkerchief with a deathly smile on her face. Zhikharev leapt convulsively around her and I watched them and thought to myself: surely Eve, who deceived God, must must have been like this horse of a woman? And I began to hate her.

Faceless ikons looked out from the dark cellar walls and the black night pressed up against the windows. The lamps burned dimly in that stuffy workshop. If one listened hard amidst all the heavy stamping and noise of voices one could hear water dripping hurriedly from the brass washbasin into the slop tub. How different all this was from the life I had read about in books! It was terrifyingly different. And in the end everyone got bored.

Kapendyukhin shoved the accordion into Salautin's hands and shouted:

'Come on, let's go!'

He danced like Vanka the gipsy, just as though he were flying through the air. Then Pavel Odintsov and Sorokin would dance skilfully and eagerly. The consumptive Davidov also moved across the floor, coughing from the dust and tobacco smoke, from that strong smell of vodka and of smoked sausage which always reminded me of tanned leather. They would dance, sing and shout, but each one of them never forgot that he was there to enjoy himself and they seemed to be setting each other little examinations to see how well they could dance and how long they could go on for without dropping from exhaustion. The drunken Sitanov kept on asking: 'How can one love a woman like that, eh?' and it looked as though he were going to burst into tears at any moment. Larionych shrugged his sharp shoulder blades and answered:

'All women are the same. What do you expect?'

The people they were discussing would then disappear without anyone seeing them go. Zhikharev would turn up at the workshop after two or three days, have a bath and then work silently in his corner for two weeks or so with a solemn expression on his face, treating them all like complete strangers.

'Have they all gone?' Sitanov would suddenly ask himself and look round the workshop with his sad, bluish-grey eyes. His face was ugly, like an old man's, but his eyes were bright and kind. Sitanov was friendly towards me and for this I had to thank my thick notebook in which I had copied out some poetry. He did not believe in God and I found it very difficult to understand which of the men loved God and actually believed in him, besides Larionych. Everyone spoke about him jeeringly, as they did when they discussed the mistress of the house, and they never took him at all seriously. However, when they sat down to meals they would all cross themselves and when they went to bed they would pray; on holidays they all went to church. Sitanov did none of this and he was considered an atheist.

'There is no God,' he would say.

'Then where did all this come from?'

'Don't know.'

When I asked him to explain *why* God did not exist he would say: 'You see, God is everything that's – up there!'

And then he would raise his long arm over his head and then let it drop down to within two feet of the floor and say:

'Man is down there! True? They say: "Man is made in the image and likeness of God" as you know very well. And in whose likeness was Gogolev created?'

This stunned me: that filthy drunken old Gogolev, who, despite his age, still masturbated. And I thought of Ermokhin, of the little soldier from Vyatka, and Grandmother's sister: what was 'godlike' about *them*?

'People are just pigs, as you know very well,' Sitanov said and when he saw how upset I was at this remark immediately started consoling me:

'Don't worry, Maximych, there *are* good ones as well. Oh yes!'

With him I felt at ease and everything seemed very simple. When there was something that he did not know he would say quite frankly:

'I don't know. Never even thought about it!'

This also struck me as unusual: before I met him I had only met people who seemed to know everything and who talked about everything.

It was strange seeing all that obscene and shameful verse written down in his notebook next to fine, soul-stirring poetry. When I spoke to him about Pushkin he would show me the *Gavriiliada**, which he had copied out.

'What's Pushkin? Just a clown! Now take Benediktov† – he's worth watching!'

He would close his eyes and quietly read to me.

> 'Just look: here is the enchanting bosom
> Of a beautiful woman ...'

For some reason he singled out three lines and read them proudly, joyfully:

---

* An anti-religious, rather lascivious poem by Pushkin. (Trans.)
† A third-rate poet whose verse was distinguished by external brilliancy and a cloying sensuality. He was very popular in the 1840s. (Trans.)

       'But the eagle's eyes
       Cannot penetrate those burning gates
       And look into the heart . . .

'Understand?'

It was very awkward for me to admit that I did not understand what made him feel so full of joy . . .

Chapter 14

THE jobs I had to do in the ikon workshop were simple. In the morning, when everyone was still asleep I had to prepare the samovar, and while the men were drinking tea in the kitchen I tidied up the workshop with Pavel, separated the yolks from eggs for the paint and then went shopping. In the afternoons I had to mix the powders for the paint and watch the craftsmen at work.

At first I found everything extremely interesting, but I soon realized that each craftsman was responsible for only a small part of the whole operation. As a result he did not like his work and suffered from excruciating boredom. I had the evenings to myself and I used to tell the men about life on the steamboat and recount stories from books. Without my noticing it I gradually came to occupy a very special position in that workshop – as story-teller. And it became clear to me before very long that all those people had seen less and knew less than I did. Almost every one of them had been placed from childhood in that cramped cage of a workshop and had been locked up there ever since. Among all the workmen only Zhikharev had been to Moscow and he spoke gloomily and didactically about it:

'People in Moscow have no time for tears, you have to watch out for yourself there!'

The rest of the men had been only to Shuya and Vladimir. When they talked about Kazan they used to ask me:

'Are there many *Russians* there? Do they have churches?'

They thought Perm was in Siberia. And they would not believe that Siberia was beyond the Urals.

'Those boats from the Urals bring sturgeon from the Caspian, don't they? That means the Urals are by the sea!'

Sometimes I thought that they were laughing at me when they said that England was the other side of the ocean and that Bonaparte was related to the Kaluga nobility. When I told them what I had seen with my own eyes, they did not believe me, but they all liked my terrifying tales and complicated stories.

Even the older men clearly preferred fantasy to fact. I

realized very well that the more improbable the event, the more fantastic a story was, the more attentively they would listen to me. On the whole reality did not interest them and they all peered dreamily into the future and turned a blind eye to the poverty and ugliness of the present. This was even more startling, since I was keenly aware of the contradiction between real life and books. Here, right before me, were living people – quite unlike those in books where there was no Smury, no Yakov the stoker, no Alexander Vasilyev the 'runner', no Zhikharev, or Natalya the laundress . . .

Davidov's trunk contained some of Golitsinsky's stories, in a tattered volume, Bulgarin's *Ivan Vyzhigin* and a small volume of Baron Brambeus. I read all these books aloud and everyone liked them. Larionych would remark:

'Reading sweeps away quarrels and noise – and that's good!'

I eagerly looked for new books, found them and sat reading to the men almost every evening: this was a marvellous time. It would be quiet then in the workshop, just as though it were late at night, and the glass balls hung over the tables looking like white, cold stars as they cast their light on hairy heads and bare skulls bowed over the tables. I could see calm, thoughtful faces and sometimes one of the men would praise an author or a hero. The men listened to me so attentively and were so gentle that they were quite unlike their real selves. I particularly loved them at these moments and they in turn were very kind to me: I felt that I fitted in. Sitanov once said to me:

'Those books are just like spring to us, when they take away the second frames and you can open the windows wide – for the first time since the winter!'

But it was difficult getting hold of new books. The men did not think of joining a library, but by being crafty I managed to get hold of books all the same, begging for them like charity. Once a chief fireman gave me a volume of Lermontov which made me really feel the power of poetry and understand why it had such a powerful influence on people.

I remember that when I started reading *The Demon* Sitanov peered into the book, then into my face, put his brush on the table, pressed his long arms to his knees and smiled as he rocked to and fro, while the chair creaked under him.

'Quiet!' Larionych said as he stopped working as well and went up to Sitanov's table where I sat reading.

The poem disturbed me in a way that was both painful and sweet. My voice broke off, I could hardly see the lines and tears welled up in my eyes. But much more disturbing was that dull, cautious movement in the workshop: the whole place seemed to be turning heavily round and round, and a magnet drew the men towards me. When I had finished the first part almost everyone was standing round the table, leaning against or embracing one another, frowning and smiling.

'Go on, go on,' Zhikharev said, pushing my head low over the book. When I had finished he took it from me, looked at the title, stuck the book under his arm and announced:

'You *must* read that again tomorrow! In the meantime I'm going to hide it.'

He locked Lermontov up in a drawer in his table and started work again.

It was quiet in the workshop and the men cautiously went back to their tables. Sitanov went up to the window, leaned his forehead against the glass and stood there as though he were frozen. Zhikharev put his brush down again and said sternly:

'That's what I call living, real slaves of God. Yes!'

He raised his shoulders, so that his head was almost hidden, and continued:

'I can paint demons! They have dark, hairy bodies, fiery red wings – I'll do them in red lead. Then the face, arms, feet . . . I'll paint them as white as white, like snow on a moonlit night.'

Right up to supper-time he fidgeted around on his stool, which was not like him at all, tapped his fingers on the table and said something unintelligible about demons, about women and Eve, about paradise and about how some saints had sinned.

'That poem is so *true*,' he insisted. 'If saints can sin with sinful women, then it's flattering for a demon to sin with a *pure* soul . . .'

The men listened to him in silence. Perhaps, like myself, no one felt like saying anything. They worked reluctantly, kept on looking at the clock and when nine o'clock came they stopped work at once.

Sitanov and Zhikharev went outside and I followed them. Sitanov looked at the stars and said:

> 'Wandering caravans
> Of luminaries thrown into space . . .*

Not many people would think of putting it like that!'

'I can never remember any of the words,' Zhikharev said, shivering in the frosty air. 'I can't remember them, but I can see that demon! It's amazing that a man could make you feel so sorry for a *demon*, that's just what he did – didn't he?'

Sitanov agreed.

'That's what you call a *man*!' Zhikharev exclaimed in a voice that was not easy to forget. When we were in the hall he warned me:

'Maximych, don't you go saying anything about that book in the shop. It must be a banned one!'

This made me feel glad, since in the same way that priest had asked me to keep quiet about forbidden books when I was at confession.

Supper was a dull affair, without the usual noise and conversation, and it was as though something important had happened to everyone, something which was making them think very hard.

After supper, when everyone had gone to bed, Zhikharev took the book out and asked:

'Come on, read it again! But slower this time. There's no hurry.'

A few men got up silently from their beds, came over to the table, sat down with their legs crossed and without bothering to put any clothes on. And once more, when I had finished, Zhikharev drummed with his fingers on the table and said:

'That's what you call living. Oh, that demon, that demon!'

Sitanov leaned over my shoulder, read a few lines, laughed and said:

'I'm going to copy that into my notebook.'

Zhikharev got up and brought the book over to his table, but on the way he stopped and suddenly started talking in an offended, trembling voice:

* From Lermontov's *Demon*. (Trans.)

260

'We're living like blind puppies and we don't know what for. God doesn't need us, nor does the demon! Job was a slave and God himself spoke to him! And to Moses as well! He also gave Moses his name: *Moi-sei**, which means man of God. But who do *we* belong to?'

He closed the book and as he started getting dressed he asked Sitanov:

'Going to the pub?'

'I'm going to see my girl friend,' Sitanov softly answered.

When they had gone I lay down on the floor by the door, next to Pavel Odintsov, who tossed and turned for a long time, started sniffling and then suddenly began to cry quietly.

'What's the matter with you?' I asked.

'I feel so sorry for everyone that I could die,' he said. 'After all, I've been living with those men for four years now. I know them all.'

I also felt sorry for them. We stayed awake for a long time, whispering about them and finding in each one of them something kind and good which made us feel even more sorry for him – in our own boyish way.

I was very friendly with Pavel Odintsov. Later he became a fine craftsman, but not for long. When he was getting on for thirty he became a hard drinker. Afterwards I met him in the Khitrovo market in Moscow walking around barefoot. I heard not so long ago that he had died of typhus. It is painful to recall how many good people died without rhyme or reason in my lifetime. Everyone becomes worn out and dies, which is only natural. But nowhere else did people wear out so terribly quickly, for no reason at all, as in Russia.

At the time I knew him he was a boy with a round head, about two years older than me. He was lively, clever and honest, and very talented. He drew birds, cats and dogs very well and was amazingly good at making caricatures of the craftsmen and used to give them all wings. He made Sitanov into a miserable looking one-legged woodcock. Zhikharev became a cock with a torn comb, with no feathers on its head, and the consumptive Davidov turned into a lapwing. But he was best of all at drawing

* In Russian *moi* means 'my' and *sei* 'this one'. Moses is *Moisei* in Russian. (Trans.)

the old engraver Gogolev as a bat with large ears, a comical nose and small feet with six claws on each of them. His white round eyes would peer out from his round, dark face, and their pupils resembled lentil seeds, and lay like slits across his eyes, which gave his face a lively, very roguish look. The men were not offended when Pavel showed them the caricatures, but the drawing of Gogolev made a bad impression on everyone and they gave the 'artist' a strong warning:

'You'd better tear it up quick! If the old man sees it he'll thrash the living daylights out of you.'

That filthy rotten old man, who was perpetually drunk, pious to the point of nausea and invariably malicious, used to tell slanderous stories about all the men to the shop assistant. The mistress was planning to marry the assistant to her niece, and consequently he already considered himself master of the whole house and everyone in it: the men hated him, but they were frightened of him, and for this reason they were frightened of Gogolev too. Pavel tried every possible way of annoying the engraver and he seemed to have made it his purpose in life not to give Gogolev a moment's peace. I also helped him, as far as I could, and the men were highly amused by our antics, which were almost always terribly crude, but they never forgot to warn us both: 'You'll cop it! You'll get beaten up by Kuzka the Beetle!' ('Kuzka the Beetle' was the nickname that the men had given to the odious shop assistant.)

We were not frightened by their warnings and we painted the engraver's face while he was asleep. Once, when he was in a drunken stupor, we gilded his nose and for three days he could not get the paint out of the wrinkles in his spongy nose. But every time we managed to make him lose his temper I remembered the steamboat and that little soldier from Vyatka, and I felt deeply disturbed.

In spite of his age Gogolev was so strong that he would often catch us in the act and beat us both up. Afterwards he would report us to the mistress. Like him she got drunk every day and as a result she was always kind and cheerful. She used to try and frighten us by banging her puffy swollen hands on the table and shouting:

'You devils up to your tricks again? Gogolev's an old man

and you should have some respect for him. Who poured acid into his wine glass?'

'It was us.'

The mistress was amazed:

'Good God! They admit it! You little devils . . . you must have some respect for an old man . . .'

She drove us away and in the evening she complained to the assistant, who angrily warned me:

'I don't understand it! You read books, the Gospels even, and yet you can still get up to tricks like this. You'd better watch out!'

The mistress was a lonely woman and touchingly pathetic at times. When she was nicely drunk on sweet liqueurs she would sit at the window and sing:

> 'No one's sorry for me,
> And I don't feel sorry for anyone,
> No one knows about my longings,
> Who will I tell of my grief?'

She would sob and sing in her quavering, old woman's voice: 'Oo-oo!'

Once I saw her take a jug of hot milk, and try to go downstairs. Suddenly her legs gave way and she fell down, banging heavily against each step, but still holding on to the jug. The milk splashed on to her dress but when she got to the bottom she held her arms out and angrily shouted at the jug:

'Where do you think you're going, you devil?'

She was not fat, but soft to the point of flabbiness, and she was really like an old overweight cat which could no longer catch mice but only miaow in sweet memory of past victories and delights . . .

Sitanov frowned thoughtfully and said:

'It was a big business in those days, a good workshop and good men worked there . . . Now it's all gone to the devil, it's all in Kuzka's paws now. We slaved and slaved, but it was all for someone else's uncle in the end! Just thinking about it makes something go snap in my head. I want to say to hell with it, climb up on to the roof and lie there the whole summer just looking at the sky.'

Pavel Odintsov thought the same way as Sitanov and as he smoked a cigarette – trying to copy the older men – he would philosophize about God, drunkenness, women, about the fact that there was less work about, that some people made things and others destroyed them, not understanding what they were doing or ignorant of their true value.

At these times his angular, kind face wrinkled up and grew old, and he would sit on the bed hugging his knees, peering at the light-blue square windows, at the roof of the shed which was heavy with snowdrifts and at the stars in the wintry sky.

The men snored and shouted in their sleep, someone seemed to be choking himself with delirious ravings and Davidov lay on his plank bed and coughed up what was left of his life. Over in one corner, with their bodies touching, lay Kapendyukhin, Sorokin and Pershin, 'slaves of God' firmly in the grip of a drunken stupor. Ikons without any faces, arms or legs looked at me from the walls. The air was thick with the smell of drying oil, rotten eggs and rubbish that had gone mouldy in the cracks in the floor.

'God, you just don't know how sorry I feel for everyone,' Pavel would whisper. 'Oh, God!'

This pity for people was beginning to worry me more and more. As I said before all the men seemed to Pavel and myself to be fine people, but their life was unworthy of them and unbearably boring. When the winter blizzards came and when everything on earth, the houses and the trees, shook and howled and sobbed, when mournful bells seemed to be ringing out for Lent, boredom flowed into that workshop in a leaden wave, stifling the men, deadening everything that was alive in them, dragging them off to the pubs – and to women, who were just as good as vodka for inducing oblivion.

On evenings such as these books did not help, so Pavel and myself tried to entertain the men in ways that we had thought up ourselves. We smeared our faces with soot and paint, acted several comedies we had written ourselves and put up a heroic struggle against boredom, forcing them to laugh. I remembered the *Legend of how Peter the Great Was Saved by a*

Soldier, and turned it into a dialogue. We climbed up to David-ov's bunk and did our act there, gaily 'decapitating' imaginary Swedes. The men roared with laughter. They particularly liked the story of the Chinese devil Tsingi-Yu-Tong. Pavel played the unfortunate devil and I acted all the other parts – people of either sex, inanimate objects, a good spirit, and even the stone on which the Chinese devil rested when he was deeply depressed after his unsuccessful attempts to do good. The men would be in hysterics and I was amazed to see how easy it really was to make them laugh, and this hurt me.

'Ah, you little clowns,' they would shout at us. 'Kill the enemy!'

But the longer I worked with them the more I could not help thinking that sorrow was closer to their hearts than joy. Gaiety was never considered an end in itself but it was deliberately exploited as a way of countering and alleviating that deadly Russian boredom. All along I had been cynical about a gaiety which was never spontaneous or natural but was forced into being only on those days when everyone felt sad. And all too often that Russian brand of gaiety quite unexpectedly and almost imperceptibly developed into a cruel drama. One of the men would start dancing just as though he were breaking free from chains and suddenly, when he had freed the wild beast in him, would throw himself like an animal on everyone, tearing, gnawing and destroying. That artificial gaiety, which was aroused purely by external stimuli, irritated me terribly. I was driven to the point where I completely forgot myself and I started telling the men stories and acting out those fantasies I had invented on the spur of the moment. How I wanted to bring out the *true,* natural joy in people! I did manage to cheer the men up and at the time they were grateful, but that boredom which I thought I had dispersed slowly returned, more oppressive than before, and it crushed everyone.

The grey-faced Larionych would say in a kindly voice:

'You're a real comedian, aren't you? God bless you!'

'A real *comfort* to us,' Zhikharev said. 'Maximych, you should join a circus, or become an actor. You'd make a very good clown!'

Out of all the men in the workshop only two went to the

theatre at Christmas and Whitsun – Kapendyukhin and Sitanov, and the older men seriously advised them to cleanse themselves of this terrible sin by bathing in one of those consecrated water-holes made in the river ice at Epiphany. Sitanov particularly liked telling me:

'Leave all this and learn to be an actor instead.'

And he would excitedly retell the sad *Life of Yakovlev the Actor* and would warn me:

'That's what can happen to you!'

He loved telling me about Queen Mary Stuart, called her a 'devil', and he was particularly delighted by *The Spanish Nobleman*:

'Now take Don César de Bazan! He was a very noble man, Maximych! An amazing person!'

He himself had something of a Spanish nobleman in him. Once, near the watch tower on the square, three firemen were beating up a peasant – just to amuse themselves. A crowd of about forty people looked on and applauded. Sitanov flung himself into the fray, hit the firemen stinging blows with his long arms, lifted the peasant up, pushed him over to the crowd and shouted:

'Take him away!'

Then he stayed where he was, one against three. The fire station was a few yards away, and the men could have shouted for reinforcements and Sitanov would have been beaten up, but luckily the men panicked and fled into the station.

'Dogs!' he shouted after them.

On Sundays the young men used to have boxing matches in the timber yards behind the Petropavlovsk cemetery where they went to fight it out with men from the cleaning department and peasants from surrounding villages. The dustmen would challenge the boys from the town with a famous fighter, a gigantic Mordvinian with a small head and sickly-looking eyes that were always full of tears. He would wipe them away with the filthy sleeves of his short kaftan and stand in front of his friends with his legs planted wide apart. He would then challenge the young men in a friendly voice:

'Come on then, I'm getting cold!'

Kapendyukhin would take up the challenge and the Mordvinian would always win. Then the Cossack, who would be covered all over with blood, would gasp:

'I don't want to live any longer until I've beaten him!'

In the end this became his purpose in life and he even gave up vodka, rubbed his body with snow before he went to bed, ate a lot of meat and practised crossing himself several times every evening with an eighty-pound weight to develop his muscles. But this did not help. So he sewed some pieces of lead into the sleeves of his jacket and started boasting to Sitanov:

'Now that Mordvinian's had it!'

Sitanov gave him a stern warning:

'Stop it, or I'll tell them you've cheated.'

Kapendyukhin did not believe him, but when the time came to fight Sitanov suddenly said to the Mordvinian:

'Stand back, Vasily Ivanych. I want to fight Kapendyukhin first!'

The Cossack went purple and roared:

'I'm not going to fight with *you*, so clear off!'

'Oh yes you are,' Sitanov said and went towards him, staring the Cossack straight in the eye.

Kapendyukhin stamped on the ground, tore the sleeves from his arms, stuffed them inside his shirt and made a hasty exit.

Both ourselves and the enemy were unpleasantly surprised, and one respectable-looking man angrily told Sitanov:

'That's not allowed, my friend. Bringing personal matters into a friendly fight!'

Everyone started on Sitanov and swore at him. He stood there for a long time without saying a word but in the end he told the respectable-looking man:

'Supposing I'd stopped someone being murdered?'

The respectable man guessed at once what he meant, took his cap off and said:

'Then we should be very grateful!'

'But don't go telling everyone!'

'Why not? Kapendyukhin is a fine fighter and we know failure infuriates men. But we'll take a look at his sleeves before he fights all the same!'

'That's *your* affair!'

When the respectable looking man had gone, our side started hurling abuse at Sitanov:

'What did you say that for? You nitwit! Kapendyukhin would have won, and now we'll all get beaten up.'

They stood there swearing for a long time, very provocatively, and they took great pleasure in it.

Sitanov sighed and said: 'Ugh, you scum!'

And to everyone's surprise he challenged the Mordvinian to a fight. His opponent took up position, gaily waved his fists and started joking:

'Let's have a little fight then. Just to warm ourselves up a bit!'

A few men joined hands and made a large circle by pushing backwards. The fighters weighed each other up and kept changing stance with right arm forward and the left guarding the chest. Experts standing around immediately noticed that Sitanov's arms were longer than the Mordvinian's. Everything went quiet and the snow crunched under the fighters' feet. One of the onlookers could not stand the strain and murmured in a pathetic, greedy voice: 'Time you started . . .'

Sitanov took a broad swipe with his right, while the Mordvinian lifted his left arm in defence and received a direct hit below the stomach. He grunted, stood back and said with pleasure in his voice:

'A young boy, but no fool!'

They started jumping at one another, punching each other's chest with their heavy fists. After a few moments both sides were shouting excitedly: 'At him, ikon-dauber. Paint him all over. Emboss him!'

The Mordvinian was much stronger that Sitanov but as he was considerably heavier he was not so quick with his fists and received two or three punches for every one he gave. But the Mordvinian's body, which had taken a lot of punches in its time, seemed none the worse for wear. He kept on saying 'Ooh' and laughed the whole time. Suddenly he dislocated Sitanov's right arm with a powerful right hook under the armpit.

'Stop the fight! It's a draw,' several voices shouted at once and the circle broke up to try and part them. Then the Mordvinian said in an amiable voice:

'Not so strong as I thought, but very quick on his feet for an ikon-painter! He'll make a good boxer, and I don't mind saying that in front of everyone here!'

Then the younger men started a general free-for-all and I took Sitanov off to the bonesetter in the hospital.

The way he had behaved raised him even higher in my esteem, made me feel more sympathy and respect for him. And on the whole he was a truthful, honest man and considered that he had done his duty, but the blustering Kapendyukhin would insist on making nasty remarks about him:

'Oh, Zhenya, you show everything! You cleansed your soul, like a samovar before a holiday and now you boast how bright it is! But your soul's made of brass and you're one hell of a bore...'

Sitanov would very calmly ignore him, say nothing and carry on with his work, or copy Lermontov into his notebook. He would spend all his free time copying out poetry and when I once suggested: 'You've got money, you can afford to *buy* the book,' he answered: 'No, it's better copying it out in your own hand.'

He would fill a page with his fine, thin handwriting, full of flourishes, wait for the ink to dry and then start reading softly:

'Without regret, without feeling
You will look upon the earth,
Where there is no true happiness,
Nor lasting beauty ...'*

After this, he would screw his eyes up and say:

'That's so true! Oh, he knows the truth so well!'

I was very surprised at the relationship between Sitanov and Kapendyukhin. When he was drunk the Cossack always tried to pick a fight with his friend, who would spend a long time trying to dissuade him:

'Get away ... Don't start anything...'

And then he would cruelly beat the drunken Cossack, so cruelly that the other men, who usually looked upon fights

* From Lermontov's *Demon*. (Trans.)

among themselves as a form of entertainment, stepped in and separated the two of them.

'One of these days we won't stop Evgeny in time and he'll *murder* him . . .' they used to say.

When he was sober Kapendyukhin, in turn, never tired of poking fun at Sitanov, mocking his passion for poetry and his unhappy love affairs. This he did in the most obscene way, but he never succeeded in making the other feel jealous. Sitanov would listen to the Cossack's jeers in silence, without taking offence, and sometimes even laughed with Kapendyukhin.

They slept next to each other and during the night they used to lie whispering to each other for a long time. These conversations worried me terribly, since I wanted to know what two people, who seemed such enemies, could find to talk about in such a friendly way. But whenever I went up to them the Cossack would growl: 'What do you want?' And Sitanov did not even appear to notice me.

But one day they called me over and the Cossack asked:

'Maximych, if you were rich, what would you buy?'

'Some books.'

'Anything else?'

'Don't know.'

'Ugh,' Kapendyukhin exclaimed in annoyance and turned away, while Sitanov calmly said:

'You see, *no one* knows, whether they're old or young! I'm telling you here and now: wealth on its own is *no good*. Everything must be used to some purpose . . .'

I asked what he meant.

The Cossack answered:

'I don't feel like sleeping, let's have a chat.'

Later, as I listened closely to their conversations, I discovered that at night they talked about things people usually discuss during the day: God, truth, happiness, the stupidity and cunning of women, the greediness of the rich, and about how complicated, incomprehensible life was. I always listened to what they said with great eagerness and it excited me. I was pleased to hear that nearly everyone was of the same opinion: that their lives were bad and must be improved! But at the same time I could see that the desire to live better did not seem to make any more demands on the men and that it did not change anything at all in the workshop. All those speeches that cast a bright light on life only opened up the depressing emptiness that lay behind it. Like straws blown across a pond by the wind, those same people who insisted that aimless drifting was absurd and degrading, were in fact drifting about in that void themselves.

They discussed things at great length and very enthusiastically, always criticizing someone, boasting, making nasty quarrels just out of nothing and hurting each other deeply. They tried to guess what would happen to them after death, while at the entrance to the workshop, where they kept the slop tub, a floor-board had rotted away, and through that damp, rotten opening came a smell of decay and a cold draught which froze the feet. Pavel and myself had stuffed the hole up with hay and rags. The men often talked about boarding it up again but meanwhile the hole grew wider and during a blizzard the wind blew through it like a chimney and everyone caught cold and started coughing. The metal flap of the ventilator made a revolting whistling noise and everyone hurled obscenities at it. But when I oiled it Zhikharev pricked his ears up and said: 'It's stopped whistling! Now it's more boring than ever in here!'

When the men came out of the bath-house and lay down on their filthy, dusty beds all those nasty smells and layers of filth did not bother anyone. There were many trivial things that made life difficult and they could easily have been eliminated. But no one did anything about them. Often they used to say:

'No one ever feels sorry for anyone else. God doesn't nor do we...'

And when Pavel and myself washed the dying Davidov, who was literally being eaten away by filth and insects, everyone laughed at us, took his shirt off and asked us to search him, called us bath-house attendants and mocked us as though we had just done something shameful and very funny. From Christmas right up to Easter Davidov lay on his plank bed, continually coughing and spitting up gobbets of stinking blood which missed the slop bucket and splashed on to the floor. At night-time he kept everyone awake with his delirious shouting.

Almost every day the men would say: 'He should be in hospital!' But first they discovered that Davidov's passport was out of date and then he began to get better. In the end they decided: 'He's going to die soon anyway!' And Davidov himself promised: 'Yes – I won't be long now!'

He had a quiet humour and was always trying to ward off the deathly boredom in the workshop by making little jokes. He would hang his dark bony face down from his bunk and announce in a whistling voice:

'Listen to the voice of one borne aloft on planks...'

And he would recite some miserable nonsense:

> 'I live on planks,
> I wake up early
> And whether I'm awake or asleep
> The cockroaches eat me ...'

'*He* doesn't let it get him down,' the men said in delight.

Sometimes Pavel and myself would climb up to his bunk and he would keep joking away to us:

'What can I give you, my dear visitors? A nice little spider – no?'

His was a slow death and he found it all exceedingly boring. He would say with real annoyance:

'I just *can't* die! It's really terrible!'

His complete fearlessness in the face of death frightened Pavel and he would wake me up at night and whisper:

'Maximych, supposing he dies here? He'll pass away one night and we'll be lying right underneath him. Oh God! I'm afraid of corpses...'

Or he would say:

'What life has he had? Why did he live? Not twenty and now he's dying.'

One moonlit night Pavel woke me up, looked at me with eyes wide open with terror and said: 'Listen!'

I could hear Davidov wheezing above us in his bunk and saying in a hurried, but clear voice: 'Come here. Co-ome...'

Then he started hiccoughing.

'He's dying, I swear it!' Pavel said and he sounded very frightened.

All that day I had shovelled snow from the yard out into the field and I was very tired. I just wanted to sleep but Pavel implored me:

'*Please* don't go to sleep, for Christ's sake don't go to sleep.'

And suddenly he sat up and shouted wildly:

'Get up, Davidov's dead!'

Someone woke up and several figures climbed out of bed. I could hear the men angrily questioning each other. Kapendyukhin climbed up to the bunk and said in a startled voice:

'Yes, I think he really *is* dead . . . he's still warm, though . . .'

Everything went quiet. Zhikharev crossed himself, snuggled back into his blanket and said:

'Well, may his soul rest in peace.'

Someone suggested: 'We should take him out into the hall.'

Kapendyukhin climbed down from his bunk, looked through the window and said:

'Let him lie up there until the morning. He never harmed anyone when he was alive . . .'

Pavel hid his head under the pillow and sobbed.

But Sitanov did not even wake up.

Chapter 15

THE snow in the fields had melted and the wintry clouds seemed to dissolve, falling on to the earth in the form of sleet and rain. The sun took longer to run its daily course, the air grew warmer and it seemed that spring in all its gaiety had in fact arrived, but was playfully hiding in the fields on the other side of Nizhny and was waiting to pour into the town. The streets were full of reddish-brown mud, little streams flowed along the passages between the shops and sparrows cheerfully hopped around the thawed patches in Arestantskaya Square. The people themselves seemed to have become as busy as the sparrows. Above all these sounds of spring, almost continually from morning until night, one could hear the tolling of Easter bells that gently tugged at the heart. In that ringing there was a pained sound, like the grumbling of an old man, and it seemed that the bells were talking about everything in icy despondency:

'That wa-as, that wa-as . . .'

On my name-day the men gave me a small, beautifully painted ikon of the holy father Alexei, and Zhikharev made a long, sermonizing speech, meant to be inspiring, that I remember to this day:

'Who do you think you are?' he said as he played with his fingers and raised his eyebrows. 'Nothing more than a little boy, an orphan, just thirteen years old. I'm almost four times as old as you. I admire you and approve of you, facing up to everything squarely. You'll get on if you always stand like that.'

He talked about God's slaves and God's people, but I could never understand the difference between people and slaves and it could not have been very clear to him either. He was a boring speaker and the men laughed at him. I stood there holding the ikon, feeling very touched and so embarrassed that I did not know where to put myself. Finally Kapendyukhin shouted to the 'orator' in a very annoyed voice:

'Stop singing a requiem for him! You've made his ears go blue!'

Then he slapped me on the shoulder and started praising me as well:

'What I like about you is that you're so friendly to everyone – that's good!'

They all looked at me affectionately, laughing very kindly at my embarrassment. A little longer and I would have roared out loud from the joy of realizing that I was a man at last and that these people really needed me.

But that same morning in the shop the assistant nodded towards me and said to Pyotr Vasilyev:

'An unpleasant boy. No good at anything!'

As usual, I was away from the shop the whole morning but when I returned in the afternoon the assistant told me:

'Go back to the house and sweep the snow off the roof and fill the cellar up.'

He did not know it was my name-day and I was convinced that no one in the house knew.

When they had finished congratulating me in the workshop I changed, ran outside and climbed up on to the roof of the shed to sweep off the tightly packed, heavy snow which had fallen in large quantities that winter. But in my excitement I forgot to open the cellar door and as a result blocked it up with snow. It was not until I had jumped down that I saw my mistake and I immediately started trying to clear the doorway. The snow was damp and it clung together in lumps. It was very hard shovelling it up with a wooden spade – I did not have a metal one – and I managed to break it in half just as the assistant appeared at the gate. The old Russian proverb: 'Grief follows close on joy' was so right!

'So-o,' the assistant said with a sneer as he came up to me. 'What sort of workman are *you*? Blast and damn! Just let me get my hands on that mad head of yours!'

He waved the shaft of the spade at me and I moved away and said angrily:

'I wasn't taken on to sweep the yard!'

He flung the shaft at my legs. I seized a lump of snow, threw it in his face and he fled, making snorting noises. I stopped shovelling and went back to the workshop. A few minutes later the assistant's fiancée came running out. She was a scatterbrained girl with pimples on her expressionless face.

'Maximych: upstairs!'

'Won't go,' I said.

Then Larionych asked me in a soft, startled voice:

'What do you mean – won't go?'

I told him what had happened. He frowned in a worried sort of way, and as he went upstairs he whispered: 'You've got a nerve!'

The workshop hummed away and everyone said nasty things about the assistant. Kapendyukhin said: 'You'll cop it now!' But this did not frighten me. My relations with the assistant had been unbearable for a long time. He hated me – all the more so because *I* could not stand *him*. However, I did want to find out why he treated me so stupidly. For example, he would scatter coins all over the shop floor. When I was sweeping I would pick them up and put them in a cup on the counter which contained a few kopeks for the poor.

When I guessed what was going on I told the assistant:

'You're wasting your time with that money!'

He flared up and shouted:

'Don't you dare try and teach *me*! I know what I'm doing!'

But he immediately tried to put himself in the right.

'What do you mean, "wasting my time"? They just fall on the floor...'

He forbade me to read books in the shop and told me:

'That's none of your business! Trying to be a Bible scholar, you little parasite?'

But he did not give up trying to catch me out with those coins. It was obvious that if a coin just happened to fall through a crack in the floor when I was sweeping it then it would prove that I had stolen it! I told him once more to stop his game, but that very same day, when I was coming back from the café with hot water, I could hear him speaking to the assistant whom they had recently taken on in the shop next door:

'Teach him to steal prayer books. A big load's arriving soon, three crates of them...'

I realized that they were talking about me and when I went into the shop they both looked embarrassed. However, I already had good reason to suspect them of some stupid plot against me. The assistant from the shop next door had worked there before. He was a good salesman but he drank too much. When he first took to drink the proprietor gave him the sack, but he took that crafty-eyed, fragile-looking assistant on again. He seemed so meek and mild, so ready to jump at his master's least command, but he was always smiling craftily into his beard and he loved making cutting remarks. He had that nasty-smelling breath which one finds with people who have bad teeth, although his were white and strong.

Once he really startled me out of my wits. He came up to me with a friendly smile and then he suddenly pulled my hat off and seized me by the hair. We started fighting and he pushed me down from the gallery into the shop. He kept trying to make me fall on to the large ikon cases which stood on the floor. If he had succeeded I would have smashed the glass and the carvings and would probably have scratched some expensive ikons. He had no strength at all, but when I got the better of that bearded man I was amazed to see him sit on the floor and cry bitterly as he wiped his broken nose.

Next morning, when the master and mistress had gone out and we were alone he said to me in quite a friendly way as he rubbed a nasty swelling on the bridge of his nose, right next to his eyes:

'Do you suppose I started that fight because *I* wanted to? Really, I'm not such a fool. Of course, I knew that you would win, because I'm weak and I drink a lot. It was the master who told me: "Hit him and try and make him damage as many things in his master's shop as possible – think of the money they'll lose!" I would never have done it myself . . . You've made a fine mess of my face!'

I believed him, and I felt sorry, since I knew that he often went hungry and that his wife beat him. However, I could not help asking:

'If they tried to make you poison someone, would you do it?'

'*He*'d make me do it,' the assistant replied in a soft voice and with a pathetic leer: 'He's capable of anything . . .'

Soon afterwards he asked me:

'Listen. I haven't a kopek, nothing to eat and the old woman howls all the time. Now you'll do it for me, won't you! Take

277

an ikon, hide it in the storeroom and I'll sell it. All right? And a prayer book as well!'

I remembered the shoe shop and the church watchman and I thought that that man would give me away in the end. But I found it hard to refuse and I gave him an ikon. I did not take a prayer book, which was worth quite a few roubles, as that seemed a really terrible crime. What could I do? Morality always has its own special logic . . .

When I had heard the assistant in my shop urging that pathetic man to teach me how to steal prayer books I became frightened. It was obvious the assistant knew that I was kind to him and that the assistant from next door had already told him about the ikon. The sheer loathsomeness of helping some-one in this way and that rotten little trap to catch me with the coins filled me with indignation and repulsion towards myself and everyone else. The next few days I spent in terrible torment waiting for the crates of books to arrive. Finally they were delivered and as I was inspecting them in the storeroom the the assistant from next door came up and asked me to give him one.

I asked him: 'Did *you* tell my *master* about the ikon?'

'Yes,' he said gloomily. 'My friend, I can't hide anything!'

This completely bowled me over. I sat on the floor and goggled at him while he hurriedly muttered something to him-self, looking confused and really pathetic:

'You see, your master guessed what was going on – without anyone's help. I mean to say, *my* master guessed what was going on and told yours!'

It seemed that I was done for, that these people had double-crossed me and that a place was already waiting for me in the juvenile penal settlement. If that was so, then it was all the same to me: if I had to drown, then it might as well be in deep water. I shoved the prayer book into the assistant's hand and he hid it under his coat and went away. But he came back immediately and let the book fall at my feet. He went away again, saying:

'I won't take it! You've had it now!'

I did not understand these words: why should I have 'had' it? But I was very pleased that he did not take the book. After this incident the little assistant treated me even more angrily and suspiciously.

I remembered all of this when Larionych went upstairs to see the master. He did not stay there very long and when he returned he looked even more crushed and subdued than ever. Before supper he looked me straight in the eye and said:

'I've tried to persuade them to let you leave the shop and work with the ikon painters. But it was no good! Kuzma wouldn't have it. He doesn't like you at all.'

I had another enemy in that house as well – the shop assistant's fiancée, who was a very flirtatious girl. Indeed, the whole workshop flirted with her and used to wait in the hall for a cuddle. She did not mind this at all and all she did was squeal softly, like a little dog. From morning until night she chewed away at something and her pockets were always stuffed with gingerbread and little cakes and her jaws were perpetually moving. I did not like that empty face with its restless, grey eyes. She used to set Pavel and myself puzzles that always had some crude, vulgar double meaning to them and she set us tongue-twisters that turned out to be obscenities. Once one of the older men told her:

'You're a shameless little bitch!'

She smartly replied by reciting the words of some bawdy song:

> 'If a girl is shy
> Then she's not fit to be a woman!'

It was the first time I had seen a girl like her and she disgusted and frightened me. The way she flirted with all the men was revolting and when she saw how I felt about it she flirted all the more. Once, for example, when Pavel and myself were helping her to boil *kvass* and cucumbers in the cellar she suggested:

'Boys, like me to teach you how to kiss?'

Pavel laughed as he replied: 'I'm better at that than you' but I told her to go and kiss her fiancé instead, and in not too friendly a tone either, which made her very angry.

'Ugh, what a rude boy! A young lady tries to be nice to him and all he does is turn his nose up! Little prig!'

Then she pointed a threatening finger at me and added: 'You wait, I'll see you don't forget this!'

Pavel took my side and said to her:

'You'll cop it from your fiancé if he finds out how you're carrying on!'

She turned her pimply face towards him and frowned contemptuously:

'I'm not afraid of *him*! With the dowry *I*'ve got I can find a dozen better than him. A virgin is entitled to lark around, but only until she gets married!'

And she started flirting with Pavel and from that time onward she told nasty stories about me when she had the chance.

Things became even harder in the shop. I had read all the theological books, and the quarrels and bickering of the Bible scholars no longer had any attraction for me, as those men always talked about one and the same thing. Only Pyotr Vasilyev still interested me by his knowledge of the darker side of human life, by his ability to talk fascinatingly. Sometimes I thought that the lonely and vengeful prophet Elijah must have looked like him when he wandered through the world. But every time I had a frank talk about people with the old man he would be kind enough to hear me out – and then he would tell the Bible scholar. He in turn would either make fun of me or angrily swear at me.

Once I told the Bible scholar that I sometimes wrote down his speeches in my notebook, which already contained poems and extracts from books. This terrified him and he quickly lurched over to me and anxiously started cross-examining me:

'Why do you do that? It's no good! Just so you don't forget them? You must stop it! You're a strange boy! You'll let me have those copies, won't you?' For a long time he tried to persuade me to hand the book over or burn it. Then he started angrily whispering things to the assistant.

One day when we were on the way home the assistant told me sternly:

'Those copies you keep on making – you'd better stop it! Do you hear? That's what the *police* are interested in.'

I was careless enough to ask:

'What about Sitanov? *He* copies things out.'

'He does? The bloody fool . . .'

After a long silence he suggested in an unusually gentle voice:

'Listen. Let me see your book and Sitanov's as well and I'll give you fifty kopeks. But only when Sitanov's not around . . .'

He must have been convinced that I would do what he wanted and without saying more ran on in front of me on his stubby little legs. When I got home I told Sitanov about the assistant's suggestion and he scowled.

'You shouldn't have told him. Now he'll get someone to steal our notebooks. Give me yours and I'll hide it. He'll get you into *real* trouble now, you mark my words!'

I was convinced that he was right and decided to leave that place as soon as Grandmother came back from the town. She had been living the whole winter in Balakhna at someone's invitation, teaching young girls how to make lace. Grandfather was back in Kunavino and I never visited him. When he was in town he did not come to see me either. Once we bumped into each other in the street. He was walking along very solemnly and slowly, just like a priest, in a heavy beaver coat. I said hullo to him but he looked at me suspiciously and said pensively:

'Oh, it's *you* . . . you're an ikon painter now . . . yes, yes. Well, get on with it then, go on!'

He pushed me aside and went on his way, just as solemnly and slowly.

I saw Grandmother very rarely. She had to keep working all the time to feed Grandfather, who was now suffering from senile mental decay and she had to look after the uncles' children as well. Mikhail's son, Sasha, who was a handsome boy, but something of a dreamer and a bookworm, gave her a great deal of trouble. He worked in the dye-works and often went from one master to another. When he was not working he would plant himself on Grandmother, calmly waiting until she found him a new job. Sasha's sister, who had made a disastrous marriage with a drunken workman who beat her and then drove her out of the house, hung around Grandmother's neck like a millstone as well.

Whenever I met Grandmother I delighted even more in her

fine spiritual qualities, but already I felt that this wonderful person had been blinded by all those fairy-tales and had no idea of the bitter reality of life: she just turned a deaf ear when I told her all that I had been through, all my anxieties and upsets.

'You must grin and bear it, Alexei!'

This was the only answer she gave me when I told her about the ugliness of life, about the way people suffered, about my unfulfilled desires – about everything, in fact, that was troubling me. I was not the most patient of people and if I did at times display that impassivity which is more characteristic of cattle, trees and stones – then it was only to test myself, to discover what strength I had, what degree of stability. Sometimes young men – just from youthful stupidity or jealousy of older men – tried to lift weights which were too much for their muscle and bone and actually succeeded. They would try to look like strong, grown-up men as they lifted those seventy-pound weights: I tried to accomplish all these things both physically and spiritually, and it was only a matter of chance that I did not kill myself or cripple myself for life. Nothing mutilates a man so horribly, destroys his capacity for suffering, as when he is subjected to conditions over which he has no control. If I finally ended up lying crippled on the ground, then I would proudly announce, when my last hour arrived, that those good people had been trying very hard, for forty years, to corrupt my soul, but that for all their persistence they had not been very successful.

I was seized even more by a wild desire to play the fool, to to make people feel stupid – and to try and make them laugh as well. I succeeded in this and I would tell the ikon painters all about the merchants in the Nizhny fair and mimic their actions. I would ape peasant men and women selling and buying ikons, the assistant skilfully swindling them, and those Bible scholars quarrelling with one another. The men would guffaw and often stopped working to watch my act, but Larionych would always advise me:

'If you *must* act, then do it after dinner. Otherwise you'll stop the men working.'

When the 'performance' was over I felt relieved, just as though I had thrown off a heavy load. For about an hour my

282

head would feel pleasantly empty. And then once again it was filled with sharp, fine nails that shifted around and became red hot. Everywhere I went there seemed to be a filthy gruel on the boil. I felt as though I were being slowly cooked in it and I thought: 'Surely life can't *really* be like this? If I go on living like these people will I ever find anything better?'

'You look angry, Maximych,' Zhikharev would say as he closely watched me, and Sitanov often used to ask: 'Who do you think you are?'

I was unable to give him an answer. Life stubbornly and crudely eroded all that was best in my soul and maliciously replaced it by some worthless rubbish. Angrily and doggedly I struggled against its power and I swam in the same river as the others. But for me the water seemed colder and it did not keep me afloat so easily as the others. At times I felt that I was falling into some abyss.

However, people began to treat me much better, stopped shouting at me as they did at Pavel, were not so rough with me and called me by my Christian name to show that they respected me. All this was very good, but it tormented me to see how much vodka men drank, how disgustingly they behaved when they were drunk, and how unnatural their relations were with women: I just could not help feeling like this even though I knew that vodka and women were the only amusements in their lives, and it brought me much spiritual anguish. Often I sadly recalled that the clever, bold Natalya Kozlovskaya called women playthings as well. But what about Grandmother? And Queen Margot? I felt rather frightened when I thought of Queen Margot: she was so aloof from everyone that I thought I must have dreamed her up from somewhere.

I began to think far too much about women and I had already made up my mind to go where the men went when the next holiday arrived. It was not simply physical desire – I was very healthy – but at times I madly wanted to embrace someone who was clever, affectionate, and sincere, someone whom I could talk to as though she were a mother and discuss all the things that troubled me so deeply. I was jealous of Pavel when he told me one night about his affair with a chambermaid from one of the houses across the road.

'It's all very funny. A month ago I flung some snow at her. I didn't really fancy her, but now we sit on a bench and cuddle each other – she's *wonderful*!'

'What do you talk about?'

'About *everything*, of course. She tells me about herself and I tell her all about *me*. Well, we kiss . . . But she's a *virgin* . . . such a good girl, I can't tell you! Cor, you're smoking like an old soldier!'

I was in fact smoking a great deal. Tobacco intoxicated me and dulled all disturbing thoughts and anxious feelings. Fortunately the taste and smell of vodka revolted me. Pavel would eagerly drink his vodka, however, and after he had had his fill would cry miserably: 'I want to go home! Let me go home!' I seem to remember that he was an orphan. His mother and father had died a long time before, and he had no sisters or brothers. For eight years he had been living with strangers.

In this restless mood of dissatisfaction with everything, which was intensified by the arrival of spring, I decided to go and work on a steamboat once again, to sail down to Astrakhan and then escape to Persia. I do not remember why I thought of Persia – perhaps it was because I liked the Persian merchants I had seen at Nizhny fair. They would sit like stone idols, airing their dyed beards in the sun and calmly smoking hookahs; they had large, dark, omniscient eyes. Of course, I could have run off somewhere there and then, but during Easter week, when some of the men had gone home to their villages and the rest stayed in town to get drunk, I happened to meet my old master (Grandmother's nephew) as I was walking across the fields above the Oka one sunny day. He was wearing a light grey overcoat, kept his hands in his trouser pockets, had a cigarette in his mouth and his hat was pushed back over his neck. His pleasant face wore a friendly smile and he had the engaging look of a man who led a life that was gay and free. Besides us there was no one else in the field.

'Good God, it's Peshkov!'

After he gave me an Easter greeting he asked how I was getting on. I told him quite frankly that the workshop, the town and everything there bored me terribly and that I wanted to escape to Persia.

'You can give *that* idea up,' he said seriously. 'What the hell do you want to go to Persia for? But I know how you feel. When I was your age I wanted to tear all over the place!'

I liked the dashing manner he had of speaking and there was something fine and springlike about him, a jauntiness in everything he said or did.

'Do you smoke?' he asked as he held out a silver case containing some thick cigarettes. This finally won me over to him.

'Look, Peshkov, come and see me again. This year I took on contracts at the fair worth forty thousand. Understand? I'll fix you up all right. You'll be a kind of foreman and supervise all deliveries and see that everyone's on time and in the proper place and that the men don't steal – all right? I'll pay you five roubles a month and five kopeks for food. But keep clear of the women. All you have to do is leave in the morning and come back in the evening – and you don't even have to see them! But if you have to see them, then don't go telling them we've met. Just turn up on the first Sunday after Easter – that's all!'

We parted good friends and he shook hands with me and even waved his hat as he walked away. When I told them in the workshop that I was leaving most of them seemed genuinely sorry, and Pavel was particularly upset. All this I found very flattering.

'Just think,' he said reproachfully, 'how can you live with peasants, with carpenters and house-painters – after us? Oh! that's called stepping down from the clergy to become a grave-digger!'

Zhikharev growled:

'A fish always looks for the deepest water – and boys run after danger!'

The men gave me a depressing and tedious send-off.

'Of course, one must try one's hand at everything,' Zhikharev said. His face was yellow from drink. 'But it's best to stick to one job from the start.'

'And for your *whole life*,' Larionych added in a soft voice.

But I felt that they were forcing themselves to say all this, from a sense of duty. The thread that had bound me to them had suddenly rotted away and snapped.

Drunken old Gogolev rolled around on his bunk and said hoarsely:

'I only have to say the w-word and everyone'll be in p-prison! I know some secrets! Who believes in God here? Eh?'

As always, the faceless, unfinished ikons were propped up against the walls and the glass balls hung close to the ceiling. For a long time the men had been working without any light in the bright spring days and the glass reflecting balls were not used. Now they were covered with a grey layer of soot and dust. I remember all this so clearly that if I close my eyes now I can still see the whole of that dark cellar, all those tables, those jars of paint on the window-sills, bundles of brushes, ikons, the slopbucket in the corner under the brass washbasins that looked like a fireman's helmet and Gogolev's bare leg dangling from his bunk like a drowned man's . . .

I wanted to escape as quickly as possible, but in Russia people like dragging out sad moments as long as they possibly can and as they said good-bye to me the men seemed to be performing some sort of requiem.

Zhikharev twitched his eyebrows and said:

'I can't let you have that book back, *The Demon* – will you take fifty kopeks for it?'

The book belonged to me – an old fire chief had given it to me and I did not want to lose my Lermontov. I was rather hurt and when I refused to take the money Zhikharev calmly put it back in his purse and announced in a completely unruffled voice:

'As you like, but you're not having the book back. It's not for *you*. It'll lead you into sin in no time.'

'But I've seen it in *shops*!'

But he said even more adamantly:

'That means *nothing*, they sell revolvers in shops!'

And he did not give me my Lermontov back. When I went upstairs to say good-bye to the mistress I met her niece in the hall and she said:

'They say you're leaving.'

'Yes.'

'If you hadn't left they would have *thrown* you out, anyway,' she said in rather an unfriendly voice – but she was trying to be sincere all the same.

The mistress, who was drunk again, said:

'Good-bye, and Christ be with you! You're a *bad* boy, far too cheeky! Although I can't say *I've* seen you misbehave everyone says you're such a bad boy!'

And she suddenly burst into tears and said:

'If my sweet little husband were alive now, my dearest one, rest his soul, he would have given you such a thrashing! But he wouldn't have driven you out. But things are different now – all they can say is clear off! Oh, where will you go? You've *no one* to turn to . . .'

Chapter 16

NOW I was in a little boat with my new master, rowing along the streets of the fair, between shops built of stone that were flooded up to the first floor. I did the rowing and the master sat at the stern and steered very badly, letting the rudder trail deep in the water. The boat clumsily darted about as it glided through the calm, brooding water from one street to another.

'Look how high that water is, to hell with it! It's interfering with building!' my master grumbled as he puffed his cigar: its smoke had the smell of burnt cloth.

'Careful!' he shouted. 'We're heading straight for a lamp-post!'

He straightened the boat and started swearing again:

'And look at the boat they've given us, the devils!'

Then he pointed out the place where, when the floods receded, they repaired boats. I could see that he had shaved himself so closely that his skin was blue, and with that trimmed moustache, and the cigar in his mouth, he did not look like a building contractor at all. He was wearing a leather jacket and boots up to his knees. A game-bag was slung over his shoulder and an expensive Lebelle rifle lay at his feet. Now and again he would nervously move his leather cap, pull it down over his eyes, puff his lips out and look anxiously around. Then he would push his cap back towards the nape of his neck – which made him look younger – and smile: evidently something pleasant had crossed his mind. It was hard to believe that he had a lot of work on his hands and that he was worried by the slow subsidence of the water: instead, it seemed that he was full of thoughts that had nothing to do with anything practical.

As for me, I just could not get over my surprise: it was so strange seeing that dead city, those straight rows of buildings with their windows boarded over. The town looked completely submerged and appeared to be drifting past our boat. The sky was grey and the sun was hidden behind a solid mass of cloud through which it fitfully gleamed – a large, silvery, wintry patch. The water was grey and cold, and it did not seem to be flowing at all. It was as though it had frozen and gone to sleep together with those empty houses and rows of shops that were painted a dirty yellow. When the pale sun came out everything shone and the water reflected the grey fabric of the sky. Our boat would then appear to be hanging between two skies. The stone buildings looked up and almost imperceptibly floated off to the Volga, to the Oka.

Broken barrels, boxes, baskets, wood shavings and straw floated around the boat and sometimes a pole or a log would rise to the surface – just like a dead snake. In some of the shops the windows were open and washing had been left to dry on the roofs of the galleries and I could see felt boots sticking out. From one of the windows a woman was looking at the grey water. A boat was moored to the top of an iron column and its sides were reflected like red meat in the water.

The master nodded at these signs of life and told me:

'The fair watchman lives over there. His job is to climb through the window on to the roof, get into his boat and sail around looking for thieves. If he doesn't find any he'll do some stealing himself . . .'

He spoke calmly and lazily, as though his mind were on something else.

Everything around was quiet, deserted and unreal, and I thought that it was all a dream. The Volga and Oka merged into one enormous lake. In the distance, on a forested hill, I could see the gay colours of the town dotted with gardens that still had a rather sombre look; but the buds on the trees had already swelled out, and the gardens and churches were clothed in a greenish, warm coat. The hollow sound of Easter bells drifted over the water and I could hear the animated noise of the town, while where we were was like a forgotten cemetery. Our boat turned between two rows of black trees and we floated up the main street to the Old Cathedral.

The cigar seemed to be bothering the master and its acrid smoke got into his eyes. Now and again the prow or side of the boat would knock against tree-trunks, and this made him shout out in an angry, surprised voice:

'What a rotten boat!'

'But you're not steering properly!'

'What do you mean?' he bellowed. 'When there's two in a boat one always rows and the other steers . . . Look over there – those are the Chinese shops.'

For some time now I had known that fair intimately. And I knew those funny rows of shops with their stupid roofs, where plaster figures of Chinamen squatted on the corners. Once, when I was with some friends, I threw stones at them and knocked some heads and arms off. But I was no longer proud of that.

'What rubbish!' the master said as he pointed at the shops. 'If only they had let *me* build them!'

He made a whistling noise as he pushed his cap back over his neck. For some reason I thought that he would have made that stone town just as boring and built it in the same low-lying area which was flooded every year by two rivers. And he would have built the Chinese shops just the same.

He threw his cigar into the water, spat in disgust and said: 'I'm bored, Peshkov! So bored. There's no educated people here, no one to talk to. I want to show off, but to whom? They're not real *people* here at all – only carpenters, masons, peasants, swindlers . . .'

He looked to the right, at the white mosque which rose beautifully above the waters on its hill and continued his reminiscing:

'I've started drinking beer and I smoke cigars now. A German lives on the floor above me – they're a hard-headed lot, blast them! It's nice drinking beer, but I haven't got used to cigars yet! After I've had a good smoke my wife will only grumble: "What's that? You smell just like a saddler." Well, we live the best we can, and we have to keep our wits about us. Come on, *you* do the steering!'

He put the oar on the side of the boat, took his rifle and fired at a plaster Chinaman on a roof. But he did not manage to hit it and the small shot splattered over the roof and walls, raising clouds of dust.

'Missed!' he said without much regret and reloaded his rifle.

'Been with any of the girls yet? No? When I was thirteen I was already in love.'

Just as though he were reliving a dream he told me the story of his first love – for a chambermaid who worked in an architect's house, where he was living as an apprentice.

The grey water softly splashed, washing the corners of buildings. A watery desert gleamed dully beyond the cathedral and the black branches of willows stuck out of it here and there. In the ikon workshop they had often sung the seminary school song:

> Oh, blue sea,
> Stormy sea . . . :

here there was deathly boredom and that blue sea must have been just the same as this watery desert.

'I didn't sleep for several nights,' the master continued. 'I used to get up and stand by her door, trembling like a little dog. It was cold in that house! At night-time her master used to go to her room and he could easily have caught me, but I wasn't afraid, oh no . . .'

He spoke in a very thoughtful voice, as though he were examining an old, worn-out suit to see if it was still fit to wear.

'She heard me, took pity on me, opened her door and said: "Come in, you little fool."'

I had heard many stories like that, and they bored me, although they did have one pleasant feature: almost everyone spoke about their first 'love' without trying to show off and without being crude; often they spoke so warmly and sadly that it was easy to understand that it was the best thing that had ever happened to them. Indeed it seemed that for many of them this was in fact the only good thing in their empty lives.

My master laughed, and shook his head as he exclaimed, surprised at himself for having told me this:

'Don't tell the wife, whatever you do! Don't say anything, or there'll be hell to pay! . . .'

He seemed to be talking not to me, but to himself. If he had not kept talking the whole time then I would have said something: in all that silence and depressing emptiness one *had* to say something, sing, play the accordion; otherwise one would have fallen asleep for ever in that dead town which was submerged in the cold grey water.

'First of all, don't get married when you're young!' he advised. 'Marriage is *very* important. *You* can live wherever you like, it's up to you. You can live in Persia, or be a policeman in Moscow. *You* can be miserable, you can steal but you can always change things. But a wife is like the weather. You can't change her. No! She's not a shoe to be picked up and thrown away.'

His expression changed as he frowned at the grey water, rubbed his hooked nose and muttered:

'Now, my friend, you must keep your eyes open.'

We sailed among the bushes in Meshchersky lake, which had joined up with the Volga.

'Row slower,' he whispered as he aimed his rifle at the bushes.

After he had shot a few scraggy-looking snipe he ordered:

'Let's go to Kunavino! I'll stay there until the evening. You can tell them at home that I've been held up by some contractors.'

After I had landed him in one of the streets in Kunavino, which was also flooded, I returned by way of the fair to Strelka, tied the boat up and sat looking at the junction of the two rivers, at the town, the steamships and the sky, which, with white feather clouds scattered all over it, was like the wing of an enormous bird. The golden sun appeared in the blue abysses between the clouds and with one look transformed the whole earth. Everything around me moved briskly, firmly and the fast current of the river effortlessly carried away the innumerable chains of rafts: bearded peasants stood solidly on them moving their long oars, shouting at each other and at approaching ships. A small paddleboat was towing an empty barge upstream, and the river caught hold of it, pushed it about, making its prow writhe like a pike. The paddleboat kept panting away as it stubbornly drove its wheels through the water that flowed so swiftly against it. Four men sat shoulder to shoulder on the barge with their feet dangling over the side. One of them was wearing a red shirt and singing. I could not hear the words but I knew that song . . .

I thought that here, on that living river, I was familiar with everything. Every object seemed close to me – and intelligible. But that town which lay submerged behind me was nothing but a bad dream, an invention of the master's, and just as hard to understand as he was. After I had grown tired of feasting my eyes I would return home feeling like a grown-up person and capable of any work. On the way I would look down on the Volga from the fortress, and from there, high up, the distant world seemed enormous and promised me whatever I wanted.

I had some books at home. A large family now lived in Queen Margot's flat: five girls, each prettier than the other, and two schoolboys. They used to give me books to read. I greedily read Turgenev and was amazed how he made the whole of life so easy to understand, so simple, as clear as the days in autumn, how noble his characters were and how good and gentle everything was in his novels. I was amazed as well when I read Pomyalovsky's *Seminary Sketches*; the life described there bore a strange resemblance to that I had known in the ikon work-shop: I myself was very familiar with the despair of utter boredom, a boredom that found an outlet in cruel practical jokes. I liked reading Russian books and they always evoked something that was at once familiar and sad. It was as though the sound of Easter bells was hidden among the pages and muffled by them and all one had to do was open the book and they would softly chime.

I read *Dead Souls* without much enthusiasm; nor did I like *Letters from the House of the Dead*. *Dead Souls, House of the Dead, Death, Three Deaths, Living Relics* – all these books with their similar titles were bound to capture my attention but they filled me with a vague feeling of hostility. Nor did I like *Sign of the Times, Step by Step, What Is To Be done?, Chronicle of Smurin Village*, or any books of that type. But I loved Dickens and Walter Scott. I read these authors with the deepest plea-sure, and sometimes I read the same book two or three times. Scott's novels made me think of a service on some high holiday in a richly decorated church – long and boring, but always triumphant and majestic. Dickens was a writer before whom I bowed respectfully: that man had succeeded marvellously in the most difficult art of showing how dear humanity was to him.

In the evenings a large crowd used to collect on the front steps of the house. There were the 'K' brothers, their sisters and some young men; the snub-nosed schoolboy Vyacheslav Semashko; and sometimes Miss Ptitsyna came – she was the daughter of an important civil servant. They used to discuss books and poetry, and all this was close and intelligible to me. I had read more than all of them. Most often they would talk about the Gymnasium, and they complained about the teachers. As I listened to their stories I was amazed at the extent of their patience. All the same I envied them for being able to study! My friends were older than I was, but it struck me that *I* was really older, more mature and more experienced than all of them. This embarrassed me, as I wanted to feel closer to them. I used to return home late in the evening, covered in dust and mud, full of impressions that were quite different from theirs, which never varied very much. They talked a lot about girls, fell in love with one and then another, and they tried to write poetry. They often asked me to help them and I eagerly grasped the opportunity of practising the art. I could rhyme very easily but for some reason my verse invariably turned out funny. I always found myself comparing Miss Ptitsyna – to whom I dedicated most of my poems – to vegetables, especially onions. Semashka used to say: 'Do you call *this* poetry? It's bootnails!'

As I did not want to be outdone in any way by the others I fell in love with Miss Ptitsyna as well. I do not remember how I expressed my love, but the affair had a disastrous ending. There used to be an old floor-board floating in the slimy green water of Zvezdin pond and once I offered to give her a ride on it. She agreed and I brought the board over to the bank, stood on it and it bore my weight very well. But when that richly dressed young lady in her lace and ribbons gracefully took her position on the other end and I proudly shoved off with a stick, the wretched thing suddenly turned over and threw her into the pond. Like a gallant knight I dived in after her and dragged her to the bank. Then I saw that panic together with the green slime of the pond had quite destroyed my lady's beauty! She threatened me with a dripping finger and shouted:

'You tried to drown me on purpose!'

She did not believe that I was really very sorry and from that time onwards I was her enemy.

On the whole, life was not very interesting in the town. The old mistress was as hostile to me as before. Her daughter-in-law regarded me with suspicion. Viktor, who had more freckles than ever, used to sniff at everyone, as though he had been mortally insulted.

The master had a great number of plans to draw up for his clients and as he and his brother could not cope with the work he asked my stepfather to help. Once I came back early from the fair – at five o'clock – and when I went into the dining-room I saw that man whom I had completely forgotten sitting at the tea table next to my master. He held out his hand and said:

'Hullo.'

I was so taken by surprise that I did not know where to put myself: it was as though the past had suddenly flared up and burned my heart.

'He looks frightened,' the master said.

My stepfather looked at me with a smile on his terribly thin face. His dark eyes had grown even bigger and he seemed absolutely worn-out and broken by the world. I thrust my hand into his thin warm fingers.

'Well, so we meet again,' he said with a slight cough.

I went away feeling weak, just as though I had been crushed. A rather cautious, ill-defined relationship developed between us. My stepfather called me by my first name and patronymic, and talked to me as though I were his equal.

'When you go shopping get me a quarter pound of Laferme tobacco, a hundred Victorsen cigarette papers and a pound of smoked sausage.'

The money he gave me was always unpleasantly warm from his hands. It was obvious that he had tuberculosis and was not long for this world. He knew this and would say in his calm, deep voice as he twisted his sharp black beard:

'My illness is almost incurable. However, if I eat a lot of meat, then I've a chance.'

He used to eat an incredible amount and while he was eating he smoked, and the only time he took the cigarette out of his mouth was when he put some food into it. Every day I used to buy him sausages, ham and sardines, but Grandmother's sister would say in a confident and spiteful voice:

'You won't cheat death by feeding it. Oh no!'

The master and mistress paid my stepfather so much attention that it became insulting. They never stopped advising him what medicine to try but the whole time they were laughing behind his back. The young mistress would say:

'Calls himself a nobleman! They say you should always sweep crumbs off the table as they breed flies,' and the old mistress would chime in:

'A fine nobleman! His jacket's worn out, it's shiny all over, but still he keeps brushing it. He's so fussy – frightened of a speck of dust!'

And the master seemed to be actually consoling them when he said:

'You wait, he'll be dead soon!'

This absurd, hostile attitude of those small tradespeople to the aristocracy only brought me closer to my stepfather. A fly-agaric mushroom was poisonous but at least it was beautiful. My stepfather, who was slowly suffocating among all those people, was like a fish which somehow had swum into a hen-house: a comparison that may appear absurd, but so was the life there. I found he had much in common with 'Just the Job', whom I could never forget. I endowed my stepfather and Queen Margot with all the best qualities I found in books, all that was best in myself, all that my fantasies and my reading had aroused. My stepfather was as remote and unloved as 'Just the Job'. He was very easy-going with everyone in the house, never spoke first and usually answered any questions very politely and precisely. I was very pleased when he started teaching the master architecture. He would stand by the table, almost bent double, and calmly instruct him as he tapped his dry fingernail on the thick drawing paper:

'Here you must strengthen the rafters with a truss – it will take the stress off the walls. If you don't the rafter will push through the wall.'

'He's damn well right,' my master murmured, but as soon as my stepfather had gone his wife said:

'I'm amazed that you can let him teach you!'

For some reason she was particularly annoyed when my stepfather cleaned his teeth and his sharp adam's apple would stick out as he rinsed his mouth after dinner.

'In my opinion,' she said acidly, 'you can do yourself an injury bending your head like that, Evgeny Vasilych!'

He would smile politely and ask:

'But how?'

'Well, because...'

Then he would start cleaning his bluish nails with a tooth-pick.

'Really, he's cleaning his fingernails now!' the mistress would say in alarm. 'He's dying, and yet he can still do that!...'

'Oh!' the master sighed, 'you've all become so incredibly stupid, you silly cows!'

'What's that you said?' asked his wife, flaring up.

The old woman would passionately air her grievances to God at night-time:

'Oh God, I'm stuck with a man who's just rotting away, and my little Viktor has no time for me...'

Viktor began mimicking my stepfather's habits, his slow walk, the confident movements of his elegant arms, his knack of tying his tie very smartly, of eating without making a noise. Now and again he would rudely ask:

'Maximov, what's French for knee?'

'My Christian name is Evgeny,' my stepfather would calmly remind him.

'All right then! What about the word for breast?'

During the dinner Viktor would ask his mother in garbled French:

'*Ma mère, donnez moisencore* salt beef!'

'You dear little frog!' the old woman would answer affectionately. My stepfather would carry on eating his meat without looking at anyone, as unperturbed as a deaf-mute.

Once the elder brother said to Viktor:

'Well, Viktor, when you've learned French you'd better get yourself a mistress.'

This was the only time I can remember my stepfather silently smiling at anything they said. But the master's wife got excited, threw her spoon on the table and shouted to her husband:

'You should be ashamed of yourself, saying such filthy things in front of me!'

Sometimes my stepfather came to see me by the back entrance. I used to sleep there, under the attic stairs, and I would read sitting by a window.

'Reading again?' he would ask as he puffed out clouds of cigarette smoke. 'What is it now?'

I would show him the book.

'Ah,' he said, looking at the title. 'I think I've read that! Like a cigarette?'

We puffed away and looked out on to the filthy yard. Then my stepfather would say:

'I'm very sorry you can't go to school. It seems you have ability.'

'But I do study . . . I read books . . .'

'That's not enough. You need to go to school, you need discipline.'

I felt like saying to him: 'Once, my dear sir, *you* went to school where there was discipline, proper teaching, and what good did it do you?'

But he seemed to suspect what I was thinking and added:

'If you have character you can get a lot out of school. Only well-educated people get on in this life . . .'

But once he offered me some different advice:

'I think the best thing for you to do is to get out of this place. I don't see the sense in stopping. It's no good to you.'

'I like being with workmen.'

'Oh? Why?'

'It's interesting.'

'Well, perhaps you're right.

But once he said:

'If you ask me the master and mistress are trash!'

I remembered Mother using that word and I could not help edging away from him.

He smiled and asked:

'You don't agree?'

'Not really . . .'

'So I see!'

'I *like* the master,' I added.

'Yes, he's a good working man. But he's so comical!'

I wanted to discuss books with him but he evidently did not like them, and more than once he advised me:

'Don't *ever* get carried away by books. You'll find that everything is painted in glowing colours in them, and is somehow distorted. Most people who write books are like the master, just small fry . . .'

Judgements like these struck me as very daring and they finally won me over to his side.

Once he asked me:

'Have you read Goncharov?'

'Yes, *The Frigate Pallas*.'

'That's a very boring book. But really, Goncharov is the cleverest writer in Russia. I advise you to read his novel *Oblomov*. That's his most truthful and boldest work. Yes, the best book in the whole of Russian literature.'

He used to say about Dickens:

'A lot of rubbish, I assure you. Now, in the supplement to the *New Times* there's a very interesting story called *The Temptation of St Anthony*. You must read that! You seem to like the church . . . you'll learn a lot from *The Temptation*.'

He brought me a whole pile of supplements and I read Flaubert's work, which was full of wisdom. It reminded me of the innumerable lives of the saints, of some of those stories the Bible scholar told me, but it did not make any particular impression. I far preferred *Memoirs of Upilio Faimali the Animal-Tamer* which was printed in the same supplement. But when I admitted this to my stepfather he calmly remarked:

'That means you're too young to read Flaubert! But don't forget the book I mentioned . . .'

Sometimes he sat for a long time with me, without saying a word, just coughing and puffing out smoke. His fine eyes had a fiery gleam about them that was very unnerving. I quietly watched him and forgot that this man, who was dying so nobly and simply, without complaining, had once been close to Mother and had treated her terribly. I knew that he was now living with some dressmaker and I felt very puzzled and sorry for her: putting her arms round that bony body, kissing that mouth which smelled of decay must surely disgust her?

Like 'Just the Job' my stepfather used suddenly to come out with remarks that no one else would make:

'I *love* hunting-dogs. They're stupid, but I love them. They're lovely animals. You know, beautiful women tend to be stupid.'

I used to think proudly: 'But you don't know Queen Margot!'
Once he said:

'Everyone who lives a long time in the same house as other people begins to *look* like them in the end.'

I wrote this down in my notebook. I waited for him to make these pronouncements as though they were gifts from heaven. It was pleasant listening to those unusual combinations of words in a house where everyone spoke a colourless language which had ossified into stale monotonous phrases.

My stepfather never spoke to me about Mother and never even so much as mentioned her name. This really pleased me and it made me almost respect him.

Once I asked him about God – I don't remember exactly what. He looked at me and said very calmly:

'I don't know. I don't believe in God.'

I remembered what Sitanov had said and told my stepfather about him; he listened to me very attentively and then he said in that same calm voice:

'He strikes me as a man who likes to reason and that kind of person always believes in *something* or other. But I simply don't believe in anything!'

'But how is that possible!'

'Why not? You can see for yourself – I just don't believe.'

There was only one thing that *I* could see – that he was dying. I was not even sorry for him, although at first I did feel a keen and natural interest in a dying relative, in death and its mysteries . . . And here was a man sitting right next to me, touching me with his knee – a warm, thinking being.

He confidently categorized people according to his relationships with them. He spoke about everyone as though he had the power of judging them and passing verdict on them, and he possessed something that I needed, or rather, something which showed me what I would do best to ignore. He was an incredibly complicated person, a storehouse of thoughts that never stopped whirling round and round. No matter how I behaved towards him, he seemed to be a part of me and lived somewhere inside me. When I thought about him his soul would cast a shadow over mine. The very next day he might disappear from the world altogether, with all that was hidden away in his head and heart, all that I thought that I could read in his beautiful eyes. When he had gone one of those vital threads that bound me to the world would snap: the memory of him would remain, but it would remain imprisoned within me for ever and become fixed, immutable, while the living and changing person made of flesh and blood would vanish . . . But these were only thoughts, and behind them lay something that one could not express in words, something that gave birth to them and nourished them, compelling one to look hard at life and demanding an answer to everything: why did it happen?

'I don't think I've got very long,' my stepfather said one rainy day. 'I feel stupid, being so weak. And I just haven't the will to do *anything*!'

Next morning when they were having tea he took special care to brush the crumbs from the table and from his knees. It was as though he were getting rid of something that was invisible to the rest of us. But the old mistress looked at him out of the corner of her eye and said to her daughter-in-law:

'Just watch him preening himself!'

Two days later he did not turn up for work and soon after the old mistress gave me a large envelope and said:

'Oh, by the way, a woman brought this yesterday afternoon. I forgot to give it to you. Nice woman she was, but I don't know if she's a relative of yours or what!'

Written in large letters on a piece of hospital paper were the words: 'If you have an hour to spare come and see me. I'm in the Martynov Hospital. E.M.'

Next morning I was sitting on my stepfather's bed in a hospital ward. He was longer than the bed and his legs stuck out through the rails at the end and his grey socks were nearly off his feet. His handsome eyes vaguely wandered over the yellow walls, then stopped on my face, and on the arms of the girl sitting on a stool at the head of the bed. She put her hands on the pillow and my stepfather rubbed his cheek on them and opened his mouth. The girl was rather plump and wore a dark shiny dress. Tears slowly trickled down her oval-shaped face and she did not take her moist, light blue eyes from his face for one second and kept staring at his bony body, his large, sharp nose and dark mouth.

'We should send for a priest,' she whispered. 'But he doesn't want one. He doesn't seem to understand anything.'

She lifted her hands from the pillow and pressed them to her breast as though she were praying. For a moment my stepfather regained consciousness, looked at the ceiling, frowned seriously and stretched his thin hand out to me as though he had just remembered something.

'Is it you? You see . . . I feel so stupid . . .'

The effort of speaking exhausted him and he closed his eyes. I stroked those long cold fingers with their blue nails and the girl gently asked:

'Evgeny Vasilyevich, please say you agree!'

'I must introduce you,' he said nodding towards her. 'A nice girl . . .'

He fell silent and his mouth opened wider and wider. Suddenly he shouted, and shrieked like a crow. He tossed around on the bed, pulled the sheets off and waved his bare arms around. The girl shrieked as well and buried her head in the crumpled pillow. My stepfather did not take long to die, but the moment he was dead he looked handsome again. I left the hospital arm-in-arm with the girl. She staggered as though she had been taken ill and she cried. In one hand she held a handkerchief crumpled into a ball. She kept dabbing her eyes with it, and crumpled it more and more, as though it were her most precious possession, the last thing she had in the world. Suddenly she stopped, pressed close to me and said resentfully:

'He didn't last until the winter. Oh God, what does it all mean?'

Then she held out her hand which was wet from tears.

'Good-bye. He thought highly of you. We must bury him tomorrow . . .'

'Can I see you home?'

'What for? It's day-time.'

I watched her from the corner of an alley: she walked slowly, like a person who had no reason for hurrying anywhere. It was August and already the leaves were falling from the trees. I did not have time to go to the funeral – and I never saw that girl again.

Chapter 17

EVERY morning at six o'clock I went off to work at the fair. The people I met there were interesting. Osip the carpenter was a greyish-looking man who reminded me of St Nikolai. He was a skilful workman and very witty. Then there were Efimushka the hunch-backed tiler, Pyotr the pensive and religious brick-layer, who also looked like a saint, and Grigory Shishlin the plasterer, a handsome man with a blond beard and blue eyes, who radiated kindness. I knew these men during the second period of my life with the draughtsman. Every Sunday they used to turn up in the kitchen looking very grave and solemn and say pleasant things, with little refinements of speech – something that was new to me. All these respectable citizens seemed thoroughly good men. Each was interesting in his own way, and all of them were very different from the evil, thieving, drunken shopkeepers in the Kunavino district.

I liked Shishlin the plasterer most of all. I even asked him if I could work with him, but he scratched his fair eyebrows with a pale finger and said softly:

'It's too early for you to be doing our kind of work. It's not easy. Wait a year or two.'

Then he lifted up his handsome head and asked:

'Things not going too well? Don't worry. Just grin and bear it. Take a firm stand!'

I don't know what use that kind advice was, but I gratefully remembered it.

The men used to come to the master's house every Sunday morning, sit on the benches around the kitchen table and have interesting talks while they waited for the master, who greeted them boisterously and cheerfully as he shook their strong hands and then sat in the corner by the door. Account sheets, bundles of banknotes appeared and the men laid them out on the table by the side of tattered notebooks: the week's reckoning had started. The master tried to cheat them as he cracked jokes, and they tried to do the same. Sometimes they quarrelled violently, but more often than not they all laughed and were very friendly.

'Oh, you're a born swindler,' the men used to say to the master.

He would answer them with an embarrassed laugh:

'And you wild animals are swindlers as well!'

'Well, what do you expect?' Efimushka admitted, while solemn Pyotr said:

'You have to steal to live. What you earn honestly goes to God and the Tsar.'

'As if I'd want to swindle *you* lot!' the master laughed. They good-naturedly agreed.

Grigory Shishlin pressed his thick beard to his chest and asked in a singing voice:

'Look, can't we work together without cheating? Can't we all live honestly, and peacefully? We're all *Russians*, aren't we?'

His blue eyes became dark and moist. At times like these he was superb.

Everyone was rather disconcerted by his questions and turned away in embarrassment.

'You won't get much out of peasants,' growled the handsome Osip and he sighed as though he felt sorry for them.

The swarthy round-shouldered bricklayer Pyotr bent over the table and said in a deep voice:

'Sin is like a swamp: the further you go into it, the harder it is to get out.'

Then the master said in the same sermonizing tone:

'What about me? If I'm bitten I jump!'

After this philosophizing the men once again tried to swindle each other and when they were all paid up and were sweating and exhausted from the mental exertion they went off to the pub to drink tea and invited the master to go with them.

My job at the fair was to see that the men did not steal any nails, bricks or planks. Each one of them had some contracts of his own apart from the work they did for my master and tried to steal building materials from right under my nose.

When I appeared they gave me a warm welcome and Shishlin said:

'Remember you asked if you could work with me? Well, look what's happened! You'll be telling *me* what to do next, won't you?'

'All right, all right,' Osip said jokingly. 'Just look after yourself and may God help you!'

Pyotr said in an unfriendly voice:

'So they've got a young crane to order old mice around . . .'

My job was sheer torture. I felt ashamed in front of those men: they all seemed to be harbouring some secret, something fine that nobody else knew about, and I had to treat them as though they were thieves and swindlers. My first few days with them were very difficult, but Osip soon noticed this and told me quite frankly:

'Now don't start getting big ideas, that's no good. Understand?'

Of course I understood nothing, but I felt that the old man could see how stupid my position was and soon we began to speak to each other quite openly about everything. He would take me aside and tell me:

'If you really want to know, the worst thief is that bricklayer Petrukha. He's got a large family and needs as much money as he can get. Watch out when you're with him, he'll steal anything – whether it's a pound of nails, a dozen bricks, a sack of lime he'll take it. He's a good man though, says his prayers, has firm beliefs, and he can read and write. And yet he loves stealing! Efimushka lives off women. He's on the quiet side and won't cause you any trouble. He's clever as well – hunchbacks are no fools! But as for that Grigory Shishlin, he's *really* stupid. He won't take what doesn't belong to him, but he'll give all he has away. He works for absolutely nothing. *Anyone* can swindle him but *he* can't do it himself. Doesn't use his loaf . . .'

'Is he a good man?' I asked.

Osip looked at me as though he were talking from a long way off and then he produced the memorable words:

'Now you've hit the nail on the head! It's the simplest thing in the world for a lazy person to be good. To be good you don't need brains, my lad!'

'And are *you* a good person?' I asked Osip.

He smiled and said:

'I'm like a girl, and when I'm a grown woman I'll tell you all about myself, so you'll have to wait! Try and find out for yourself what I'm really like. Go on!'

He upset all my preconceived ideas about him and his friends. It was difficult to doubt the truth of what he said and I could see that Efimushka, Pyotr and Grigory considered that handsome old man cleverer and better informed in all practical things than themselves. They asked his advice about everything, listened to what he said very carefully and treated him with great respect.

'Do us a favour, give us some advice,' they used to ask him.

But once, after Osip had given them some, the bricklayer calmly said to Grigory:

'He's a heretic.'

Grigory smiled and said: 'And a clown.'

The plasterer gave me a friendly warning:

'Watch out, Maximych, you have to be careful with that old man. He'll twist you round his little finger before you know where you are! These old men can do a great deal of harm – if you give them half a chance!'

But I did not understand a thing he said. It seemed that the most honest and upright man was Pyotr the bricklayer. He spoke about everything very briefly, but with an infectious enthusiasm. Most often he thought about God, hell and death and used to say:

'Hey, however much you struggle, whatever you hope for in this life, you'll all end up in the grave!'

He suffered from continual stomach-ache and there were days when he could not eat anything. Even a small slice of bread sent him into terrible convulsions and made him violently sick. Efimushka the hunchback also appeared to be a kind and honest man, but he always struck me as comical, even mad at times, like a harmless imbecile. He was perpetually falling in love with different women and spoke about them all in exactly the same way:

'I'm telling you straight. She's not just a *woman*, but a flower in cream! Oh-o-oh!'

When the lively housewives from Kunavino came to wash the shop floors Efimushka would climb down from the roof, stand in some corner, screw up his grey, bright eyes and purr like a cat, opening his mouth so wide that it reached his ears.

'What a succulent little morsel God's sent me! What joy he's sent me from heaven. Just look at this flower in cream. How can I ever be grateful enough for such a present? Her beauty's set me alight!'

At first the women laughed at him and shouted to each other: 'Just look at that hunchback pining away. Heavens!'

Their jeers did not in the least upset him; his face with its prominent cheekbones grew dreamy and he talked as though he were delirious. Cloying words flowed from him in an intoxicating stream and clearly went to the women's heads. In the end one of the older women told her friends in a startled voice: 'Just listen to him suffering – like a young boy!'

'Sings like a bird.'

'More like a beggar at the church door!'

But Efimushka did not look like a beggar to me. He stood there as solid as a thick block of wood. His voice began to sound even more appealing, his words became more seductive and the women listened in silence. He really seemed to be melting them with his sweet, heady words. These scenes used to end with him shaking his heavy angular head after morning break and saying to his friends in amazement:

'What a sweet, *dear* little woman. First time in my life I've laid my hands on one like *her*!'

Efimushka did not boast when he told us about his conquests. Nor did he laugh at his victim like the others. All he did was look grateful, full of joy, with his grey eyes wide open in surprise.

Osip shook his head and exclaimed:

'Ugh, you're a tough one, and no mistake! How old are you?'

'Forty-four. But that's nothing! Today I've grown five years younger, it's just like I've been swimming in the river, in the fresh water. I feel so healthy, at peace with *everything*! But would you think such women existed, eh?'

But the bricklayer said to him sternly:

'When you're fifty you'd better look out. Then you'll pay bitterly for those filthy habits of yours!'

'Yes, you've no self-respect, Efimushka,' Grigory Shishlin agreed with a sigh.

It struck me, however, that the handsome workman was in fact jealous of the hunchback's success with women.

Osip surveyed everyone from under his evenly twisted silvery eyebrows and started telling jokes:

307

'Every little Mary has her likes and dislikes. This one likes spoons, that one spangles or earrings; every little Mary grows into a grandmother...'

Shishlin was married, but his wife had stayed behind in the country so he used to take a lively interest in the women who came to wash the floors as well. They were all very easy and each one was ready to do 'a little overtime'. In this hungry quarter of the town earning money this way was looked upon like any other kind of work. However, that handsome workman did not lay a hand on the women, but watched them from a distance instead, with that peculiar look of his, as though he were feeling sorry for them – or for himself perhaps. And when they took the initiative and started flirting with him and tried to tempt him he would laugh in an embarrassed sort of way and walk off.

'As for you lot!...' he would say to the other men.

'What did you say? You're a funny fellow!' Efimushka would reply in astonishment. 'How can you let a chance like that slip?...'

'I'm married,' he would remind them.

'But surely your wife won't find out?'

'Wives always find out if you've been unfaithful. You'll never deceive *them*, my friend!'

'But how *can* she find out?'

'I don't know really. But she's bound to find out if she's faithful herself. If I'm faithful and she betrays me, then *I'll* know...'

'But *how*?' Efimushka shouted, while Grigory calmly replied: 'That I don't know.'

The roof-tiler flung out his arms excitedly and said:

'Wha-at! You can't *really* know if someone's faithful or not, you stupid nit!'

The seven men who worked for Shishlin treated him rather unceremoniously, not as their master at all, and behind his back they called him a weakling. When he arrived at a site and saw that they were lazing around he would take a spade and, like an artist in his work, would start digging himself, while he shouted to the men in that friendly voice of his: 'Come on, let's get started then!'

Once when I was carrying out my own angry master's orders I said to Grigory:

'Your workmen are no good.'

This seemed to surprise him.

'Well, what of it?'

'That job should have been finished yesterday morning, but they won't get it done today even.'

'True, they won't finish it . . .' he agreed and after a short silence added cautiously: 'Of course, I can see that, but I feel too ashamed to hurry them up. After all, they're from *my* village. What's more, it's said "By the sweat of thy brow shall ye eat bread", and that means *everyone*, you and me. Both of us do less work than the men, so it's not right for us to drive *them* hard.'

He was a thoughtful person and was in the habit of wandering down the deserted streets of the fair and suddenly stopping on one of the bridges over the Obvodny canal. He would stand there for a long time at the railing, gazing into the water, at the sky, and along the Oka. I would catch him up and ask:

'What are you doing?'

'What?' he would say with an embarrassed smile, as though I had just woken him up. 'I was just . . . I just stopped to have a look . . .'

'God's taken care of *everything*,' he would often say. 'The dear sky and the earth. Rivers flow and steamboats sail – all because of him. You can go wherever you like on a steamboat. To Ryazan, or Rybinsk, Perm, even as far as Astrakhan! I've been to Ryazan. Not much of a town, and very boring – more boring than Nizhny. But Nizhny is a fine place really. It's so lively! It's more boring in Astrakhan. The chief thing about Astrakhan is the Kalmuks. I don't like them. I don't like any of those Mordvinians, or Kalmuks, Persians, Germans and tiny little nations . . .'

He would speak slowly and he always seemed to be looking carefully for someone who had the same opinions – and this person was invariably Pyotr the bricklayer.

'They're not really people, they pass everything by,' Pyotr would say confidently and angrily. 'They were without Christ when they were born, and they ignore him now.'

At this Grigory would liven up and beam all over his face:

'Whether that's right or wrong, I like a *pure* nation like the Russian, with eyes that look straight and true! I don't like Jews and can't understand why God needs little nations like them. It all must have been very cleverly thought out.'

The bricklayer would add gloomily:

'Very clever, but there's a lot of things on this earth we could do without!'

Osip, who had been listening very attentively, would chime in and say in a sneering, caustic voice:

'Yes, you're right, there's a lot we could do without – all your sermons for example! Oh, you mad lot! You should all be flogged!'

Osip kept to himself, but I could not really understand what he agreed with or what he was arguing against. Sometimes it seemed that he could not care less about anything and that he agreed with everyone and with everything they thought. But most often I could see that everything bored him and that he thought that most people were half-wits. He used to say to Pyotr, Grigory and Efimushka:

'Oh, you little pigs!'

They would reply simply by smiling – not very cheerfully or enthusiastically – but they smiled all the same.

The master gave me five kopeks a day for my food. This was not nearly enough and I often went hungry. When they saw this the men invited me to have breakfast and the midday snack with them. Sometimes the sub-contractors themselves asked me to go to the pub and have some tea. I eagerly agreed, as I liked being with them, listening to the slow way they had of speaking and their strange stories. My knowledge of theological books gave them a lot of pleasure.

'You've stuffed yourself enough with books, your gizzard must be full of them!' Osip said staring at me with eyes the colour of cornflowers. It was difficult to make out their exact expression as the pupils always seemed to be dilating and melting away.

'You'd better remember this: learn what you can, it'll come in handy one day. When you grow up, you must become a monk and comfort people with your learning. Or you must become a millionaire.'*

'*Missionary*,' the bricklayer corrected him and he really sounded most annoyed.

'Wh-at?' Osip asked.

'They're called *missionaries*, surely you know that! Are you deaf? . . .'

'All right then, a missionary, so he can argue with heretics.' Then he turned to me:

'Why don't *you* become a heretic then – it's very profitable. With brains and heresy you can make a good living.'

Grigory laughed in bewilderment while Pyotr said softly:

'And magicians don't do too badly either, or any sort of pagan or non-believer.'

But Osip retorted at once:

'But magicians have no *learning*, it just doesn't seem to suit them!'

And then he would tell me a story:

'Now listen hard. A poor peasant used to live in our village. He was called Tushka, and he was a miserable, insignificant devil. Just like a feather he was and he went whichever way the wind blew. He wasn't a workman, but he didn't laze around either. So one day, as he had nothing better to do, he went on a pilgrimage for two years, and when he came back he looked a different man. His hair was down to his shoulders, and he was wearing a skull cap and a red leather cassock. He goggled at everyone and told them straight: "Repent, O cursed ones!" And why shouldn't they repent, especially the women? And everything turned out all right for him. Now Tushka was well-fed, now Tushka was drunk, now Tushka was terribly pleased with the women . . .'

The bricklayer angrily interrupted:

'But that's not the point, whether he was well-fed or drunk!'

'What *is* the point then?'

'It's in *what he said*!'

'Well, I didn't try to find out exactly what words he used.'

* The mistake is more obvious in the Russian, with *missioner* meaning missionary. (Trans.)

'We all know Dmitry Tushnikov* quite well,' Pyotr said, flaring up, while Grigory silently lowered his head and peered into his glass.

'I'm not going to argue,' Osip said in a pacifying voice. 'I'm just telling Maximych all about these so-called roads to happiness . . .'

'But all other roads lead to prison.'

'Not very often!' exclaimed Osip. 'Not all roads lead to the priesthood either: you must know where to turn off . . .'

He always teased religious people a little – such as the plasterer and the bricklayer. But if he did not like them, then he cunningly concealed the fact. It was impossible to understand what he really thought of people. But he seemed kinder, gentler with Efimushka. The roof-tiler did not take part in these discussions about God, truth, religious sects, about the misery of human life, all of which were very popular topics. He would place his chair sideways to the table, so that the back did not press against his hump, and calmly sit there drinking glass after glass of tea. Suddenly he would prick his ears up, look round the smoky room, listen intently to the chaotic noise of voices, then spring to his feet and rapidly vanish: this meant that a creditor had turned up. He owed at least a dozen people money, and since some of them used to beat him up he would escape while the going was good.

'What's that lot getting all worked up about?' he would say, completely nonplussed. 'I'd pay them if I had the money, wouldn't I?'

Osip would tell him off as he went: 'Ugh, you old parasite!'

Sometimes Efimushka would sit there a long time deep in thought, blind and deaf to the world. His face, with its high cheekbones, would soften and his eyes seemed even kinder.

'What are you thinking about now, you old soldier!' they would ask.

'I was thinking that if I were rich, I'd marry a real lady, from the nobility, a colonel's daughter, say. God, wouldn't I love her! She would burn me up with love! Yes, I was once repairing a roof for a colonel's country house . . .'

* The full surname, of which Tushka is a diminutive. (Trans.)

Pyotr interrupted hostilely: 'Yes, and he had a widowed daughter. We've heard all that before!'

But Efimushka rubbed his knees with the palms of his hands, rocked on his chair and continued:

'She'd come out into the garden, in a beautiful white dress. I'd look down from the roof and ask myself why I needed the sun, or the wide, wide world at all. All I wanted was to be a dove and to fly down to her feet. She was just like a sky-blue flower – growing in cream! With a woman like that you'd pray for bed-time all day long – and for the rest of your life!'

'And what would you eat?' Pyotr would ask sternly.

But Efimushka was unruffled:

'Good God! What does a man need? Anyway, she'd be rich!'

Osip would laugh, and say:

'And when do you expect to start leading this life of luxury then?'

Women were Efimushka's sole topic of conversation. He was an unreliable workman: sometimes he would work extremely well, very quickly – and then things would start going wrong. His wooden mallet would be heard lazily hammering away at a roof, carelessly leaving knot holes everywhere. He always smelled of grease and oil, but he had his own special healthy, pleasant smell, very like freshly-cut wood.

It was interesting discussing any topic with the carpenter – interesting but not very pleasant, since what he had to say always disturbed me deeply, and it was difficult to know when he was speaking seriously or merely joking. Best of all I liked discussing God with Grigory. He loved talking about God and was a firm believer.

'Grisha,' I used to ask, 'do you know there are people who don't believe in God at all?'

He would calmly smile and say:

'How can that be?'

'They just say: there *is* no God!'

'Oh! To hell with them! I know that already.'

He would wave away an invisible fly and say:

'If you remember, King David said: "Only a madman says

in his heart that there is no God." Yes, that's what lunatics used to say. But you can't live without God.'

Osip seemed to agree and said:

'Take Pyotr's God away and he'll do you some terrible evil!'

Shishlin's face would become very forbidding. He would finger his beard (his nails were caked with lime) and say in a mysterious voice:

'God is part of all flesh. Your conscience, all that is deep within you, comes from God.'

'What about your sins?'

'Sins come from the flesh, from Satan! Sins are on the *outside*, like the pox. The man who thinks most about sin is the one who sins the most. If you don't think about sins, you won't commit any! Satan, who is master of the flesh, tries to fill you with sinful thoughts...'

The bricklayer sounded rather doubtful:

'That's not quite true...'

'But it *is*. God doesn't sin, and man is created in his image and likeness. It is the *image*, the flesh that sins. But the inner likeness cannot sin, it's a... likeness, pure spirit...'

He smiled triumphantly but Pyotr grumbled:

'But that's not so...'

Osip then asked the bricklayer:

'If I understand you right, if you don't sin, then you can't repent, and if you can't repent, then you won't find salvation.'

'But is *that* any better? If you forget the devil you'll stop loving God – that's what wise old men used to say.'

Shishlin hardly drank at all, and it took only two glasses to make him tipsy. His face would turn pink, his eyes became child-like, he would almost start singing:

'Yes, that's all lovely. We live our lives, do a bit of work and we have enough to eat, thank God. Oh, it's a wonderful world!'

He would start crying and his tears would trickle down on to his beard and glisten on the silky hairs like glass beads. I found this frequent praise of life and those glistening beads of sweat most unpleasant: Grandmother was much more convincing, spoke more simply when she praised life, and was much less opinionated than those men. These discussions kept me in a continual state of tension and aroused vague feelings of anxiety. I had read many stories about working men and I could already see the vast difference between men in books and those in real life. In books all workmen seemed to be unhappy. Whether they were good or evil, they were inferior to real workmen in thought and expression. Workmen in books spoke less about God, religious sects and the church and more about the 'authorities', the land, truth and the burdens of life. They even spoke less about women, and what they did say was far less crude and much more friendly. For the real-life working man women were only a source of amusement – but a dangerous one: with women one always had to be cunning or else they would get the upper hand and ruin one's life. Working men in books seemed to be either good or bad, and that was the end of it. Real ones, however, were neither good nor bad and as a result they were terribly interesting. However much a real workman poured his heart out one always felt that he was holding something back, something he did not wish others to know – and it was perhaps this that was most important. Out of all the men in the books I had read I preferred Pyotr in the *Carpenters' Guild*.

I wanted to read this story to my new friends and so I took the book to the fair. I often had to spend the night in some workshop, often because I just did not want to go back to the town while it was raining or because I was so tired that I simply did not have the strength to go home.

When I told them that I had a book about carpenters they were all very interested, especially Osip. He took the book from me, turned the pages over and mistrustfully shook his ikon-like head.

'It's all about *us*! Ugh, the devils! Who wrote it – a gentleman? Hm, I thought as much. Gentlemen and civil servants are capable of anything. If God can't find something out, then a civil servant will! That's how they get their living.'

'That's a bit careless of you, Osip, talking about God like that,' Pyotr observed.

'Far from it! What I say means less to God than a snowflake or one drop of rain on my bald head. There's no doubt about it – none of us will ever reach God.'

He suddenly poured out a stream of sharp words, like sparks flying from a flint stone and he used them like shears, to nip off anything that contradicted what he said.

Several times during the day he asked:

'Come on now, Maximych. Are you going to read to us?'

When they had knocked off work they went and had supper with Osip and later Pyotr turned up with his mate Ardalyon, and Shishlin came with a young boy called Foma. They lit a lamp in the shed where they slept and I started reading. They listened silently, without moving, but after a short while Ardalyon said angrily: 'I've had enough!' and left.

Grigory was the first to fall asleep. His mouth stayed wide open in astonishment, and soon he was followed by the carpenters. Pyotr, Osip and Foma, however, moved closer to me and listened very attentively. When I had finished Osip immediately put the lamp out and from the stars I could tell that it was already midnight. Then Pyotr asked out loud in the darkness:

'What's the point of that book? Who are they attacking?'

'It's time to go to sleep,' Osip said as he took his shoes off.

Foma turned away without saying a word.

Pyotr persisted with his question:

'I said, who are they attacking?'

'The person who wrote it will tell you!' Osip said as he lay down on his bunk.

'If it's stepmothers, then it's a sheer waste of time,' the brick-layer continued. 'It won't make them any better. If it's Pyotr, then it's also a waste of time: his sins speak for themselves. You're sent to Siberia for murder and that's all there is to it! There's no need for that book at all, we all know what the punishment is. A waste of time, I say. Well?'

Osip did not say a word. The bricklayer continued:

'They should have something better to do than poke their noses into other people's business. Just like a mothers' meeting! Well . . . good night . . . it's time to go to sleep.'

For a moment he stood in the bluish square of the open door and asked:

'Do you agree, Osip?'

'What?' the carpenter's sleepy voice echoed across the room.

'Nothing. Go to sleep...'

Shishlin turned over on his side in the same place where he had been sitting. Foma lay down on some ruffled straw next to me.

The whole suburb was asleep now and in the distance I could hear the whistle of locomotives, the heavy thunder of iron wheels and the sound of shunting. The shed was filled with the noise of snores, all pitched in different keys. I felt awkward and waited for someone to say something – but no one did. Then suddenly Osip said in a soft, clear voice:

'Don't believe any of that, mates. You're young and have a long life in front of you. Live on your wits and remember what you see, it'll always stand you in good stead. Are you asleep, Foma?'

Foma replied eagerly: 'No!'

'All right. Both of you can read and write, but don't believe everything you read. People can print what they like, and we can't do anything about it!'

He let his legs dangle down from his bunk, propped his arms on the edge of the planks, leaned over towards us and went on:

'What are we supposed to make of books? They're written to denounce people, that's for sure! – carpenters for example, or any other working man. But a gentleman's different! Books are never written without some reason but always in defence of something...'

Foma said in a deep voice:

'Pyotr was *right* to kill the contractor!'

'No, he was *wrong*. It's never right to kill a man! I know you don't like Grigory, so stop thinking those things. We're all poor. Today I'm boss and tomorrow I'll be a workman again'.

'I didn't mean *you*, Osip.'

'It's all the same.'

'You're right!'

'Wait, I'll tell you why that book was written,' Osip interrupted Foma, who was now very angry. 'It's a very *crafty* book. There you have a landowner without a peasant working for him, and a peasant without a master! Now, the landowner was having a rough time of it, and so was the peasant. The land-

317

owner became weak and stupid, and the peasant grew into a terrible boaster and drunkard, and he became ill and very touchy into the bargain! But in the days of serfdom landowners had a better time of it. Now the landowner covered up for the peasant, and the peasant did the same for the master, and as a result they were both well fed and had peace of mind. Now I'm not saying things were better under serfdom. It was no good for a landowner if his peasants were poor. Only if they were well-off. But they had to be stupid as well so he could keep them under his thumb. *I* should know, as I was a serf for forty years. You can read it on my skin!'

I remembered that Pyotr the cab-driver who cut his throat had said the same about gentlemen and landowners and it very much distressed me to hear that Osip's opinion coincided with that evil old man's attitude.

Osip touched my leg and went on:

'You must discover the real meaning of books, of *anything* that's written down! Everyone has a reason for doing *something*, and it only seems as if they're doing it for nothing. Books are written with a reason – to befuddle you. You can never get anything done without brains – you can't even use a chopper or make a bast-shoe without them . . .'

He went on like this for a long time, then lay down on his bed, but jumped up again, filling the quiet, dark room with his wonderful sayings:

'They say landowners and peasants are different kinds of people altogether. That's not true. We all come from them, only lower down. Of course, a gentleman has books to learn from, while we have to learn from knocks and bruises. A gentleman's arse is whiter than ours – that's the only difference! No, it's time the world was changed and they stopped writing books. Everyone should ask himself who he is. He'll answer that he's a man, like anyone else. And what's the master? Only a man – just like himself! So what's the difference if God expects a few more kopeks from the master – we're all equal when it comes to paying our debts . . .'

Towards morning, when the light of dawn had made all the stars vanish, Osip said to me:

'So you see, *I* can write too. I've said things I never even

318

thought of before. But don't believe everything I said! I wasn't being serious, I just couldn't get to sleep . . . You lie there and you think of something to pass the time to make you drop off: "Once there was a crow, it flew from the field to the hill, from hedge to hedge, and lived its life. Then it died and rotted away." Where's the sense in it? There just *isn't* any . . . Come on, let's get some sleep, it'll soon be time to get up . . .'

Chapter 18

LIKE Yakov the stoker, Osip assumed huge proportions and blotted out everyone else from me. He was very similar to Yakov in many ways, but at the same time he put me in mind of Grandfather, Pyotr Vasilyev the Bible scholar and Smury the cook. While he reminded me of these people, who were already firmly implanted in my memory, he left his own deeply engraved pattern in me and he seemed to eat into my memory like oxide into a bronze bell. It was obvious that he had two completely different ways of thinking. During the day-time, when he was working with the other men, his lively, simple thoughts struck me as more practical, easier for me to understand than during tea-breaks or in the evenings, when he went with me into the town to see his godmother who sold pancakes, or at night, when he could not sleep. He had his own special, precise way of thinking and his thoughts assumed many different forms like a flame in a lamp: they shone very brightly but I could not discover their true identity, which of them was closest and dearest to Osip. He seemed far cleverer than any-one I had ever met and in his company I felt the same as with Yakov the stoker: I dearly wanted to find out what he was really like. But he was elusive and would wriggle out of my grasp, making it impossible to pin him down: what was the real truth about this man and when could I believe what he said? I remember him telling me once:

'Go on, try and find out for *yourself* where I'm hiding!'

My pride was hurt, but this was not all: it became almost my sole purpose in life to understand that old man, to discover the truth about him. For all his elusiveness his character was very stable. It seemed that if he were to live another hundred years he would still be the same, firm and steady among a lot of terribly unstable people. The Bible scholar had this same im-movability but I did not find it very agreeable. Osip's stability was something altogether different and much more pleasant. The unsteadiness of the people around me was all too painfully evident and their clownish leaps from one predicament into

320

another always upset me. But I was no longer surprised by these inexplicable jumps, which gradually destroyed all my interest in them, with the result that I no longer loved them as I used to.

Once, at the beginning of July, a drozhky with some of its screws loose came tearing up to the site where we were working. A drunken, bearded driver sat gloomily hiccoughing on the box. He had lost his hat and had a cut lip. Grigory Shishlin, who was also drunk, was rolling around in the drozhky and a plump red-cheeked girl wearing a straw hat with red ribbon and glass cherries on it, with a parasol in one hand and rubber galoshes over her bare feet, tried to hold him still. She brandished the parasol, rocked to and fro, laughed out loud and shouted:

'The devil! The fair's closed. There *isn't* any fair, and he said he was taking me there!'

Grigory, who was dishevelled and looked as though he had just undergone the most terrible tortures, climbed down from the drozhky, sat on the ground and said to us with tears in his voice:

'I must kneel and pray – I've committed a terrible sin! I just got an idea . . . and I sinned! Efimushka said to me: "Grisha! Grisha! Stop it." He's right! Will you ever forgive me? I'll make up for it, I swear! Efimushka's right when he says we only live once but I'll never do anything like this again . . .'

The girl was choking with laughter, and she shook her feet so hard her galoshes came off.

The driver gloomily shouted:

'Let's get out of here quick! Loudmouths! Come on, the horse'll pass out soon!'

The horse, which was an old, worn-out nag stood there foaming at the mouth as though it had been struck by lightning and the whole scene was unbearably funny. Grigory's workmen split their sides when they saw their master with that tarted-up girl and a driver who seemed to have gone out of his mind. Foma was the only one who did not laugh and he stood by the shop door next to me and muttered:

'The filthy pig! And he's got a lovely wife at home!'

All this time the driver had been in a mad hurry to get away.

Finally the girl climbed down, lifted Grigory up into the drozhky, laid him across her lap, waved her parasol and shouted:

'Let's go!'

When those good-natured workmen had finished laughing – they were really jealous of their master – they obeyed Foma's furious shouts and went back to work: evidently Foma did not like seeing Grigory made to look such a fool.

'And he calls himself the boss!' he muttered. 'Only another month and he would have been back home . . . But *he* couldn't wait.'

I felt annoyed for Grigory's sake: that girl with the cherries in her hat looked so ridiculous next to him, it was a terrible insult to his dignity. I often used to wonder why Grigory Shishlin was in charge and Foma Tuchkov a mere workman. He was a strong young man with a fresh complexion, .curly hair, an aquiline nose and grey, clever eyes set in his round face. He was not like a workman at all, in fact, and if someone had bought him good clothes he would have looked like a merchant's son from a good family. A morose sort of person, he said very little, and when he did speak he always came straight to the point. As he could read and write he looked after the contractor's accounts and worked out estimates. He knew how to get the best out of the men but was not very keen on working himself. Often he would say in his calm voice:

'Life's too short for all this work we have to do.'

He spoke disdainfully about books:

'They'll print *anything* these days . . . and it's all a load of rubbish anyway!'

But he listened to everything that people said very attentively and if something really interested him he would insist on knowing every single detail; he always seemed to have something at the back of his mind. Invariably he judged everything by his own criteria.

Once I told Foma that he should become a contractor and he answered lazily:

'If it's a question of a few thousand roubles, then it's worth going after. But to mess around for the sake of a few kopeks is a sheer waste of time. No, I'll have a look round first and perhaps I'll go into the monastery at Oranki. I'm good-looking, strong and some merchant's widow might fancy me! You never know! After only two years a boy from Sergatsk found happiness and married a girl from the town. They were carrying the ikon round the houses at the time and she spotted him.'

He had thought it all out very carefully, and he had heard many stories about men who had had an easy time after being a novice in a monastery. I did not like these stories, nor his way of thinking, but I was sure he would end up as a monk.

When the fair opened Foma startled everyone by taking a job as a waiter in a pub. I would not say that this came as a complete surprise, but his friends just would not leave him alone. On holidays, they would go to the pub to drink tea and have a laugh together before they left.

When they arrived they would start shouting as though they owned the place:

'Hey, waiter! Curly, over here!'

He would go over to them with his head held high and ask: 'What do you want?'

'Don't you recognize your own friends?' they would reply.

'I've got no time to mess around!'

He felt that his friends despised him and just wanted to have some fun at his expense. He looked on them with dull expectant eyes, and his face would become wooden, expressionless. But he seemed to be saying to himself: 'Any more from you lot and I'll...'

'Want a little tip?' they would ask. They deliberately fumbled around in their pockets for a long time but did not give him a single kopek in the end.

I asked Foma why he had become a waiter, when he really wanted to be a monk.

'I didn't want to be a monk,' he answered, 'but I won't be a waiter for very long.'

Four years later I met him in Tsaritsyn, still working as a waiter. And afterwards I read in the papers that Foma Tuchkov had been arrested for attempted robbery with violence.

I was particularly struck by the story of Ardalyon the bricklayer – the oldest and best workman Pyotr had. This cheerful man of forty who had a thick black beard also set me wondering why Pyotr was in charge and not him. He rarely touched vodka and almost never got drunk. He knew his job very well, performed it lovingly and the bricks flew in his hands like red doves. Next to him the sickly, hypocritical Pyotr seemed completely out of place in the workshop.

Ardalyon often used to talk about his work:

'I'm building stone houses for other people and a wooden coffin for myself.'

He used to lay the bricks with gay abandon and shout:

'Come on, mates, let's work for the glory of God!'

He told everyone that next spring he was going to Tomsk, where his brother-in-law had taken on a big contract for building a church, and wanted him as foreman.

'It's all been arranged. I love building churches.'

Then he said to me:

'Why not come with me! Life in Siberia's very easy for someone who can read and write. You can't go wrong!'

I agreed and Ardalyon shouted triumphantly:

'Fine! But I'm not joking . . .'

He treated Pyotr and Grigory with good-natured mockery, the way an adult treats children, and he told Osip:

'Big-heads! All trying to show me how clever they are! You'd think they were playing cards: one of them says "Look at my flush," the other says "I've got trumps."'

Osip replied rather vaguely:

'What do you expect? Boasting is only human. All young girls like to show off their breasts when they walk along the street.'

'They all moan and groan but they rake the money in just the same!' Ardalyon persisted.

'Well, Grigory doesn't rake it in!'

'I'm talking about *myself*. If I had my way I'd escape into the forest or the desert. Oh, I'm so bored here, I think I *will* move on to Siberia in the spring.'

The workmen were envious of Ardalyon and said:

'If we had someone there, like Ardalyon's brother-in-law, then we wouldn't say no!'

Suddenly Ardalyon disappeared. One Sunday he left the workshop and for three days no one had the faintest idea where he was. Anxious guesses were hazarded:

'Perhaps he's been beaten up?'

'Suppose he went swimming and got drowned?'

Finally Efimushka appeared and said:

'Ardalyon's gone on a binge.'

'What are you talking about?' Pyotr shouted disbelievingly.

'He's gone on a spree, got drunk. He's burned himself up inside – just like a lime-kiln! Seems his wife has died.'

'But he's a widower! Where is he now?'

Pyotr angrily went off to try and save Ardalyon, but only got a violent beating.

Osip said to me as we went:

'Now there's a man who lives a good life until suddenly some devil gets inside him and he goes berserk. Take a lesson from *that*, Maximych . . .'

We came to one of those cheap little houses in the 'gay village of Kunavino' and were met by a thievish-looking old woman. Osip whispered something to her and she led us into an empty little room which was as dark and filthy as a cattle-stall. A large fat woman was sprawled out asleep over a bed. The old woman poked her in the side and said:

'Get up, you lazy bitch, get up!'

The woman jumped up in fright, rubbed her face with the palms of her hand and asked:

'Good God! Who's this? What's happening?'

'It's the police,' Osip said sternly. The woman groaned and disappeared. Osip spat as she went and announced:

'She's more frightened of the police than she is of the devil!'

The old woman took a small mirror off the wall, lifted up a piece of wallpaper and said:

'Look, is that him?'

Osip looked through the opening in the wall.

'That's him all right. Get that girl out of here!'

I had a look through the hole as well. A lamp was burning in a tin can on the sill of a heavily shuttered window in a room the size of a dog kennel – just like the one we were in. Next to the lamp a cross-eyed Tartar girl was standing mending a shirt. Behind her I could see Ardalyon's bloated face propped up on two pillows with his rumpled black beard sticking up in the air. The girl shuddered, hurriedly put the shirt on, went past the bed and came into our room. Osip looked at her and spat again:

'You filthy little bitch!'

'And you're an old fool,' she answered laughing.

Osip had to laugh too and he pointed a menacing finger at her. Then we went into that pigsty of a room. Osip sat on the bed at Ardalyon's feet and for a long time he tried to wake him without any success. Then he muttered:

'Well, let's wait a bit, then we'll go . . .'

Finally Ardalyon woke up, gave Osip and myself a wild look, closed his red eyes and mumbled:

'Well now . . .'

'What do you think you're doing?' Osip said calmly, without any reproach. But he sounded gloomy all the same.

'I went mad . . .' he explained, wheezing and coughing.

'Why?'

'Well, you know . . .'

'There'll be a terrible row . . .'

'Well, when it comes . . .'

Ardalyon took an opened bottle of vodka from the table and started swigging. Then he offered Osip some:

'Like a drop? I think there's some savouries somewhere . . .'

The old man poured some vodka straight into his mouth, gulped it down, frowned and cautiously started chewing a slice of bread.

The befuddled Ardalyon said in a limp voice:

'See, I've got mixed up with a Tartar girl . . . It's all Efimush-ka's fault . . . She keeps saying she's a young orphan from Kasi-mov and came for the fair.'

Broken Russian came from the other side of the wall:

'Tartars is best like a young chickings. Tell 'im to push off, 'e's not yer farther.'

'Yes, that's her all right,' Ardalyon mumbled vaguely as he peered through the hole.

Ardalyon turned to me and said:

'Now look, mate . . .'

I waited for Osip to tell Ardalyon off, give him a sermon, and make him feel embarrassed and regret what he had done. But nothing of the sort happened. They sat side by side, shoulder to shoulder, and talked calmly in monosyllables. It was very sad seeing them together in that dark, filthy kennel. The Tartar girl said something funny through the hole in the wall, but they ignored her. Osip took a smoked roach from the table, banged it on his boot and carefully started taking the scales off. Then he asked:

'Blown all the money?'

'There's enough left for Pyotr.'

'Will you be all right now? You'd better go to Tomsk right away.'

'Why Tomsk?'

'Changed your mind then?'

'I would go if some *strangers* had asked me . . .'

'What's the matter?'

'Well, there's my sister and brother-in-law . . .'

'Go on.'

'I don't fancy being at the beck and call of relatives . . .'

'But you have to be under people wherever you go . . .'

'All the same . . .'

They spoke in such a friendly but serious way that the Tartar girl stopped trying to tease them, came into the room, silently took her dress from the wall without saying one word and vanished.

'She's very young,' Osip said.

Ardalyon looked at him and said without any annoyance:

'It's all that troublemaker Efimushka's doing. Doesn't want to know about anything except women. But that Tartar girl's a lively little thing . . . a bit frolicsome . . .'

'Watch it, or you'll be in *real* trouble,' Osip warned him and when he had finished taking the scales off the roach he started saying good-bye.

On the way back I asked Osip:

'Why did you go and see him?'

'Just to have a look. He's a friend isn't he? I've seen lots of cases like that. A man lives quietly then all of a sudden he goes berserk,' he said, repeating what he had said earlier. 'You must keep off the vodka!'

But a minute later he said:

'But without it life's so boring!'

'Boring without *vodka*?'

'Yes! After a drop or two you seem to be in another world!'

Ardalyon did not go away however. A few days later he turned up at work but soon disappeared again. In the spring I met him with a lot of tramps breaking up ice around barges in a backwater of the river. We were very pleased to see each other and went off to the pub for tea, during which he started boasting:

'Remember what a workman I used to be? Well, I'll tell you straight I was a magician in my trade. I could have earned hundreds.'

'But you didn't.'

'All right then, I *didn't*!' he shouted proudly. 'To hell with work!'

He swung his arms about as he spoke and attracted everyone's attention by his provocative remarks.

'Remember what that sly little thief Pyotr said about work? "It's a stone house for other people and a wooden coffin for yourself." That's work for you!'

Then I said:

'Pyotr is ill, he's frightened of dying.'

But Ardalyon shouted:

'I'm ill as well. Perhaps my soul's in the wrong place!'

On holidays I often went down from the town to Millionnaya Street, where tramps went to find shelter, and I could see that Ardalyon had in no time at all become an accepted member of the 'golden company'. Only a year before Ardalyon had been cheerful and behaved very respectably. Now he shouted at people, adopted a special, gangling way of walking, and spoke very provocatively, just as if he were trying to pick a quarrel or start a fight. He never stopped boasting:

'See how I'm treated here. Just like a *leader*!'

He did not worry about the money he earned and gave it away to tramps. He stood up for weaklings and when a fight broke out he would try to make the tramps feel sympathetic, often saying to them:

'That's not right, mates. You must be *fair*!'

So they gave him the nickname 'Fair' – which he was very pleased with.

I tried very hard to have a close look at those people crammed together in that old and filthy stone sack of a street. They were all people who had rejected normal life, but they appeared to have made a life of their own instead, one which was free from masters and really quite cheerful. With their boldness and 'couldn't-care-less' attitude they reminded me of those barge haulers Grandfather spoke about – men who easily turned into bandits or hermits. When there was little work about they were not averse to petty thieving from the barges and steamers, but this did not worry me. I could see that stealing was part of the fabric of their lives, like grey threads in an old kaftan, and at the same time I understood that these people sometimes worked with great enthusiasm, not sparing any effort when the work had to be done very quickly – when there was a fire or the ice was breaking up, for example. On the whole there was something more festive about their lives than other people's. But Osip noticed that I was friendly with Ardalyon and warned me in a fatherly way:

'Look here, son, my old stick-in-the-mud! Why are you so friendly with that crowd from the Millionnaya? Mind you don't get hurt!'

I told him as best I could that I liked those people who led carefree lives and who did not do any work.

'They're just like birds in the sky,' he interrupted, smiling. 'Why? Because they're lazy, there's nothing to them and the thought of work gives them the willies.'

'But what *is* work really?' I retorted. 'They say that by "honest toil" you won't earn yourself a stone house!'

It was easy for me to talk like that as I had heard that proverb all too often and felt how true it was. But Osip got angry with me and shouted:

'*Who* says that? Only fools and idlers. You shouldn't listen to such things. Ugh! Only people who are jealous, the failures, say idiotic things like that – wait until your feathers grow before you try and soar! But I'm going to tell the master how friendly you are with them, you wait!'

And he went and told the master, who gave me a warning in Osip's presence:

'Peshkov, keep away from Millionnaya Street. There's only

thieves and prostitutes there. You'll end up either in prison or hospital, so keep away!'

I tried to visit the Millionnaya without their knowing but in the end I was obliged to give it up.

Once I was sitting with Ardalyon and one of his friends, Robenok, on the roof of a shed in the yard of one of the doss-houses. Robenok was telling us an amusing story about how he managed to walk all the way from Rostov-on-Don to Moscow. He had been a sapper in the army and held the Order of St George. His knee had been smashed in the Turkish war and he walked with a limp. He was short and thick-set, and was incredibly strong in the arm. This arm was no use to him at all, however, as he could not get a job because of his bad leg. Some sort of illness had made all his hair fall out and his head was like a new-born baby's. His reddish eyes glinted as he started telling me his story:

'Well, it happened in Serpukhov. A priest was sitting on the palisade, so I said to him: "Please give something to a hero from the Turkish wars."'

Ardalyon shook his head and said: 'You're lying, lying.'

'Why should I lie?' Robenok asked, without taking offence, while Ardalyon grumbled in a lazy, didactic sort of voice:

'You're a liar! You should get a job as a night watchman – lame men always become watchmen. But all you can do is limp around doing nothing and tell lies . . .'

'Well, it was only meant as a joke, just to make you laugh!'

'You'd do better to have a good laugh at yourself! . . .'

Out in the yard, which was dark and filthy although the weather was dry and sunny, a woman suddenly appeared. She was shouting and waving some sort of rag.

'Who wants a skirt? What do you say, friends?'

Some other women came out of little doorways in the house and crowded round her. I recognized her at once – it was Natal-ya the laundress. By the time I jumped down from the roof, she had already sold the skirt to the first buyer and had quietly slipped out of the yard.

'Hello,' I said joyfully, as I caught her up outside the gates.

'What's that?' she asked as she looked at me out of the

corner of her eye. Then she suddenly stopped and shouted angrily:

'Good God! What are *you* doing here?'

I was rather touched and embarrassed at the same time when I saw how frightened she was at seeing me in a place like that, but I soon managed to explain that I was not living in the street but came only now and then to have a look round.

'To have a look round?' she asked in a sneering, angry voice. 'What on earth have *you* come to look at? People's pockets or women's bellies?'

Her face looked tired. There were deep shadows under her eyes and her lips drooped, limply. As she stopped by the pub door she said:

'Come on, let's have a cup of tea! At least your clothes are clean, not what you expect round here. But there's something about you I don't trust...'

But once we were in the pub she began to trust me (or so it seemed) and as she poured the tea out she started telling me a very boring story about how she had woken up only an hour before we met and that she had not eaten or had a drink yet.

'Last night I was really plastered when I went to bed and I still can't remember where I went drinking or with whom...'

I felt sorry for her and embarrassed, and I wanted to ask her where her daughter was. But after she had drunk some vodka and some hot tea she began to speak in the same crude, excitable way as all the women in that street. When I asked about her daughter she seemed to sober up at once and shouted:

'What do *you* want to know for? Oh no, you won't get your hands on her if I can help it!'

She drank some more tea and vodka and continued her story.

'As far as I'm concerned my daughter just doesn't know I exist. Who am I? A laundress. And what kind of mother was I to her? She's had education – and that's something! She left me to go and work for a rich friend, as a teacher I think.'

After a brief silence she said softly:

'So that's your game! Are you after a laundress, or is it a tart you want!'

I saw at once that she was a prostitute – there just wasn't any other kind of woman in that street. But when she herself told

331

me this my eyes filled with tears of shame, of pity, for her. It was as though this confession had literally burned me – and this was a woman who not very long before had been so independent, clever and full of character!

'Ugh!' she said as she looked at me and sighed.

'Get out of here! I'm telling you for your own good. If you stay here much longer you're finished!'

She seemed to be talking to herself – very brusquely and softly – as she leant over the table and drew something with her finger on the tray.

'And what's my advice to you? Well, if my own daughter couldn't do what I told her ... I even shouted to her: "You can't abandon your own mother, can you?" And she replied: "I'm going to kill myself." She went to Kazan to train as a midwife. Well, that was fine. But what about *me*? Whom could *I* cling to? To the next person who came along...'

She was lost in thought and said nothing for some time, moving her lips up and down without making any sound at all: clearly she had forgotten all about me. Then the corners of her lips drooped, her mouth turned into a crescent. It was horrible watching her wrinkled lips tremble as they silently told some story. A tuft of hair had fallen from under her scarf and lay over her cheek and curled round her small ear. A tear dropped into her tea, which by then was cold. She pushed the cup away and pressed her hands hard to her eyes, squeezing out two more tears. Then she wiped her face with her scarf.

I could not stand it any longer and I quietly got up and said: 'Good-bye!'

'What did you say? Go to hell!' she shouted, waving me away.

All the time I had been sitting there she had forgotten about my existence and I went back to the yard, to see Ardalyon. I knew that he would come with me to catch some crayfish, but first I wanted to tell him all about that woman. By the time I got back, however, both he and Robenok had disappeared from the roof. While I was looking for them in that chaotic yard there began one of those scandals so typical of the street. I went through the gates and immediately bumped into Natalya, who was sobbing, wiping her bruised face with her scarf and tidying her dishevelled hair with her other hand. She was walking along the passage between the shops like a blind woman, with Ardalyon and Robenok following. Robenok said:

'Give her another one!'

Ardalyon caught up with her and shook his fist. Natalya turned and looked at him. Her face was terribly beaten, and her eyes burned with hate.

'Go on, hit me!' she shouted.

I caught hold of Ardalyon's hand and he looked at me in amazement:

'What do *you* want?'

All I managed to say was:

'Don't *touch* her!'

He burst out laughing.

'Who is she – your mistress? Good old Natasha, ate her *kasha*!'

Robenok laughed as well and slapped himself on the ribs. For a long time both of them called me all the names under the sun, which terrified me. While they were hurling obscenities at me Natasha made her escape. Finally I lost my patience and butted Robenok in the chest, knocked him over and ran away.

Long after that I did not dare go near Millionnaya street, and the next time I saw Ardalyon was on the ferry.

'Where did you get to?' he asked in a delighted voice.

When I told him how sick it made me just remembering how he had beaten up Natasha and called me all those filthy names he laughed good-naturedly and said:

'But we weren't being *serious*! We only did it for a joke. And why shouldn't we beat her up if she's a prostitute? All women get beaten, especially the likes of her. We were really only larking around. I know that beating someone up is not the same as a good telling-off!'

'But why should *you* try and tell her? Does it make you feel better?'

He put his arm round my shoulder and said sneeringly:

'But that's why our life is so ugly – no one's better than anyone else. I know that all right – inside out, every way!...'

He was rather drunk and in a very cheerful mood. He looked

333

at me with gentle compassion – just like a kindly teacher having to deal with a stupid pupil.

Now and again I met Pavel Odintsov. He was more frisky than ever, dressed like a dandy, spoke to me very condescendingly and kept on telling me off:

'What kind of job is *that* supposed to be? It'll be the finish of you... Those workmen!'

Then he sadly told me the news from the ikon workshop:

'Zhikharev is still mixed up with that big cow. Sitanov's really got the miseries and never stops drinking ... Gogolev was eaten by some wolves. He was on his way home for Christmas and some wolves found him lying dead drunk and ate him up!'

He burst into laughter and continued his comical story:

'Of course eating him made *them* drunk as well! They all became very gay and started trotting through the forest on their hind legs, like circus dogs. Howling away they were. And one day later they were all dead!'

I listened and started laughing as well. But I felt that the ikon workshop and all that I had gone through there were now miles away – and this made me feel sad.

Chapter 19

DURING the winter there was hardly any work at the fair. As before, I had many trivial little jobs to do in the house. They took up the whole day, but I was free in the evenings. Once again I had to read novels which were serialized in *Niva* and the *Moscow Leaflet*, and which I found most unpleasant, to the master and mistress. During the night I managed to read some good books on my own and I tried to write poetry. Once, when the women had gone to midnight mass, the master stayed at home because he was not well and he asked me:

'Viktor's been laughing at you. He says you're writing poetry now. Is that true, Peshkov? Read me some then.'

It was awkward to refuse and so I read him a few poems. Clearly he was not very impressed, but he said all the same:

'Keep it up, keep it up. Perhaps you'll be a Pushkin one day! Have you read Pushkin?

> 'Are they burying a household sprite,
> Or giving a witch in marriage?

'In Pushkin's day they still believed in household sprites. He himself didn't believe in them – he was only joking!'

'Yes my friend,' he added pensively, 'it's time you went to school, or it'll be too late. God knows what you're going to make of your life! Be sure you hide your note-book somewhere safer, or else the women'll find it and have a good laugh. Women like hurting you . . . *ever so* deep down . . .'

For some time now the master had been quiet and pensive and kept anxiously looking round. Even the sound of a bell frightened him. Sometimes even stupid little things made him terribly angry and then he would start shouting at everyone and run out of the house, coming back drunk late at night. One felt that something had happened in his life that no one else knew about, something that had broken his heart. Now he lived hesitantly, reluctantly, out of sheer habit.

When there was a holiday I used to go for a walk from dinner time until nine, and after that would go and sit in the pub on

Yamskaya Street. The landlord was a fat man who was perpetually sweating. He was a passionate lover of singing. All the choristers from almost all the neighbouring churches knew this and used to meet in the pub. In return for a few songs he would give them vodka, beer and tea. The choristers were a drunken lot and not very interesting. They sang without any enthusiasm, just for the drinks, and almost always they would sing hymns. Because even those pious drunkards thought a pub was not quite the place for hymns the landlord would take them up to his room and I had to listen to them from the other side of the door. But peasants and workmen often sang in the pub as well and the landlord went round the town looking for singers himself, sought them out among peasants who came into town on market days and invited them over. The singer always sat on a chair by the bar, beneath a small barrel of vodka, and his head would be silhouetted against the bottom as though in a round frame.

The best singer was a small thin saddler called Kleshchov and he sang particularly fine songs. He had a dishevelled nondescript look and his reddish hair stuck out in large tufts. His little nose was very shiny, like a corpse's, and his tiny, sleepy eyes never moved. He would shut them, lean his neck against the barrel, stick out his chest and start singing rapidly in his tenor voice, which despite its softness, triumphed over everything:

> 'Oh, how the mist fell on the open fields,
> And concealed far distant paths.'

At this point he would stand up, leaning with his waist against the bar, bend backwards and sing very soulfully as he gazed at the ceiling:

> 'Oh, where will I go,
> Where will I find the broad highroad?'

His voice was not at all powerful, but it never seemed to tire. It was as though he were weaving all the dull noises of the pub into one silvery chord, and his sad words, sighs and exclamations conquered everyone – even the drunks became incredibly serious and looked silently down at the tables. My heart would break, almost bursting from those powerful feelings that good music always arouses – and this singing, miraculously, touched the very depths of my soul. The pub would become as quiet as a church and the singer looked just like a kindly priest. He was not preaching, but was praying with all his heart and soul for all mankind, giving voice to his thoughts on the misery of existence. Bearded men looked at him from all directions and childlike eyes blinked pensively in their brutish faces. Sometimes one of them would sigh, and this only emphasized the triumphant power of the song. At moments like these I thought that everyone else was living a false, fictitious life and that the real life of humanity was here!

Lysukha the fat-faced street trader, a repulsive woman, who lived the shameless life of a prostitute, sat in one corner. She was hiding her head between her plump shoulders and crying, and her impudent eyes gently moistened over. Not far from her a gloomy bass singer Mitropolsky was sprawling over the table. He was a young man with lots of hair and huge eyes set in his drunken face and he looked like an unfrocked priest. He would peer into the glass of vodka in front of him, lift it up to his mouth, then put it back carefully on the table – for some reason he could not bring himself to drink it. While Kleshchov sang everyone in the pub seemed to have gone dead, and it was as though they were listening to something long-forgotten, something that was near and dear to them.

When Kleshchov had finished singing and modestly sank down on his chair the landlord smiled with pleasure as he handed him a glass of vodka and said:

'Very good, of course! Although you don't sing as much as you talk, you're a *master*, it goes without saying. No one could ever say anything else about *your* voice . . .'

Kleshchov took his time over his vodka, carefully cleared his throat and said softly:

'*Anyone* with a voice can sing. But to bring out the soul of the song – only *I* can do that!

'All right then, don't boast about it!'

'Those who've got nothing to boast about don't boast!' he said in the same soft voice, but rather more insistently.

'You're very stuck-up, Kleshchov!' the landlord exclaimed, deeply annoyed.

'I don't *stick* myself higher than my soul,' Kleshchov replied.

The gloomy bass singer Mitropolsky snarled from his corner:
'What do *you* understand about this ugly angel's voice, you scum?'

He never agreed with anyone, argued with everybody, made wholesale accusations and almost every holiday was cruelly beaten by the singers and by anyone else who felt like it. The landlord loved Kleshchov's songs, but he could not stand the man himself. He went around complaining to everyone about him and was obviously trying to humiliate him and make a laughing-stock out of him. The pub regulars, Kleshchov included, knew this.

'A fine singer, but he's too stuck-up. Needs taking down a peg or two,' he would say, and some of the men would agree.

'Yes, he really thinks a lot of himself!'

'But why? A good voice is God's gift, he didn't have to *work* for it,' the landlord persisted. 'And what is a voice, anyway?'

The men would agree: 'True, but it's not the voice itself, it's how it's used.'

Once, after the singer had cooled down a little and left, the landlord started trying to persuade Lysukha:

'Marya, why don't you try and get off with Kleshchov, make him spend a bit on you, eh? It won't cost you anything!'

'I would if I were a bit younger,' she replied.

The landlord said in a loud, heated voice:

'What do you have to be young for? Go on! I'd like to see him twine himself round you! Think how he would sing if you made him pine from love. Go on! I'd be terribly grateful!'

But that large, fat woman would not do it. She lowered her eyes, played with the fringe of the shawl covering her breast and said in a monotonous, lazy voice:

'You need a *young* girl for that. If I were a bit younger I wouldn't hesitate.'

The landlord almost always tried to get Kleshchov drunk, but after he had sung two or three songs – accompanying each one with a glass of vodka – the singer would carefully wrap a knitted scarf round his throat, pull his cap down tight over his shaggy head and leave. Often the landlord would try and find someone to compete with Kleshchov. The saddler would sing his songs and the landlord would praise him as usual and then say excitedly:

'Oh look, another singer's just turned up. Come on, show what you can do!'

The new arrival would sometimes have a fine voice, but I cannot remember anyone else singing so simply and with such feeling as that small, insignificant-looking saddler.

'Hm,' the landlord would say with a note of regret, 'that's very good, of course. You must remember that the voice is up here and the soul is down below . . .'

The men would laugh and say:

'You can see for yourself, no one can beat the saddler!'

Kleshchov would survey everyone from under his reddish, bushy eyebrows and say to the landlord calmly and politely:

'You're wasting your time! You won't find anyone better than me, my gift comes from God!'

'We *all* come from God.'

'You can ruin yourself giving me drinks but you'll never find anyone else!'

The landlord would turn purple and rumble:

'How do *you* know, eh?'

But Kleshchov persisted:

'And I'm telling you again that singing is not the same as cockfighting.'

'Think *I* don't know! But why go on at me?'

'I'm not going on! I'm only trying to tell you. If songs are only meant to amuse people, then they must come from the devil!'

'That's enough now! You'd better sing some more . . .'

'I can always sing, even when I'm asleep,' Kleshchov agreed, carefully clearing his throat before he began.

All the trivial little things in life, all stupid words and thoughts, all that was vulgar or prosaic and connected in any way with the pub, miraculously vanished like smoke. Everyone felt the breath of a new kind of life which was thoughtful, pure, full of love and sadness. I envied that man for his remarkable talent, for his power over people which he used with such amazing skill. I wanted to get to know this saddler better, have a long talk with him, but I did not have the courage to go up to him: Kleshchov looked at everyone so strangely with those whitish eyes – it was just as though he could not see people at all. There really was something very nasty about him and I could not bring myself to like him although I wanted to – and not only when he was singing. It was unpleasant seeing him pull his cap down over his head like an old man and ostentatiously wrapping his red knitted scarf round his neck. He always spoke the same way about that scarf: 'My girl friend made that for me, a little girl . . .'

If he was not singing, he would solemnly puff himself up, rub his dead-looking, frozen nose and reply very reluctantly, in words of one syllable, to people's questions. Once when I went and sat next to him and asked him something he replied without even looking at me: 'Clear off, you little brat!'

I liked the bass singer Mitropolsky much better. When he turned up at the pub he would slink into a corner like a man with a heavy weight on his shoulders, kick a chair into place and sit down with his elbows on the table and his great hairy head hanging down on his knees. He would drink two or three glasses of vodka without saying a word and noisily clear his throat, which made everyone shudder and turn towards him while he looked challengingly back at them with his chin propped on his knees. His mane of shaggy hair gave a wild look to his bloated, swarthy face and straggled all over it.

'What you all looking at? What you gaping at?' he would suddenly ask in a thunderous voice.

Sometimes they would answer:

'A hobgoblin!'

There were evenings when he drank in silence and left without saying a word, scraping his boots over the floor. But sometimes I could hear him accusing people, trying to imitate the language of the prophets:

'I am the incorruptible servant of my Lord and I accuse you, like Isaiah! Woe to the city of Ariil, where filthy devils and swindlers and all the nasty scum of this world wallow in the mud of their obscene lust! Woe to ships on the sea carrying miserable wretches through the universe! I mean you – drunkards, gluttons, refuse of this world! There is no end to you, oh cursed ones, and mother earth will not receive you into her bowels . . .'

His voice was so vibrant that even the window panes rattled, which pleased his audience no end. They showered their prophet with praise:

'Gives you a right old drubbing with his tongue, the hairy mongrel!'

But for all this it was easy to make friends with him: one just had to offer him a drink and some food. He would ask for a carafe of vodka and a piece of bull's liver – his favourite snack.

When I asked him what books I should read he answered fiercely by firing a question straight back at me:

'What do *you* want to read for?'

But when he saw how he had upset me he relented and asked:

'Have you read Ecclesiastes?'

'Yes.'

'Well, carry on with it and read nothing else! All the wisdom of the world is there, only those stupid sheep over there don't understand. That is to say, *no one* understands. But who are you? Can you sing?'

I said that I couldn't.

'Why not? One *should* sing. It's the most stupid way of passing the time.'

Someone at the next table asked:

'But why do *you* sing then?'

'Well, I'm lazy! And what of it?'

'Oh, nothing.'

'I'm not surprised to hear you say something so idiotic. Everyone knows you haven't a brain in your head. And you never will have. Amen!'

He spoke like this to everyone, including me, although he would treat me more kindly after a few more drinks and once he even said with a note of surprise in his voice:

'When I look at you I really can't make you out! *What* are you, *who* are you and why? But to hell with you!'

I really could not understand his attitude to Kleshchov. He would listen to his songs with obvious pleasure, sometimes even with a warm smile, but he never made friends with him and always spoke rudely and disdainfully about him:

'He's a blockhead! He knows how to breathe, he understands what he's singing about, but he's an ass all the same!'

'But why?' I asked.

'It's just *him*!'

I wanted to have a talk with him when he was sober, but then he would only start bellowing and look at everyone with his sad bleary eyes. Someone told me that this man, who was a confirmed drunkard, had studied in the Kazan Academy and could have become a bishop, but I did not believe this. However, when I was telling him about myself and happened to mention the name of Archbishop Chrysanth he shook his head and said:

'Chrysanth? I know him. He was my teacher and benefactor. I remember him from the Kazan Academy. Chrysanth means golden, as Pamva Berynda rightly says. Yes, he was golden, that Chrysanth.'

'Who was Pamva Berynda?' I asked.

Mitropolsky answered very abruptly:

'That's nothing to do with you!'

When I got home I wrote down in my notebook: 'Must read Pamva Berynda at all costs.' It seemed to me that this Pamva Berynda would give me the answers to the many questions that were troubling me. The singer loved using names I had never heard before and many strange combinations of words and this infuriated me.

He would say: 'Life isn't Anisya.'

And I would ask: 'Who's Anisya?'

'A very useful woman,' he would reply and he would be highly amused at my bewilderment.

Those little sayings of his together with the fact that he had studied in an academy made me think that he knew a lot. For this reason I found his reluctance to speak very annoying and even if he did condescend it was impossible to understand what he was talking about. Perhaps I was not asking the right questions? All the same he left something in my heart. I liked the drunken audacity of his accusations, which were based on the sayings of the prophet Isaiah.

'O filth and scum of this earth,' he would bellow, 'the most their sockets – behind her head, and as she slipped down, her back, neck and then her bluish face banged against the seat and the footboard until she finally fell on to the road, hitting her head on the paving stones.

The driver whipped the horse and drove off, while the house porter caught hold of the girl's legs and pulled her backwards on to the pavement as though she were a corpse.

I went mad with rage and ran up to them. Fortunately as I ran I either must have thrown away or deliberately dropped my foreman's long spirit-level and this saved both the house porter and myself from something very unpleasant. After I had punched him and knocked him over I ran up the steps and desperately rang the bell. Some wild-looking people came running out. I was in no state to explain anything to them and I left, picking up my spirit-level on the way.

I caught the driver up. He looked down at me from his box and said approvingly:

'Yes, you got rid of him all right!'

I angrily asked him how he could allow a house porter to treat a girl so disgustingly but he calmly replied with a look of disdain:

'To hell with them! They paid the fare when they put her in the cab, so why should I care who gets beaten up?'

'But would they have *killed* her?'

'Oh yes, it's no trouble at all killing girls like her.'

He said this in such a way that I thought he had tried it himself – and not only once. After that I saw the house porter every morning. I would walk along the street and there he was, sweeping the road or sitting on the front steps as though he were waiting for me. I would go up to him and he would get to his feet, pull his sleeves up and issue a preliminary warning:

'Well, I'm going to break your neck!'

He was over forty, short and bandy-legged, with a stomach the size of a pregnant woman's. He smiled as he looked at me with his radiant eyes – they were so kind and cheerful that it was in fact terrifying to look at them. He was a poor fighter and his arms were shorter than mine. After two or three scuffles he would give in, lean back against the gate and say in a startled voice:

355

'You wait, I'll get you – you devil!'

These little fights bored me and once I said to him:

'Listen, you fool, keep away from me. Please!'

'But why do you keep picking fights?' he asked sneeringly.

I replied by asking him why he made such vile mockery of women.

'What's that to do with *you*? Feel sorry for that girl then?'

He fell silent, wiped his lips and asked:

'Do you feel sorry for cats as well?'

'Yes, cats as well!'

Then he said:

'You're a fool – and a liar! You wait, I'll show you!'

I had to walk down that street as it was the quickest way to work. But I started getting up earlier in order to avoid that man. However, I saw him three weeks later – he was sitting on the steps stroking a smoky-grey cat. When I was two or three steps from him he leaped up, caught the cat by its legs and with one blow smashed its head against a flagstone, splashing me with its warm blood. Then he threw the cat at my feet, stood by the yard gate and asked:

'Well, what do you say to that?'

There was nothing else for it. We rolled over the yard like two dogs.

Afterwards I sat in the long grass on the slope, almost driven insane by an inexpressible despair. I bit my lips to try and stop myself from roaring and bellowing like a wild animal. When I remember this even now I shudder from terrible feelings of nausea and wonder how I did not go out of my mind or kill someone. Why, you may ask, am I telling you all these abominations? So that you should know, my dear sirs, these are not things of the past – far from it! I know that you prefer beautifully told, fictitious horrors: the fantastic and the terrifying give you an agreeable thrill! But I know what is *really* terrifying, the horrors of everyday life, and I claim the indisputable right to shock you with stories about it, to make you take stock of your own lives and the world in which you live. We *all* live vile dirty lives – that's the point of these stories! I love people and I would not wish to horrify them. But I will not be sentimental nor conceal the terrible truth with the tinsel words of a beautiful lie. We must go forward into life! We must take from it into our hearts and heads everything that is good and humane so that it becomes a living part of us.

Those people's attitude to women particularly maddened me. I had had my fill of novels and I looked upon women as what was best and most meaningful in life. This opinion was confirmed by Grandmother, by her stories about the Virgin and Vasilisa the Wise, by the unfortunate laundress Natalya and by those hundreds, by those thousands of glimpses, smiles with which women, who are the true mothers of creation, embellish our life which is so sadly lacking in joy and love. Turgenev had sung the praises of women. All that was good in them I saw in the beautiful and memorable image of Queen Margot. Heine, and Turgenev in particular, gave me much precious material for this idealization.

When I returned home in the evenings from the fair I would stop on the hillside, by the wall of the fortress, and watch the sun setting beyond the Volga. Fiery streams flowed in the sky and my beloved river turned purple and blue. At such moments the whole earth resembled an enormous convict barge; it was like a pig that an invisible ship was lazily towing somewhere. But most often I thought about the great size of the world, about the towns that I had got to know through books, about foreign countries, where people lived differently. In those books written by foreign authors life was portrayed as purer, more pleasant and less laborious than the life which slowly and monotonously seethed around me, and this alleviated my anxiety and made me dream constantly of the possibility of a different life. And I never gave up thinking that one day I would meet a simple, wise man who would lead me on to a broad bright path.

Once, when I was sitting on a bench by the fortress walls, Uncle Yakov turned up. I did not notice him coming and at first I did not recognize him. Although we had been living in the same town for several years, we met only on rare occasions, purely by chance and very briefly.

'You've grown a lot,' he said jokingly, giving me a shove.

And we started talking as though we were complete strangers. From Grandmother's stories I knew that during the time I had been away Uncle Yakov had finally gone bankrupt, had spent what was left of the money and was now out of work. He had been working as an assistant to an inspector at a convict stage, but things turned out badly. The inspector became ill and Uncle Yakov started organizing wild drinking sessions in his room for the convicts. The authorities found out and he was dismissed and sent for trial, charged with letting the convicts out 'on the town' at night. None of the convicts actually ran away but one of them was caught when he was doing his best to strangle a deacon. The investigations dragged on for a long time. The case did not go to court however and the convicts and wardens managed to clear my benevolent uncle. Now he was unemployed and was supported by his son who sang in the then famous Rukavishnikov church choir. He spoke strangely about his son:

'He's become so serious, so *solemn*. Sings solo. You've hardly had time to get the samovar ready or clean his clothes before he begins to lose his temper. But he's a very tidy boy. Keeps himself neat and smart.'

Uncle Yakov had aged considerably. He was filthy and shabby and he now had a bloated look. His hair, which had been so thick, had now thinned considerably, his ears stuck out and the whites of his eyes and the morocco leather of his shaven cheeks were covered with a thick network of little red veins. He talked in a series of jokes but it seemed that there was something in his mouth that was getting in the way of his tongue, although all his teeth were perfect. I was glad of the chance to speak to a man who once knew how to live a gay life, had seen a great deal and who evidently knew many things. I clearly remembered his lively, comical songs and I can still hear what Grandfather said about him: 'When he sings, he's King David, but in business he's a venomous Absalom!'

Respectable-looking people passed us by along the promenade – well-dressed young ladies, civil servants and officers. But Uncle was wearing a worn-out autumn coat, a crumpled cap and reddish-brown boots. He shrank back when people went by and he was clearly ashamed of his appearance. We went into one of the pubs along the Pochainsky ravine and sat by the window that looked out on to the market.

I said to him:

'Do you remember how you used to sing:

'A beggar hung his socks out to dry
And along came another and stole them . . . ?'

When I repeated the words of the song I suddenly understood
the hidden mockery in it for the first time and at once I realized
how clever – and spiteful – my uncle was.

He poured some vodka out and said pensively:

'Yes, I've had a good time. I've lived a little! But that song's
not mine, a teacher from the seminary wrote it. Can't remember
his name for the life of me. He's dead now. We were good friends.
He was a bachelor, but he took to drink and then he died –
from frost-bite. It's impossible to count how many people I
knew took to drink! You don't drink then? Well keep off it,
there's plenty of time. Do you see Grandfather often? Miserable old devil! I think he's going mad.'

After a few vodkas he livened up, looked fresher and tidier
and began to speak with more enthusiasm. I asked him what
happened to the convicts in the end.

'Didn't you know?' he asked. Then he turned round,
lowered his voice and said:

'Well what *are* convicts after all? I'm not their judge!
People are only people. Let's all be friendly and gay, that's
what I say. There's a song that goes:

'Fate is no obstacle to joy!
Even though it may grind us down,
We will live for laughter's sake –
Only a fool lives otherwise . . .'

He laughed, looked through the window out on to the
darkening gully which was littered with boxes along the bottom, smoothed his whiskers and went on:

'Of course, they were glad of a drink as it's boring in prison.
Well, as soon as roll-call was over they'd come straight to my
room. There would be vodka and savouries. Then the fun
would begin and music would come from Mother Russia! I
love songs and dancing and some of the convicts were marvellous at it – really amazing. One of them had chains on and of
course you can't dance in *them*. So I decided to take them off,

359

not a word of a lie! They know how to get them off themselves, anyway, without a smith – a very crafty lot they are. But the story that I sent them into town to steal is a load of rubbish. No one proved it!'

He fell silent and looked through the window on to the gully where old-clothes men were shutting up their stalls. Iron bolts grated, rusty hinges creaked and falling planks made a hollow sound. Then he gave me a gay wink and said softly:

'To tell you the truth, one of them really did go out at night. Only it wasn't a convict but a thief from round here, from Nizhny. His mistress lived with him at Pechorka, not far from here. And the affair with the deacon was a pure mistake – he was taken for a merchant. It was in the winter, during a snow-storm *and* at night-time. People were wearing fur-coats, so who could tell if it was a merchant or a deacon, especially if they were in a hurry!'

This struck me as very funny and Uncle laughed too and said:

'Good God! To hell with them all!'

At this point Uncle quite unexpectedly – and for no apparent reason – lost his temper, pushed away the plate with the savouries, screwed up his face with a look of repulsion, puffed at his cigarette and murmured in a dull voice:

'They all steal from one another, then they catch one another, send each other to prison, to Siberia, hard labour, so what's it to do with me? To hell with the lot of them . . . I've my own soul to save!'

I suddenly thought of the hairy stoker who often said 'To hell with it'. And he was called Yakov too.

'What are you thinking about?' Uncle softly asked.

'Did you feel sorry for the convicts?'

'Oh yes! You'd be amazed: they were *real* human beings! Sometimes you'd look at them and think: "I'm not fit to lick their boots, although I'm in charge." They were a clever lot of devils, very crafty . . .'

The vodka and all that reminiscing had put Uncle in a very good mood. He leaned on the window sill, waved his yellowish hand with a cigarette stub stuck between the fingers and said in a perky voice:

'One of them was blind in one eye. But he was an engraver and a master watchmaker. He'd been sentenced for forging bank notes and had escaped. You should have heard him talk. Pure fire! He did not speak, but sang, just like a solo, and he'd say: "Tell me, why can the treasury print money and *I* can't? Please explain!" But no one could. No one – and me included! And I was the boss! Another was a famous thief from Moscow, didn't say much, but quite a dandy. He used to say – very respectfully though: "People work until they go stupid, but I don't want any of that. I've been through it all: you work and work and all the more fool you! You're left with a kopek to get drunk on, seven kopeks which you lose at cards and five to buy some love. And then you're poor again and hungry. No, that's not for me!"'

Uncle Yakov leaned towards the table, blushed right up to the crown of his head and continued his story. He was so excited that even his little ears started quivering.

'Oh yes, my friend, those men are no fools. They're dead right. To hell with all this working for nothing! If I ask myself, for example, what kind of life I've led I feel ashamed to recall it even. It's been all fits and starts, everything I've ever done has been underhand. Grief is one's very own, but joy is always stolen as they say. Now my father would shout at me: "Don't you dare!" Then the wife would say: "You can't!" So in the end you're too frightened to spend a rouble even. I've let life slip by and now I'm an old man and my own son's servant. Why should I try and hide it? I wait on him, all meek and mild, and he starts shouting at me like he was a gentleman. Calls me father, but all I hear is "servant". Was I born for this kind of life? Did I slave away just to be a servant to my own son at the end of it all? And even if it weren't for this, why have I lived? What pleasure have I had out of life?'

I did not pay much attention to what he was saying. All the same, I did tell him rather reluctantly, without really expecting him to answer:

'*I* don't know either what kind of life to lead . . .'

At this he grinned and said:

'Well . . . does *anyone* know? *I've* never seen anyone who did! People live the way they're used to.'

Once again he started speaking angrily and now he sounded offended:

'I once had a man from Oryol under me, convicted of robbery with violence. He was a nobleman and a marvellous dancer. He used to have everyone in fits when he sang about Vanka:

> 'Vanka walks through the graveyard –
> Now that's very simple!
> Oh, Vanka, come now,
>   Stick your nose out a bit further!

'Now I did not think this was funny at all, but it was so true! However much you run around, you won't see further than the graveyard in the end. And then it'll be all the same, whether you're a convict or a warder . . .'

He grew tired of talking, finished his vodka and looked with one eye, just like a bird, into his empty carafe. Then he silently smoked another cigarette, blowing out the smoke through his whiskers.

'No matter how you strive, however much you hope, you can never escape the grave,' Pyotr the bricklayer often used to say, and he was a man who was quite different from Uncle Yakov. This was not the first time I had heard sayings like these. I did not feel like plying Uncle with any more questions: it made me feel sad being with him and I was sorry for him. I still remembered the lively songs he used to sing and the sound of his guitar which brought a little joy in the midst of that gentle sadness. Nor did I forget the gay Tsyganok and as I looked at my dishevelled Uncle Yakov I could not help thinking: 'I wonder if *he* remembers when Tsyganok was crushed by the cross?' But I did not want to ask him. I looked into the gully which was now filled to the edge with the damp gloom of an August night. The smell of apples and melons wafted towards us. Lamps flickered along the narrow road into the town and everything was so familiar. Soon the steamer from Rybinsk would sound its siren and then another, bound for Perm.

'We'd better be going,' Uncle said.

As he stood by the pub door shaking my hand he advised me jokingly:

362

'Now don't get down in the dumps. You do get depressed, don't you? Say to yourself: to hell with it! You're still young. The most important thing is never to forget that saying: "Fate does not stand in the way of gaiety." Well, good-bye! I'm off to evening mass!'

My carefree uncle left, leaving me even more confused by what he had said.

I went up to the town and then out into the fields. There was a full moon, and heavy clouds drifted across the sky, blotting out my shadow with their own dark shadows. I bypassed the town, going across the fields instead, and I came out at Otkos, near the Volga. Here I lay down on the dusty grass and for a long time I looked at the river, at the meadows and at the motionless earth. Those shadows were slowly crossing the Volga. When they were above the water meadows they became brighter, as though they had been washed in the river. Everything around me was half asleep, every sound was muffled. Things moved reluctantly, just out of sheer necessity and not from any passionate love of movement and life. And I dearly wanted to give that earth a hard kick – and myself as well – so that everything, myself included, would start spinning round in one joyful whirlwind, in a festive dance where people were in love with each other, in love with a life which had been begun for the sake of another, which was beautiful, bold and honest. And I thought: 'I *must* do something, or I'll be finished.'

On dull autumn days, when one cannot see the sun nor even feel its warmth and when one forgets its existence altogether – on autumn days like these I often wandered through the forest. If I lost my way completely and grew tired of looking for the right path I would grit my teeth and go straight through thickets, through rotting undergrowth, across swamps full of slippery clods of earth and I would always come out on the main road in the end. So I decided to do something. That autumn I went to Kazan in the secret hope that I might somehow manage to enrol as a student there.

MORE ABOUT PENGUINS
AND PELICANS

For further information about books available from Penguins please write to Dept EP, Penguin Books Ltd, Harmondsworth, Middlesex UB7 0DA.

In the U.S.A.: For a complete list of books available from Penguins in the United States write to Dept DG, Penguin Books, 299 Murray Hill Parkway, East Rutherford, New Jersey 07073.

In Canada: For a complete list of books available from Penguins in Canada write to Penguin Books Canada Ltd, 2801 John Street, Markham, Ontario L3R 1B4.

In Australia: For a complete list of books available from Penguins in Australia write to the Marketing Department, Penguin Books Australia Ltd, P.O. Box 257, Ringwood, Victoria 3134.

In New Zealand: For a complete list of books available from Penguins in New Zealand write to the Marketing Department, Penguin Books (N.Z.) Ltd, P.O. Box 4019, Auckland 10.

TOLSTOY

War and Peace

Few would dispute the claim of *War and Peace* to be regarded as the greatest novel in any language. This massive chronicle, to which Tolstoy devoted five whole years shortly after his marriage, portrays Russian family life during and after the Napoleonic war.

Anna Karenin

In this masterpiece of humanity Tolstoy depicts the tragedy of a fashionable woman who abandons husband, son and social position for a passionate liaison which finally drives her to suicide. We are also given a true reflection of Tolstoy himself in the character of Levin and his search for the meaning of life.

Childhood, Boyhood, Youth

These semi-autobiographical sketches, published in Tolstoy's early twenties, provide an expressive self-portrait in which one may discern the man and the writer he was to become.

The Cossacks

The three stories in this volume illustrate different aspects of Tolstoy's knowledge of human nature.

Resurrection

Tolstoy's last novel reveals the teeming underworld of Russian society; the rotten heart of his country.

Henry Troyat
Tolstoy

'Nothing less than this magnificent, massive, 700-page biography could even begin to do justice to one of the most complex, baffling and grand men that ever lived ... a masterly book. M. Troyat would have to be invented if he did not exist as the ideal biographer' – *Sunday Telegraph*

GORKY

My Childhood

Translated by Ronald Wilks

My Childhood, which appeared in 1913, is the first part of Maxim Gorky's autobiographical trilogy. The ordinary experiences of a Russian boy in the nineteenth century are recalled by an altogether extraordinary man, whose gift for recapturing the world of a child is uncanny. Across the vision of the boy perched above the stove the Russian contrasts flicker – barbaric gaiety and deep gloom, satanic cruelty and saintly forbearance, clownish knaves and holy fools. A shutter in the mind closes: thirty years later the pictures develop, as fresh, as vivid, as exotic as when they were snapped.

My Universities

Translated by Ronald Wilks

Published in 1923, *My Universities* is the third, and Lenin's favourite, volume of Gorky's autobiography, recording his life from 1884 to 1888 when he was twenty.

Frustrated in his desire to become a university student, Gorky seeks an education in clandestine discussions with revolutionaries and in arguments with religious fanatics and eccentric schoolteachers. He encounters a bewildering variety of people; from aimless drifters to half-demented visionaries, from the consumptive atheist Shaposhnikov, with his pathological hatred of God, to theological students who hold orgies in brothels and Klopsky, the despicable Tolstoyan who seduces two sisters.

Throughout this volume, Gorky repeatedly stresses his disenchantment with the workers and the peasants – with their apathy, drunkenness and inertia. He submits himself to a ruthless self-analysis, and describes his attempted suicide. In common with *My Childhood* and *My Apprenticeship*, *My Universities* offers incidents of enormous breadth and variety, and writing of rare power and intense conviction.

THE PENGUIN CLASSICS

Each year we are glad to add a few more titles to our ever-expanding list of Classics. This does not just mean works by Latin and Greek writers, but the most comprehensive collection ever of classic works from all countries – China, Japan, India and Iceland as well as Europe – all in new translations.

A selection

OVID

The Erotic Poems   *Translated by Peter Green*

Orkneyinga Saga   *Translated by Hermann Pálsson and Paul Edwards*

ZOLA

The Earth   *Translated by Douglas Parmée*

MARIVAUX

Up from the Country/Infidelities
The Game of Love and Chance
Translated by Leonard Tancock and David Cohen

Three Sanskrit Plays   *Translated by Michael Coulson*

SHIKIBU

The Tale of Genji
Translated by Edward Seidensticker

iniquitous among you live in glory, while the good ones are persecuted. The dreadful day will come, and you will repent. But then it will be too late, too late!'

My brief acquaintance with this man had a curious ending. In the spring I met him in the fields near the camp. He was striding along like a camel, shaking his head, looking very lonely – and very bloated with drink.

'Going for a walk?' he asked hoarsely. 'Come along with me then . . . I like walking. But I'm not feeling too well, no . . .'

We walked a little way without saying a word and suddenly we saw a man at the bottom of a pit. He was in a sitting position with one shoulder propped against the side. His coat stuck out higher than his ears – just as though he had been trying to take it off but had not succeeded.

'Must be drunk,' the singer said as he stopped.

But under his hand, on the young grass, lay a large revolver and not far away was his hat, with a freshly opened bottle of vodka next to it. Its neck was half buried among the green blades. The man's face was hidden under his coat, as though he were covering himself up from shame.

For a minute we stood there in silence. Then Mitropolsky planted his legs wide apart and said: 'He's shot himself.'

At once I understood that the man was not drunk, but that he was dead. This was so unexpected that I just did not want to believe it. I remember not feeling any fear or pity as I looked at that large smooth skull sticking out of the coat and at that ear which had turned blue. I simply could not believe that a man could kill himself on such a gay and warm spring day. Mitropolsky rubbed his unshaven cheeks with the palm of his hand as though he felt cold and then he said in his rasping voice:

'An oldish man. His wife must have left him, or else he spent someone else's money.'

He sent me back to the town to fetch the police, while he sat down on the edge of the pit letting his feet dangle down. He shivered and huddled up in his threadbare overcoat.

When I had told the police that a man had shot himself I ran back, and while I was gone Mitropolsky had finished off the vodka and greeted me by waving the empty bottle.

'*That*'s what finished him!' he screeched furiously, flinging the bottle on to the ground so that it smashed to smithereens.

A policeman came running after me, peered into the pit, rather sheepishly crossed himself and then asked Mitropolsky:

'And who are you?'

'That's nothing to do with you.'

The policeman thought for a moment and then asked, rather more politely:

'I don't understand. There's a corpse lying here and yet *you're* drunk!'

'I've been drunk for twenty years!' Mitropolsky proudly declared and thumped himself on the chest. I was certain that he would be arrested for drinking the vodka.

People came running from the town and a stern-looking police officer drove up in a drozhky, climbed down into the pit, lifted up the man's coat and peered into his face.

'Who saw him first?'

'I did,' Mitropolsky said.

The police officer looked at him and said threateningly,

'Oh ho! Good day, my dear sir!'

About fifteen people had arrived by now. They were all breathless and seemed terribly interested in what had happened as they circled round the pit and looked into it. Someone shouted: 'It's a clerk from our street. I know him.'

Mitropolsky had taken his cap off and staggered about in front of the police officer trying to argue with him and shouting something that was very hard to make out.

The police officer shoved him in the chest, making him slump backwards on to the ground. Then he slowly took a piece of rope from his pocket, tied the singer's hands, which were already in their usual place behind his back, and started shouting angrily at the spectators:

'Clear off, you scum!'

Another, older-looking policeman came running up. He had moist, red eyes and his mouth was gaping from the effort. He took hold of one end of the piece of rope which was tied round the singer's hands and quietly led him off to the town. And I went back as well feeling very depressed. Those 'prophetic' words still echoed loudly in my memory: 'Woe to the city of Ariil!'

I had seen something really horrible: the police officer taking the rope slowly from his coat pocket, while the 'dreadful prophet' meekly placed his hairy red hands behind his back and crossed one wrist over the other very neatly, as though from habit. I soon found out that the 'prophet' had been taken away under police escort.

Soon afterwards Kleshchov disappeared. He married very well and went to live in a district where a saddlery had just been opened. I spoke to my master so enthusiastically about the saddler's songs that he once said: 'We must go and listen then,' sitting down at a little table opposite me with his eyebrows raised in amazement and his eyes wide open.

All the way to the pub he made fun of me and for the first few minutes just laughed at me, the people there and the stifling smells. When the saddler started singing he sneered and started pouring beer into his glass. But he only half filled it and suddenly he said: 'Oho, the devil!'

His hand shook as he gently put the bottle down and began listening very attentively.

'Oh yes, my friend,' he said with a sigh when Kleshchov had finished, 'he really *can* sing, damn him! He even warmed me up a bit!'

The saddler started singing again and gazed at the ceiling with his head flung back:

> 'A young maiden walked across the fields
> Away from the rich village.'

'How that man can sing!' the master muttered, smiled and shook his head.

Kleshchov overflowed with song, just like a shepherd's pipe:

> 'The beautiful maiden says to him
> I'm only an orphan, no one needs me . . .'

The master whispered: 'Good,' blinking eyes that had now reddened. 'Oh, damned good!'

I looked at him and felt glad. The heart-rending words of that song which drowned all other sounds in the pub rang out even more powerfully, beautifully and soulfully:

'In our village they're not very friendly
They don't invite a maiden like me to parties.
Oh, I'm poor and badly dressed,
I'm no good for a daring youth . . .
A widower proposed to me, so he could have a housemaid –
I don't want to bow to such a fate! . . .'

My master burst out crying and was not at all ashamed of it. He sat there with his head bowed, twitching his hooked nose and the tears trickled down on to his knees. After the third song he said in a very agitated voice:

'I can't stop here any longer . . . I just can't breathe. Those smells! Let's go home!'

But once we were out in the street he said:

'Come on, Peshkov, let's go and have a bite in the hotel . . . I don't want to go home yet.'

Without haggling about the price he climbed into a cab and did not say a word the whole way. In the hotel he sat down at a small table in a corner and immediately started pouring out his spleen in a soft angry voice, continually peering over his shoulder:

'That old goat's really upset me. I've got the blues good and proper! Now, *you* can read and think for yourself – tell me, it's a devilish life, isn't it? You live your life, forty years go by, you have a wife and children, but no one you can really talk to. At times you're dying to pour your heart out, yet there's no one. You talk to your wife but she doesn't understand. And what *is* she after all? All she can do is have children and look after the house. She'll *never* understand me, we're poles apart . . . As they say, a wife is a friend until the first child comes along. And as you can see, there's not an ounce of life in mine – a lifeless lump of meat. So to hell with her! Oh, I'm really fed up, I can tell you . . .'

He gulped down some cold, bitter beer, did not say anything for a while and twisted his long hair. Then he continued:

'On the whole, my friend, people are just *scum*! You talk to the men, don't you? There's cheating going on the whole time, some really vile things, I know that all right. *All* of them are thieves. And do you think that what you say gets through to them? Not one little bit. Yes, Pyotr and Osip are swindlers. They tell me everything and talk like you do about me . . . What did you say?'

But I was too amazed to say anything.

'Oho,' he said smiling. 'You were *right* to want to go to Persia although you won't understand what they're talking about there. It's a different language! But all you hear in your own language is nothing but filth, anyway . . .'

'Does Osip talk about me?' I asked.

'Of course! What did you think? He talks more than anyone else. He's a real gossip, a real crafty piece of work! No, Peshkov, words are no use to anyone. True? And what the hell is truth anyway? Just like snow in the autumn that falls on mud and melts. All you have is more mud. So you'd better keep your mouth shut . . .'

He drank glass after glass of beer without its having any effect on him and he began to talk more quickly and angrily.

'There's a proverb: Silence is golden. Oh, my friend, I feel sad, so sad! The saddler was quite right when he sang: "In our village they're not very friendly." Men are like orphans on this earth . . .'

After taking another look round he lowered his voice and said:

'Once I thought I'd found a real friend. I met a woman here, a widow whose husband had been sentenced to Siberia for forging banknotes – he was being kept in the town prison before he was sent away. I got to know her. She didn't have a kopek, so she took up *you know what*. A pimp introduced me. I took a good look and saw what a lovely woman she was. A beauty – and quite young as well. Really wonderful! I saw her once or twice and said: "How come, when your husband's a crook and you yourself live dishonestly, you don't follow him to Siberia?" But she *was* going to follow him to the penal settlement, oh yes! Then she said: "Whatever he's done I still love him. For me he's a *good* man. Perhaps he committed the crime for my sake. And I'll sin with you for *him*, as he needs money. He's a gentleman and is used to living well. If I lived on my own then I would be respectable. You're a good man too, and I like you a lot, but don't talk to me about that again . . ." So I thought "To hell with it!" I gave her all I had on me –

347

eighty roubles or more and said: "Forgive me, I don't want to see you any more, I just can't." I left and that was the end of that . . .'

He fell silent again and suddenly the drink began to take effect. He slumped forward in his chair and muttered:

'I went to see her six times. You can't imagine what it was like! I may have gone as far as her door *another* six times – but I just could not bring myself to go in. And now she's gone, for good . . .'

He put his hands on the table, tapped his fingers on it and whispered:

'Please God, don't let me ever meet her again. Please! If that happens I'm finished! Let's go home now. Come on!'

We got up and left. The master staggered about and snarled: 'That's life for you, my friend . . .'

The story he had just told me came as no surprise and for a long time I had been thinking that something very unusual was going to happen to him before long . . . But I was extremely depressed by what he said about life, especially about Osip.

Chapter 20

FOR three years I worked as a foreman in that dead town among empty buildings, supervising the workmen when they broke up the clumsy stone shops in the autumn and when they built them all over again in the spring. The master made sure that I really earned my five roubles. If they were laying a new floor in the shop I had to choose a quantity of earth to cover the whole area to a depth of two feet. The tramps were paid a rouble for laying the earth and I got nothing. But when I was supervising them I could not keep my eye on the carpenters as well, and they unscrewed locks and handles from doors and stole various little fittings. Both the workmen and sub-contractors tried in every way they could to cheat me and steal things. They did this almost openly, as though they were under some obligation to carry out a dreary routine and they were not in the least angry if I caught them, but showed surprise instead and said:

'You have to slave away for five roubles as though they were twenty. It's too funny!...'

I told the master that if he made a rouble from the work he got out of me he always lost ten times more because of the stealing, but he would only wink and say:

'Don't try and fool me!'

I realized that he suspected me of being an accomplice in the thieving that was going on. This made me dislike him strongly, but I did not feel offended. Such was the order of things: everyone stole and even the master liked to take what belonged to other people. When the fair had closed and he had started inspecting the shops (which he was under contract to repair), if he happened to see a samovar that someone had left behind, crockery, a carpet, scissors, and sometimes a crate of goods even, he would smile and say:

'Make a list and take it all to the storeroom!'

Then he would take the things home in a cab and make me check the inventory several times.

I did not like property: I did not want anything and found

349

that even having a lot of books around was a nuisance. I possessed nothing except a small volume of Béranger and the songs of Heine. I wanted to buy some Pushkin but the only book-seller in the town, a spiteful old man, was asking too much.

I hated furniture, carpets, mirrors, or any of the clumsy things that were crammed into the master's room and the smell of paint and varnish only irritated me. On the whole I did not like any of the master's rooms, as they reminded me of trunks stuffed with old rubbish. It disgusted me to see the master dragging other people's property from the storeroom, perpetually adding to the junk that already surrounded him. The rooms in Queen Margot's flat were crammed full of furniture, but it was beautiful.

In general life struck me as illogical and absurd and there was far too much that was so obviously stupid and meaningless. There we were rebuilding shops. In the spring they would only be flooded once more and the water would warp the floors and damage the front doors. The water would recede and the planks would lie rotting. Year in year out, for the past ten years, the water had flooded the fair, ruined the buildings and the bridges. These annual floods caused enormous loss to the tradespeople and everyone knew that something had to be done about them and that they would not stop of their own accord. Every spring the ice would break up and cut the barges and dozens of little boats to pieces. People would groan and then start building new boats which the ice would smash up again the following year.

All this rushing about and rebuilding was so incredibly absurd.

I would ask Osip what he thought about it and he would laugh aloud in amazement:

'Think you're clever, don't you? And what's it to do with you anyway? Eh?'

Then he would look at me a little more seriously. But his light-blue eyes, which were very bright and clear for an old man, still seemed to be laughing at me:

'How clever of you to notice! You never can tell, knowing that it might come in handy one day! Now listen to me.'

And he would start talking again in his dry voice, generously sprinkling his sentences with silences, unexpected comparisons and all sorts of jokes.

'Now people complain that there's not enough land. In the spring the Volga tears away at its banks, takes the land away and piles it up to make shoals. Then people start complaining that the Volga is getting shallow! The spring floods and summer rain dig gullies and the earth goes into the river again!'

He spoke without compassion, without malice, and seemed to be deriving pleasure from his knowledge of the way people complained about life: although what he said coincided with my thoughts on the subject it was unpleasant listening to him. I remember that not a single summer went by without the forests beyond the Volga catching fire. Every July the sky would be covered with a pale yellow smoke. The purple sun, blotted out, looked down on the earth like a bad eye.

'Forests are stupid really,' Osip would say. 'They belong to gentlemen, the government. A peasant doesn't have forests. Towns burn down – that's of no importance either. Rich people live in towns and you don't have to feel sorry for them! Take villages. Just think how many are burned down in the summer. Not less than a hundred, perhaps. That's some loss!'

He laughed quietly.

'There's property all right – but there's no brains to go with it! You and me aren't working for ourselves, for the land even, but for fire and water!'

'Why are you laughing?' I asked.

'Why not? You won't put fires out with tears, but they swell the flood water.'

I knew that this handsome old man was cleverer than anyone I knew. But was there anything he really hated, anything he loved? I kept wondering about this, but he went on adding his dry words to the fire burning inside me:

'Just you watch how people don't do very much when it's a question of saving their own strength or other people's. Why does your master make you run around the whole time? And what does a little drop of water really mean? It's impossible to calculate, even the most learned man couldn't tell you. If a hut burns down you can knock another together. But when a good peasant is ruined for no good reason at all you won't ever put that right. Take Ardalyon for example, or Grisha – remember the time he lost his temper? He's stupid, but he has a good heart. That Grisha catches fire like a bundle of straw. Women just fall on him – like worms attacking a corpse in the forest!'

I used to ask him just out of curiosity:

'Why do you have to tell the master what I think?'

He would explain in a calm, even affectionate, voice:

'So that he knows that you have harmful thoughts in that head of yours. He's the one who should teach you – who else is there? I don't tell him because I'm trying to be spiteful, but because I feel sorry for you. You're no fool, but there's some devil stirring things up in your head. If you steal I won't breathe a word. I'll even keep quiet if you go after the girls. And I won't even tell them if you start drinking! But I'll always tell the master about the other tricks you get up to, so there!'

'I don't want to talk to *you* any more!'

He silently picked at the dried tar on his hand with his fingernails. Then he looked at me with his kind eyes and said:

'You're lying! Of course you want to talk to me. Who else is there? No one at all . . .'

He was a tidy man who kept himself very clean and suddenly he reminded me of Yakov the stoker, who could not care less about anything. And sometimes he put me in mind of Pyotr Vasilyev the Bible scholar, and sometimes Pyotr the cab-driver. Sometimes he seemed rather like Grandfather – in one way or other he looked like all the old men I had seen in my lifetime. They were all incredibly interesting, but I felt that it was impossible to be with them for long, as they made my life oppressive and repulsive. They seemed to eat one's soul away and their clever sayings choked my heart with a thick reddish rust. Was Osip a good man? No. Was he evil? No. But one thing was clear – he was very clever. His mind startled me by its ingenuity but at the same time it had a deadening effect on me and finally I came to feel that he was hostile to me in every possible way. Dark thoughts boiled up within me: 'All people are really strangers, in spite of their friendly words and smiles. No strong feelings of love bind *anyone* to this earth. Only

Grandmother loved life and everything in the world – only Grandmother and wonderful Queen Margot.'

Sometimes similar depressing thoughts grew into a thick dark cloud and life became stifling and unbearable. But what other life was there and where could I go? There was no one to talk to besides Osip. So I began to talk to him more and more.

He listened to my excited babbling with obvious interest, cross-examining me and trying to worm something out of me. He would calmly say:

'A woodpecker's stubborn – like you – but it's not terrible to look at and no one's frightened of it! In my heart of hearts I advise you to go into a monastery and live there until you come of age. Then you'll be able to comfort those in need of spiritual help with inspiring words! You will lead a peaceful life and the monks will profit from it! I do advise you to do this. You're not fitted for earthly things really.'

I did not want to go into a monastery, but I felt that I had lost my way and that I was running around in a vicious circle and understood nothing about life. It was all very depressing.

Life became like a forest in autumn. The mushrooms had already been gathered and there was nothing to go there for. It seemed that I knew every tree by heart.

I did not drink vodka or go after girls – books took the place of these two methods of self-intoxication as far as I was concerned. But the more I read the harder it became to live the empty useless life that everyone around me seemed to be leading.

I was only just fifteen, but sometimes I felt like a grown man. In some peculiar way I had swollen up inside and everything I had gone through, had read and worried about lay on me like a heavy weight. As I looked deep inside myself I found that my stock of impressions was like a dark storeroom crammed with piles of different things – and I had neither the strength nor the ability to sort them all out. But all these heavy burdens, despite their enormous number, did not weigh down on me for long but tossed me up and down like the sea rocking an unsteady ship. I had a strong aversion to the misfortunes, illnesses and sufferings of others and in fact I was quite squeamish: when I saw anything cruel – blood, beatings, even verbal mock-

353

ery, all of this produced a feeling of physical repulsion which quickly developed into a kind of cold fury, and I too would fight like an animal and feel terribly ashamed of it afterwards. At times I wanted to beat up those who tortured others and I threw myself into the fray so blindly that even now I feel ashamed when I recall those fits of despair caused by my feelings of sheer impotence.

There were two persons living within me. One of them had experienced far too much that was filthy and nasty and had as a result become rather timid. This person who was crushed by his knowledge of the horror of everyday life had begun to look upon it distrustfully, suspiciously, with a helpless feeling of compassion for everyone – even for himself. This man dreamed of a quiet, solitary life with books and without any people, of a monastery, of a life as a forest-warden, of living in a railway-man's hut, of going to Persia or working as a night watchman on the outskirts of some town. There were fewer people in this kind of life and one was more remote from them. The other man had been baptized by the holy spirit that he had read about in books written by honest and wise men. Although he realized how terrible reality was, how insuperable its horrors were, although he felt that its strength was enough to tear his head off or trample his heart under its filthy boots, he still persisted in defending himself, clenching his teeth, baring his fists, and was always ready for a quarrel or a fight. This man transferred his love and compassion for people into deeds and like a hero from a French novel he would pull his sword from its scabbard and take up a fighting stance.

At that time I had a bitter enemy – a house porter from one of the brothels in Malaya Pokrovskaya street. I met him one morning as I was going to the fair. He was dragging a dead-drunk woman down from a cab box outside a front door. He had caught her by the legs and her stockings started coming off. Then he stripped her to the waist, bellowed and laughed, and spat on her body as he pulled her about in the most disgusting way. The girl slid down from the box in a series of bumps; she was terribly dishevelled, did not appear to see anything that was happening to her and her mouth was wide open. She had put her soft arms – which appeared to have been pulled out of